Where Joy Starts

Applewood Hill Book 3

Angela D. Meyer

Darlene Books

Darlene Books

Where Joy Starts © 2022

Angela D. Meyer

ISBN 978-0-692-89634-1

This novel is a work of fiction. Names, characters, places, and incidents either are the product of the author's imagination or are used fictitiously. Any resemblance to actual events, locales, organizations, or persons living or dead is entirely coincidental and beyond the intent of either the author or the publisher.

Cover design by Roseanna White Designs

Printed in the United States of America

Welcome to the Mosaic Collection

WELCOME TO THE MOSAIC COLLECTION

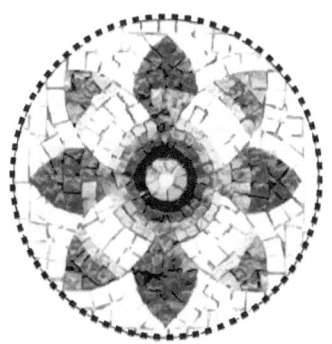

We are sisters, a beautiful mosaic united by the love of God through the blood of Christ. Each month The Mosaic Collection releases one faith-based novel or anthology exploring our theme, Family by His Design, and sharing stories that feature diverse, God-designed families. All are contemporary stories ranging from mystery and women's fiction to comedic and literary fiction.

We hope you'll join our Mosaic family as we explore together what truly defines a family. If you're like us, loneliness and suffering have touched your life in ways you never imagined; but Dear One, while you may feel alone in your suffering—whatever it is—you are never alone!

Subscribe to Grace & Glory, the official newsletter of The Mosaic Collection, to receive monthly encouragement from Mosaic authors, as well as timely updates about events, new releases, and giveaways.

Learn more about The Mosaic Collection at
https://www.mosaiccollectionbooks.com

Join our Reader Community, too!
www.facebook.com/groups/TheMosaicCollection

Books in the Mosaic Collection

Eye of the Storm by Janice L. Dick
Totally Booked: A Book Lover's Companion
Lifelines by Eleanor Bertin
The Third Grace by Deb Elkink
Crazy About Maisie by Janice L. Dick
Rebuilding Joy by Regina Rudd Merrick
Song of Grace: Stories to Amaze the Soul
Written in Ink by Sara Davison
Out of the Storm by Janice L. Dick
Open Circle by Stacy Monson
The Heart of Christmas: A Mosaic Christmas Anthology III
Broken Together by Brenda S. Anderson
Every Star in the Sky by Sara Davison
Where Healing Starts by Angela D. Meyer
All Things New: Stories to Refresh the Soul
Into the Flood by Milla Holt
Through the Blaze by Milla Holt
A Whisper of Peace: A Mosaic Christmas Anthology IV
Twice Told Tales by Chautona Having
Within the Storm by Milla Holt

Learn more at

www.mosaiccollectionbooks.com/mosaic-books

CHAPTER ONE

Elinor

With four words, the doctor exhumed the truth. "You can't have children."

Relief mingled with fear. Briefly. Elinor thought she had buried the past forever. Guilt replaced her relief as tears stung her eyelids.

The receptionist tapped the end of her pencil against the desk, breaking through the cacophony of thoughts running through Elinor's mind. "Do you want to make an appointment for you and your husband to come in and talk to the doctor together? We have an opening next Friday at two."

James. Lifting her chin, Elinor perched her sunglasses on her nose. "I need to check my husband's schedule. I'll get back to you." She turned on her heels. She marched through the door, then moved down the hall and past the water fountain to the elevator. Mocking her from their perches on the walls, the scenes of families laughing, families having picnics, families playing at parks, and parents beaming over their babies glared down at her.

The elevator door opened, and a crowd poured out toward her. Every head seemed to look her way. She sidestepped into the stairwell. Leaning against the wall, she replayed the appointment in her mind. A shudder ran up her spine. *How can I tell James that my choices from the past have stolen our future?*

"Excuse me. Do you need help?" An older gentleman with wrinkles around his eyes furrowed his brows to match the compassion in his voice.

Her response stuck in her throat. Nodding, she hurried past him, down the stairs, through the lobby and out into the sunlight. Lowering her gaze lest anyone feel the urge to greet her with some inane cheerful wish for her day, she dug keys out of her purse as she zigzagged through the car lot to James's BMW.

She slid into the driver's seat, leaned back against the headrest, and allowed herself the luxury of tears. She remembered another doctor visit in another time and place. The loneliness, the pain, the regret. Shaking her head against an onslaught of emotions, she started the car.

Her phone rang out the Piano Guys' Rockelbel's Canon in D. *James.* Pushing regret aside for the moment, she swiped her thumb across the screen. "Hey, sweetheart. I'm kind of in the middle of things. Can it wait till I get back?"

"Sure. Is something wrong?"

"No. Just a bit distracted."

"You sound like you've been crying."

The love in his voice almost gave her reason to hope that no matter what, even the inability to have kids, he would keep loving her. But she knew how important a family was to him. He talked about it often enough.

"I'm fine. I'll talk to you soon." Elinor forced cheerfulness into her voice.

"I love you. More than you know."

"I love you, too." She tossed her phone into the passenger seat, then glanced in the rearview mirror. Sadness welled up in her throat. She wiped moisture from the corner of her eyes and performed a bit of makeup repair. James deserved to know what the doctor had said, but she needed time to get her emotions in order. How could he love her if he knew the whole story?

Shoving that part of history out of her mind, she popped in a Piano Guys CD. Maybe that would help her get in a passable mood before facing James.

CHAPTER TWO

Elinor

E linor had stopped at three flea markets on her way home from the doctor's yesterday, then once her emotions were securely tucked away, she had returned to the Applewood Hill Bed and Breakfast. She had taken full advantage of her position there as assistant manager to ensure she didn't linger too long with anyone capable of reading through the thin veneer protecting her heart. Like her husband, James, or her sister, Karen, who owned the place.

This morning, she had woken up curled in her husband's arms. Equilibrium restored, she decided to hang on to another day of peace before she told him the state of their future. Pausing her effort to tug another box of flea market finds out of the foyer closet, she allowed her thoughts to meander through her memories.

James wanted to be a dad and would have made an amazing one. He always had time for her niece and nephew and loved playing with them when he wasn't working. And he was gentle when they interrupted, no matter what he was doing.

She didn't think she would be a good mother and had no desire to test that theory, but she had never come out and told James that she didn't want any children. Her heart walled itself in every time he talked about it. And now, it wasn't even a choice. She dreaded his disappointment. Regardless, tomorrow she would tell him.

The scent of freshly baked cinnamon rolls wafted into the hallway from the kitchen, pulling Elinor out of her reverie. She was tempted to forget the project in the foyer and dive into comfort food. Instead, she promised herself a roll after she finished.

Elinor checked the time and kicked off her favorite pair of heels. Two hours before the lunch crowd. Enough time to work her magic. She chose the latest Piano Guys album on her music app and stuck in her ear plugs.

Tasked with bringing a fresh look to the bed and breakfast, Elinor enjoyed hunting for the perfect props at flea markets and estate sales across the county. She reached for a stack of framed prints, excited about sprucing this place up. Karen had told her she could wait till after Christmas, but Elinor needed something to occupy her mind.

Half an hour later, the enticement of sweets forgotten, Elinor stared at the new picture grouping on the wall. Frowning, she flicked her hair over her shoulder and reached for the largest frame. She jumped when hands encircled her waist and one of her earplugs was tugged free of its confines.

"There's the prettiest girl in the state." James pulled her close and nibbled her ear.

Shivers ran up Elinor's spine as she giggled. She leaned back into her husband, the top of her head bonking his nose.

"Ow. Be careful with the smeller."

Elinor laughed. Karen had dubbed James "Mr. Darcy" early in Elinor's relationship with him. It was fitting. He was just like she had imagined Mr. Darcy when she first read *Pride and Prejudice* in her high school days. The epitome of handsome. She was glad when the movies finally caught up with her imagination. Plus, James's rich English accent, and aristocratic air he wore when it benefited him, gave a certain flair to his job as manager of the bed and breakfast. The name and reputation stuck. At least in public. To her, he would always be the gentle attentive man who won her heart—one day, flower bouquet, and "as you wish" at a time.

"And everyone thinks you're so proper."

He chuckled. "Little do they know."

She loved him more than she had ever loved anyone, yet even after being married for over a year, she didn't understand why he loved her.

"How's your day so far?" His breath fluttered past her ear.

This love, this connection, was why she had kept her secret. She wasn't brave enough to risk losing it. Banishing her melancholy, she returned play with play. "Nothing exciting. By the way..." She reached into a bag and pulled out a wrapping-paper tube. "I found something for you the last time I went out to the flea market. Forgot to give it to you."

"What I've always wanted. A cardboard sword."

She swatted him. "Be nice or I might give it to someone else."

"I'm behaving."

Ignoring his antics, she slid out her gift and unrolled it to reveal a movie poster of *The Princess Bride.*

He wrapped his arms around her, lifted her from her feet, and spun her around. "You're always doing such nice things for me."

"Put me down." She squirmed to get away.

Setting her down, he laughed and peppered her with kisses. "Only if you promise to focus on us tonight."

"Hmm." She murmured. "What did you have in mind?"

She blushed at his whispered suggestions, despite the lack of audience. Stepping back, she placed her hands on her hips. "Then you better let me finish my work." She gave him a quick peck on the cheek. A night spent shutting out the world together was the perfect antidote for her uncertainties. Maybe in his arms she could find the courage to tell him about her past.

"I suppose I can wait."

They both turned at the sound of yapping from the porch, heralding the appearance of a small dog the size of a large rodent as it tore through the door toward them. It skidded to a halt at their feet. Growling, it planted its tiny paws in as fierce a stance as a dog its size could muster.

"I hate Chihuahuas." Elinor muttered. James forgotten, Elinor and dog stared at each other until an older woman with white hair walked up behind her dog. As tall as Elinor without heels, her posture slumped like she carried the weight of the world on her shoulders. Her eyes cast down, she appeared sad.

Smoothing her skirt, Elinor offered a smile. "May we help you?"

Oblivious to either Elinor or James, the woman held one hand to her back and groaned as she bent to pick up the dog. Cradling it in her arms, she ran her hand down its back like a mother would smooth a troubled child, and then murmuring in the dog's ear, she held out a treat. The animal lapped it out of her palm.

Thinking the woman might be hard of hearing, Elinor reached out to touch the woman's arm. "Ma'am?" The beastette in the woman's arms snapped at Elinor. She jerked back and crossed her arms.

The woman looked Elinor over from head to toe, then glanced at James. Shaking her head slightly, the woman harrumphed. "I need to check in."

Elinor had a feeling that her talent as hostess was about to be sorely tested. "Do you have a reservation?"

The woman raised an eyebrow, then walked back to the front desk.

Elinor looked sideways at James. He barely restrained a smirk. Elinor narrowed her eyes at him, then put on her best demeanor before they followed the woman. "We'll just pull up your reservation. What is your name?"

"Mrs. Helen Granger. And this is Wrinkle. And yes, I called ahead about him."

"Wrinkle?"

The woman giggled. "From *A Wrinkle in Time* by Madeleine L'Engle."

"Well..." Elinor glanced at James, who shrugged, leaving her to fend for herself on the matter. She looked more closely at Wrinkle. The skin did seem to crinkle around the eyes. "It's a unique name."

The woman slapped the counter with the palm of her hand. "Young people these days. Probably haven't read the book.

Madeleine L'Engle was my favorite author as a kid. Just get me checked in." The woman pulled her pet closer and stroked its back.

Elinor refrained from shaking her head or letting loose her voice of frustration. She looked at the computer. A three-week stay. "What brings you to the Applewood Hill Bed and Breakfast?"

The woman looked up, her eyes soft and moistened with tears. "Visiting my kids. First time since my husband died a few years ago." She pulled out a handkerchief from an unseen pocket and dabbed at the corners of her eyes. "Want to see pictures of my grandkids? Let me just put Wrinkle down and I…"

"Mrs. Granger, you need to hold on to Wrinkle for now. We can't have him getting underfoot with our other guests."

"What about the pictures?"

Elinor hesitated at the hope in the woman's expression. She seemed so lonely. "Can you show me later? After you get settled and make sure Wrinkle is in his kennel."

The woman looked down at her feet. "My family doesn't like Wrinkle. That's why I'm staying here. Do you like Wrinkle?"

Before Elinor could find a reply in her heart for that, James reached over to pet the woman's Chihuahua. "We'll make sure Wrinkle feels at home."

When James spoke, the woman's eyes lit up and she grasped his arm. "Your accent…" A tear escaped its captivity. "My husband was from England."

The woman's countenance glowed as he showered Wrinkle with attention.

James always knew the right way to handle the difficult situations. A task Elinor seemed to fail in.

She grabbed the key. "Here you go. Room 108. James, if you have this, I need to finish that project before lunch."

He took the key from her and held onto her hand for a moment. "Go out with me tonight before…?" He wiggled his eyebrows at her.

Elinor blushed at his inference and glanced at their guest. Mrs. Granger smiled, seemingly glad to be in on a bit of romance. Maybe the woman wasn't so bad after all. "What did you have in mind?"

"If I told you, it wouldn't be a surprise. Just be ready by six."

Mrs. Granger clapped. "Oh, I like the sound of this."

Elinor laughed. "I'll be ready." She waved and turned to go.

"Before you go. I almost forgot to tell you we got an inquiry about the Applewood from France."

"France?" Elinor froze.

"An investment company with a branch in Kansas City. Looking for a place to do retreats."

"Paris is a lovely place. My husband and I visited there on our honeymoon. Never made it back, though." Mrs. Granger giggled. "It's so romantic."

James laughed. "Maybe I should take my wife there, someday."

Elinor listened to the exchange. She felt exposed as she attempted to make sense of what James had said. It had to be a coincidence. *It couldn't be...not now. Not him.*

Mrs. Granger winked at Elinor. "You've got you a good catch here, young lady. Don't you let go of him."

Elinor forced herself to engage in the conversation. "I don't intend..."

"Mrs. Elinor. Mrs. Elinor." A blur of energy zipped through the foyer from the direction of the kitchen. The young girl flung herself into Elinor's arms. "You smell good, Mrs. Elinor. Miss Karen told me to hang out with you for a while. I got to hug Miss Karen's baby. Why is Hope still bald? Will she have red hair just like her mama? My hair looks just like my mama's."

"Hello to you too, Clarice." Elinor laughed at the bundle of delight in her arms and gave an apologetic glance with a mouthed "sorry" toward Mrs. Granger, who grinned and waved off the idea that this interruption was a problem.

When Elinor's oldest sister, Joanna, had begun working at the Huddle, an after-school center in downtown Kansas City, no one had expected it to last; not just because it was court ordered, but because Joanna was...Joanna. Yet she'd connected with Clarice. Go figure. And when Joanna headed off to the recovery program in Colorado, the family promised to look out for the girl. She had become a regular fixture at the bed and breakfast and visited as often as someone could pick her up.

Elinor placed a kiss on the girl's cheek. "It's good to see you, too. And, yes, I think Hope will have red hair like her mama. I saw red fuzz the other day."

Laughing, Clarice hopped down and placed a fist on one hip, thrusting her other hip to the opposite side. "So, what we gonna do?" She flipped her braids over her shoulder.

Elinor wondered how the child's grandmother got her to sit long enough to do her homework. At nine years of age, the child had spunk, despite the events of her life.

Clarice's grin drove away the darkness gathering inside of Elinor. "You have a suggestion I suppose?"

Clarice nodded, her bouncing hair emphasizing her enthusiasm. She clapped her hands. "Can we go see the horses at Mr. Charles' stable? And ride them? Please?" She drew the "please" out into a sentence-worth of sound.

Elinor laughed. "I have to finish my work first, but I think I can arrange that this afternoon."

James cleared his throat and raised an eyebrow. He pointed to himself and Elinor.

Drats. By the time she fed Clarice after visiting the stables, then took her home, it would probably be too late to enjoy going on a date. She wrapped her arms around James's waist. "Do you mind if we go out tomorrow night?"

"As long as you're in by curfew. There are some things that I want to talk about." He wiggled his eyebrows.

Mrs. Granger giggled.

Elinor felt her cheeks heat up. "Meet you for dessert in the dining room around eight?"

"I'll be there." He kissed her, then turned back to check in their guest.

"Ewe."

Elinor laughed. "Did Grammie come this time?"

Clarice shook her head. "Grammie isn't feeling well. I hope she doesn't die."

Elinor dropped to her knees and gathered the child into her arms. "Don't even think that way. Let's pray right now. You want to say it?"

The girl nodded. "Mr. Jesus, please make Grammie better. And don't let her die. I love her lots, You know. Amen. Oh, and thank You for Miss Joanna's family. Was that okay, Miss Elinor?"

"Perfect." Clarice's mom was a junkie, married to an abuser. Grammie had full custody. Elinor joined her own silent prayer to the girl's. *Lord, take care of Clarice.*

CHAPTER THREE

Elinor

Well past dinner, Elinor returned from taking Clarice home. The afternoon spent riding horses had been a welcome reprieve, but now with the inquiry from France back on her mind, she became uneasy. Maybe it wasn't him. It wouldn't make sense. Relishing the quiet, she pulled out leftovers and popped them in the microwave. A hot bath sounded nice. After retrieving her food when the microwave dinged, she grabbed her tea and headed to the formal dining room.

Going in backward to push open the swing door, Elinor noticed James walk toward her. Tonight was supposed to be for each other, but she felt like running away, her emotions too much on the surface. He waved. She tilted her head toward the dining room. At least they could enjoy their eight o'clock dessert date.

"I'll grab dessert and be right in."

Tired of keeping up a front, she longed to tell him. She thought that time together would give her courage, but since she heard about this inquiry from France, dread had infected her mind. Forcing a smile, she looked up at her beloved when he walked into the room.

James set two plates of apple pie on the table then knelt next to Elinor's chair and pulled her into a hug. "I don't think I've told you enough today how much I love you."

Elinor played along with their back-and-forth love remarks that had started on their honeymoon. "How much is that?"

"All the way through our life together and back."

Elinor swallowed the knot of tears stuck in her throat. She didn't deserve his love. *God, help me.* She leaned into his hug. "I love you too." She would tell him. Tonight. She needed to get it done without any more delays.

James moved to his chair, leaned forward, and took her hands in his. "What would you think about—"

"—I need to tell you something." Elinor spoke at the same time.

James sat back in his chair. "What's up?"

Elinor shook her head. "No, you go first."

James smiled. "I think we need to take a vacation before the holiday busyness and spend quality time together without getting interrupted."

"That would be nice." If he still wanted to go after she told him.

James kissed her hand. "I watched you with Clarice today. You're countenance changes when you're with her. This vacation might even give us a chance to try starting that family we've been talking about."

"*You've* been talking about it." Elinor's hand flew to her mouth.

"*We've* been talking about it."

"No. You have. I've been listening." She couldn't stop the words from tumbling out. She blinked back tears. Instead of telling him the truth, she was putting up defenses again.

"Are you saying you don't want kids?"

"I'm saying, I'd like to be asked."

"So, do you? Want to have kids?"

Elinor caught her bottom lip between her teeth. "It's more than that. I can't..."

"But the bottom line is you don't want kids? Why didn't you say something sooner? Why did you let me keep hoping?" James stood up and paced from her to the buffet and back.

"Would you have married me if you knew how I felt?"

He stopped in front of her. "Don't accuse me of things I didn't say."

"When we were dating, you told me you didn't marry your childhood sweetheart because you wanted kids and she didn't."

He wrinkled his forehead and tilted his head.

Elinor's voice rose. "Seems it's always about your plans." She stared at James. *Love me enough for both of us, James, please don't give up on me.* But the words lost their way somewhere between her mind and her heart.

"You've been holding onto that? Don't you think if I had really loved her that part wouldn't have mattered? I can't believe this." He looked away from Elinor then back. "Never mind." He shrugged and strode out of the room, then slammed the door back against the wall.

Scooting her plate out of the way, Elinor dropped her head onto her arms and wept. *God, give me strength. I don't know how to do this.* She startled when a hand settled on her shoulder. She glanced up at Karen. "How much did you hear?"

"Just raised voices. Want to talk?"

Elinor shook her head as tears streamed down her cheeks.

Karen dropped to her knees and held Elinor close until her tears were spent.

CHAPTER FOUR

Elinor

E linor had returned to an empty apartment last night after having words with James and crying on Karen's shoulder. She assumed he went for a drive as he often did when he needed to clear his mind. But when midnight arrived and he hadn't shown up or called, she wandered out into the bed and breakfast and found him asleep on the library couch.

She went to bed alone, and was aware of him coming in during the early hours of the morning. It was the first time they had slept apart because of a disagreement. She didn't like it and had lifted a silent prayer for help.

He joined her in bed, curled up next to her and whispered promises of love. She lay still, pretending to sleep, soaking in the warmth of his words, and trying to believe every one of them. Not too long after, she fell back asleep wrapped in his arms.

When Elinor woke up this morning, there was a fresh cup of coffee on her bedside table, along with a note of apology for his harsh words to her during their disagreement. Her tears dripped onto the note. He deserved to know the truth.

An hour later, Elinor strode through the kitchen of the Applewood Hill Bed and Breakfast carrying two file boxes. The chatter of staff in the breakroom and the click of her heels on tile filled the momentary stillness of the kitchen. She enjoyed this time of morning. Guests fed, quiet before the noon rush, and the aroma of breads and desserts fresh from the oven filling the air with temptation.

Her gaze landed on a counter full of apple pies. Her mouth watered, and she thought about absconding with a pie and a box of ice cream. Shaking a mental finger at herself, she gazed longingly at the sweets as she backed out the doorway and headed to Karen's house.

Her sister and brother-in-law, Karen and Barry, had moved back into their house behind the Applewood Hill last month. Almost a year to the day following last year's tornado. After that storm's destruction, it had made sense for Karen and Barry to stay in her and James's attached apartment space and for them to take over the honeymoon suite. Karen's baby being in residence in the honeymoon suite next door to guests wouldn't have gone over too well.

The last year had felt like an eternity. Other than their trip to New York City, where they apartment-sat for Karen's old friends, their newlywed stage was put on hold. As the managers of the bed and breakfast, residing in the honeymoon suite put them only a knock away from their guests' beck and call.

Hushed disagreements left hanging between her and James simmered anxiousness in her heart. She liked things settled. Still, James showered her with his love. He was a better husband than she deserved. And for the most part, excluding discussions about having kids and the possible appearance of a man who—she shuddered—didn't belong in her life, they were happy.

"Thanks for bringing over the last of our boxes." Karen held open her back door as Elinor approached.

"I should have worn my tennis shoes." Elinor kicked off her heels inside the door.

Karen laughed. She took the boxes from her sister and set them on the table. "I've been telling you that for years."

Elinor rolled her eyes.

"How are you doing after last night? Did you get things worked out with James?"

Elinor shrugged. "It's more like we just moved on."

Karen gave her sister a hug. "If you need to talk, you know where to find me."

Elinor nodded. "Thanks."

"Ti.Ti."

Elinor bent down and waited for Hope to toddle her way. Still bald except for a bit of fuzz over her head, she turned one year old last month. Unable to say "Aunt Elinor" yet, "TiTi" had become Hope's name for her aunt.

Elinor wrapped her arms around Hope and held her close. Despite Elinor's insecurities about having her own kids, she loved her niece. A miracle in the middle of a storm. She still couldn't believe that Joanna, of all people, had delivered Hope in the basement in the middle of a tornado when no one could get to them. Joanna surprised everyone though, including herself.

Hope squirmed to get down, then toddled back to her toys. Elinor reached for a brownie, cooling next to the stove.

"Those are for Barry."

"It's only one. As a thank-you for carrying over your boxes?"

"You're incorrigible."

Elinor grabbed a brownie, then slipped her shoes back on. "Thanks, sis."

"Why do I try?" Karen threw her hands up in the air and laughed as Elinor opened the back door.

"By the way, I'm taking Alita to see Blake next week." Elinor paused in the doorway.

"What changed her mind about seeing him?"

"Guess I'll find out." Elinor waved as she headed back to the bed and breakfast to finish her latest redecorating project.

It was hard to believe that her older brother, Blake, had been incarcerated since shortly after the same tornado that destroyed

Karen and Barry's house. Several months before the tornado, he had robbed a convenience store and killed a man in the process. He hid out down in Oklahoma for a while, but when he came back to Missouri the police finally caught up with him. From what she understood about the crime, he had reacted in the middle of a PTSD flashback. Still, he had the gun. Refusing a plea based on his condition, he had received a stiff sentence. It was sad how war had messed with his mind.

This would be the first time his wife, Alita, had been to see him since he had been sentenced. Elinor had been reluctant to make another the trip so soon after her last visit, Blake being so belligerent. But the family had made a commitment with each other to visit him regularly, so she went when it was her turn. Besides, she was curious why Alita wanted to go. When she agreed to shop flea markets and estate sales on the way back as a thank-you for Elinor's keeping her company, that had sealed the deal.

CHAPTER FIVE

Elinor

D ecorated with reds, yellows, oranges, and browns to usher in the season, the large oval table in the private dining room delighted the senses. Elinor placed an arrangement of orange mums on the table between tall candlesticks, then stepped back. Setting the table for the Sunday family dinners afforded her the opportunity to practice her hostess skills. And to show off a bit. Not sure the family appreciated it, though. But it was satisfying. For the most part, paper plates would do the trick. But Sundays, she insisted that if dinners were required, so were the nice dishes.

Karen walked up beside her. "You have a flair for this. You need to start a business."

"Might spoil the fun."

"Maybe. Something to think about, though."

"There's my girls." Charles strode into the room and tossed his ever-present cowboy hat onto the table. After putting an arm around each of his daughters he pulled them into a hug. "Where is everyone?"

"Barry should be here any minute with Hope. Albert and Haley are on their way. Not sure about the others." Karen gave her dad a sideways hug before excusing herself to the kitchen. "Better check on the roast."

Elinor rearranged a fork that was slightly askew, then chided herself. When her dad was in the room, she reverted to her old compulsion to get everything perfect. Forcing her hands to her sides, she watched the man she hadn't quite made peace with yet. He wore a rough-around-the-edges look, but that came with his outdoor lifestyle. Between caring for the orchard and the stables, and spending days outside hunting, the sun beat down on his skin more than any indoor lighting, leaving his skin leathered. And though he sported graying hair, he carried himself like a young man. He probably would have thrived in the old west.

He moved away from the buffet when Karen and Barry carried in more food with Hope toddling behind them. Karen had lucked out in the handsome-husband category, marrying an Indiana-Jones-looking corporate type. With black hair. Elinor laughed to herself as her thoughts came out just as jumbled as Clarice's words.

Alita followed close behind with a bowl of fruit, her honey-brown hair swaying back and forth just above the shoulders. Married to their brother Blake, now in prison, Alita maintained her involvement in the family. "Where should I put this, Elinor?"

"At the end is good."

A commotion in the foyer announced the entrance of Annie and Charlie—Albert and Haley's kids—just before they barreled through the doors. Annie sported the familiar red Hannigan hair while Charlie took after his dad with dark brown locks.

"Grandpa." The twins ran straight for Charles. Annie wrapped her arms around his waist while Charlie stood to the side, head hanging as if in disgrace.

Charles ruffled his grandson's hair. "What's up, cowboy?"

Albert walked up behind his son. "He didn't like a decision I made."

Charles nodded at Albert, the youngest of his five kids. "That happens." Charles gave Albert's wife, Haley, a hug. "Did you bring my favorite dessert or did your husband eat it all before you got it out the door?" He angled his head toward Albert.

Haley laughed. "I'll bring it next time. This time, just cookies." She handed her dish to Elinor to be placed on the buffet.

"I'll try and be patient. But your strawberry rhubarb pie is hard to wait for. Best crust ever." Charles looked around the room. "Looks like it's time to pray. Link up."

The family gathered around in a circle, hand in hand. Elinor watched her dad pray. His joy was evident. When he first began this tradition of family dinners, they all found excuses not to come. No one held any interest in healing their relationships with each other or their dad. He resorted to threatening them with receiving nothing in his will. He wasn't wealthy, but he owned the orchard, house, stable, lands, and a decent-looking bank account. Enough to serve as motivation.

At first, reluctance prevailed, but unity forced for these moments together. Getting along was a pretense and they only prayed out of duty. She looked around the circle. Still with room for growth, these dinners were no longer a farce, but a time of thankfulness. Content, she bowed her head while her dad prayed.

"Dear heavenly Father, bless our family. Bless Joanna in Colorado and Blake in prison. Keep them in Your care. Draw them ever closer to You. Bless this food as we eat together and thank You for those who prepared it. In Jesus's name, amen."

"Amen, dig in." Charlie ran for the buffet table. Annie followed close behind.

"It's hard to believe Hope is a year old." Like it was yesterday, Elinor remembered Hope's birth.

"Time flies." Karen placed Hope in her highchair and snapped a bib in place.

"Have you heard from Joanna?"

Karen scattered crackers on Hope's tray. "She called last week. She said she enjoys working at the rehab facility now that she's finished her program, but she doesn't want to stay there indefinitely."

"Think she'll come back?" Elinor retrieved the rattle that Hope threw on the floor.

"She said she would try and make it for the holidays, but she was elusive with details."

"That's Joanna for you." Elinor caught the rattle before it landed on the floor again.

Barry set his plate down and kissed Karen on the cheek. "You go on and get your food. I'll watch Hope."

Elinor followed Karen to the buffet. She smiled at James across the dining room. Since their argument a few days ago, he had gone out of his way to shower her with affection. He grinned back as he set his plate down and pointed to the chair next to him then back to her. She nodded and gave him a thumbs-up. Thankful for his love, she tangled herself up comparing it to what she knew of love from her growing up years.

Try as she might, she found it difficult to accept his love. Especially lately with her past pursuing her. *God, I know it in my head, but my heart is having a hard time catching up. Help me figure this out before I lose James.* They had rearranged their missed date for this coming weekend. She hoped she could find the strength to say what needed to be said.

"Hey, sis. How's it going?" Albert joined her in line.

Elinor startled out of her thoughts. "Keeping busy." She picked up a plate and began to fill it.

"Think you could spare a couple hours for your brother?" He looked at her with puppy dog eyes. "I could use your decorating expertise at the church this week."

"What's up?"

"Getting ready for the church's twenty-fifth anniversary celebration. And the golden-agers and the twenty-somethings are vying for control. Need an outside hand in the matter."

"I see how it is. Put me into the pot of hot water."

"Yep. They won't be able to resist your smile."

"Right. When did you need help? Alita and I are going to visit Blake on Monday."

"Don't need you till Friday. Will you do it?"

"Are you giving me a choice?"

"Nope."

"Fine." She marched to the table and sat in her unofficially reserved seat.

Albert sat beside her and nudged her elbow with his. "If you don't want to help, I understand."

She nudged him back. "No, I'll help. Sorry to get grumpy on you."

He shrugged. "Did you get any of the sweet potato casserole? I'll go get you some." He scooted back his chair.

"I'll get it later if I want any." She placed a hand on his arm.

"You sure?"

"I'm not a kid anymore."

"Just trying to be nice." He slumped back in his chair.

Elinor gritted her teeth. After Karen left home and the brunt of Dad's anger fell on them, Albert often took her punishments for her. He did lots of things at school and church for her that she could have done for herself. And he still stepped in uninvited to do things for her then got upset when she refused his help. She had resented him in high school, treating her like she wasn't able to take care of herself, and she resented him now.

Counting to ten, she unclenched her hands under the table and forced herself to relax. "I appreciate it, but I already have a full plate. See?"

He shrugged. "You're missing out."

"Halloo. Where is everybody?" Elinor turned as Mrs. Granger poked her head through the door, her white hair now a familiar sight around the bed and breakfast.

Karen greeted the older woman and gave her a hug. "Remember, we only serve breakfast on Sunday."

"Oh." Her eyes echoed a sadness Elinor hadn't seen since her dad stood over the bed of her dying mother three and a half years ago.

"My family went up to St. Joe and the Pony Express Museum. They didn't think I would enjoy going." She looked around the room, her gaze lingering on the kids. "I just hate leaving Wrinkle in his kennel all the time."

"Why don't you join us?" Karen guided the woman further into the dining room.

Mrs. Granger's eyes lit up. "You wouldn't mind?"

"Making you a place right here." Charles moved a chair next to his. "Maybe later you can show my grandkids your dog."

"Yes, please." Annie and Charlie chimed in together.

You would have thought the woman had just won a million-dollar sweepstakes. She stood up straighter and her step lacked its shuffle as she headed to the buffet.

Looking over the selection, she laughed. "This is fun. Thank you." She loaded up her plate and sat next to Charles. Barely touching her food, she engaged with the conversation.

The transformation in the older woman amazed Elinor. Belonging, being wanted, made all the difference.

CHAPTER SIX

Elinor

E linor wove the car through traffic on their way through Kansas City. She glanced over at Alita staring out the window at the passing scenery. "Looks like you have a lot on your mind."

Alita shrugged. "Mind if I turn on the radio?" She reached for the dial.

"I have Piano Guys CDs in the glove compartment."

"I was thinking a bit of country?"

Elinor bit back a groan. At least it wasn't rap or hard rock. "We can take turns. You choose first."

Alita found a station then settled back in her seat. "Thank you for going with me to see Blake."

Elinor glanced at her sister-in-law. "How come you waited this long to go?"

"At first I planned to divorce him." Alita played with a string from the hem of her sweater.

"I hear a 'but' in there."

"Staying married didn't make sense. But Karen made me promise to pray about it."

"She has a habit of doing that." Elinor chuckled.

"True."

The music from the radio enveloped them as they drove. Waiting for Alita to gather her thoughts, Elinor's gaze landed on the fields empty of livestock and crops on either side of the highway. Bare trees stood at attention against a brilliant blue sky. Not a cloud to be seen; the sun gave an illusion of warmth.

Alita turned down the radio. "Every time I picked up the phone to call my lawyer, I would get nauseated. I couldn't make myself go through with it. Then last Sunday, Albert preached about second chances."

"You decided not to divorce Blake?"

"Pretty much."

"You're a better woman than I am." Elinor reached over and placed a hand on top of Alita's.

Alita wiped her eyes with the back of her sleeve. "Don't say that. I have thought so many awful things about Blake. If your brother hadn't said those things from the pulpit, I would probably still be bent over the toilet throwing up about the matter." She shrugged.

"I'm glad you asked me to come along."

"I'm glad you agreed to come."

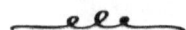

After an hour wait, then going through the lengthy check-in process, Elinor and Alita stared through the glass at Blake, arms crossed, tattoos labeling him according to every vice he ever encountered. With his hair cropped short in a military regulation cut, he looked every bit a stereotypical tough guy standing guard against threat. Blake gave Elinor a cursory glance, then ignored her. She felt like an intruder as she scrunched into her chair, attempting to give them a semblance of privacy. She had told Alita to come in on her own, but she insisted Elinor come.

There was a tenderness in Blake's eyes as he watched his wife, and his voice didn't hold the edge Elinor heard the last time she came to visit with Karen. One of the benefits of state supplied meds, she was sure.

Alita picked up the phone that allowed visitors to communicate with prisoners. "Hello."

"You should have stayed away."

"How are you?"

"You don't want to hear about prison." He looked down at the counter in front of him.

"I want to hear about you."

"Why?"

Alita pulled her lower lip between her teeth and looked up at the ceiling as though in thought. "I talked to the boys last week."

Blake narrowed his eyes. "They still after a pound of my flesh?"

"They have a lot of hurt, but I'm hopeful they'll come around."

"Right. And how's that? They have a religious experience or something?"

She touched the glass then looked down at the counter in front of her. "I'm just hopeful."

"Why now? I thought we were done." He looked into her eyes then away.

"I did, too"

"Did?"

Alita glanced at Elinor, then back at her husband. "Karen challenged me to pray about it."

"She should mind her own business."

Alita touched the glass that separated them. "I'm not going to divorce you." Moisture rimmed her eyes.

Blake touched the glass as if he could feel her hand against his. He squeezed his eyes shut. "I'm not worth it."

"Everyone deserves a second chance."

"Not me."

"Everyone."

He shook his head and leaned back in his chair. "You're better off without me. File the papers and move on."

"No."

They stared at each other until Blake pushed his chair back and stood. "Move. On. You deserve more than I ever gave you." He hung up the phone and touched the glass one more time as he mouthed the words "I love you" before the guard led him away.

Elinor leaned over and hugged her sister-in-law as she contemplated what Blake just did. Trying to do right by Alita. She hadn't expected that.

CHAPTER SEVEN

Elinor

E linor snuggled into James. After getting back late last night from the prison, she and James had spent the evening sipping tea in front of the fireplace. They'd chatted until early this morning before following their hearts into each other's arms. An immunization against the fears incubating in her heart.

"Honey?" James caressed Elinor's cheek. "I know you don't like to talk about having kids. Please help me understand."

She twirled a strand of her hair around her finger. How could she explain this truthfully without going into all the details? She wanted to wait until they had more uninterrupted time to tell him everything. "I'm not sure how to explain it. Would it help that I like having you to myself?"

He held her gaze for a few seconds then sat up on the opposite edge of the bed.

Elinor scooted close behind him and rested her hand on his back. He stiffened under her touch. Squeezing her eyes shut, she bit her lip.

He turned and searched her face. "I appreciate that, but I know there's more."

"I'm scared." She whispered as tears trickled down her cheeks. *Of telling you the truth. Of being a good mother when I already rejected one child. Of losing you.*

"What?"

She brought her knees up under her chin. "I'm scared."

He caressed her cheek. "What are you scared of?"

"Having kids."

"Why didn't you tell me?" He wiped her tears with his thumb.

"You've never made it a secret how important having kids was to you. I hoped I would grow into it, but the thought still terrifies me." She pleaded with her eyes. "I can't lose you."

James tucked her hair behind her ear. "Not going to happen. You're stuck with me."

She gave him a weak smile. "Why do you love me so much?"

"You're my gift from God. He knit my heart to yours the first moment I laid eyes on you. I believe you were helping Karen with a little old lady at the bed and breakfast. Made you late back to work at that antique place, if I remember Karen telling it right. You were so kind. And beautiful. Something inside me connected with you unlike I had with anyone else. You brightened my day every time you stopped by the Applewood."

"You never told me that." She wiped an escaped tear.

"The secret's out. Think any less of me?"

She shook her head.

"Why would I think any less of you for being scared?"

Elinor stilled under his gaze and shrugged, throwing more dirt on top of her secret. Doubt threw another shovel full on top. How could he keep loving her if he knew all of it? Maybe that person from France wasn't the man she thought he was. Maybe her past could remain hidden. She sucked in a deep breath on the edge of a sob.

"Let's just open the discussion of having kids, without the pressure of a when. Get a green light from the doctor. I'd like to dream a bit about a mini-Elinor running around. Tour some houses that have enough bedrooms. Think about living somewhere other than where we work."

"It would be nice not to wake up to the sounds of the bed and breakfast." She leaned against him

"We'll still have that family, but only when you're ready. Can we start there?"

"I think I can handle talking about it." This weekend she would have to tell him she already went to the doctor. Tell him what the doctor said and why. No matter what, he deserved the truth. But for now, she relished his assurances too much to bring it up.

CHAPTER EIGHT

Albert

"Where do you want all this stuff? Elinor reached for one of the boxes that was labeled Christmas decorations.

"There's a reason I asked you to help." Relieved that Elinor had come to sort through the decorations, Albert was in good spirits today. His energy level was higher than usual. He leaned against the doorframe and watched her work. She had a knack for making things beautiful, that was for sure. No wonder Karen had hired her at the bed and breakfast. He was thankful every time Karen shared their sister's time and skill with him. Especially on a Friday during one of their busier days.

"If it were up to me, I wouldn't use any of this stuff in the storage room."

"Then we would have World War Three on our hands. Can't you spruce it up without demolishing these...precious gems?" Albert scrunched up his nose when an unpleasant smell drifted his way as Elinor opened the box. "What is that?"

"Ewe." Elinor pulled out an outdated flower arrangement and plopped it on the floor. "It smells mildewy and needs to go. I don't care what anyone says."

"Agreed." He picked it up, holding it as far away from his body as he could and took it outside to the trash bin.

"Yoohoo."

Albert looked up at the woman headed his way. No. Glancing down at the odorous bouquet, he grimaced. Surely the smell would be enough to convince Mrs. Bowing that her once wonderful creation had seen its last days. "Hello, Mrs. Bowing. I didn't expect you today."

She stopped in front of him and took the bouquet out of his hands. "Obviously. It's a good thing I arrived when I did." She nodded toward the dumpster. "No doubt, my great-grandmother's flower arrangement would have been lost to my family forever."

Albert bit back a sharp reply. "Perhaps it's time they resided in your own home. Given the sentimental value they hold for you."

"Are you kidding? My husband would have a fit if I brought them home. They belong right here, in the very building my grandmother got married in." She marched up the stairs and into the foyer. "And I hope that sister of yours hasn't brought her high airs with her for the decorating party."

"Party?" Albert followed Mrs. Bowing close behind.

She set the vase down on a table near the door. "You didn't think I would leave the other girls out of it, did you?" She went back to the door and looked outside. "They should be here any time, now."

Elinor glared at him from the door of the storage closet.

He shrugged and mouthed, "I'm sorry."

"You owe me." She mouthed back.

He gave her a mock salute before he turned to the older women chatting among themselves as they entered the building. How would he get through this afternoon? He loved every member of his congregation, but lately it felt like all he ever got from them was complaints. Expectations with no freedom to accomplish what needed to be done. He looked heavenward and lifted a silent plea. *Lord, I don't know how much more of this I can take.*

Mrs. Bowing, along with the other ladies, planted themselves in front of Albert and waved Elinor over to join them. "We've decided to let Elinor decorate the bathroom. We'll take care of the rest."

Elinor raised an eyebrow. "Mrs. Bowing, you don't need to hand something off to me to make me feel good. I am not offended in the least if you want to handle this without me."

The women's faces filled with relief.

"If you're sure." Mrs. Hansom, sporting a velour leisure outfit and down-to-the-shoulders thinning hair, laid a hand on Elinor's arm. "You're very gracious young lady."

Just then, the door to the foyer popped open. A group of young mothers clomped into the building, young children in tow. A baby cried and several toddlers chased each other, yelling in delight.

Albert held his breath. He could anticipate how this would go and he didn't want to be here to see it unfold.

Mrs. Bowing huffed and turned to Albert. "We don't need them to help us."

One of the young mothers walked toward them. "What can we do?"

Mrs. Bowing hesitated a moment then led the way to the storage room. "Pull all of these boxes out. Our old joints can't do all that lifting and tugging like they used to."

The young woman smiled. "We'd be happy to." Two other ladies joined her, and they began the task of hauling boxes of decorations from the storage room.

Albert motioned for Elinor to follow him back to his office.

"They're wound tighter than necessary." Elinor sat in one of the chairs in front of the large picture window, then draped her legs over one arm, leaning against the other.

Albert sat across from her. "Just a bit." He leaned his elbows on his knees and rested his forehead in his hands.

"You too?"

He looked up. "That obvious?"

"Why don't you pastor somewhere else?"

He shrugged. "Likely be the same anywhere I went."

"You'll be fine. Always are."

He snorted. He didn't feel fine. "How's the married life?"

"Changing the subject?"

"If it works."

"It's good. I suppose."

"You suppose. Why can't you just be happy with what you have?"

"What's that supposed to mean?"

He ran a hand through his hair. "Forget I said it."

"No. I'd like to hear what's on your mind."

"Look, I'm just tired. I shouldn't have said that." He always opened his mouth at the wrong time.

"When did we stop getting along?" Elinor crossed her arms and waited.

"After Europe?" Albert wondered where Elinor was headed with the line of thought. "We did pretty good before that, though."

"Ha. I remember it differently."

"What do you mean?"

"You treated me like a china doll. Critiqued my every move."

"I was trying to protect you from Dad."

"At what cost?" Elinor twirled a strand of hair between her fingers.

Albert pointed at her hair wrapped tight around a finger. "Haven't seen you do that in a while. Not since…" Albert stopped himself. He thought she had worked through everything with their dad. At least she came across that way. Of course, neither of them had the same kind of issues Joanna and Blake had. "What's going on?"

"Nothing. Even if there were, I can take care of myself, now. Thank you very much." Elinor swung her legs around to the front of the chair.

"Do you dislike me so much for trying to protect you?

"I just wanted to be my own person."

"Is that why you had a double life while we were in high school?"

"I wouldn't call it that."

"I remember how unhappy you were in high school and the lengths you went to change things."

She narrowed her eyes and glared at him. "I'm not you, I couldn't just suck it up and keep going."

"It was deceitful."

"Like pretending everything is fine when you're obviously ready to move on from this pastoring life isn't deceitful? Take care of your own issues before you start poking around in someone else's. Besides, that was a long time ago."

He shouldn't have let her push him into telling her what was on his mind. She was good at that. Did it all the time growing up. And then she acted like she was better than him, while she was the one leading a double life. If their dad had ever found out, Albert wouldn't have been able to stand in the way of her punishment.

She never got in and out of trouble and she wasn't easy with the guys or partied with the drug heads, but her stack of fashion magazines she kept in her locker at school gave her plenty of ideas on how to present herself to the world. She must have had an entire wardrobe stashed in there, too. She always arrived early, and by the time class started, she wasn't the quiet mousy kid that Dad knew.

"What about taking Dad's money for your senior trip to Europe?"

Elinor stood and waved her hands in the air like an orator making a grand point. "You critiqued me, Dad did, Mom did. I just wanted to figure out who I was for myself."

"Did you? Figure that out on the trip?"

"That was the plan. What about you? You figured out who you are yet?"

Albert stared at his sister and thought about what to say. Nothing came to mind. "This is getting us nowhere, Elinor. Don't feel like you have to stick around." Leaving her to stare after him, he sulked out of his office and into the gaggle of women, fluttering around, posting faded and musty decorations about the building. This was the last place he had the heart to be. There was no way he could prepare for Sunday. He would have to come back tomorrow. At least it should be quiet.

Saturday morning came too soon. Especially after a late night in front of the television when sleep eluded him. But it couldn't be helped. Albert dropped the kids off at a friend's house for the day and headed to the church with every intent to finish the sermon, but the church ended up not being the quiet refuge he imagined.

The ladies were back, preparing for the twenty-fifth anniversary celebration, and the noise distracted him from focusing.

By noon, they were done. Albert waved them on their way and locked the door behind them. He didn't want any needy members coming into the building seeking his counsel today. Albert mentally shook a shame-on-me finger at himself.

Even though he hadn't worked with the group today, he found himself deeply resentful of their intrusion into his mental space. He never used to feel this way about the people in his congregation. All he ever wanted to do was serve them. He loved them, but lately he couldn't stand a day with them around. Where had he lost his way?

He worked till midafternoon when brain fog settled around him. Giving his outline a once-over, he printed out a copy and shut down his computer as he prepared to leave. Tonight, he and Haley were headed over to their friends' house. The football game on a wide screen TV for the guys, video games for the kids, and who knew what their wives would do. If Haley were to ask him right now, he didn't have the energy to think about spending the evening with Mitch and Izzy.

He eyed the sofa. A nap sounded heavenly. A glance at the clock told him a power nap would have to do. But maybe that would help him get ahead of this brain fog, so he could at least pretend to enjoy tonight. He set a wake-up alarm on his phone then turned the notifications and ringer off. Relaxing into the cushions, within minutes he fell asleep.

"Albert?"

Haley's soft voice talked to him in his dream.

He smiled into her blue green eyes. Framed by bouncy red hair, her face brightened the dark thoughts of his dream. Why did she look so worried? He reached for her but grabbed air instead. Where did she go? He listened for her voice. It was louder now.

"Albert?"

A bright light pierced the darkness. He closed his eyes against the sudden onslaught, then felt the cool touch of her hand against his cheek. He grinned at her. "This is a nice surprise."

"I've been trying to reach you. Finally decided to use that key you gave me eons ago. Do you realize what time it is?"

He sat up and grabbed his phone. "No way. I just lay down for a power nap."

Haley sat next to him and rubbed his back. "We need to head over to Mitch and Izzy's."

"I don't know what's wrong with me. A two-hour nap?"

Haley stood up. "We can talk about it on the way."

Albert's stomach clenched up. He didn't need her pestering him about what was wrong, especially not in front of the kids. "I want to talk now."

Haley sat back down. "You haven't been sleeping well at night. Maybe that's the problem."

He looked at her. "I guess you have it all figured out."

"No, I just..."

His irritation grew. Nerves on end, he recoiled at her defense. "You just what?"

"Look, I'm not trying to start anything. You said you wanted to talk." She held up her hands in surrender. "If you don't want to go tonight, that's fine, but I'm going and I'm taking the kids. They've been looking forward to this for a long time." She stood and walked toward the door.

"Haley." He followed her into the hallway. "I'm sorry. I don't like the way I've been acting. I just don't understand what's gotten into me lately or what to do about it."

"I don't know either, Albert." She reached her arms around his neck.

He held her tight as though she were a lifeline in a raging sea. She had no idea the depth of his turmoil lately. He had managed to avoid talking about it, but his behavior was catching up to his raw emotions. He didn't like the possibilities of where that might take him. Shaking off the foreboding, he breathed in her musky fragrance, his muscles relaxing.

He would go tonight. For her. "A night out would probably be good for me. The kids with you?"

She shook her head. "We can pick them up at the house when we drop off one of the cars."

"Let me grab my bag."

CHAPTER NINE

Albert

Albert looked in the rearview mirror. Annie and Charlie sang another one of their camp songs. Again. Determined to make tonight fun, he bit back a plea for silence. They were almost to Mitch and Izzy's house, anyway.

"Albert."

The panic in Haley's voice drew his gaze back to the road. He swerved and missed side swiping a car coming straight at them, traveling with their tires on the center line. He swore. "Stupid driver." He glanced in the rearview mirror and then sideways at Haley. The kids got quiet but didn't look his way. Haley stared out the window. He was tired of watching his every word. He tapped his thumbs against the steering wheel. People in his congregation swore. But if he let out the occasional word, they acted like the world was falling apart.

He turned down their friends' drive. At least Mitch and Izzy were laid back. Not serving-beer laid back, but certainly not judgmental. He could relax tonight.

The kids scrambled out of the car and dashed for the door. Not waiting for anyone to answer, they opened it wide and hurried inside. Albert held Haley's hand as they strolled to the house. He leaned over and kissed her on the forehead. "Love you."

"Me, you."

"Now, three."

"Now, four."

"Love you more."

Haley giggled and squeezed his hand.

He grinned at their silly back-and-forth that anchored him to his commitment to his wife. Born during the rough childbearing years, it never failed to warm his heart toward her. He scrunched his mouth in a frown. Lately, they hadn't had enough of these moments between just the two of them. Maybe a weekend away would help him. The kids could stay with Mitch and Izzy. He would check with them tonight.

Mitch opened the door and took the casserole dish from Haley. "My favorite?"

"Would I dare bring anything else?"

He laughed and slapped Albert on the back. "Better hold on to her."

"Wouldn't dream of not." Mitch's words felt like a reprimand. *I haven't done anything wrong.*

They tossed their jackets over the back of the couch, then joined Izzy in the kitchen, where she was finishing up dinner prep. She glanced up from the chopping board. "Mitch, could you check the steaks?"

"Got it." He glanced at Haley and Albert and rolled his eyes. "After all these years, she thinks I'll burn the meat."

Izzy threw a towel at her husband's head. "Go."

He gave her a mock salute, grabbed his coat, and headed to the sliding door to the patio. "It's a good thing there's no snow on the ground or you would have to grill the meat yourself." Laughing, he ducked as wadded-up paper towel sailed his way.

At that moment, Mitch's two kids, Madison and Ethan, dashed through the kitchen. Near the same age as Albert's kids, who followed close behind, they were always moving. They bumped into the table and glasses full of ice water wobbled and threatened to fall over.

Albert laid a head on the table to steady it. "Watch out, kids." His raised voice brought the kids sliding to a halt. Madison and Ethan looked at their mother with questions in their eyes.

Izzy's head jerked up. "You don't have to yell. They're just being kids. Chill out, Albert."

He supposed her smile was expected to soften her words. He hadn't yelled at the kids. A gentle bark, maybe, but they needed to be reminded where they were. He glanced at Haley staring at the floor. Why was she upset? He tamped down his rising frustration and smiled. "Sorry. Been a long day."

Izzy narrowed her eyes, looking back and forth between her two guests. Pretending not to notice, Albert sidestepped closer to Haley and put an arm around her shoulders. She stiffened.

Fine. "I'm going to go check on Mitch. Maybe he needs a bit of help with the meat." He scooped up his coat and followed his friend outside. Closing the door with an extra measure of gusto, Albert stepped out on the patio and slipped into his coat.

Mitch glanced up from turning the meat.

"Women." Albert leaned against the railing and crossed his arms.

"Had enough female chatter?"

"Something like that."

Closing the lid on the grill, Mitch raised an eyebrow at Albert. "What?"

"You're a bit touchy." Mitch sat at the patio table then waved Albert over to join him. "What's going on?"

Staring at Mitch, Albert sat and leaned back in the chair. Had Haley been talking to Izzy? He drummed the arm of the chair with his fingers. "Nothing." Why did everyone want to get in his business?

"We've known each other, how long, now?"

Albert shrugged. "About six years."

"Try closer to nine. Our first Sunday, you weren't even there. You were at the hospital with your wife and new babies."

Albert grinned. "And we've been hanging out ever since. What's that got to do with anything?"

"I know when something isn't right. Spill it, man."

Albert looked out over the yard toward the sunset. He shivered as a breeze blew across the yard. He wasn't sure he knew how to talk about the mess currently in his head. Besides, he was a pastor. How would Mitch respond?

"Not sure. I'm tired. All the time. Edgy. I get mad at the drop of a hat. But it doesn't make sense. All in all, life is good. I see the way Haley and the kids look at me when I lose it." He glanced across the table at Mitch.

Mitch wove his fingers together and placed his elbows on the table. "Sounds like my brother. At least what he was like a year ago."

Albert bounced his knee up and down. What kind of quick fix would Mitch throw his way. Buck up and move on? "He's better now?"

Mitch nodded. "He was diagnosed with depression. Got a prescription and..."

"I do not have depression." Albert scooted his chair back and stood.

Mitch held up his hands. "Not saying you do. But it might be worth a trip to the doc's."

"My life is too good for me to be depressed."

"My brother had more issues with what happened as a teenager than he did with the present. Never took care of it and it creeped up on him."

Albert paced like a caged animal. "I can handle this without being labeled as depressed and pumped with drugs."

"Think about it?" Mitch returned to the grill. "I better get the meat in. They're going to send out a search party if we don't come in soon."

Albert stomped across the patio and into the house, leaving the door wide open. He didn't need everyone snooping around in his head. He grabbed Haley's coat and handed it to her. "We're leaving."

Haley looked from him to Izzy and Mitch.

"I said we're going. Get your coat on. Kids, come on."

"I was looking forward to the evening." Haley hugged her coat to herself.

Albert felt ready to explode. *I can't yell at my family. I have to keep it inside.* He took a deep breath and found his self-control. "I'm tired, Haley. I should have said something before. Please, can we just go home?"

Izzy stepped over to Haley and put an arm around her. We can get her and the kids home. Would that work?"

Albert looked at Mitch and shrugged. "Sure. If that's what you want." As he marched to the door, he heard Haley burst into tears.

"I just wish I knew what was wrong. Maybe there's something I could change."

"It's not you, Haley." Mitch's voice followed him out into the chilly November air. "Albert, wait up." Mitch hurried after Albert.

Albert stopped and waited next to his car. "What?"

"If you decide you want to talk, call me."

Albert gave a curt nod and slid into the car seat. "Thanks for bringing my family home."

Home alone, waiting for his family, he thought of the sermon outline lying on his desk and discovered an urge to disappear and avoid another Sunday in the pulpit. Then what would he do? Preaching was all he knew.

CHAPTER TEN

Albert

Albert waited while the choir finished their last song. He dreaded preaching today. With his focus off the entire week, preparation had been spotty at best. The last two days had been the worst. Dealing with the ladies decorating for the church's anniversary celebration next week had interrupted what little concentration he'd mustered, but then falling asleep during the only time he had to work? Why did Mitch have to bring up his state of mind last night? Albert pinched the bridge of his nose. He needed focus. *God help me.*

Albert couldn't remember the time when his prayers had been for anything other than his own survival. He longed to be in that place again with an easy back-and-forth with God throughout his day. Not just for himself, but for those in his congregation and his family. Thinking about it aroused an overwhelming exhaustion in his spirit.

A subject to contemplate at another time. As the choir filed off the stage, he walked up to the pulpit. He had preached so often, he could do this in his sleep. Facing his congregation, he pulled out a smile from some unknown resource inside himself. The humorous anecdote spilled out of his mouth without a thought, but then in the middle of an idea, his mind went blank. Stumbling to find his place in his notes, he apologized to the audience, then cut things short after one point being made in its entirety. Better to end on an up note. He made his way to the back exit to greet people as they left and steeled himself to receive the sure-to-come critique of his sermon.

Mitch approached him. Pulling Albert into a hug, his friend whispered a prayer of blessing and reaffirmed his offer to listen if needed. Moisture gathered in the corners of Albert's eyes until he glanced at the next person in line.

Mrs. Bowing. Dread filled Albert and he wanted to dash back to his office, lock the door, and cry. *I'm a grown man, for goodness' sake.* Sucking in his breath, he smiled, and prepared his mind to be beat into the ground with her harsh opinion of him.

"Mrs. Bowing. So good to see you."

Arms crossed, she looked at him long and hard, then seemed to come to a decision. Relaxing her stance, she leaned over and patted his arm. Looking behind herself as though she was concerned about who might hear her, she whispered, "You look tired, Albert. I think you're pushing yourself too hard. Why don't you go home and take a nap?"

Albert pulled back slightly, eyebrows raised, surprised at this twist in his expectations.

Mrs. Bowing chuckled. "You ever met my husband?"

"No."

"No matter." She lowered her voice again. "I understand depression. That's all. A nap, young man. Okay?"

Albert nodded, all the while feeling as though he had been gut punched. He did not have depression. He shook off the feeling of impending doom as he greeted the next person in line.

After what seemed an eternity, he was alone in the empty sanctuary. In the foyer, his family waited.

He walked down the aisle and knelt at the front. "God, I'm coming up empty and don't know what to do. I could use a bit of help." Looking at the cross hanging on the wall at the back of the stage, he bowed his head. The soft steps of shoes on carpet alerted him to someone's approach and he rose from his prayer spot.

"You okay, honey?"

Albert nodded. "Just taking a minute with God."

Back in the foyer, Elinor marched up to him, musty old flowers in her hand. "We need to do something about these. They are ugly and outdated, and besides that, they stink."

"No, I think those are just fine." Whether or not Albert agreed with Mrs. Bowing's assessment, her kindness meant a lot.

Elinor tilted her head. "Someone put something in your coffee this morning?"

Albert managed a chuckle. "Maybe we could deodorize them somehow? You're always reading those DIY and home improvement magazines. Surely there's an idea or two in there we could try."

"Fine. I'll see what I can do." She pivoted away from Albert and walked back the way she came.

Barry pointed Elinor's way with his thumb. "What's got into her?"

"A minor difference of opinion."

"That would do it. Hey, still game to go see Blake this week?"

Albert bit down a sarcastic remark about his older brother. "Sure, what time?"

"I can get away from the bed and breakfast tomorrow or Tuesday. Which is best for you?"

"Tomorrow is fine." Albert wanted to get his duty to family out of the way. "Wait, it will have to be Tuesday. Tomorrow, I'm meeting with the church board."

"Can you be ready by six so we can beat rush hour out of the city?"

"Why not?"

"Doing anything today? Want to watch the game on the big screen later today?"

"Thanks, but I think I just want to go home and take a nap." Albert followed Barry out and locked the door. Maybe he should just take a week off. Sleep the whole time. Like that would ever happen. Haley would have a to-do list made up in no time.

CHAPTER ELEVEN

Albert

Albert climbed into Barry's car. "How about those Chiefs?"

"Glad they're on a winning streak." Barry pulled out of the driveway.

"Right. All I ask is not another season like 2012."

"Glad I missed that one." Barry merged onto the highway then reached toward the console. "Radio?"

Albert shrugged. "You're driving."

Barry dropped his hand and glanced at Albert.

Albert reached for the knobs. "I don't mind."

Christian music filled the air. Hoping to avoid conversation about their upcoming visit with Blake, Albert leaned back in his seat and closed his eyes. His gut churned over yesterday's meeting with the church board. Concern for his wellbeing had been the topic of their conversation. He clenched his fists. Sunday's sermon had sent them scrambling to talk behind his back. He cursed. Glancing sideways at Barry, he waited for a reprimand.

"What's up?" Barry turned the volume down on the radio.

"Just resting."

"And I have season tickets to the Chiefs."

"I didn't sleep well last night." At least that part was true.

"I've never heard you swear before."

"Fine, you want to know what's going on? Yesterday, the church board informed me that I need to take a sabbatical."

"That sounds like a good thing."

"A three-week vacation is a good thing. But they expect me to take three months. And they didn't give me a choice. Told me if I don't take the time, they will have to let me go. As it is, I have to undergo a review after my time off to see if I'm fit to be their pastor."

"What did Haley say?"

"I haven't told her yet." Albert looked down at his clenched fists.

"Need to do that."

"I know. I will." Albert stared out the window. "I just don't want to disappoint her."

"I get that."

"And I don't want her to jump at the chance to make a honey-do list."

"Give her a chance. She probably knows better than anyone that you need a sabbatical to rest, not just to work on something else."

Albert glanced at Barry. Had he been talking to someone behind his back? Albert shook off the feeling that clawed its way into his mind. "It feels like this is just an excuse to ease me out."

"Are they paying you during the sabbatical?"

"Yeah."

"Doesn't sound like they're trying to get rid of you."

"What if they don't want me back after the sabbatical? Being a pastor is all I know."

"I have a feeling you'll find your way. Don't give up on yourself."

Albert snorted. "And what am I supposed to do with myself for three months?"

"What kinds of things do you like to do, but never have the time for?"

"Plenty."

"Do those things. Rest. Maybe volunteer somewhere. Spend time fasting and praying."

"When you put it that way, it sounds like I'll be having a great time. Why doesn't it feel that way?" After holding up his hand when Barry started to respond, Albert turned up the radio and looked out the window. "I'm done with this topic. Don't worry. I'll figure it out." He checked his watch. Two more hours before he had to put on his pastor face to see his brother. Leaning his head back against the headrest, he drifted off to sleep.

Barry and Albert watched through the glass as Blake took a seat opposite them. He nodded and leaned back in the chair. "The familial duty visit."

"How are you?" Albert drummed his fingers on the table.

"Peachy." Blake glared at each of them in turn.

Wishing he could be anywhere but at a table across from his brother, Albert shifted in his chair. Time off from being a pastor would give him an excuse to avoid these awkward conversations. Blake would laugh him out of here if he found out. He didn't want them here anyway.

Barry cleared his throat. "Karen says hello. She'll visit closer to Christmas."

Blake sneered. "Tell her not to bother."

"Wouldn't keep her from coming."

"Whatever." Blake looked down at the table then back up at Barry. "How's Alita?"

"She stops by the Applewood Hill most weeks. That dog of hers is smart. Goes hunting with Dad sometimes." Barry turned to Albert. "Didn't she say she's thinking of getting another one?"

"No clue." Albert shrugged then glared at Blake. "Besides, I heard you told Alita to move on. What do you care how she's doing?"

Blake snorted and placed his hands in front of himself on the table. "If it's all the same to you, I have a manicure to get back to."

The two brothers glared at each other.

"Guys. Stop it. Blake, Albert has a lot on his mind. I don't think he meant anything by it." Barry looked from one brother to the other. "Cut him a break. He's having a rough day."

"I'm going to be having a rough day for the next...oh...several years. Welcome to the club."

"Whatever. You ready to go, Barry?" Albert scooted his chair back.

Barry turned to Blake. "Did you get the Bible I sent?"

"And the note. What a load of..."

Barry held up his hand. "Just think about it."

"I'm out of here." Blake stood and the guard led him away.

Albert shrugged and followed Barry out to the check-in point where they gathered their keys and wallets.

"I think that went well. Not." Albert stuffed his hands into his pockets.

"He'll come around."

"Yeah right."

"I get it Albert. You're discouraged. You're exhausted. But turn down the cynicism. Please."

Albert followed Barry to the car. Rolling his shoulders, he shook out the tension before climbing into the car. Maybe he should take up yoga or meditation. Right. Like that would go over well with the church board. No matter what he ended up doing, likely there would be someone overlooking his every action to make sure it was up to snuff.

Watching the scenery pass by in a blur, he didn't bother breaking the silence that settled over the car for the entirety of their trip home.

CHAPTER TWELVE

Elinor

E linor's date with James had been delayed *again*. Pausing at the end of the hall, Elinor watched James as he worked. The week had been so busy, they hadn't had much time to talk, but James hadn't pressured her and their time together each night had been sweet. She treasured each expression of his love for her. He deserved the truth. Tonight, he would know everything.

Straightening her posture and taking care not to click her heels on the floor, Elinor approached James from behind. With a pastry from the kitchen, and a cup of tea, on the tray she held, she eased closer to the desk and placed it at his elbow.

He twirled around in his chair. "Gotcha." Catching her around the waist, he pulled her into his lap before she slipped away. "You can't just drop a treat and run." He nudged her in the ribs.

She squirmed away from his finger and giggled. "Stop it. You'll start a laughing fit I won't be held responsible for."

"Fine. But I reserve the right to resume tickling later tonight." He held up both hands.

"If you can catch me." She scooted out of his lap.

"I do like a challenge." He picked up his fork. "What kind of treat did you bring me this time?"

"Taste it first." She watched him put a bite in his mouth. He closed his eyes as though thinking hard about the flavors. He took another bite, then glanced her way. "Apples?"

She nodded. "What else?"

"Pure deliciousness." He finished off the sweet, then set the saucer at the edge of the desk.

She leaned down and gave James a peck on the cheek, then picked up the saucer and headed down the hall as the front door opened. She glanced over her shoulder. Light, spilling across the foyer of the Applewood Hill Bed and Breakfast, blinded her from identifying the newcomer.

"Are you the manager?" That voice. A shudder ran down her back at the sound of the rich accent cloaked in a smooth, deep timbre.

Elinor moved to the alcove under the stairs, out of sight. The past reached out and grabbed her, wrapping her in memories of a season so full of promise that, for a brief time, she had dared to believe. All her hopes that it wouldn't be him calling from France vanished like smoke blown away by a strong wind. Even after all the years, she would know that voice anywhere.

"I called you earlier about possibly using your facility for a company retreat." His voice continued taunting her.

"Welcome to the Applewood Hill. I'm James."

"Nice to meet you, I'm Remí."

Elinor peeked around the corner to see the man whose voice transported her back in time. Still in the shadows. She waited.

"I can give you a tour, then we'll stop by my office to go over details to help you make a decision about whether or not our location will work for you." James got up from his seat.

"That would be great." The man stepped into the light. A splash of gray now lightening the dark brown of his hair, he wore the same smile that was so familiar to her heart. Half smirk, half invitation. His eyes reminded her of dark chocolate.

Not now. Elinor leaned against the wall. Catapulted back in time, she was tempted to ignore the reality of what kind of man he had proven to be. Old feelings she thought long dead stirred her heart. She shook her head. No.

Once the men were walking up the stairs, Elinor rushed to her apartment. After locking the door, she ran to her bedroom and pulled clothes, shoes, and boxes of nostalgia out of her closet.

"Where is it?" Half her belongings were in the middle of the floor before she stopped her frantic search at the sight of the neon-green photo album. Nibbling on her bottom lip, she grabbed the album and plopped on a chair next to the bed.

She rested her forehead on the cover of the album. Since the day she returned from Europe, other than the briefest of glances when it unearthed itself on moving days, she had buried the album and all the memories it contained in the back of her closet and her mind. Until today. Taking in a shuddering breath, she opened the album. Pictures from back when you could hide them, instead of losing them on the pages of the Internet, stared back at her. "Thank you, God, for small mercies."

She glanced at the clock and estimated about an hour before someone came looking for her, but it didn't take long for her past reality and humiliation to pull her into a downward spiral. She had bought into every promise Remí made her. Then he completely humiliated her. Threw her and everything they had away like so much rubbish. Dread rose like bile in her throat.

Elinor slammed the album closed and tossed it aside before her thoughts rambled too far down that pathway. *How did he come to call the Applewood Hill in the first place?* The sensation of someone watching tapped her on the shoulder. "If he comes...if he says anything to James..." She shook her head. *No. Please, God, no. Surely Remí won't say anything. Why did I put off telling James the truth?*

Glancing at the time, she hurried to put her closet back in order. Half an hour later, clothes back in place, she realized she had left the album out, and contemplated the best place to hide the evidence of her past.

The key turned in the lock to their front door.

"Elinor?" James's footsteps sounded on the other side of the bedroom door.

Elinor jammed the album between the mattress and box spring. She would find a better place for it later. "In here."

He leaned his head in the door. "Would you like a cup of tea?"

"Sure."

James led the way to the kitchen. "Guess what?" Filling the tea kettle with water, he waited for Elinor to catch up.

"I'll bite."

"The guy I told you about from France? That was him just now. Remí Bonnet. He just booked the whole place for a company retreat for his Kansas City branch. It's for top executives and their wives the week after Thanksgiving. Great business for the Applewood."

"What's the company name?" Avoiding his eyes, Elinor reached for the mugs.

"RJB Investments. Headquarters in France."

"How in the world did he find us?" Emotions simmered under the surface of Elinor's words.

"They were scouting for the perfect place. Read that article in the *Kansas City Star* last year. You gave a glowing review of the bed and breakfast in the interview, and it impressed him."

A suspicious dread crawled up her spine. The same feeling inspired by her compulsion to draw the curtains in case someone watched. She laced her words with sarcasm. "A bunch of high-power executives and their fancy-pants wives running around this place?"

James touched her cheek. "You seem to have a lot on your mind, let's talk later."

She nodded. Anything to get out of this conversation. She needed to think.

"I love you." He gave her a quick kiss before he returned to work, tea forgotten on the counter.

Please, God, show me how to preserve my marriage. An urge rose in her heart to tell him the truth. All of it. Now. No more hiding.

Just as quickly, doubt took hold. How could he love her once he knew?

CHAPTER THIRTEEN

Albert

The light bulb blinked off then on in the murky shadows of the garage. Albert berated himself for not packing his hunting gear last night. It would have gotten his mind off the sabbatical. Instead, he'd sat up long after his family went to bed and stewed about it.

Albert had told Haley about the board's decision when he got back from the visit with Blake earlier this week. She acted relieved and encouraged him to follow the board's recommendations. He was happy not to be handed a to-do list. But he still wasn't sure what it was he needed to figure out. He shoved it to the back of his mind. He had three months to work on it.

The light flicked off and stayed off. Muttering to himself, he grabbed a flashlight and went back inside for a new bulb. A few minutes later and the light continued its blinking routine, revealing the culprit to be the wiring. One more thing that needed repair. Albert cursed.

He pulled out his Remington. He was looking forward to hunting with his dad. Other than a bit of chit chat on the way out to the deer stand, he counted on it being a quiet day as they waited for the perfect deer. Not that he expected to bring anything home; his dad was the better shot. The bed and breakfast would have venison on their menu for the holidays. If not from today's hunt, then his dad would go out till he got one.

After loading his gear into the truck, he retrieved the cooler and filled it with water bottles and the sandwiches Haley had prepared last night. Glancing at the clock, he decided he didn't have to leave immediately to pick up his dad.

Going back inside, he opened Charlie's door. He had been pestering Albert about going on the kids' turkey hunt a local hunting club sponsored. Charlie took the hunting safety course last summer, as well as archery lessons. He just needed a bit more practice.

Closing the door, he moved on to Annie's room. Her bed lamp still on, a book lay open on the covers next to his daughter. He slipped across the floor, moved the book, and turned off the lamp. Placing a kiss on her forehead, he regretted the times he spoke harshly or ignored his kids altogether. He longed for days when he fully enjoyed their kid zest for life. *Lord, I'm so tired of this roller coaster I'm on.*

Entering his own bedroom, he heard the rhythmic breathing of his wife, and walked across the carpet to the side of the bed where she lay. He knelt beside the bed. "I love you so much."

She smiled in her sleep, reaching an arm around his neck. She pulled him close. "Hmmm..."

He smiled at her sleep-awake moment, tiredness beckoning him back to bed, instead of out into the early morning chill. He stood and looked down at Haley. He'd better leave, or they wouldn't get to the deer stand early enough to beat the dear. He kissed her on the cheek and turned to leave. At the door, he glanced over his shoulder. *Will I ever feel normal again?* Cursing under his breath, he sucked in the emotional turmoil and headed for the car.

Albert drummed his fingers on the steering wheel as he waited for his dad to load his hunting gear in the back of the pickup. He looked at the time on his phone. "Hurry up, Dad. Sun's going to be up before we get there."

Charles leaned in through the open window on the passenger side. "If you can't be patient waiting on me to load my gear, you're going to be a bear in the stand. That will scare the deer off for sure." He pulled back from the window and patted the side of the car. "Be right back. I'm going to grab my coffee."

Albert leaned his head back against the headrest and closed his eyes. He'd left his coffee mug sitting on the counter. It was going to be a long day. Boots crunching on gravel alerted him to his dad's return. He opened his eyes.

"Here, son." His dad leaned in the window and handed Albert a mug before he climbed into the truck. "Didn't see yours. Reckoned you might need this."

Albert held the mug up in a mock cheer. "Now, I can survive the day."

Of all the days for Dad to be chatty. At least he had been quiet in the stand. Mentally shutting out his voice, Albert walked with him to the car. Sans dear. His dad would be back, but next time, Albert planned to decline the invitation sure to be extended.

Albert considered his wife's goodbye. If only he didn't chase that warmth out of her eyes when she was awake. He shook his head. Maybe this sabbatical would end up being a good thing. The quietness registered in his brain and he noticed his dad staring at him.

"What's on your mind, son?"

Albert looked straight ahead. He might as well come out with it. Everyone would know soon enough when they made the announcement at church. "I've been put on sabbatical."

Charles nodded and looked Albert in the eyes. "Time to sort things out?"

"What things?" Albert furrowed his brow.

"Whatever it is that's been bothering you all these years."

"What are you talking about?"

Charles shrugged. "Can't say. Just know something eats at you."

"Nothing eats at me."

"When there's anger, usually is something."

"Who are you to..."

Charles held up a hand. "I've been there. That's how I know."

"You're right, you've been there." Sticking his hands in his pockets, Albert stared off through the trees. He was not like his dad. Not in the least.

Charles put a hand on Albert's shoulder. "If you ever want to talk about it...the past. Anything."

"It's not going to happen. Let's just get home." He shrugged off his dad's hand and hurried ahead to the truck.

Albert pulled into his driveway and sat, his mind returning to the conversation with his dad earlier in the day. Banging a fist on the steering wheel, he swore. Penned in from every side with opinions about the state of his own mind and heart. He was tired of it. Why did everyone think this sabbatical had to be about more than just getting rest? He was tired. That was all.

He opened the car door, then paused and watched his family through the front window of the house. Charlie and Annie were throwing pillows at each other. The familiarity of the scene caused his heart to ache. When was the last time he had joined in on their antics instead of yelling at them to stop? Haley walked into view, caught the pillows, and pointed to the couch. The kids plopped down with arms crossed.

Albert was relieved that Haley took care of the incident before he got in the door. Determined not to spoil the evening, he quieted the thoughts stewing in his mind. He slammed the car door and went inside. "I'm home."

Charlie looked at him over the back of the couch. "Did you get a deer?"

Albert shook his head.

"Good." Annie stuck her tongue out at her brother.

He grimaced back at her.

"Kids. Stop it." Haley shook her finger at the kids before giving Albert a hug. "You're here to rescue me, right?"

"They been causing trouble?"

"No more than usual. I'll tell you all about..."

The sound of liquid sizzling on a hot burner preceded a burnt smell. Haley scurried back to the kitchen.

"Drats. Back to square one." She set the pot in the sink and ran water into it. Steam rose when cold met hot. Pushing her hair off her forehead with the back of her arm, she grabbed a rag and wiped up the mess on the stove. "By the way, Mitch called."

Albert frowned. Not where he wanted to go with the night. He leaned across the counter. "Pizza?"

"Meat lovers?"

"You got it." Albert pulled out his phone and called the Westfall Pizzeria to place an order. Sliding his phone in his pocket, he grabbed his keys. "Who wants to help me pick up the pizza?"

The kids hopped off the couch and ran for the door.

Haley mouthed, "Thank you," as Albert turned to throw her a kiss before following Charlie and Annie to the truck. Wishing this moment was more than just a reprieve from the usual tension that filled their home lately, he smiled back. Maybe, after he rested up, they could return to the way things used to be.

CHAPTER FOURTEEN

Albert

Albert sat up in bed and glanced at the clock. *Eight Thirty? Just as well.* Less than a week after being relegated to a sabbatical, it would be awkward to sit in the sanctuary where he usually preached. The board was going to make the announcement today. Maybe he would go next Sunday. He hoped Haley wouldn't make a big deal over it. Yesterday had ended well over pizza and a movie and he wanted to keep it that way.

He headed to the kitchen, where he heard sounds of breakfast conversation.

"Charlie, go wake up your dad."

The sound of a chair scooting across the floor preceded the rushing form of his son rounding the corner before skidding to a halt. "Dad, breakfast is getting cold." Dressed in khakis and blue button-down shirt, Charlie appeared more grown-up than child.

The words felt like a slap to Albert. He couldn't even get up on time to eat with his family. What kind of dad was he? He followed his son back to the kitchen.

Charlie plopped back in his chair. Haley wiped her hands on her apron. "There's an omelet and pancakes on the table. I need to go finish getting ready."

"Thanks." Albert gave Haley a quick hug and kiss before sitting at the table. Reaching for the pancakes, he paused at the look on his kids' faces.

"You coming to church, Dad?" Annie lowered her eyes and took a bite of her eggs.

"Look at him, Annie." Charlie elbowed his sister. "The answer is obvious, don't you think?"

Albert tensed and pointed his finger at Charlie. "Assumptions are never a good thing."

"But I'm right, aren't I?"

"Be respectful, young man." He picked up his fork and stabbed a bite of pancake.

"Whatever." Charlie got up from the table and picked up his plate.

"Sit down."

"I'm just clearing off the table."

"Don't talk back to me."

Annie's fork clattered onto her plate. Albert glanced over at his daughter looking down at her lap, then back at Charlie glaring at him. So much for any connections made last night.

"Leave my plate, I'll eat later." Exiting the kitchen, he almost bumped into his wife.

Haley let out a deep what-am-I-going-to-do sigh, then glanced at the kids. "Go get in the car, we're running late. Don't worry about the dishes. Dad will take care of them while we're gone." She looked back at Albert and raised her eyebrows, daring him to contradict her.

He nodded.

"I'll be right out." Haley waited till the door to the garage opened and shut before speaking. "You realize you're crushing your kids?"

"I can't get anything right in your eyes."

"I guess it's a good thing you're not preaching!"

Albert slumped against the wall as Haley stormed past him.

Hand on the garage doorknob, she paused. "I'm sorry, Albert. I shouldn't have said that." And then she was gone.

Every nerve in his body taut, he slid down to the floor and rested his forehead in his hands. How did he stop the noise clamoring in his soul? Every piece of conversation, every obstacle he came up against, every expectation of others felt like pin pricks against his skin about to burst the balloon of emotions bottled up inside. He couldn't remember not feeling this way. When would it stop? Or would it? *God, have I completely screwed everything up?*

He pushed himself up off the floor, then headed back to bed and crawled under the covers.

The noise of the dishwasher being loaded brought Albert out of his sleep. He groaned. He hadn't gotten to the dishes like Haley wanted him to, and now she would be mad. He pretended to be asleep when he heard the door open.

"Albert?"

"Hmmm?"

"You coming to family dinner at Karen's?"

Albert's eyes popped open. "You serious?"

"Why wouldn't I be?" Haley stood with her hands on her hips, glaring at him.

"Because I'm still in bed?"

"You slept the whole time?"

"I was just so tired. I'm sorry about the dishes. I was going to get up and do them before you got back."

"You could have set an alarm. Never mind. We'll be leaving in about half an hour. I need to take care of the mess in the kitchen and throw together a salad. If you decide you want to go, be ready." She marched out of the room and slammed the door behind her.

Tomorrow. He would start fresh tomorrow. He rolled over and didn't wake up till after dark when the bed moved beside him. He glanced at the clock. *Ten o'clock? Seriously? I slept all day?* He waited for sleep to return, but after what seemed like an eternity, he decided waiting was futile. It wasn't happening. Careful not to wake Haley, he eased out of bed. In the kitchen, he scrounged for snacks then settled in front of the television for a Netflix marathon. And no one to disturb him.

CHAPTER FIFTEEN

Elinor

O ctober flew by faster than Albert's hamster used to, escaping from its cage when they were kids. Elinor tossed another bag of Halloween candy into the shopping basket for the Applewood Hill Harvest Party next week. "Think that will be enough?"

"Two for each carnival game?" James laughed. "Remember the crowd last year? And we have an ad in the Westfall paper this weekend."

"True. Good thing we have a membership here. Let's get twenty more bags. That along with the candy the bank is donating, we should have enough. And if we don't use all the candy, we can donate it to the Huddle. I know those kids will eat it up. Speaking of which, have you heard from Clarice's grammie yet?"

James shook his head as he piled more candy into the basket. "Think she'll be up to going to Clarice's presentation tonight?"

"I hope so. Clarice understands her grammie isn't doing well, but it would mean a lot. At least we'll be there."

"I think Karen and Barry are coming, too."

"What's going to happen to Clarice if Grammie...I can't even think..." Elinor blinked back a gathering of tears. "I need to talk to Joanna about it."

"Good place to start." James pushed the cart out into the main aisle. "Let's price the supplies for the RJB Investments retreat while we're here."

Elinor's mood dampened at the mention of Remí's impending invasion of her life. He had lured her into believing him and now she paid the fools tax for the price of her trust. Clenching her fist, she glanced around for James, who had disappeared from the aisle in front of her. Spotting him near the Halloween costumes, she headed his way. She hoped the truth didn't come out by way of Remí. He'd ruined her life once and she wasn't about to let him have a second run at it.

Ever since he showed up, she had been debating when to tell James. But life picked up the pace this time of year. She would need to talk to Karen and plan a time when she could get James away from the Applewood, despite the full schedule on the calendar. Satisfied with her plan, she focused on the present.

"What are you doing in the kids' costumes?" Elinor came up behind James and encircled her arms around his waist.

"Wondered where you went." James turned partway and gave her a quick peck on the forehead. "Look at these princess costumes. I can just see a mini-Elinor running around in one someday."

Elinor coughed. "Someday. Maybe."

"Maybe?"

Elinor glanced down, avoiding his gaze. "She might want to be a ninja, you know."

James laughed. "Either way, she'll be the best dressed kid on Halloween night."

"We need to be going if we're going to pick up Clarice and eat before her presentation."

"As you wish."

If only it were that simple. Elinor rested her hand on his arm as they made their way to the checkout.

———ele———

Applause followed the performance by the children's choir. Elinor leaned over to James. "I think Clarice is next." The musical show featured several solos and duets in addition to the choir performance. Clarice's school was full of talented students.

The audience stilled as the curtains opened. A spotlight shone on one lone child. Standing as still as a statue, Clarice stared out into the audience. Elinor held her breath. Would Clarice give in to stage fright? The pianist began playing the tune now familiar to Elinor. Then Clarice opened her mouth and began to sing. Her voice, clear and strong, carried to every corner of the auditorium.

The lyrics to "Somewhere Over the Rainbow" washed over Elinor. If she were Simon Cowell, she would push the golden buzzer. But then, she was biased. The song ended and there was silence for the briefest of moments before the whole room exploded in applause. Clarice raised a fist in the air and began twirling around on the stage. Celebration, Clarice style. Elinor made a mental note to talk to Joanna about voice lessons for their young friend.

CHAPTER SIXTEEN

Elinor

E linor's phone sang out James's tune. Turning on her blinker, she glanced into the rearview mirror before moving into the left turn lane. She savored the thought of their upcoming date. Thankful Karen allowed them to take time off, Elinor's mood dimmed when she remembered one of her goals tonight. But fun first, then the truth.

Elinor parked at the store, then checked her messages from James.

Power Play. North?

She texted back.

"Absolutely!"

He responded.

"Meet @b&b in 30 min drive down together?"

She checked her watch.

"CU @4"

She added a kissy face emoji, then tucked the phone into her purse.

An hour later, they pulled into a parking spot at the Power Play KC. James hopped out of the car and hurried around to open Elinor's door. When she climbed out of the car, he pulled her into his arms and began dropping kisses on her neck.

She felt a flush rise on her cheeks and leaned back, still caught in his arms. "Everyone is looking."

"They're just jealous." He released his embrace. "You ready?"

"You bet."

He tucked her hand into the crook of his arm and laughed. "What do you want to do first?"

"Go-carts, then let's try the zip line before the line gets too long."

"I'm glad we got here when we did. This place can get packed."

———ele———

Three hours later, after multiple races around the track and trips on the zip line, then laser tag and bumper cars, James and Elinor grabbed a couple of slices of pizza before calling it quits.

"That was fun." Elinor linked arms with James. "Thanks for a fabulous evening."

"It was good to laugh."

"True that."

"Let's go for a drive."

"Can we get ice cream on the way?"

"Sounds good to me." James opened the car door for Elinor and waited for her to get settled. He leaned down and gave her a kiss, then walked around to his side of the car and got in. "How about Culver's?"

"Mmm. I can taste a Salted Caramel Pumpkin Mixer already."

"I think I'll be daring and create my own tonight."

She wiggled her eyebrows at him. "Really now?"

"But don't get any ideas."

Pretending to be offended, Elinor huffed. "Whatever could you mean?"

"You know what I mean." He shook a finger in her direction.

The last time they went to Culver's, she decided she liked his Mixer better than hers and convinced him to trade. "You could have said no."

"Right." He laughed as he headed north on Highway 169.

"Where are we going?"

"Taking the scenic route?"

"Promise a girl ice cream…"

James laughed and took the clover leaf exit onto 152 and headed west toward I-29. "Happy now?"

"You're my hero."

"Is that all it takes?"

"It helps."

Half an hour later saw them back on the road with ice cream. Elinor eyed James's Mixer sitting in the cup holder. "Can I have a taste?"

"Now it starts."

Elinor gave James a playful swat on the arm.

"Fine. Help yourself. You're incorrigible."

She grabbed his Mixer and took a bite. "This is good. Hey, now where are we going?"

"You already got my ice cream. Now you're just going to have to wait and see where we're going."

"Fine." Elinor grinned and settled back in her seat. She enjoyed this playfulness between them. It brought happier times to mind. James would make a good father. She looked his way. "You seem deep in thought."

"How about we load up Charlie, Annie, and Clarice and take them to Power Play?"

"We could make it a whole family outing. That would be a blast."

"Let's do it. Maybe after Christmas. It's going to be too busy before then with the RJB retreat and Christmas at the bed and breakfast."

Elinor agreed. "I'll talk to everyone and get it on the calendar sometime in January."

"And someday, we can bring our own kids. I can imagine a little daredevil Elinor taking that zip line like a pro."

"I'm no daredevil." Pasting on a smile, she attempted to ignore the thoughts racing through her mind.

"True. But I think our girl will have the best of both of us."

She slapped at his arm. "Since when are you a daredevil?"

"Since I married you."

"Ha." Elinor tensed. She knew he didn't mean anything by it, but somehow it felt like a jab at the murky waters of her emotions lately. She looked out the window. *He loves me. He loves me. He loves me.*

"Elinor?"

"Huh?"

"I was asking if you thought she would sport the Hannigan red hair or your blond hair."

Elinor tensed. "I don't know...red?"

James tapped on the steering wheel with his thumbs. "You agreed we could talk about having kids. That's all I'm doing."

"It feels like more."

"It's not. Can you just take what I say at face value?"

She nodded. "I'll try."

"Thank you." He reached across and took her hand. "I love you."

She nodded and squeezed his hand. "I love you, too. I'm sorry."

He rubbed his thumb against the back of her hand. "We'll get through this."

She nodded. "I just..."

"Shh...we don't have to talk about it anymore tonight. Music?"

"Sure." Elinor relaxed as the sounds of instrumental worship music filled the car. Hanging on to James's hand, she turned her head toward the window as her heart cried out to God. *Help me be the wife James deserves.*

CHAPTER SEVENTEEN

Elinor

"That should do it." Karen tossed the empty can of whipped cream into the trash then licked her fingers.

Elinor laughed at the smiley face staring back at her from the top of the pan of Jell-O. "The kids will love it."

Karen picked up the pan and headed toward the dining room as their dad came in the back door.

"Want me to take that in?" Charles held out his hands.

"You and Elinor grab the potatoes when the timer goes off." She nodded toward the stove.

Charles leaned against the counter next to Elinor. "I'm heading out to see Blake this week. Talked to the pastor leading the prison ministry out there. It sounds like a good program. He visited with Blake a bit and thinks Blake might be willing to meet with him again. Hard to see, but glad for it."

"Tell Blake hi for me."

Charles nodded. "By the way, you're looking good, today."

"Thanks." She ducked her head and opened the oven to check on the scalloped potatoes.

He never was one to compliment her. In fact, if she had ever worn what she wore at school back to the house, he most likely would have burned the clothes and called her names. He wasn't much of an encourager back then. But this felt good. The edges of her mouth lifted.

"I still remember the day I first saw you in one of those fancy outfits you brought back from your senior trip to Europe."

She stood up straight and looked at him. He had noticed?

"You looked so strong and sure of yourself."

Little did he know it was all an act. "I guess traveling abroad does that to a person."

"That's when I knew you were going to be okay." He scuffed his boot heel against the floor. "Even after..."

She placed a hand on his arm. "It's over. Let's not talk about it."

His eyes glistened, and he shook his head. "In all this time that I've been trying to make amends, you keep avoiding me. But not talking about it isn't healing. The way I treated you was wrong. Can you forgive me?"

The timer for the potatoes went off.

Nibbling on her lip, Elinor grabbed the hot pads and pulled out the pan and set it on the counter. How did she answer him? She didn't stew about it. She knew he had regrets and had changed. Although they didn't have a close relationship and she couldn't see that happening, it was good, though a bit awkward at times. Forgiveness? It hadn't happened with a grand epiphany, but she supposed she had forgiven him along the way. And no matter how she felt saying it, her dad needed to hear the words. "Yes, Dad. I forgive you."

"Thank you, the words mean a lot." He pulled her into a hug. "I love you more than you know."

Elinor stepped back. No matter how much their relationship had improved, hugging him still felt awkward. "Better get the food in there. We've got a hungry crew."

He nodded and grabbed the potholders. "I'll get the pan. You get the door."

The chaotic noise of the family coming together made her think of a fox getting loose in a chicken house. That was her family all right.

Charles gathered everyone around and offered a prayer for their meal. At the sound of amen, Charlie goosed Annie. Annie squealed and tried to poke her brother back. He took off running with her close behind. Haley tried to catch them as they weaved in between and around the family.

Charlie bumped into the table as he rounded the room. He knocked over a chair, water glasses sloshed, and the centerpiece fell over. Charlie slid to a stop and Annie collided with him. They took one look at each other and let out a wave of laughter. Hope started crying.

Barry soothed Hope's tears.

James stepped forward and righted the chair.

Elinor grabbed a towel and swiped at the spilled liquid.

Albert marched over to his kids and glared down at them. "What do you think you're doing?"

"We were just playing, Dad."

Albert's tone intense, he shook a finger at them. "You made a mess is what you did. All you can think about is yourself. What about being considerate of everyone else for a change?"

The room grew silent, and the family watched the scene unfolding. Haley stepped up behind the kids. "Take it easy, Albert."

"Take it easy? They need to learn some manners."

"Everyone is watching." Haley whispered.

Albert looked around the room. "What?"

James cleared his throat. "No harm done."

Albert glared at James and snorted.

The door knocked against the wall as Alita backed into the dining room. Her purse hung over her shoulder, and she carried a large dish in one hand and balanced a bag in the other. Turning around as the door shut behind her, she took in the scene before her. "Did I miss something?"

Albert shook his head. "Haley, I'm leaving. Are you coming?"

"No."

"Fine. Get a ride home then." He strode out of the room and stomped through the kitchen toward the back door. Barry nodded at Karen, then followed Albert.

"I'm sorry." Haley drew Charlie and Annie close. "Maybe we shouldn't have come."

"Nonsense." Karen moved closer to the small family and put a hand on each of the kids. "I think you guys need time with family, don't you?"

Haley nodded.

"Then why don't you come over to the house after lunch and hang out. We'll pull out board games and make brownies. How does that sound, kids?"

Annie and Charlie gave up a bit of a smile.

"For now, go get your food." Karen remained by Haley's side while the kids picked up plates and filled them with food. "You'll get through this. We're all with you."

"Thanks, Karen. That means a lot."

CHAPTER EIGHTEEN

Elinor

"Where are we going?" Elinor turned in the car seat to get a better view of her husband.

James had kidnapped her from the kitchen, much to her distress at leaving behind her duties. He'd assured her that Karen had approved of their little field trip and had agreed to cover Elinor's duties. With no argument left, she allowed him to abscond with her.

"It's a surprise." James's grin widened.

"Just a hint?"

"Nope."

"Fine."

"Don't look so worried. We're just having fun. Dreaming a bit."

"Dreaming?" Elinor's breathing clinched. "Oh, we must be checking out new beds."

James chuckled. "Very punny."

Looking straight ahead, Elinor combed her fingers through her hair. *Lord, please help me not ruin this time James has planned.*

"Almost there. It's all in the spirit of dreaming about our future family. No pressure."

Elinor nodded at James's reminder as she tugged on her hair, now caught between two fingers. She cringed and placed her hands in her lap. They entered a housing development, and she wrinkled her brow. "So, what are we talking about here? Window shopping for baby clothes?"

"Something a bit bigger."

"Like...?"

"Like...this." James pulled over to the curb and put the car in park. He pointed to the house they now sat in front of, a for sale sign in the front yard. "There's an open house today. Thought we could walk through without the pressure of needing an agent yet. How about it?"

Elinor looked up at the house and squelched an excitement rising inside her. It was beautiful. She caught her bottom lip between her teeth. "It's big."

James turned off the car. "Come on. Let's see the inside."

"No pressure?"

"No pressure."

Elinor smiled and climbed out of the car. "How many bedrooms does it have?"

James grinned. "Five."

Elinor batted at his arm. "How many kids do you want, anyway?" This lighthearted approach to the subject of kids was easier to deal with. Maybe today wouldn't end in disaster.

"We'll want a guest room and maybe an office. That would leave one for us and two for kids."

"Smooth. Nice save."

James laughed and opened the door to the house. They stood in the entryway and took in the view. The tiled foyer opened on the left into a large family room. On the right, a curving staircase led up to the second level. Elinor leaned in to James when he put his arm around her. Voices from further back in the house drew them through the living room and into the kitchen.

A large-framed woman glanced over at them from the counter, where she stood talking to another couple. "Come on in. come on in. Be right with you." Her southern drawl draped them in welcome.

She waved her hand toward the table. "Feel free to look around while you wait. There's info on the kitchen table."

James took Elinor's hand and led the way to the table. He picked up a floor plan. "Wow, three thousand square feet."

Elinor stared at the property informational sheet and gulped down a rather loud exclamation of disbelief. She leaned over to James and whispered, "Yeah. And look at the price."

"Dream a bit. Please?"

"I'll try."

"Well, how are you two doing today? So nice to have this sunshine. Better to enjoy these windows, I say." The real estate agent joined them at the table. "I'm Genny Day." She held out hand to Elinor.

"Elinor. This is my husband, James." She shook Genny's hand.

Genny then shook James's hand. "Newlyweds? I just love showing houses to newlyweds. Come on, I'll give you the tour. I like to start upstairs and work our way down. That work for you?"

They followed Genny up the stairs and drifted through two of the bedrooms. Each one boasted a large walk-in closet and double windows that filled the space with light. Across the hall, a large closet invited storage of sheets, towels, and toiletry items.

Elinor clapped her hands. "This would be great space."

Genny nodded. "The ladies like this space. And don't worry, James, I think you'll like the garage."

They peeked into the hall bathroom next. "This bath is fairly basic. But wait till you see the master bath." Genny gushed about the multi-sprayer shower and companion hot tub.

Elinor gripped James's arm. There was no way they could afford something like this. Why were they even here?

James leaned down and whispered in her ear. "No pressure. Just dreaming."

Elinor relaxed her death grip on his arm and repeated his words to herself. The tension released from her shoulders and neck as the agent led them into another bedroom.

"While those first two rooms are perfect for office or guest room space, these two are perfect for the kids. Each room is a mirror of the other with large walk-in closets and huge windows." She opened a door on the wall between the rooms and stepped back to let them walk through. "In between, you'll find a sitting area and bath. You could use the space for the nursery or playroom. Windows all around, with the ledge coming up high enough, kids can't easily climb up without you there. The builders thought of everything."

Except my heart. Elinor put a hand on her chest. Tears welled up in her eyes. Turning away from James and Genny as they chatted about various features in the house, Elinor walked to the window overlooking the backyard, which spread out behind the house further than the space between the Applewood Hill and Karen and Barry's house. A large tree sat in the middle of the yard and begged to be climbed. She knew in a heartbeat that James would be leading that adventure. Most likely he would build a treehouse before…Elinor fought against panic settling around her like a cloak.

This house represented all the hopes and dreams James had for their family. What would their dreams consist of when he knew the truth? What dreams would be left? She had put off telling him the whole story for so long, it was getting harder and harder to think about doing. Especially with Remí showing up. She pulled her hair over her shoulder and combed her fingers through the strands.

Forcing her mind onto happier topics, she settled her nerves and turned around. "The room is lovely."

James looked out into the yard. "Perfect for a treehouse, isn't it?"

"Perfect." Feigning interest in the woodwork, Elinor made her way to the door. "Let's see the master bedroom."

Genny expressed delight in each feature of the house. Her enthusiasm was contagious, and Elinor had a hard time remembering this was all just an exercise in futility, especially when she toured the spacious kitchen. It was perfect for hosting parties, and the large pantry had more storage than she could imagine using on her own. The laundry room just inside the garage promised easy processing of a large family's wash load.

James carried on like a kid in a candy store over the garage and storage space for tools and equipment. Elinor always saw him as the manager of the inside of the bed and breakfast and never realized how much he wanted to care for his own home. Her gaze lingered as their eyes met. She hoped the look that filled his eyes remained after her lack became obvious.

CHAPTER NINETEEN

Elinor

"Clarice! You look adorable." Karen stopped midstride through the foyer of the Applewood Hill and hugged their young friend, whom Elinor had just brought in.

Clarice twirled her blueberry taffeta dress. "Miss Joanna sent it to me. She said I was a princess. See the crown?"

Elinor pointed to the tiara sitting on top of her head.

"She wrote a note to Grammie and said she would see us at Christmas. Did you know that Miss Joanna was coming back at Christmas? I hope she comes back to live here 'cause then I could see her all the time." She twirled and threw out her arms, flouncing her attire.

Karen laughed. "You could, indeed." She turned to Elinor. "How was Grammie?"

Elinor shook her head and mouthed, "Not good."

Karen nodded. "Clarice, you want to help Elinor get the candy passed out to all the carnival games?"

Clarice jumped up and down and clapped her hands. "Can I eat some?"

"That depends."

Clarice plopped her hands on her hips and narrowed her dancing eyes. "On what?"

"Do we have the kind of candy you like?"

"I like all kinds of candy. But especially chocolate. Did you get lots of chocolate?"

"You should be good." Karen straightened Clarice's dress. "There are two red wagons out front loaded with baskets of candy. Pull them around to the games and leave a basket at each. Can you handle that while I talk to the community volunteers?"

Clarice gave Karen a salute. "Yes, ma'am." Clarice grabbed Elinor's hand and dragged her out the front door.

"Mrs. Karen is funny."

Elinor tapped Clarice 's nose. "Let's get to work so we have time to play."

"And eat the candy."

They laughed as they pulled on a wagon to make their rounds.

The games had been set up in the field between the bed and breakfast and the orchard. Volunteers from Westfall had worked all week to mow and trim and clear off any troublesome plants to make room for the event. Then since early morning today, more had come to set up the games. Mrs. Granger had even participated. She'd giggled like a kid, relishing the night ahead, hinting at her own costume she planned to wear. For now, it felt like the quiet before the storm. Workers had hurried home to feed families and come back dressed up, ready to man the booths.

As Elinor and Clarice left candy at each station, Clarice rated her favorites. The ring toss, a gigantic bop the mole game, and dunk the town's high school baseball team were at the top of her list. The human checkers game and the bouncy house came in a close second. But the rest of the games were for the little kids, according to her.

Done with their job, the two joined Albert, Haley, Annie, and Charlie on the porch, where they watched the cars pull up the drive and park. Parents and kids piled out and headed to the games. Mrs. Granger joined them on the porch, decked out as the best fairy godmother Elinor had ever seen. Many of the bed and breakfast guests joined in on the fun as well. Last year, they raised a handsome sum for the local charity. They expected to raise even more this year.

Annie, in a dress the color of the sea and with a tiara on her head, hugged Clarice and grabbed her hand. "Can Clarice come with us to all the games? Please?"

"Do I have to hang out with princesses all night?" Charlie, dressed as a ninja, crossed his arms.

"How about just us guys hang out? Albert tussled his son's hair.

"Really?" Charlie's eyes lit up.

"What do you say, Haley?"

"That would be great. Are you sure?"

"Why wouldn't I be sure?" Albert crossed his arms, voice edged with frustration.

"Just asking."

"I offered. Isn't that enough?"

Charlie moved next to his mom and mirrored his dad's stance. "I can go with the girls, dad. It's okay."

"No, it's not."

Charlie mumbled and looked down at his shoes. Elinor watched the scene unfold. "Guys..."

Albert shut her up with a glare and stepped closer to Charlie. "What did you say?"

Charlie stepped back and shook his head.

"Albert, please." Haley put a hand on his arm.

He looked his wife in the eye. Stepping back, he ran a hand through his hair. "I'm trying. I am."

Haley put an arm around Charlie. Glancing at Albert, she tilted her head toward their son.

Albert nodded. "I'm sorry, Charlie. I blew it. Forgive me?"

Charlie nodded and glanced up at his dad.

"If you still want to go look at the games with me, we can. How about it? Give me a second chance?"

Haley nudged Charlie forward. "Go ahead."

Charlie offered his dad a half grin and followed him off the porch toward the games.

"I'm sorry." Haley pulled Annie close to her side.

Elinor hugged her sister-in-law. "No sorry necessary. You're not responsible for my brother's choices."

"Thanks. Do you mind if we take Clarice with us?"

"Not at all. Go have fun."

Grabbing the two princesses by the hands, Haley led the way toward the games. "We'll see you later. All sugared up and raring to go."

Elinor laughed and waved. She jumped as arms circled her waist, then leaned into the embrace of her love.

"I've been waiting to get you alone." James pulled her backward into him. "You are so good with Clarice. Someday that will be our child all dressed up." He kissed the curve of her neck.

Elinor leaned back into him. *Just enjoy the moment.* "Hmm."

"Getting any closer to doing more than think about our own kids?"

Feigning the need to take care of a nearby plant that had fallen over on the porch, she slipped out of his arms. When the pot of mums stood righted, she returned to his arms, facing him. "What happened to not rushing it?"

He wrinkled his brow and tilted his head. "What's going on?"

"I want to make you happy. It's just..." She looked down and fought the tears.

He tipped her chin up with his finger. "You do make me happy."

She returned his gaze with her own tear-filled one.

He brushed away the tears. "Yes, I want kids. But I love you, and even if we never had kids, I would be happy."

She leaned her cheek against his chest, soothed by the sound of his heartbeat.

He cupped her head against him. "One of these days, you'll believe me. No matter how long it takes, you're going to know I do love you and you, you alone, make me happy."

CHAPTER TWENTY

Elinor

Elinor helped Mrs. Granger gather up the remaining evidence of game night at her dad's while he and James checked on the horses. The evening had been a respite from the busyness at the bed and breakfast during the Harvest Carnival earlier in the week.

Mrs. Granger was a pleasure to be around. For her dad, too, as the night obviously showed. This was the first woman her dad had spent any time with since her mom died. He needed someone. Of course, with Mrs. Granger halfway across the country, Elinor wasn't sure that anything could come of it. She laughed. Mrs. Granger had gone all out at the carnival. Dressed up as a fairy godmother she'd handed out candy all night. She was a hit with all the kids. When her own family stopped by, they almost walked right past her. Mrs. Granger got a kick out of that. Elinor wondered why in the world they didn't care to be around her more than they did.

A grin tugged at her heart. James had been so reassuring of his love after the carnival. *Tonight. I will tell him I can't have kids.* At least start with that. No matter what. Pausing, her mind twirled through each scenario of how she imagined this might play out. *Stop it. This isn't helping.*

Surprised at the touch of a hand on her arm, she attempted to focus on the here and now.

"What is it, dear?" Mrs. Granger's soft voice penetrated her fog.

Tears escaped before she could stop them. Mrs. Granger rubbed her back. "Do you want to talk?"

"Not really."

"Marriage?"

Elinor pulled back and looked at the older woman in front of her. Mrs. Granger shrugged. "I was married for a lot of years, you know."

"He wants kids."

"And you don't."

"There's more to it than that."

"Does he know?"

Elinor shook her head.

Mrs. Granger sighed. "It's been my experience that secrets do far more harm than good. They did in my family."

"But I'm afraid."

Mrs. Granger nodded. "I was too. Should have ignored the feeling."

"I can't."

"Just barrel through them. I've seen the way he looks at you. What are you afraid of?"

Resentment brewed in Elinor's heart at the ease with which Mrs. Granger tossed out advice. Elinor shrugged. "What if he stops loving me?"

"The negatives we imagine are typically bigger than the reality."

"But..."

"You girls done cleaning up in here yet?" Charles poked his head into the family room. "Anyone up for coffee?"

"We'll be done before the coffee is ready." Mrs. Granger leaned closer to Elinor. "Just get it done." Tears welled up in her eyes. "My family still might be talking to me if I had overcome my fears."

Elinor wrinkled her eyebrows in question.

"That's a story for another day. I know it's hard, but you can do it."

Elinor and James arrived back to a quiet bed and breakfast. All the guests were in their rooms or not back in yet. The night manager was on duty, so they slipped into their apartment unnoticed.

All the way home, Elinor had thought about what Mrs. Granger had said. She hesitated just inside the door and took a calming breath. After taking off her jacket, she tossed it onto the couch. Time to do this. Holding her head high, she followed the noises to the kitchen.

James glanced over his shoulder at her as he prepared to brew of pot of coffee. "There you are. Thought I was going to have to send out a search party."

She offered him a hesitant smile. "We need to talk." She caught herself holding her breath and let it out slow and easy.

He set down the bag of coffee beans. "I'm at your disposal. Want coffee to go with our conversation?"

"No thank you." No question of him not following her, she headed to the living room. Settled into the overstuffed easy chair, she looked across the coffee table at her husband. His eyes radiated love to her. How could she disappoint him like this? Logic told her it wasn't her fault, but what would he think?

As if sensing her discomfort, he got up and moved closer, sitting on the edge of the coffee table right in front of her. He held her hands. "What is it?"

Tears escaped, despite her efforts to contain them. She bit her lower lip. "The doctor says I can't have kids."

"What was that?" He leaned in closer to hear the quiet words.

"I can't have kids."

He sat back with a surprised expression. "That's why you've been so upset when I talk about kids."

"Are you mad?"

"Why would I be mad? You are the love of my life. I love you no matter what. You didn't choose this." He moved to her side and wrapped her in a hug as the tears overcame her.

She melted into his embrace. But there were other things she *had* chosen. Would he be so forgiving of that?

Still holding her, he leaned back enough to look her in the eye. "Did the doctor say what the problem was?"

I can't do this. Not now. "Can we talk about it later?"

"As you wish." He brushed a stray tear from her cheek and pulled her back into his arms.

Holding tightly to her husband, she nestled into the nook of his arm. *Lord, do I have to tell him the whole story?* She knew the answer as soon as the question left her heart. She sucked in a quick breath and bit her lip against the pain growing in her soul.

CHAPTER TWENTY-ONE

Elinor

E linor paused before getting out of her car and joining the others at Dad's stables. She leaned her head back and listened to the ending of Piano Guys' *Peponi*. Last night, James had pledged his love no matter what. *But...* "No. He loves me and that's that." Grabbing a tissue, she blew her nose, glad for the upcoming distraction of a fall outing on horseback. Thankful it wasn't below freezing yet, she grabbed her jacket and gloves and stepped out of her car as Karen approached.

"I got a letter from Joanna." Karen waved an envelope between them.

"How is she?"

"She sounds great. But come on. I'll fill you all in at the same time." Karen looped her arm through Elinor's, and they headed toward the stables. Alita and Haley waved to them from where they sat on the top rung of the corral. They jumped down and joined them at the nearby picnic table.

"Open it, already." Alita sat on the edge of the table with feet propped on the attached bench.

"Hold your horses." Karen pulled out Joanna's letter, then sat next to Alita and cleared her throat before reading.

Dear Karen (and probably Elinor, Alita, and Haley),

I'm coming home for Christmas. I should be there no later than the second

week of December. Life is good here, but time for a few changes. I'll tell

you all about it when I get there. And don't bother trying to squeeze it out of me.

LOL.

Love you all! Joanna

PS Give Clarice a big hug for me.

"That's it?" Haley grabbed the letter and read it to herself.

Alita picked up the envelope and looked inside. "No way she can keep us in suspense for over a month."

"She just did." Elinor busted out laughing. The others joined in.

Karen hopped down and dusted off the back of her pants. "Who's ready to ride?"

The girls saddled up their mounts, and opting to aim for the treehouse, headed down the trail that wound its way along the road passing in front of Dad's house and orchards then through the woods. Haley, not joining into the sister banter, brought up the rear with Elinor in front of her.

When the trail widened, Karen slowed and joined Haley. "Want to talk?"

Haley shrugged.

"Albert?"

Haley nodded and looked away. "I feel so alone lately. Albert takes everything I say the wrong way and gets upset over the smallest thing. It's like I've lost my best friend. And my mind."

Elinor glanced over her shoulder. "You've got us."

"I know. But I live with Albert. And what do I tell the kids?"

"The truth." Alita dropped back to join the conversation.

"Which is what?" Haley shook her head. "He won't go to the doctor because he doesn't want to be labeled as depressed. Besides, he keeps saying that he should be able to get over whatever this is because he's a Christian. A pastor."

"I'm sorry, Haley. I didn't realize it had gotten so bad." Karen reached over and touched her sister-in-law's arm.

"That's part of what makes me so mad. He can hold it together when he's around everyone else, but as soon as we walk in the door at home, it's like a dam breaking. I want to be supportive, but I don't know how. I don't understand this thing that has a hold of him. He acts like he's the only one hurting, but I need support, too."

"Have you considered going to a counselor? That helped when I was working though things with Blake." Alita nudged her horse past the bushes, where it was attempting to nibble the leaves.

"I would love to, but we don't have the money. I think the church might pay for it, but first I have to convince Albert to go that route." Alita huffed. "I'm sorry, I don't mean to take it out on you guys."

"No sorry needed." Elinor stopped her horse and edged forward till her knee touched Haley's. "What can we do? You know you can count on us."

Haley allowed the tears to come. Alita and Karen joined Elinor, edging their mounts closer to Haley. They reached out and touched her, lifting their voices in praying for Haley as she struggled with Albert's depression. Haley's sobs slowly subsided, and she took the tissue Alita offered. "Thanks. You don't know how much your support means to me."

Promising to be there for her, each of the girls leaned over and gave Haley a hug before turning their horses back to the trail.

"That might have been a much-needed therapy session, but I need to have fun. Who wants to race?" Haley urged her horse forward as she yelled the challenge over her shoulder.

The others followed in close pursuit. Ten minutes later, they stopped at the edge of the clearing surrounding the treehouse which Blake and Joanna claimed as their own when they were kids. After

Blake landed in prison and Joanna headed to Colorado, Charlie and Annie had begged Grandpa to fix up the hangout for them. He had complied, complete with a picnic table beneath its shadow. The clearing was the perfect spot for the horses to graze while the ladies enjoyed lunch.

Karen dismounted and grabbed her saddlebags. "Ready for lunch? I've got the sandwiches." She headed toward the picnic table.

"I've got the hot chocolate." Elinor dismounted and glanced over at Alita. "Did you remember the dessert?"

"How could I forget my super deluxe double fudge brownies?" Alita laughed. "I mean a girl needs her chocolate."

Haley laughed and set out apples and a bag of cut-up vegies. "Did anyone remember paper goods?"

The girls all looked at each other and busted out in another round of laughter.

"Guess it's less to clean up." Karen handed out the sandwiches.

"Anyone ready for Christmas besides me?" Elinor passed around the thermos of hot chocolate.

"Let's enjoy Thanksgiving first." Alita munched on a carrot.

"And the decorating." Karen tossed an apple from hand to hand.

"What about Black Friday?"

Everyone looked at Haley like she had grown a beard.

"What?" Haley shrugged her shoulders.

"Thought you hated Black Friday." Karen shook her head.

Haley laughed. "Albert's sentiments, actually. If you don't mind, I would like to join you guys this year."

"Absolutely. But are you ready to get up at five in the morning?" Elinor leaned forward onto her elbows.

Haley grimaced. "Sure?"

Everyone laughed then began chattering about which stores were likely to have the best deals this year.

CHAPTER TWENTY-TWO

Elinor

E linor slammed the lid to the trunk and juggled an armload of flea market and estate sale finds she and Alita had found yesterday after horseback riding. She'd gotten back too late to unload last night but had time before family Sunday dinner to move her treasures to storage.

James held the door open as she entered through the kitchen entry. "Do you need help?"

Elinor shook her head.

He followed her to the storeroom. "You sure?"

"I'm sure."

"I'll put those up." He took the bags dangling from her fingers.

"I can manage." She took the bags back.

He put on a puppy dog face.

"Fine. They go on the back shelf." She handed the bags to him and waited. She was sure he wanted something. She crossed her arms and tapped her toe.

He completed his self-assigned task, then he grabbed her hand. "Come with me." He made a beeline for their apartment. Once inside the privacy of their quarters, he wrapped her in his arms. "I've missed you."

Elinor melted into his arms.

"Can we skip the family dinner?"

"You know how Dad feels about that."

"Can't blame a man for trying. As a matter of fact, I have a surprise for you." He released his hug and walked over to his desk. "It's actually not for right away. It's a bit down the road, but I know how much you're dreading that retreat for RJB Investments. I wanted you to have something to look forward to. This is our next vacation." James handed a flier to her.

She gasped at the image of a beautiful old Victorian house with mountains rising in the background. A bed and breakfast in Colorado that she had been dreaming about going to someday. "How did you know?"

"I have my ways. I booked a suite for us in January for a belated anniversary celebration. And I already cleared it with Karen for time off. She agreed we were both due a vacation. I don't think your dad's Sunday dinner will be a problem."

Elinor wrapped her arms around James's neck and allowed the tears to fall. She didn't deserve his love. "Thank you."

"Women crying when they're happy is one thing I never get used to." He wiped the tears from her cheeks.

"It will be one of my favorite memories. I know it already. But for now, we better join the family before they come looking for us."

James wiggled his eyebrows. "Imagine how compromising that could be."

Blushing, Elinor swatted his arm. "You better behave."

"But that's no fun."

Elinor laughed. Grabbing his hand, she led him out of their apartment to join the family.

CHAPTER TWENTY-THREE

Albert

Haley snuggled close to Albert as they watched *The Wizard of Oz*, one of Haley's favorite movies. Annie and Charlie were tucked in bed, and they had time to themselves. Albert determined not to give in to the churning in his mind. He needed this time with his wife.

"Honey, can I ask you something?"

"Yes, I love you." He looked down and touched her nose with the tip of his finger.

She smiled up at him and giggled.

"You think that's funny?" He donned a mock hurt look.

She shook her head. "I'm just enjoying the moment."

"Me, too." He kissed the top of her head. "What was it you wanted to ask?"

She played with her hands as though she were nervous. "It's about your moods lately."

He leaned forward, resting his elbows on his knees. "I don't know what's wrong with me, Haley. Life just feels too big right now."

She rubbed his back with one hand. "I'm glad you're getting this sabbatical, but what about seeing a doctor?"

He fought back the retort sitting on the edge of his tongue. "I don't think I need a doctor."

"What then?"

He shrugged, then stood and walked to the window. The moon lit up the backyard bright enough to see Haley's winterized garden beds. The ones he promised her he would get to last spring and never did. He swore under his breath.

"Why don't you at least give Mitch a call?"

"So he can tell me to go to the doctor?"

She shrugged. "I don't know."

"That makes two of us." He leaned his forehead against the glass. Why couldn't this have just been a pleasant Friday night?

"Honey?"

"What?" He cringed at his sharp tone.

"I love you. That's all." She got up from the couch and went to their bedroom.

As soon as she left the room, he sank to his knees on the floor. "God, when will this end? I'm so tired." In the quietness of the empty room, he rested his head in the palms of his hand and allowed the tears to come.

The next morning, Haley found Albert sprawled out on the couch. "Sweetheart?"

Albert threw an arm over his eyes.

She touched his shoulder. "It's morning."

"It's Saturday. I'll get up in a minute."

She padded toward the kitchen. The fridge opened and closed. Pans came out of the cupboard. Ice poured from the ice maker. The kids bantered back and forth.

He grimaced. No silence for the weary. The smell of coffee lured him to a sitting position, then he stood and stretched his arms over his head. Half an hour later, after a shower and breakfast, he loaded the kids into the family car to take them over to a friend's house for the day. He turned the key. Nothing. He swore under his breath and tried the ignition again. He tried to turn on the lights. Zilch. He got out and slammed the car door. The kids climbed out and waited next to the car.

Haley came out into the garage. "I'm so sorry. I completely forgot to tell you it wouldn't start."

"How can you forget something like that?" He narrowed his eyes at Haley then turned to the kids. "Get in the truck." The kids' eyes widened, and they scurried outside to the truck.

"I don't have time for this, Haley."

"I said I'm sorry." She crossed her arms and matched his glare.

He drummed his thumb on the roof of the car where it rested. "Call the tow truck. Have them take it to the garage." Pivoting away from her, he stomped to the car.

Charlie and Annie kept their eyes down when he climbed into the cab. Pulling out of the driveway, he glanced at his kids. He hated himself for pushing his family away. He bounced his left leg as he considered his behavior.

Over a year ago, before Joanna went to that rehab center in Colorado, she voiced her opinion loud and clear about his acting like their dad. He denied it, but it didn't take long to realize she had been right.

He made a concerted effort to avoid their dad's path after that and it worked until about a year after Hope was born. Seeing Joanna turn her life around and be so accepted and forgiven by the family had stirred up his anger and resentment. Since then, each day seemed worse than the last, gathering momentum like a huge snowball rolling down a hill.

Regardless, he was not going to a doctor. Pressing his foot against the pedal, he increased his speed going around a curve. He pulled the wheel to bring him closer to the middle line. A car came around the curve coming the opposite way. Albert sucked in a breath and eased up on the speed, moving to the outside of his lane. Glancing in the rearview mirror, he saw the kids' eyes wide open. How could he be so stupid? He couldn't go around scaring his kids. *God, help me. I'm at a loss here.*

CHAPTER TWENTY-FOUR

Albert

A lbert stared at the big screen TV. A morning marathon of classic TV shows served its purpose to numb his mind. After nearly driving into a head-on collision while the kids were with him on Saturday, he clamped down on his emotions and managed a tolerable weekend. He even went to church. Afterward, though, he hustled out of that building faster than he used to do as a kid. He saw no sense putting up with clicking tongues and pats on the back from people who thought they understood what was going on in his head. Haley hadn't been too happy, but at least he went.

The cheesy lyrics from *Gilligan's Island* blaring from the television signaled the start of another rerun. Exciting. He turned off the TV and tossed the remote on the coffee table. He related well to the inhabitants of the island, forever hoping to get off. Hopes dashed every time rescue looked near.

Glancing at the clock, he groaned. Lunchtime. The kids were at school and Haley was shopping. With the Hyundai still in the shop for another week, he was stuck at the house. He went to the kitchen and rummaged through the fridge for food. Good thing Haley was shopping. Not much choice. He grabbed an apple and walked out onto the back patio. Come spring, he would follow through on his promise and help Haley bring her garden to life. Why had he let it go so long? It would take up all his spare time to help her. He kicked the metal patio chair and cursed at the throbbing in his toes.

He tossed the apple core out into the yard for the squirrels, then headed back into the house to look for a crunchy snack. The cupboards yielded single-serve size bags of chips. Shrugging his shoulders, he plopped back down on the coach. Haley should be home soon with real food. Of course, he could order pizza. Now there was an idea. But Haley would probably harp about their budget and how inconsiderate it was of him, since she had plans to cook supper. Fine. He crumpled the chip bags and tossed them on the floor.

His phone notifications alerted him to a call from Haley. He swiped the screen and tapped the speaker option. "You almost home? I'm hungry. Should I wait?"

There was a pause on the other end.

"Haley?"

"I won't be back till this afternoon. I'm sorry. I have some things I need to do."

"Like what?"

"We'll talk when I get home. Why don't you order a pizza?"

"Sure. I'll see you later." Why did Haley have to do that? Couldn't she tell him over the phone? He closed the phone app and leaned his head back. He needed to get out of the house. He bounced his left leg as he debated the issue at hand. Scrolling through his favorite contacts, he tapped on Barry's number. Typically, the least intrusive person in the family. A promised pizza and a half hour later, he had a ride.

The aroma of fire-cooked pizza promised a decent meal if not decent company and conversation. He didn't feel like talking, but Barry seemed to be in the mood. Albert glanced away as Barry talked about possibly going back to college sometime in the next year. Good for him. A meat lover's style pizza was all that Albert wanted to contemplate for the next half hour.

After the waitress brought their drinks and took their order to the kitchen, Barry leaned his forearms on the table. "Do you have any plans for your sabbatical?"

"Get through it and get back to preaching."

"Hmm."

"You think I shouldn't be preaching?" Albert crossed his arms.

Barry held up his hands as if in surrender. "I didn't say that. But your church board gave you a sabbatical for a reason."

Albert looked out the window to his left. "They think I'm depressed."

"Are you?"

"Just a bit stressed."

"Hmm."

Albert glared at Barry. Why did he think Barry was a good idea for a ride? Because anyone else would have given him more grief. He cursed under his breath.

"I know a good counselor."

"Don't need a counselor. What I need is everyone staying out of my business."

Barry tapped the table with his fingers. "Want to come volunteer at the soup kitchen with me tomorrow?"

"Why would I want to do that?"

Barry shrugged. "Helping others can get our minds off our own problems."

Albert glared at Barry, then pulled out his phone and scrolled, ignoring his brother-in-law the best he could until the waitress finally brought their pizza to the table and refilled their water. The two men each dished up two slices and ate in silence. By the time they had finished all but one slice, the waitress had returned with the check. Barry snatched it up before Albert could.

"Trying to bribe me to serve at that place?" Albert hated the bitterness laced through his voice, but he was too tired to censor it.

"If I thought it would work, I might try." Barry tossed a five on the table for tip, then stood. "It's your call. Let me know if you want to come and I'll pick you up. They need us there by ten in the morning."

"Right." Albert scooted back his chair. "You ready?"

"Sure." Barry stopped at the cashier and paid their bill, then led the way to his car.

Albert slammed the door and stomped past Haley. He slouched onto the couch and turned on the TV.

Haley followed him into the living room. "Did you have lunch?"

"Trying to keep track of me?"

"I want to know if I need to fix you something to eat."

Albert glanced up at Haley. She looked like she was about to cry. What now? "You told me to have pizza. I had pizza. Where have you been?"

"I went shopping. And to see a counselor at Hillside Community Church in town."

"You what?"

"You heard me."

"Why would you do that?"

"I needed perspective."

"On what?"

"How to be the best me for you during this season of your life."

"What is that supposed to mean?"

"What it sounds like."

He snorted. "What did you figure out?"

"I plan on getting a job."

Albert rose from the couch and walked over to his wife. "We agreed you wouldn't work outside the home."

"We weren't counting on this particular season. We need to adjust. I need space and I don't think it's going to be you getting out of the house. I applied at three places while I was out. It won't be full time. But it…"

Albert took a step closer and leaned over Haley. "You're right it won't be full time. It won't be at all."

Haley cringed. "Please. Don't shout."

"I'm not shouting."

"Mom?"

Albert looked behind him where Charlie and Annie watched from the door. Albert took a step back. "I'm sorry. I didn't mean to…go ahead and do what you want." He sagged back onto the couch. Couldn't he get anything right? Maybe the church was better off without him.

CHAPTER
TWENTY-FIVE

Albert

Albert wiped another table and picked up trash left by one of the homeless men that frequented the soup kitchen. After his unintentional intimidation of his family last night, Albert did some hard thinking and decided to take Barry up on his invitation to serve at the Westfall shelter where he and Karen donated their chef's time to cook one meal a week.

Albert hated to admit it, but it did feel good to get out of the house and do something meaningful. He couldn't remember the last time his work had felt full of purpose. There was always so much pressure and so many expectations from his congregants. He always came up against someone who wasn't pleased with his effort. Here, he just served, and people were grateful.

"You about done?" Barry slapped Albert's back.

"Just finished."

"They need help in the kitchen. Someone had to leave because of a family emergency, so they're short staffed. Are you good if we stay for another hour or so?"

Albert shrugged. "Not like I have anything else to do." He tossed the dishrag into the basket for dirty rags and followed Barry. "What do they need us to do?"

"Clean pots and pans."

Albert groaned.

"I know. Not my favorite job either. But it will be good for us."

"How do you figure that?"

"Exercise. Lift those pots and pans. And it's a hot job, too, so figure we can sweat off part of a pound while we're at it." He patted his stomach. "Get ready for our Thanksgiving feast."

"In your dreams." Albert grabbed an apron and pair of rubber gloves. "You want to wash or dry?"

"Drying of course."

"Why did I bother asking?" Albert laughed. He reached for the first pan and scraped the edgings of food into the sink with a garbage disposal. "We could take turns."

Barry shook his head. "You're doing a fine job. I don't want to interrupt your flow."

"Ha. Right." Albert focused his energy into washing instead of talking and made quick work of it. But no sooner did he think he was done than one of the cooks stopped by the sink with another pan. Did this ever end?

"How's Haley doing with the sabbatical?" Barry stacked another pot at the end of the counter.

Albert snorted. "She likes it just fine. Announced yesterday she plans to get a job. Something about getting space away from me. Guess who's going to be left with the cooking and running the kids around."

"And that's a problem?"

Albert paused and looked at Barry. "Yeah. Actually, it is."

"Why?"

"Because it's her job."

Barry raised his eyebrows. "While you do what?"

Albert dropped the pan he was holding into the water and turned to glare at Barry. After pulling off the rubber gloves, he tossed them into the drain rack. "I wish everyone would get off my back. Nobody gets what's going on."

"I'm listening." Barry leaned against the counter.

He wasn't expecting that response. Even Albert didn't get it. How did he explain that? "I don't need everybody knowing my business."

"What about going to a counselor?"

"The only place I want to go right now is home. You ready?"

Barry met Albert's glare with a look of kindness. Albert wanted to crawl into a hole. The church board was right. He had no business pastoring right now.

Maybe I should find a counselor.

Barry shrugged. "Sure. Let me tell the manager we're leaving."

Albert wiped the last counter off and looked around. Haley would be surprised that he cleaned the house. He even caught the laundry up. Lethargy had begged him to stay in bed this morning, but he forced himself to get up. Despite how the volunteering at the soup kitchen had ended, Albert had been inspired.

He was sick and tired of everyone on his case. Yesterday, he gave in to the pestering and went to his doctor, who concluded that Albert did indeed suffer with depression. His doctor prescribed an antidepressant and encouraged him not to rely solely on drugs, but to find a counselor, eat healthy and exercise. Especially since it might take time for the medication to make a difference. He hadn't told Haley yet. No "I told you so" for him.

Besides, Albert got all the housework done today and felt good. Without the benefit of meds. Maybe he could beat this on his own. *Yes.* He grabbed paper and pen and sat down to make a list of what he would do every day to win the battle. Get up every morning even when he didn't feel like it. Exercise every day. Maybe a membership to the gym. Good sleep. Eat healthy. Do all the housework and drive the kids around without complaining. Stop being angry at everyone. Spend two hours in Bible study every day. Focus on the positives. Find somewhere to volunteer. What else did Haley take care of? Errands. Shopping. Albert paused and looked at his list. How did Haley do it all?

His mind wandered to when the sabbatical would be over. Did he still want to be a pastor? He didn't know anything else. He would have to go back to school. Or start his own business. Tapping his pen on the table, he bounced his leg up and down. He had no clue. *Guess I should do some research.* In the meantime, there was plenty to keep him busy.

He glanced at his watch and dropped the pen on the table. Whistling, he headed for the garage. Time to make a dent in the mess out there. If Barry could see him now. He opened the door to the garage, stepped out, and groaned. He'd forgotten how much of a mess it was. Pastoring hadn't left much time to keep things in order. Piles of boxes, furniture ready to refurbish, and a large collection of odds and ends filled the half of the garage opposite the door.

"Am I the only one who has enough sense to put things where they go?" He swore and kicked the closest box. Must be. Closing his eyes and taking a deep breath, he focused on the shelves at the front of the garage. He would start there. He pulled his toolbox down and placed forgotten tools back in their home. He could only blame himself for this one. He glanced over his shoulder. But that mess was another story. After half an hour, Albert returned the toolbox to the overcrowded shelf.

He checked briefly inside each box or bag on the shelf for anything of value, then tossed most of it into a garbage bag. This was the way to do it. Grinning, he rummaged around and found more of his supplies for working on the house and car and set them next to his toolbox on the shelf. He stood back and looked at his work. Nodding, he brushed off his hands. "One shelf down and..." Albert looked around him. A wave of tiredness swept over him, stealing any desire he had to clean and organize the garage. There was always tomorrow.

Adding the one full garbage bag to the bin outside, Albert returned to the kitchen for something to eat. He would catch a quick nap then get supper started. Haley would be impressed. He set his alarm for an hour and fell asleep as soon as his head hit the pillow.

"Albert? Albert?"

Albert heard Haley say his name like it came through a tunnel. He felt a nudge on his arm and turned away from her voice. "I'll get up in a little bit."

"Albert, I could use help with supper and the kids now."

He groaned. Wasn't it enough that he cleaned the house? "Sorry. I must have slept through the alarm."

"Are you going to help?"

"I'll be out in a bit. Just need to wake up."

"Fine." Haley closed the door behind her when she left the room.

"Fine." Albert turned to the wall and drifted back into his dream. The sound of kids bickering bolted him from the bed. *Can't Annie and Charlie be quiet?* Albert swore. What time was it anyway? He glanced at the clock. *Nine o'clock? How in the world? Haley is going to be mad.* Forcing himself out of bed, he padded across the floor. Cracking the door open, he peeked into the hallway. Quiet had again descended on the house. The droning of a TV program explained where the kids were. He moved down the hall to find Haley. He paused outside his office when he heard her voice. Sounded like she was on the phone.

"I'm afraid we can't come to your game night this weekend."

There was a pause while she listened.

"No, I'm sure the kids will survive."

Another pause.

"Albert? No, he...we just had some things come up."

Haley's voice became more insistent. "Really. We can't come even if you change the time. Oh, I'm sorry. I just saw the time and I need to go. I'll talk to you Sunday."

Albert peeked into the office when he heard Haley hang up the phone. She folded her arms on the desk and put her head down. "God help me be strong. Pull Albert out of this depression." Her shoulders shook as quiet sobs interrupted her prayer.

He backed away from the door and leaned against the wall. Sliding down, he sat on his haunches with elbows on his knees. She canceled the outing because of him? He rested his forehead in his hands. Couldn't he get anything right? He sucked in a breath. Haley was already tired of all this. If he didn't' get a grip soon, would she ever consider leaving him?

CHAPTER TWENTY-SIX

Albert

H aley leaned over the couch and gave Albert a hug from behind.

"Hey. What's up?" Irritated at the interruption, he looked up from the game on TV.

"When you were cleaning in the garage the other day, did you put my box of scrapbooking stuff somewhere?"

"Not that I remember. Why?"

"It was a red box on that shelf you organized. Karen gave me a plastic tub to store things in and I planned to switch things over and scrapbook today. But I can't find it."

The red box? Albert gave himself a mental kick. He barely looked in those boxes. And the sanitation truck came yesterday. One more mark against him. He turned sideways on the couch, so he could see her and rested his hand on hers. "I'm sorry, honey. I must have thrown them out, but I'll get you more supplies."

"Didn't you even look inside?" Haley's voice rose, and she clenched her fists at her side. "There were pictures in there, too. Of the kids when they were little. Before we went digital and stored everything on the computer. How am I supposed to replace those?

And even if I could replace them, what money would I use? Get it together already." Haley turned and hurried out of the room, but not before Albert saw her tears.

He turned off the television and tossed the remote onto the coffee table. How could he make that right? She'd made it obvious he couldn't. He was a royal jerk. Swearing under his breath, he went to the kitchen. "I didn't choose this. I hate it. Why can't she get that?" He mumbled to himself as he dug around in the fridge. Looked like a run to the store was in order if any of them were going to eat. He slammed the fridge door and turned. Haley stood in the doorway staring at him. What had he done this time?

"We're out of food."

"I've been interviewing for a job."

"Guess I should have gone shopping yesterday." Albert shrugged.

"Probably. Then maybe the pictures would still be here."

They stared at each other for a long moment until Albert broke the silence stretching stretched between them. "I'm trying." He shook his head. "I was waiting to tell you, but I went to the doctor and got a prescription."

"It's not working."

"Doc said it could take a while. What else can I do?"

"Counseling."

"No."

"Do you want to get over this?"

"The meds..."

"I'm glad you're on medication. I am. It's a good thing. An important part of the picture. But you need more than pills."

Albert hung his head. The pastor getting counseling? How would that go over? But if it made the difference between losing and keeping his family...

"Think about it?"

"Sure." He shrugged his shoulders.

"I hope you mean that. Something needs to change. Think of the kids. What do you want them to remember about their dad? That he gave up?"

Was that what he was doing? He felt like he was drowning. How did he fight that?

Haley crossed her arms and hugged herself. "I'm sorry. I know you didn't choose this. But I'm struggling with this, too. Let's get through Thanksgiving, then figure out next steps. Maybe give Mitch a call? Izzy told me he's left several messages. Will you promise you'll do that much?"

"I promise."

Tears welled up in Haley's eyes. "Thank you." She grabbed the keys from their hook. "I love you, Albert. I do. I won't leave you, but I'm tired." She headed to the garage door. "I'm going shopping. I may stop by Karen's. I'll pick up the kids on the way home."

"Haley?"

She turned back.

"I'm sorry about the pictures."

"I know. I'll see you later."

Sitting at the kitchen table, Albert pulled out his phone and tapped Mitch's number. A few rings and his friend picked up. "Can we talk?" Albert had no idea what he was supposed to say, but he could at least keep this promise to his wife.

Mitch and Albert dug into Westfall Pizzeria's signature Nachos Supreme. Usually, this was his favorite dish in the place, but Albert set his portion aside after one bite. It didn't taste as good as he remembered. He shook his head. He couldn't even muster up the energy to care.

"Talk to me." Mitch stuffed his mouth with another nacho topped with mango salsa, smoked gouda cheese, and salmon.

Albert shrugged. "I'm driving my family crazy, but I can't seem to help it. My doctor prescribed antidepressants, but those take a while to kick in. Haley asked me to go to a counselor, but...I don't know...honestly, I just don't want to."

"Why not?"

"Why would I?"

"'Cause your wife asked?"

"But I don't need counseling."

"Sounds like pride talking." Mitch scooped another serving of the appetizer onto his plate.

Albert sat back in his chair. Was he allowing pride to get in his way? He used to accuse his dad of pride. And his dad's pride led to anger and judging everyone else as worse than himself. Was he just as guilty? How had he taken a path he swore he would never go down?

Mitch tossed his napkin onto his now empty plate. "You know, there is more than one way to lose your family. Refusing to do your best to overcome this will drive them away. Emotionally if not physically. Saw it happen with my brother and his family. Good news though, his wife is moving back in time for Thanksgiving."

Albert bounced his leg and drummed the table with his fingertips. "I don't suppose you have a counselor to recommend?"

"The one my brother sees." Mitch pulled a business card out of his wallet and handed it to Albert. "I think you'll like this guy. My brother does and he's a harder head than you."

"Now you're calling me names? What happened to brotherly love?"

Mitch smiled and shrugged. "You know I still love you, man, but you can't get past this if you don't face the truth."

"I have a feeling I'm not going to like what I find."

"Maybe. But getting to the other side?"

"I know. Sweet." Albert shook his head. The words he often used to encourage others came back to prod him forward. It was time to live what he had preached to others. He took a deep breath. "I'm going to call right now and make an appointment before I back out. You mind?"

"Not at all. I'll get a box for the leftovers while you do."

"I'll just step outside." Albert held up the card. "Thanks."

"Sure, I'll send you the bill." Mitch grinned.

Albert smirked. "I'll meet you outside."

CHAPTER TWENTY-SEVEN

Elinor

Forcing herself to focus on the words to the worship song, Elinor dropped the flier onto the seat beside her and took a deep breath before she joined in singing. Why hadn't she paid attention to upcoming events? She could have come up with a reason not to be in church today.

James leaned over and whispered in her ear. "I'm looking forward to the presentation. How about you?"

Elinor smiled and nodded but kept singing. She fully expected the sales pitch on the way home. But no way would she consider adoption. It would be one more thing to remind her how badly she was messed up and how lacking she was.

After two more songs, a prayer, and the offering, the preacher got up and introduced the local Christian adoption agency, which would speak before the sermon. They came to encourage people to consider adoption and to offer a class for those who wanted to understand the process. Out of the corner of her eye, she watched James. At almost every point, he nodded. When ushers offered packets of information, he took one. At the end of the service, he hurried to their display and cornered one of the representatives.

Elinor found someone else to talk to well out of view. She didn't want to be lumped together with his excitement. Or put on the spot in their conversation.

When it was time for the building to be locked up, James helped carry the agency's materials to their car. Still asking questions. Elinor groaned. It would be a long day.

Scooting the pan of scalloped potatoes into the oven next to the roast to warm up, Elinor reflected on the morning presentation. James had talked about it the entire way home from church. Relieved at his uncharacteristic talkativeness, Elinor's turn to share her thoughts was spared till after family dinner, although she was fairly certain what the topic of conversation would be around the table. She didn't want anyone to ask her opinion. Probably unavoidable. But she could hope.

Elinor set the salad, a pan of brownies, and a basket of bread on the counter. She checked the roast, then poked her head into the dining room. "A little help, please?"

Haley, Charlie, and Annie joined her and each grabbed something to carry.

"Hey, kids. What's got you looking so sad?"

"Dad didn't come." Annie followed her brother back into the dining room.

"What's up?" Elinor placed a hand on Haley's arm.

Haley shrugged her shoulders. "Albert and I had a disagreement about me getting a job. He roused himself for a couple of days, helped around the house. But mostly, it's like he doesn't care about anything. I hurt for the kids, but I don't know what to do."

"I'm so sorry, Haley. Is there anything I can do? Watch the kids? Take you with me on more shopping expeditions?"

Haley laughed under her breath. "I'm not sure what I need, but thanks for the offer. It means a lot."

Elinor gave her a hug. "Let me know if you think of something."

Haley swiped a stray tear from her cheek and nodded. "For now, we better get the food in before we have a riot."

Elinor laughed. "Don't you know it."

Plates full and everyone seated around the table, the conversation turned to adoption. James fed the topic with extra information he had gleaned from the presenters. He smiled at Elinor but didn't draw her into the discussion.

Stomach in knots, Elinor checked on the buffet for an excuse to move. Twirling a strand of hair around her finger, she contemplated what it would be like to take in someone else's child as her own. James thought she would be a good mother. Clarice and even Hope seemed to respond well to her. But she didn't deserve to have a child. She gave a sharp tug on her hair when James mentioned to the whole family that they would like to adopt. All eyes turned her direction.

She shrugged and took a seat next to James. Mustering all the strength she could, she patted James on the arm. "A discussion for just the two of us. I'm sure everyone understands." She looked around the table. Her eyes landed on Karen, a silent plea sent to her sister.

Karen nodded. "Absolutely. Now, how about Thanksgiving for five hundred?"

Laughter rippled through the family and the subject of the holidays took center stage.

"Let's have Thanksgiving at the house." Charles grinned. "It's about time we brought the bird home to roost. Don't you think?"

"I like it." Barry leaned forward on his forearms.

"And how about us guys take charge and cook the meal?" Charles grinned at the men.

James groaned. "You had to go there."

"Yep." Barry laughed and turned to Karen. "What do you think, honey? Think we're up to the task?"

"You better be. I'm taking Dad up on the offer."

"I like it." Haley nodded.

"Me to." Elinor snickered and elbowed James. "You'll be the one getting up early this year."

He wiggled his eyebrows. "You still have the guests to think about."

Karen cleared her throat. "Actually, as of yet, we have no guests for Thanksgiving weekend. I think I'll keep it that way. It's about time we had a weekend off."

Conversation stopped when someone knocked on the dining room door before it cracked open. Mrs. Granger, hair styled, clothes stylish, looking the part of royalty, peeked inside the room.

"There you are." Charles hurried over to greet her. "I'm glad you could come. You look lovely today." He tucked her hand into the bend of his arm and led her to a chair next to his at the end of the table. She smiled up at Charles.

Albert looked at Elinor and raised an eyebrow.

"I know. Right?" She poured a refill of her coffee from the carafe setting on the table.

"How long has this been going on?" Alita leaned over to Elinor and tilted her head toward their dad and Mrs. Granger.

"I haven't seen her with anyone but Dad recently. She even tagged along with James and me to Dad's place for table games. They cracked us up all night. She actually got all his jokes. And before we left, they made plans for Dad to teach her how to ride a horse."

"What?" Haley and Alita spoke together.

Elinor nodded and the three of them focused on eavesdropping.

Mrs. Granger tucked her hair behind her ear. "I wish I didn't have to go back this week. I'm having a wonderful time. I'm glad I extended my stay."

"Me, too." Charles laughed. "You're welcome back anytime, Helen. You wouldn't even have to tell your family."

She giggled. "I think that's a great idea."

Haley, Alita, and Elinor looked at each other and covered their mouths, stifling a laugh.

"They're too cute." Elinor whispered.

"What are you three whispering about?" Karen came up behind them.

Elinor angled her head toward their dad and Helen.

Karen looked at the two, heads bent together in conversation, then glanced back at her sister. "I guess I've been too busy to notice." She laughed, then made her way around the table and gave Helen a hug. "Next time you come, the room is on us."

Mrs. Granger looked up at Karen and scrunched her shoulders. "Even if I bring Wrinkle?"

Karen laughed. "Even if you bring Wrinkle."

Elinor snuggled next to James on their couch. She picked up her tea and took a sip. "I'm looking forward to a Thanksgiving out of the kitchen."

"Ha, ha. I think I'll clock your dad next time I see him."

Elinor gave him a soft jab in the ribs. "Be a good sport."

"I promise I'll be good." He kissed the top of her head then leaned his head back against the couch. "What movie did you pick out?"

"*Princess Bride*."

"Great choice." Grabbing the remote, he turned on the television and fast forwarded through the previews. "What did you think of the presentation this morning?"

Elinor caught her breath and almost spilled her tea. "I haven't had much of a chance to think about it."

"First impressions."

"I guess I'm willing to think about it. I don't want to disappoint you."

"I don't want this to be about you not disappointing me. Yes, I want kids. You'll be a great mom. I do want to explore the possibility of adoption, but would not having kids change how I much I love you? Not on your life. And I don't want to have kids, any way they come, until you have that secure in your head. So, for now, let's just pray about it."

Elinor nodded. "Thank you." She snuggled under his arms. "Can we just snuggle? No movie?"

James turned off the television. "As you wish."

Elinor stared at the ceiling for what seemed like hours after James feel asleep, his gentle snoring indicating his unawareness of her plight. Glancing at the clock, she moaned. *Only half an hour since we went to bed?*

She slipped out of bed and headed to their apartment kitchen where she set the tea kettle to boil and pulled her favorite mug and a box of chai tea from the cupboard. Holding her housecoat in place with her arms wrapped around her waist, she paced. Her mind roamed back to the year she graduated from high school. The year everything changed.

Leaning against the frame of the eating nook window, she stared at the full moon shining into the house above the café curtains. She culled through the memories one by one. The man. The love. The choices. The lost future. *How could I have been so...trusting? God, can I ever make it right?* James deserved so much more. Not a woman incapable, physically or emotionally, of being a mother to his children. The whistle blew on her tea kettle. Startled, she wiped her tears with the sleeve of her housecoat and shuffled over to the stove and poured hot water over the tea bag.

Before the tea finished steeping, tiredness overwhelmed her. Thoughts of her past continued bombarding her. She had avoided those thoughts for years. But after Remí showed up, everything reminded her of what was and what now couldn't be.

"Remí." She whispered his name like she used to.

At the end of the day, when he came back to his apartment. To her. And it was just the two of them. Alone. *Why couldn't you have been who you said you were?* But would she have wanted him over James? She covered her mouth with her fingertips and shook her head. She couldn't let herself think that way. Remí had proved his lack of character. But still...what they had...it came back to haunt her now. Tempting her with empty promises.

Setting her tea mug on the coffee table, she lay on the couch and pulled the snuggle blanket over herself. Tears, held captive till now, overthrew her desire to forget. Curling into a ball, she fell into a restless sleep full of images trampling her peace.

"No! Don't take my baby!" Tears filled her heart. Elinor wrestled the snuggly blanket and looked around in the semidarkness, disoriented. Her eyes stung with saltiness oozing out of them. She hugged her knees to herself and rocked side to side. Haze veiled the difference between reality and nightmare. Loss grabbed at her insides and pulled them out. She moaned. "No." Throwing back her covers, she abandoned the fight against the images playing in her head.

An empty room. Empty arms. Hot water running over her. Watching the water swirl around her feet before it disappeared down a drain. Pain gripped her middle. She shook off the despair grasping for a hold on her soul. Moaning, Elinor thrashed against the unseen.

A hand against her forehead brought relief to her desperation. She leaned into the strength. Tears subsided. Her breathing eased.

"Elinor?" The voice whispered like the morning air after a storm.

She curled into the voice and rested. Peace cloaked her from the world. Light penetrated the darkness, and she opened her eyes. "James?" Had she spoken any of the nightmare?

"It's me, sweetheart."

Still disoriented, Elinor nodded.

"What were you dreaming about?"

Sighing, she held his hand against her cheek. "Emptiness. I was dreaming of emptiness. Don't leave me." She wrapped her arms around his neck and pulled him close. "I don't like the emptiness."

James held her close. "I will never leave you, my love. Never. And when you're ready to talk about whatever is bothering you, I'll be here."

CHAPTER TWENTY-EIGHT

Albert

Albert pulled off at the rest stop. The sounds of the road faded, and he leaned back his car seat. Quiet. Absolute quiet. No kids. No wife. Nobody. He was beginning to think this retreat idea was a good thing. After the fight with Haley last week, he'd stayed home from the Sunday family dinner. He couldn't pretend that everything was normal when everyone knew it wasn't. Monday, he followed through on meeting with the counselor.

The blare of a horn interrupted his moment of peace. His car rocked as another vehicle sped past him. Too fast for passing through a rest stop. And too close. He swore. Whoever that was could have hit him. Looking around the parking area, he noted a gray, dinged-up jeep partway out of its parking space further down to his right, the direction the speedster had come from. Albert's car would have been hit if that guy's tail hadn't been sticking out forcing the speedster to swerve. He offered a quick prayer of thanks for protection and headed back to the highway.

Last week, his dad offered to pay for a retreat if he decided to take one like the board suggested. Rental car, place to stay, food, however long he needed. Probably a guilt offering, but after hashing the idea over with the counselor, Albert had finally decided to take his dad up on the offer regardless, and made plans.

When he got home from his appointment, he told Haley what he had in mind. She didn't blink. Just asked him to call every day and let them know he was safe. He promised to text her when he arrived at his stop each night. But he needed space and time to think. Having to relay details about his day was not going to be part of his retreat. By the time the kids got home from school, his bag was packed, and the rental car delivered. They didn't seem to mind the fact that he would be going on a trip for a while. He left Tuesday once the kids left for school.

Heading west, he drove straight across Kansas. The mountains seemed like a good destination. According to the forecast, weather wouldn't be a problem. Of course, if he stayed very long, that might change.

Last night, he stayed in an offbeat little place just northwest of Topeka off a two-lane highway. This morning, he got back on 70, but after two hours of heavy traffic and the near miss at the rest stop, traveling two-lane roads sounded more his speed. At least for daytime driving. Taking the next exit, he stopped at a diner promising the world's best hamburgers. After supper, he would find a place to stay nearby, then in the morning, resume travel on a more peaceful two-lane road. Even if it took longer.

Someone pounded on Albert's motel door, and he bolted upright. Still dark. He glanced at his clock. Five o'clock?

Whoever it was pounded again.

"Hold your horses. I'm coming." Albert put on his jeans and pulled a T-shirt over his head. He peeked through the door to make sure it wasn't a crazed kid high on something Albert didn't want to deal with. The manager of the hotel stood under the light. Leaving the chain in place, Albert cracked the door. "You realize what time it is?"

"Sorry. It's just someone backed into your car and they're in a hurry to get out of here. Thought you would want to talk to them before I let them scoot on down the road."

"Could have called."

"Tried. You're one heavy sleeper."

Albert nodded. "Let me get on my shoes and grab my jacket. Meet you in the office?"

Half an hour later, insurance information in hand and rental company notified, Albert headed back to his room. He would have to stick around till lunch to give the rental place time to deliver his replacement car. He paused outside his room and looked out across the road. The sun was just beginning to color the sky with a pink glow. The brown stubble in the fields and bare branches of nearby trees covered in frost created a lacy filter for the light to shine through. God's artistry at work. It wasn't a bad place to be stuck. Albert breathed in deeply. He missed this. Just being still. Taking in God's world around him. His mind had gotten so clogged up that he had been missing out. Why had he allowed things to get so bad?

That was what he needed to figure out. Something inside him had caved in and he couldn't seem to get enough air to breathe. He felt trapped. But he didn't have to figure it out in a day.

The manager had said there was a diner about a quarter mile away. Claimed they served the best cinnamon rolls around. Not sure that was saying much, but Albert didn't have anything to lose. As long as they served coffee, he would be happy. He checked that the door to his room was locked and then walked toward the promised land of cinnamon laden rolls.

When he arrived at the diner, the parking lot was full. Likely the only place around to get a plate of food if you wanted something besides what was being served at home. The shopkeeper's bell on the door jingled as he came in, and the waitress waved at him.

"Help yourself to coffee over there against the far wall and find a seat. Be with you when I can. Menus are on the table." The middle-aged woman turned her flirtations back to the men at the counter and Albert found his way over to the coffee and an empty table. She would be a while.

About fifteen minutes later, the waitress meandered over to his table, setting a plate covered with one gigantic cinnamon roll in front of him, then topped off his coffee. "Name is Kayla. Your omelet is cooking."

"Huh?"

"You look like an omelet sort of guy. Am I wrong?"

"What kind?"

"The guys call it the monster meat omelet. Official name is much less descriptive."

"Meat sounds good. Do you do this all the time?"

"Order for people? It's my specialty." She laughed a pleasing join-me-if-you-can sort of laugh.

Albert couldn't help but smile. "Not much else to do around here?"

"Oh, you're a smart one. Must not be from around here."

"Guilty as charged."

A man entered the diner, and the waitress gave him wave before turning back to Albert. "Enjoy your treat. I'll be back with your omelet in a jiff. Right now, I gotta go place an order. He looks like the scrambled egg variety."

Albert laughed. How he missed laughing. He picked up his fork and dug in. He widened his eyes. The motel manager might be right. This was fantastic. Taking another bite, he watched the interaction between the newcomer and the mind-reading waitress. The man seemed agitated. He kept glancing over his shoulder toward the door. Albert glanced outside the window and noticed a car sitting off to the side. Albert squinted. Looked like there was someone sitting in the front seat and two heads just topping the back seat. Albert watched the waitress deliver the plate of eggs and one of their infamous rolls to the table. He held up his hands in a stop motion. She placed her hands on her hips and shook her head then went back to the kitchen. She returned with a box and their ticket. The man dug out money from his pocket and handed it to Kayla before he boxed up the food and left.

Albert watched him through the window. The man's shoulder's drooped as he walked to the car.

Kayla came over and set his omelet down in front of him. "It took all the money he had just to get one omelet and the roll. Looks like he has a whole family to feed. Sad, isn't it?"

"Do you know him?"

She shook her head.

"Put in an order for enough to feed that family. And feed them well. I'm paying." Albert jumped up from his seat and ran after the man. Within minutes, he reentered the diner carrying a toddler in his arms, followed by the man carrying their infant daughter. His wife and a young boy in early elementary school were close on the man's heels.

Kayla filled the table with omelets, hash browns, bacon, sausage, and cinnamon rolls.

Hesitating before he filled his plate, the man looked at Albert. "Why are you helping us?"

Albert shrugged. "You had a need and I was able to help."

"Thank you." The man's wife teared up.

Albert waved off the thanks and grinned at the enthusiasm of the young boy. "My pleasure. Now fill up." His phone rang, and he glanced at the number. The rental company. He excused himself and picked up. His car would arrive in less than half an hour.

On his way out the door, Kayla stopped him. "Thanks for what you did for that family."

Albert waved and headed back down the road. It felt good to help. Not because he was required to as their pastor. Just because.

He grabbed his bag from his room and headed to the motel office. He bumped into a man with a baseball cap pulled down, throwing a shadow across his face. The man mumbled an apology and continued out to his car. Albert checked out and once his car arrived, loaded up. Considering the time, he probably wouldn't make it to Colorado tonight. Maybe he would find another gem of a diner along the way. He grinned in the first moments of anticipation he had felt in a while.

Turning out of the parking lot, he caught a glimpse of the man he had bumped into, now leaning against a nondescript beat-up jeep. Albert glanced back. The man looked away and tossed a cigarette butt on the ground. Wrinkling his brow, Albert shook his head and refocused on the road in front of him. With the sun at his back and a new map on the seat next to him, Albert decided to head onto highway 24. No more four lanes for a while.

CHAPTER TWENTY-NINE

Albert

I t was about three in the afternoon when Albert turned off Highway 24. A steepled church stood near a diner. *Hole in the Wall Diner?* Albert shook his head. Next a full-service gas station and a one-sided block of stores filed down the road before disappearing around a bend. A one-lane road shot off between the church and diner, and another at the end of the row of storefronts.

Driving around the bend, a sign announced the presence of a camp down a graveled road only a brave person would dare drive. Nothing else enticed him to keep going. Albert pulled over onto the wide shoulder and made a sharp left U-turn. The diner seemed to be the best place to get information without getting lost.

The two customers at the counter glanced over their shoulders when he entered, then nodded before going back to the coffee and newspapers in front of them. Voices floated out of the kitchen. Through the open window into the back, Albert saw a waitress and a man, possibly the cook, talking. Voices raised. The woman, not much older than Albert, pointed her finger at the man and shook it, then pointed to the stove. The man gestured wildly with his hands, took off his apron and threw it down. The woman lifted her head and closed her eyes. Almost as if in prayer. Then she turned and made eye contact with Albert, and offered a wry smile.

"Be right out. Go ahead and find a seat." The waitress removed her glasses and squeezed the bridge of her nose. She looked tired and frustrated. Wavy brown hair escaping a loose bun added a distracted feel to the picture.

Albert chose the corner booth to his far left and picked up the almost sticky menu lying on the table. Usual fare. Easy enough.

"What brings you to our wonderful area of the state?" The waitress set a mug in front of him and held up a pot of coffee.

Albert nodded. "Just traveling through. Hoping to find a motel for the night. Anything around?"

The woman laughed. "Nope. But you're in luck. Our cook just quit. Part of his pay is getting to stay in the cottage out back. Nothing fancy. He'll be gone within the hour. I'll give my husband a call and okay it with him. That work?"

"Perfect."

"If you want food, though, it will have to be something I can cook. And that won't be much."

He waved aside her explanation. He was thankful he had mainly come in for information. "Just the coffee would be fine."

She poured his cup then started to walk away. Pausing, she looked upward, then turning back, she appeared to size him up. "You don't happen to cook, do you?"

Albert chuckled. "Not looking for work."

"You in a hurry?"

Albert shook his head. "I don't think I qualify as a cook."

"You're here. Can you cook eggs? Scrambled and fried?"

Albert nodded, deciding to play along.

"Hash browns?"

"Sure."

"Can you brew coffee?"

"Yep."

"Use a microwave?"

"Pretty sure. Haven't blown up anything yet." Albert laughed.

"Can you reheat things in the oven?"

"My wife may argue that I can't, but I make do."

"I like your sense of humor. Listen, we just need someone for a week while we replace that deadbeat who just walked out in the middle of the shift. And those guys..." She pointed over her shoulder at the cowboys at the counter. "...no offense, but they wouldn't know a coffee pot from a fry pan. What do you say? Room and board plus whatever I can wrangle out of my husband for you?"

"I don't know..."

"Think about it till he gets here?"

Albert held up his hands in surrender. "Sure. Why not?"

"Good. Name's Jennifer. My husband is Bill."

"Albert." He shook her hand before she headed back to the kitchen, then contemplated what was to come of this offer as he sipped his coffee.

Albert enjoyed a hearty supper with the owners of the café, before making his way to the tiny cottage behind the diner. He tossed his duffle bag onto the couch, then took a quick walk around his temporary home. Somehow, the couple had managed to convince him to help out. Not sure why they trusted him, but considering the last guy, hopefully he came across as more trustworthy than that. Besides, he supposed they were desperate.

Cooking. Ha. Wait till he told Haley. Remembering his promise, he shot off a quick text and let his wife and kids know where he was, then he turned off notifications and plugged in his phone to charge.

Albert grabbed his Bible out of the duffle bag and settled onto a couch that was in great need of new stuffing. Opening the well-worn book, Albert's thoughts wandered. Restless, he paced around the living room. *God, I don't even know what I'm looking for on this trip. I need...peace. How do I find it?*

He felt guilty for not feeling guilty for taking off by himself. He should have been able to stay at home and deal with things. Rubbing the back of his neck, he paused at the window and drew back the curtain. The moonlight shimmered through the branches of the now bare trees. Turning off the light, he ambled out onto the porch and sat on the stairs.

Stars splotched the dark veil of the evening sky. Like someone had taken a paintbrush full of paint and flicked it at a blank canvas. Breathing in the calm of the country night, Albert rested. Nothing demanded his attention. Not even the road and the need to get further down it. Not his church and family full of expectations. Forcing his mind off the very things that began to lure him back toward a state of near panic, Albert leaned against the porch rail and closed his eyes.

A favorite Psalm came to mind. "The Lord is my Shepherd; I shall not want. He makes me lie down in green pasture and leads me beside quiet waters."

The rest of Psalm 23 ran through his heart. *Thank You, God for this moment. For this place to rest.*

The rest of the week passed in a blur of cooking, laughter, and camaraderie among the town folk, who were understanding of his trial-and-error style of preparing food. Their gentle poking at his efforts welcomed him into their midst as one who belonged. He found himself smiling more than not about how cooking at a diner could prove a useful part of his retreat.

Nighttime found him soaking in the wonder of God's creation from the front row stadium seat on the porch of the cottage. Breathing, resting, talking to God like he hadn't in a long time. But he wasn't yet ready to go home. He didn't know what God was leading him to, though he was confident this stop was a part of the plan.

Conversation at the Hole indicated that most of the regular customers as well as the owners belonged to the church next door. They uncovered the truth of his journey and were supportive of his search. By the time Saturday night and his replacement arrived, the diner regulars had wrangled a promise from him to attend Sunday service before he hit the road again.

Early Sunday morning, Albert packed his bag and loaded the car, then hiked down a trail branching off behind the cottage. It had invited exploration from his first day. He checked his phone and confirmed he had about two hours before church started. Setting a leisurely pace, he followed the winding trail. He imagined that during the summer, this place would offer a refuge from the harshness of life. When he got home, one of the first things he would do when the weather permitted, would be to clear out the trail Haley had created on their property.

Two hours later, he arrived at the building that housed the family of God in this part of the country and walked into a still empty building. His boots echoed on the wooden planks. The smell of old hymnals reminded him of church in his youth. There had been a lot of good in the middle of the bad during those years. Despite his dad's anger and rejection, other Christians had come alongside to help his mom.

But boundaries between those helping and the sanctity of marriage were broken and when their dad discovered the truth, he rejected the only child he had ever shown any real love to.

Albert hit the back of the pew he stood beside. If he felt rejected, even though his dad only showed him and Elinor a grudging acceptance, he couldn't imagine how Karen felt having the rug ripped out from under her.

Memories flooded through him, pulling a mingling of joy and grief. Anger and peace. His mom had been lonely, hurt, abandoned. A part of him understood, but another part of him judged. Harshly. He shook his head. Had he ever fully, wholeheartedly forgiven?

The door opened behind him and one of the old cowboys who sat at the counter every day walked in. He patted Albert on the back. "Glad you came."

"Thanks. Me, too." Albert shook his hand.

He found a seat in the middle of the sanctuary on the right-hand side. Each member of the congregation welcomed him like a long-lost friend with a pat on the back, a hug, or a handshake. Albert fought back tears that heralded a belonging that he had never quite felt with his family. He pulled out a hymnal and turned to his favorite one, "How Great Thou Art." He recalled the first time he heard the song. It was during a thunderstorm. It still came to mind every time thunder crashed and lightning lit up the sky. He allowed the goodness of the memory to chase away any negative thinking and focused on the service.

Surprised by the potluck feast laid out after church in his honor, Albert enjoyed every piece of fried chicken, serving of mashed potatoes, and piece of pie he managed to eat. Grinning, he accepted the offers of leftovers the congregation piled into a cooler and handed to him. He wouldn't need to buy food for a while.

He promised to stop back through on his way home and climbed into his car. Driving away, he glanced into the rearview mirror at his new friends waving him on to the next part of his journey. Humming, he pulled onto the two-lane highway that had already led him to part of his healing. In another day and a half, he could sleep in view of the mountains.

Albert's overnight stop didn't have the warmth of the cottage behind the Hole, but it was clean and included a free breakfast. The early morning sun reflected in his side-view mirrors as he pulled back onto the highway. Whistling, he turned on the radio and pushed the search button. Surely there was a Christian radio station around.

Last night, he had talked to Haley and the kids. They sounded guarded, but glad to talk. The kids carried on about their school activities, and Haley had kept it upbeat, no news about broken-down appliances. He had asked Barry and Karen to look in on her in case she needed anything, so he didn't worry on that front.

He gave up on the search to discover a relevant radio station and turned it off, instead thinking about what the end of this sabbatical might look like. Would he return to pastoring? At this point, the thought made him weary. Before he could figure out what to do with his life, he had to figure out what was going on with his soul. Why did it take a forced sabbatical to bring any peace to his soul?

With him deep in thought, the next couple of hours passed in a blur. A growl from his stomach demanded feeding. He had plenty of leftovers, but the billboard ahead invited him to stop at a famous local eatery. Steak and potatoes would hit the spot. On the side of the road next to the billboard, an SUV-type vehicle sat. The back left tire was flat. A man stood at the back of the car looking inside where a spare tire should be. He backed away from the car with hands on his hips.

Albert wondered if he should stop as he drew closer. *Why not?* He had no place to be by a certain time. The man seemed frustrated. Pulling over in front of the vehicle, Albert realized it wasn't an SUV, but a Jeep. An older model, gray Jeep. Was it the same one he'd passed already? A glance toward the man now walking toward him confirmed it. Weird. What were the odds? Like how many times had he left a store at the same time as someone else only to find they were parked next to one another. He lifted a quick prayer heavenward and climbed out of his car.

"Need some help?"

The man jerked his thumb in the direction of his Jeep. "No spare." He held up his cell phone. "No service."

Albert checked his phone. "Me neither."

"Would you mind giving me a ride to the next exit?"

"Hop in."

The man held up his hand. "Be right there." He ran back to his Jeep and locked it, then slid into the front seat next to Albert and removed his hat. "Appreciate it. Name's Gabe."

"Albert." They shook hands and Albert pulled back into the flow of traffic. "Where you headed?"

"Ultimately, California. Have a job waiting for me out there. But I'm enjoying the journey, so I'm taking my time. What about you?"

"Colorado."

"What's waiting for you there?"

"Sabbatical."

"You must be an educator or a pastor, then."

"Pastor."

"Needing a break from the grind?"

Albert glanced at the man sitting next to him. "You're getting a bit personal, aren't you?"

"It's a talent I have. I'm sorry if I overstepped."

"No worries. My board instructed me to take a few months off to get my head together. West sounded good. I started driving and here I am."

"Colorado is a good place. That exit up ahead will be fine for my purposes."

"Same one I was looking for." Albert pulled into the gas station and stopped. "I'm heading over to a steak place I saw advertised." He pointed past the gas station. "Want to join me?"

"I better be getting back to my car. But thanks, man." He pulled a slip of paper out of his wallet. "Here. If you're interested. Phone number for a guy I know. Name's Joe. He and his wife, Abigail, have a place near the mountains. Southwest of Colorado Springs. They rent out cabins, but sometimes trade work for rent. Might be worth looking into. Who knows, I might see you out there."

"Appreciate it." He stuck the paper in his pocket. "I'll check it out." He waved at Gabe and headed down to the steak joint. About a mile down the road, he noticed Gabe's hat in the seat next to him. He pulled over onto the shoulder and executed a sharp U-turn and went back to the gas station. Inside, Gabe was nowhere around. The attendant confirmed that someone meeting Gabe's description had made a call then headed east on the highway hitchhiking.

He must be going back to his car to meet the tow truck. Albert shook his head. The guy was nuts. Well, he wasn't going to chase him because of a stupid hat. Back at his car, he decided to skip the steak dinner and grab leftovers instead. After he made a phone call to Joe.

Albert looked around the cabin. Well-kept and snug, it contained a working fireplace, an eat-in kitchen, one bedroom, a bath, and a living room. The colors were a neutral beige with bits of blue thrown in here and there. A large picture window in the living room offered an unobstructed view of the mountains in the distance. "I'll stay." He walked to the front door where Joe stood.

"Good. We need a strong back around here to help us get us caught up on a few things." Joe slapped Albert on the back. "Come to the main house at six a.m. for breakfast. You can meet my wife, Abigail, and I'll give you a tour, show you what we need help with. For tonight, there's food in your fridge." He walked out onto the porch, then turned around. "You said the guy's name was Gabe?"

"That's what he told me."

Joe scratched the top of his head. "Can't recall an image of the man. But then, I've met a lot of people in my years. I'm sure it will come to me. Good night."

CHAPTER THIRTY

Elinor

E linor watched as the woman entered the bed and breakfast. A bit taller than Elinor, the woman boasted kind eyes that made you feel like you had known each other for years. She lit up when she noticed Elinor. She held out her hand. "I'm Bijou Bonet. I'm looking for the manager. James Abbott."

The smooth timbre of the woman's voice washed like a lullaby over Elinor. She shook Bijou's hand. "It's a pleasure. I'm James's wife, we manage the bed and breakfast together. How can I..."

Bijou's accent snapped connections into place. This was Remi's wife.

She cleared her throat and coughed. "Excuse me. How can I help you?" She wondered if the woman knew Elinor's connection to her husband.

"I need to go over details for the wives at the retreat. Would this be a good time, or should I come back?"

"Now is fine. Let me arrange for someone to watch the front desk."

Once she had a replacement for desk duty, Elinor led the way to Karen's office.

"You have a wonderful place here. I see why my husband chose it. The decor is lovely. The atmosphere very welcoming."

"Thank you." Elinor could only hope that her presence here had nothing to do with Remi's choice, but she doubted it. She motioned for Bijou to sit in a chair opposite the desk. "I believe my husband went over most of the details with your husband. What are your concerns?"

Bijou's laugh reminded Elinor of windchimes tickling her ear with their notes. "It is not with your bed and breakfast that I have concerns. It is my husband. Men do not see with the same eyes as women."

"And you want to be sure the wives are pampered just a bit."

"Exactly. The minute I laid eyes on you I knew you would understand."

Bijou appeared to view beautifying the world like Elinor did. Elinor couldn't help but wonder if in another life they would have been good friends. Her soul sighed in regret. But she could enjoy this moment working together with Bijou to provide something refreshing to these women on the retreat.

Leaning forward on her elbows, she raised her eyebrows. "What did you have in mind?"

The meeting took three hours. They plotted and planned and laughed. Gifts for the women on their arrival. Transportation to a local day spa for the one day out of the retreat when their spouses would be in an all-day meeting. If the weather was snowy and Elinor could talk her dad into it, a sleighride. And a romantic candle lit dinner in their rooms for the ones who desired it.

"The wives will love it. Thank you. Bijou laughed. "I never got your name."

"Elinor."

With her eyebrows furrowed as though puzzled, the woman paused for half a beat. She shook her head slightly and the smile was back. "I enjoyed our planning session. I think you are a kindred spirit."

Elinor nodded. "I agree."

Bijou paused at the door and turned back. "Have you ever been to France?"

"I went to Europe for my senior trip." Karen kept her smile intact while fighting her fear.

Bijou nodded. "Who knows, perhaps we crossed paths all those years ago."

"I suppose it's possible." Elinor cringed at the flatness of her words, the obviousness of her feelings. If she didn't know before, Bijou must know now.

Bijou offered Elinor a warm smile then took her hand. "Thank you for your work on this. I will see you soon."

CHAPTER THIRTY-ONE

Elinor

James leaned over and handed the church bulletin to Elinor. He pointed to the first announcement.

Volunteer at a Crisis Pregnancy Center? Elinor felt like a deer in the headlights.

"I've been thinking about how many couples can't have kids, not just us. It's so sad these women feel like they have no choice but to choose abortion. Maybe we could influence some of them to keep their children. Or give them up for adoption."

Tugging on a strand of her hair, she twirled it around her finger.

"Elinor?"

"I...sorry. I got distracted." She dropped her hand to her lap. "It's certainly something to think about. Talk after church?"

"Perfect." He gave Elinor a peck on the cheek. "Thanks. This means a lot to me."

Elinor focused on the words to the song now projected onto the wall and joined her voice with others in worshipping God .

Taking the long way back home after church, Elinor listened while James chattered about the Crisis Pregnancy Center. She clasped her hands in her lap and fought the emotions spinning in her gut like a merry-go-round. She offered the appropriate responses to his enthusiasm and wondered how she would get out of the service project.

Helping at the CPC would be a constant reminder of how broken she was. What joy was in that? It didn't matter that the project consisted of sorting through donations in their facility. The possibility of encountering these women who were so desperate that they would end the life of their child overwhelmed her. The whole idea took her back to a time she didn't want to revisit. Tears seeped out of her eyes, shut against the onslaught of emotional pain. Why was he so bent on helping at this place?

"Elinor?" James touched her hands.

She startled. "Sorry. Just thinking."

"About the Crisis Pregnancy Center."

"Why are you bent on helping? And the March for Life? You seem so passionate."

"You know I've always wanted to be involved. It just never worked out."

"I've never asked why, but it just seems so important to you."

James drove past the Applewood Hill. "We need to talk."

"About?"

"There's something you don't know about my old girlfriend."

Elinor turned and stared at her husband. "What?"

"We were young. And..." the pause lingered like the threat of an incoming storm.

"And?"

"It wasn't just that she didn't want to have kids. She had an abortion."

Elinor widened her eyes.

"It was our baby."

Elinor gasped. If James left his girlfriend because she had an abortion, where did that leave Elinor? It became hard for Elinor to breath. She closed her eyes and willed her heart rate to slow. Squeezing her fists until her nails bit into her skin, she felt the tension in her lungs release. Counting to ten in her head, the panic attack eased off.

"Elinor? Say something. I was a young believer. We made a mistake. But an abortion? Our child? I couldn't get past it at that point in my faith. It wasn't till later..."

Elinor felt trapped. Between two terrible truths. How could her marriage survive?

"Elinor?"

"I need time to process."

"Sure." Disappointment laced his words. "I understand. Want me to head back to the Applewood?"

"Please."

"As you wish."

Back at the bed and breakfast, Elinor unbuckled as James parked, then hurried out of the car and into the bed and breakfast. Getting busy with lunch prep would give her needed buffer.

"Catch."

Lost in her thoughts, Elinor looked up just in time to dodge the incoming roll. Charlie attempted to act innocent. Barry, sitting next to Charlie, looked only a speck more innocent than their nephew. Welcoming the intrusion to her melancholy, Elinor narrowed her eyes. She knew how to play this game. Grabbing a roll off her plate, she turned her shoulder to the guys and took aim out of the corner of her eye. "Have you heard anything from Albert?" She launched her missile sideways over her shoulder. Barry's startled cry told her she'd hit her bullseye.

Haley covered her mouth and giggled. "I can't believe you did that."

"Shh. Don't let on. Karen will kill me." Elinor leaned in with a conspiratorial whisper.

Haley grinned and nodded. "Albert called me last week. He seemed more relaxed than I've heard him in a long time. You'll never guess what he's doing."

Barry joined the conversation. "What's Albert up to now?"

"He agreed to help cook at a diner in exchange for room and board."

"What? My little brother?" Karen turned from where she stood next to the buffet. "No way."

Haley laughed. "Apparently, they were desperate. He said he would tell me the whole story later."

"Mom says maybe he'll learn a thing or two." Charlie rolled his eyes.

Charles' deep laugh thundered along with the rest of the family. "Good to see Albert getting back in the saddle helping people."

Haley agreed. "It seems to be doing him good."

Charles leaned forward and placed his elbows on the table, hands fisted under his chin. "I propose a change in topic. How about the church service project at the CPC? Sounds like a family activity to me. Who's in?"

Discussion ensued about logistics, and someone suggested they play games and eat dinner together after serving.

Karen turned toward Elinor. "You've been quiet. Are you going to join us?"

Elinor shrugged. "We hadn't decided yet what we'll do."

Tapping his finger on the table, James gave her a funny look, but didn't say anything.

"I'm getting a headache. I need to take something. Maybe ice my neck a bit and rest. I was on for cleanup. Do you guys don't mind if I bow out?" Elinor scooted back her chair.

James rubbed her back. "I think I can manage in your place."

She gave him a smile of appreciation and headed toward their apartment before anyone else could voice their concern.

An hour later, headache receding, Elinor paced in her apartment. Everyone else was excited to volunteer at the CPC. *Can I do it?* She imagined walking into that building with confidence. Her breath caught in her throat, and she felt hot. Seeing one of those girls would be too much like looking in the mirror. Her breathing sped up and the walls felt like they were closing in.

The door to their apartment opened then shut with a thud. She hurried from the bedroom to the adjoining bathroom before James could corner her into a conversation. She turned on the faucet and splashed her face with cold water.

"Elinor?" James knocked on the bathroom door. "I'm back."

"Be right out." Leaning against the wall, she prayed for strength and calm. She took several deep breaths until her heart rate slowed down. Straightening her skirt, she glanced at herself in the mirror and nodded. *Ready as I'll ever be.*

Elinor found James in the kitchen pouring tea. He looked up and smiled. "Thought you might like a bit of chai tea."

"Thank you." Elinor took her mug and sat at the table. "How were the kids on clean up?"

"I had to mop."

Elinor laughed. "Make them do it next time."

"Believe me, I plan to." He sat down catty corner from Elinor. "So...can you let me in on what you're thinking? About what I shared?"

"Why didn't you tell me before now?"

"I moved past it and thought it didn't affect us."

She nodded. That she understood. Maybe now would be the perfect time to share her past. Hope he could move past it like he was asking her to do with his past. But would he look past the abortion? The words stuck in her throat.

"I guess, though, that is part of why I want to look into adoption."

"That makes sense."

"Does that mean—"

"Whoa. It doesn't mean anything. I'm still not sure."

James held up his hands. "Not trying to start anything."

"Adoption still reminds me too much of what I can't give you."

"Why are you still on that? I love you no matter what."

"I'm supposed to believe that, after what you told me?" Elinor recognized anger, frustration, and confusion splayed across his features. How much worse would it be if she just told him the truth? She pleaded with her eyes for his understanding and opened her mouth to share her secrets. "I don't deserve to be a mother. How could I be when I've..."

"Stop, Elinor. Please. Abortion isn't the same as not being able to have kids. No one could be more deserving than you. The love you have for everyone. And when I see you with Clarice and with Hope, I know you would be good for our kids."

She reached for his hands. How had they traversed to here from his past? "A part of me wants to adopt, but there are things..."

"I can't figure it out. I know you. I know your heart, and this resistance to helping someone in need isn't you."

"That's what I'm trying to tell you. You don't know me like you think you do. If you did..." Elinor leaned her forehead against the dining room window, the willingness to share her secrets fading with the day's light.

James paced back and forth between the dining room and their living room. "Maybe you're right and I don't know you. Help me understand."

Elinor tried to keep the tears at bay, but they came anyway. *Say it. Just say it.* "I'm trying to. I've done things..." She looked into James's eyes and stopped at his barely concealed look of *I've had enough.* The words wouldn't come out the way she wanted. Breaking down in tears, she chose the safer confession. "I'm just afraid. I don't want to lose you."

James stuck his hands in his front pants pockets and stared at Elinor. "I know you're afraid. But I won't walk away from us because we end up not having kids—whether our own or adopted. What will it take to convince you that I love you no matter what? He pulled her into his arms. "I'm not going anywhere."

If only I could believe that. She leaned into his embrace. *I've got to make this work!* "We can keep talking about adoption. But I'm still not sure."

He let out a moan. "Elinor." He walked back to his tea, picked up the cup, and then set it down. "Don't do this just to make me happy."

"So, if I said a flat no to adopting, you would drop it?"

He raked his fingers through his hair. "Probably not."

"Now what?" Elinor held out her hands in a plea.

"I don't know." He took her hands in his. "But I do know that I won't leave you. I promise." He kissed the palms of each of her hands. "I have to get back to work, but we'll talk later."

Silence settled around Elinor as James left. Why hadn't she just blurted it out? A volcano of emotions erupted inside of her. Dropping to her knees, she grabbed her middle. Silencing the cries, she groaned as tears, long held back, poured out of her. Curling into herself, she lay on the carpet until she was spent. Light had begun to wane when she finally moved from her place of spent regret and fear and crawled under the covers of her bed, fully clothed. *What now, God?*

Closing her eyes, she hid all her anxiety under the cover of sleep.

CHAPTER
THIRTY-TWO

Elinor

E linor loosely draped an evergreen garland on the hooks around the doorframe. Stepping back, she examined the effect then readjusted till it was evenly spaced. Having Thanksgiving at Dad's and closing the Applewood Hill for the weekend relieved the time pressure of getting Christmas decorations up.

"When will Karen and Haley be back with Clarice and Grammie?" Alita pulled out a wreath and set it near the piano.

"Should be anytime now. Good thing. I'm ready for that pizza." Elinor looked around the space. The library promised to look amazing when they were done. Then next week, they could tackle the remainder of the bed and breakfast before the RJB Investments retreat. She looked forward to giving each room a Christmas makeover. Especially with the new trinkets she'd picked up over the last year. Even if she did dread the particular crowd that was coming.

"Did Karen invite Helen like she threatened?"

Elinor laughed. "Yep. Didn't work out. It would have been a great surprise for Dad."

"They did seem to have something going, didn't they?"

"I hope there is. Mom's been gone three and a half years. Dad deserves someone."

"We're here!"

Clarice, Charlie, and Annie burst through the doorway. Supporting Grammie, Haley followed the burst of energy lighting up the room. Karen brought in their bags and headed upstairs with them.

"Happy Thanksgiving!" Elinor set the garland down and welcomed the young girl who warmed the hearts of the entire Flannigan clan. "You ready for the weekend?"

Clarice wrapped her arms around Elinor's neck and nodded. "Grammie doesn't feel good. She's really, really tired."

"We'll take good care of her. Make sure she gets pampered."

"And can we Skype with Joanna? I miss her. I have so much to tell her. She doesn't know I get to be in the Christmas pageant at the Huddle. I hope she's here for that. Will she be home in time for Christmas? I'm making a special gift for her 'cause I don't have money to buy her one. Do you think she'll like it? Will we get to see the horses tomorrow at Grandpa Charles' place?"

Elinor laughed. "Slow down, girl. I can't keep up."

Clarice giggled. "Grammie says I talk too much. But I don't think..." She clamped a hand over her mouth and laughed. Squirming out of Elinor's arms, she grabbed Charlie's and Annie's hands. "Come on." They ran to the boxes of decorations. "Can we put up the tree this weekend?"

"Absolutely. We're going to pick it out at the tree farm on Saturday."

"Yay." Clarice twirled around the foyer. "Decorating the tree is my favorite."

"What's going on down here?" Karen came back downstairs.

Clarice ran over to Karen and hugged her around the waist. "Thank you for letting Grammie and me stay here for the whole weekend. It's going to be so much fun. Which room do we get to stay in? Will the window be in the front or the back? The front is great 'cause you can see who is coming before they get here. But the back is great too 'cause..." Eyes sparkling, Clarice clamped her hand over her mouth again.

"Do you want to pick your room?" Karen bent down on eye level with Clarice.

"Can I?"

Karen nodded.

Clarice ran to Grammie on the couch where Haley had made her comfortable. "We get to pick our own room." She looked at Karen. "Can we stay in the biggest one?" The one with a fireplace?"

"I had a feeling you would pick that one. I already put your bags in there."

Clarice clapped her hands. "We're going to have so much fun. Thank you."

A knock sounded on the front door.

"Must be the pizza. Want to help me?" Elinor motioned for Clarice to join her.

Clarice skipped to the front door then danced back and forth across the foyer while Elinor paid the delivery guy.

"You're as good a dancer as you are a singer." Elinor tussled Clarice's hair.

"Thank you." Clarice bowed. "Grammie says if I didn't dance, she would be climbing the walls." Clarice snickered. "Can you see Grammie climb the walls? She says dancing is the only thing she's seen that settles me down." Clarice grinned. "When I dance, I settle down in here." She thumped her chest. "And I then I can focus on my homework. And if I focus on my homework, Grammie lets me watch that dancing TV show. I get good ideas on what to try." She did a spin and slide on the wooden floors. "Can I carry one of the pizzas?"

Elinor handed Clarice one of the pizzas and made a mental note to talk to Joanna about dance lessons along with those singing lessons for the young girl. Maybe for a Christmas gift.

"Hey everyone. Pizza."

They set the pizza on the library table next to the paper plates and soda.

"I'm glad we decided to close up the bed and breakfast this year for Thanksgiving. This is much more relaxing." Karen draped garland along the shelves and stepped back to examine her work. "For once, I have time to help decorate."

"Has Barry given you any hints about what they're cooking tomorrow? Other than the turkey, of course." Haley laid out more garland, ready to be hung.

"His lips are sealed. Even told us we aren't allowed to come by before noon. Very secretive, if you ask me. He did say we would all be very pleased and very stuffed."

Alita laughed. "Stuffed I believe. Probably pleased, but my money is on them catering something worthy of our taste buds."

"They did seem pretty sure of themselves." Elinor helped Karen secure the rest of the greenery around the library.

"We need a backup plan." Haley helped herself to the pizza and sat down.

"Too late for that. Guess we'll have to settle for beans and weenies if they burn the turkey." Karen laughed.

"Karen?" Clarice tugged on Karen's sleeve.

"What is it, sweetie?"

"I'm tired."

Karen glanced at Grammie, whose head leaned against the back of the chair, eyes closed. "Looks like Grammie is, too."

Clarice nodded and hid a yawn with her hand.

"Come on." Karen took her hand. "Haley, will you wake up Grammie and bring her up?"

CHAPTER THIRTY-THREE

Albert

Joe swung the ax at the base of the tree. Albert took his turn at the base. His notch wasn't nearly as deep as the older man's. Albert was sure the older man would make this into an illustration.

"See that notch, son?"

Albert grinned and nodded.

"Takes experience and work to go deep with each swing. More of that than natural skill. And if I quit too soon? I won't reap the benefit of a stack of firewood to last the winter. Kind of like most things in life. Wouldn't you say?"

"Do you ever run out of ways to illustrate your point?"

The old man had been driving home the same point in one way or another the entire week. The man wasn't about to let Albert just give up and quit on what waited for him back home. There would come a day that Joe would send Albert packing. He was sure of it.

The man's laughter echoed across the snow. "Why would I want to do that?"

"No idea." Albert's laughter rang out with Joe's as he swung his ax again.

Joe had promised to keep him busy, and he had. Albert had cleaned out all the cabins on the property, gone hunting with Joe for the Thanksgiving turkey, shoveled snow from the walk and drive, helped take enough food to feed an army to the soup kitchen, and today they were chopping enough wood to warm up the entire state of Colorado. Not much time for anything beyond eating, work and sleeping. But Thanksgiving was day after tomorrow and a few days off from labor had been promised. Albert grinned. He was ready to do a bit of exploring. Joe had pointed out the best trailheads that promised an afternoon of solitude.

"Time for a break, son." The old man set his ax to the side and went over to the pickup. He pulled down the tailgate and dragged the cooler to the edge, then climbed up beside it. "Abigail packed us good stuff." He handed a sandwich to Albert. "Unless you want your pie first, like me." Joe took a big bite out of the slice he held cradled in a napkin.

"Don't mind if I do." Albert retrieved his piece of pie and hopped up to the tailgate. "Mmm. Don't tell my wife, but I think your wife's pies are the best I've ever had."

"Your secret's safe with me."

The two ate in silence till all the food was gone. Albert leaned against the inside of the pickup bed. "You promised me you would tell me the rest of your story once I proved myself. Are you satisfied yet?"

Joe took a gulp of coffee from his thermos. "Just waiting for you to ask again."

"Out with it, then."

Joe wiped his mouth then threw the napkin in the cooler. "Well, now...where were we?"

"You were born and raised here on this mountain. Your mom died when you were in high school. You and Abigail met in California during college, came back to Colorado to work for your dad. Inherited the place when he died early from a heart attack. Your brothers gave you no rest about it for years, but you've managed to make peace with them. You quit talking when I asked if you had any kids. Made me promise not to ask Abigail."

Joe nodded. "Sounds about right. Kinda hard to talk about." He hopped down from the bed of the truck. "Come on. Want to show you something."

Albert slammed the tailgate closed. "Where to?"

Joe tilted his head toward the trail leading to a lookout. "Let's walk." Stuffing his hands in his pockets, the big man took the lead.

Albert watched the man, whose shoulders slumped forward as he walked ahead of Albert on the trail. Almost as if a large burden had been laid across his back. Albert was almost sorry to have asked about the man's kids but felt there was a reason he needed to know. That it was part of why he had come here.

Joe stopped at a curve in the trail. A rocky area to their left overlooked a valley and the mountains beyond. He waited there for Albert to catch up. "See this?" Joe traced a bird carved into the bark of a tree next to the rocks.

Albert stared at carving.

"My oldest, William, carved that. About a year before he left. The other two kids left soon after." He stuffed his hands back in his pockets. "Always wanted to leave this place to them. They're still in the will. I just don't know if they would ever come back and claim the place." Joe kicked at the dirt at his feet. "Probably sell it." He shrugged and walked further up the hill with Albert close behind.

"What happened to cause..."

Joe held up a hand to stop Albert. "All in good time."

They walked in silence for about half an hour, then Joe paused and looked off into the distance. "Storm is moving in. We better get back to the house. Probably not much snow in those clouds, but enough to cause trouble on these back roads. Come on."

Back at the house, Joe waved Albert to join him in the barn. "Might as well take care of the stock before dinner." The men each took a bucket to measure out feed for the horses. "We have three kids."

Albert glanced over his shoulder at Joe. "All boys?"

Joe shook his head. "One girl in the mix." The old man smiled. "My, how she could light up a room. Jennifer. Spittin' image of her mother at that age."

"What are your boys' names?"

"William and Michael."

"Good names."

Joe nodded. "William was named for my father. Michael for Abigail's. After college, the oldest, William, kept his promise to come back and work the place." Joe paused in the middle of scooping up a bucket of feed. "That would have been twenty-one years ago. Relations were bumpy, but we managed. For a while. Michael graduated three years after him and joined us. But it was too late by then."

"What happened?" Albert whispered his question, afraid to jolt Joe out of his storytelling.

"I happened." Joe thumped his chest with the flat of his palm. "Me." Joe tossed the bucket into the bin of food and stomped toward the door. "Finish up in here. Abigail should have supper by then."

Albert watched the man go. What had caused so much strife between him and his kids? Albert scooped up more feed and thought about his own family. A feeling of dread descended in the barn. He looked behind him as though he expected his dad to walk through the door at any moment. That was how much weight he imagined Joe's kids gave to their father. Albert needed to be careful, or he would judge a man as lacking who had done nothing but give of himself since Albert arrived. Surely Joe wasn't the same man he used to be. Didn't he deserve another chance?

By the time Albert showed up to the big house for supper, Joe had gone to bed. Abigail looked sad as she dished up a plate of food and handed it to Albert. "Joe said it will be a later start tomorrow."

"Thanks." Albert sat at the table. "Join me?"

Abigail carried a steaming mug of something to the table and sat across from him. "Haven't seen Joe so worked up since the boys left."

Albert paused with the fork halfway to his mouth and glanced over at Joe's wife. This thing cut deep. He set his utensil down. "Sounds like I may owe you an apology. Got him to talking about your kids."

She offered him a soft smile and placed a weathered hand over his. "I'm glad you got him to talk. Needs to be kept out in the light, not locked up where it can fester. Finish your food up and join me in the family room."

Half an hour later, holding his own steaming mug of coffee, Albert joined Abigail. She glanced up from the photo album she was thumbing through and patted the couch next to her.

"These are my kids." Page by page, she walked him through the memories of her heart. She stopped on an image of a young William and Michael with their dad at that same lookout where Joe had taken Albert.

"They look happy."

"Despite the bumps in the road, they did manage to have plenty of happy times together."

"What happened?"

"Joe didn't tell you." A tear slipped out of her eye. She wiped it away and took a deep breath. "I can only tell you my side of things."

Albert nodded and waited.

"Joe was tough on the boys. There was the usual tug-of-war between rebellious child and disciplinary parent. He had a gentle side, but that mostly showed up with their sister. Overall, *they* had a decent relationship." Abigail took a sip of her coffee.

Albert placed a hand on her arm. "You don't have to tell me this."

She covered his hand with her own. "I'd be obliged if you would let me. I need to keep this out in the light, too. There's no one left at the church now who walked through it with us. And I feel awkward bringing it up after so many years."

Albert nodded. "I've been told I'm a decent listener."

She gave him a small smile then looked away. "While the boys were in college, Joe had an affair."

"I'm so sorry, Abigail."

"It went on even after the boys came home. I didn't know about it at the time. They found out before I did." She set her mug down on the coffee table. "I don't know who they were maddest at, him for having the affair, or me for being so stupid so as not to see it."

Albert scooted closer and put his arm around her the way he would have his own mother had she still been living. They sat that way for a time before she reached for a tissue.

"We weren't Christians at the time, so had nothing to guide us toward having a good marriage. We just did the best we could. It didn't work out so well." She got up and paced around the room. "Once I found out, I more or less lost it. I was angry. Had no clue what to do. That was the last straw. The boys left. Told their sister. Don't know if she would have ever come back or not. She ended up eloping."

"You guys follow Christ now."

Abigail turned and smiled. "That is the brightest spot in this story. It's the only reason we're still together and have hope that someday our kids will come back into our lives." She walked over to a shelf and pulled out another photo album. "Where is that picture?" She thumbed through the book until she found what she wanted. "Here he is." Placing the album on the coffee table on top of the other album, she pointed at a man leaning against their pickup truck. "Mike. He was the first person we took on and traded work for room and board."

Albert squinted. The man looked like Gabe. But ages didn't match up.

"About a week after the boys vacated the premises to who knows where, he shows up at our door asking if we needed any work done around the place. Joe jumped at the chance now that we were down two. That man walked his talk, I tell you what, and bit by bit, he brought us closer to Christ." She laughed. "We always call him our guardian angel. Like to think about entertaining angels unawares, you know." She patted Albert's arm. "Took a while to convince us to go to church with him. But once we did, I think we had already both made up our minds to become Christians. He left soon after that, and the pastor and his wife took up where he left off. They counseled us through the restoration of our marriage. God did a work there." Abigail's eyes sparkled. "We found meaning to our lives even in the middle of hurting over what happened with our kids."

Albert sat amazed at the transformation in Abigail as she told their story. From despair to hope. That was what he needed. "What one thing made the biggest difference?"

"Forgiveness."

Albert leaned back into the couch. He knew the importance of forgiveness. Preached it. To his congregation and to his family. Thought he had walked it, but now he wondered.

Abigail got up from her chair. "A few years ago, on our fortieth anniversary, Jennifer sent us a picture of her and her brothers. Here." She held out a framed photo to Albert. He stared at the image of two men and a woman as Abigail pointed to each. "The tallest one is Michael, then of course, Jennifer is in the middle and the man wearing a baseball cap is William."

"Where are they now?" Albert stared at the image he held in his hand. Jennifer reminded him of someone. Maybe a different color hair? He couldn't place her. Probably an actress.

"Don't know exactly where the boys are. Jennifer mentioned being in the state once when Joe called to check on a legal matter. We think Michael is in the Midwest and William is on the West Coast."

"Good looking kids." Albert handed the photo back to Abigail.

She held the picture close to her chest. "I miss them so much."

"Do they know you became Christians and worked things out in your marriage?"

"We told Jennifer. She used to call from time to time. Hopefully, she passed it on. Don't think it will make much difference unless they're willing to forgive. Joe is afraid too much has happened. I try to keep hoping, but it's hard. It helps to talk about it. Thanks for listening."

"You need to find someone to lean on through this. Someone to pray with about it."

She nodded. "You're right. I'll think about talking to the ladies in the prayer group. They are so young, though."

"You might be surprised what kind of insight and encouragement they can give you. And that you can give them. You might be able to help a young marriage in trouble."

"You're right. I've allowed this to consume me too long and make it all about us. I've got to look around me and see who I can encourage."

"You're going to be just fine, I do believe."

Albert lay in his bed Thanksgiving morning, looking up at the ceiling, waiting for the early morning light to begin filtering into the cabin. Leaning on one elbow, he pushed back the curtains covering the window his bed sat next to. He never tired of seeing the sunlight's first refraction of the day bouncing off the snow high up in the mountains. If he and Haley ever moved, he could see living in a place like this. But he wasn't sure that he wanted to continue being a pastor, and if he didn't go back to pastoring, what would he do for work out here? He wasn't a rancher. What would he do anywhere, for that matter?

Plopping down on the bed, he let out a pent-up breath. *Lord, I'm not sure what to do.* Joe had advised him to stay busy with his hands and give the rest space to work itself out in Albert's heart. There was some truth in that. For the last week, even though he worked from sunup to sundown, he had more rest in his soul than he could remember having in any season of his life. A part of him longed to be able to do this for the rest of his life. But he knew the day would come to run toward his future. When Joe would tell him to go.

Albert got up and dressed, then hurried to the big house for his coffee and to help get things ready for incoming guests. Before shooing him down to his cabin last night, Abigail had explained they would be having guests join them for Thanksgiving dinner. Ten of them, to be exact. She promised details when he came for breakfast.

He gave a quick knock on the kitchen door before entering. A note on the table told him to help himself to a plate of food. By the time he had eaten and stacked his plate, Abigail was at his elbow giving him directions.

"A busload of kids traveling back home to the middle of nowhere in Kansas from a youth event broke down. They landed in our neck of the woods, being as they knew one of the families in our congregation. Knowing our cabins are typically empty this time of year, they called late yesterday afternoon, asking if we could take in about ten of them till the bus gets fixed. With it being a holiday weekend, no telling when Gus will get back to his garage. Anyhoo, good thing you cleaned up those cabins last week. Going to bunk the eight guys in the two cabins near yours. The two girls they're sending will stay in the house."

Abigail's face lit up. "I'm hoping they like to cook. I can pass on a recipe or two."

Joe laughed. "Sounds like a party."

"Not sure those kids' parents think so, but I'll take it." Abigail raised her eyebrows.

"So, what do you need me to do?"

"Help me get the turkey in the oven. Then check on Joe and see what he needs before the kids arrive." Abigail opened the oven.

Albert lifted the pan. "This thing is heavy."

"With all these kids arriving on our doorstep soon, it's a good thing you guys brought home a fat one."

Albert slid the turkey into the oven, then grabbed his mug of coffee and headed to the barn. He found Joe spreading fresh hay in the horses' stalls. "Need any help?"

"Last stall." Joe kept working with his back toward Albert.

"Anything else?" Albert grabbed a pitchfork and headed to the indicated stall.

"Nope." Joe backed out of the stall he'd just finished and latched the door before hanging the pitchfork on its hook in the tack room.

Albert watched the man's agitated movements a moment before he broke the silence. "Did I do something?"

Joe paused and leaned a hand against the wall of the tack room. He shook his head.

Albert walked over to his friend. "If it's about yesterday..."

Joe shrugged.

"Abigail filled me in."

Joe nodded.

"I'm sorry about your kids."

Joe took off his hat and rubbed a hand over his face. "It's hard to revisit. I wasn't a good dad. I loved my kids, but I don't remember encouraging them much. All I ever got growing up was noise about everything I did wrong. And I mean everything. That's what I knew, it's what I did as a parent. It wasn't right. Tearing down their spirit like that. And then what I did to my wife." Joe reached for the pitchfork Albert held and entered the last stall. "What's done is done."

"There's always hope."

"You sound like her."

"There's truth in what she says."

"Talking from experience?"

Albert stared at the man like a deer in the headlights.

"Not so easy when it's your own life, is it?"

Albert hadn't experienced hope in so long, he'd forgotten what it was like. He felt thirsty for it at the thought.

Joe nodded. "You get it."

"I have to believe there is hope. I have to." Albert sat on a nearby upturned barrel.

Joe came out of the half-finished stall and leaned against the wall. He stuck a piece of straw between his teeth. "There are days it's not an easy task." He closed the stall door. "I'll finish the stall later. Better get these chairs up to the house before Abigail starts hollering for them."

A couple of hours later, two vans pulled up to the house, and kids tumbled out with bags in tow.

Abigail threw open the door. "Come on in and get out of the cold."

Kids ranging in size from petite to basketball-player height ushered in chaos as they tossed their bags in a pile along the wall. kicking off snow-covered boots, they hurried to the fireplace and stretched out cold hands toward the warmth. Not a one refused the offer of a warm mug of cider as they chattered about their adventure and took turns grilling Joe about the ranch. He straightened his posture and stood proud as he extolled the benefits of living on the mountainside. Joy spoke through his words, despite his earlier momentary conflict with hopelessness.

That's what I'm missing. Joy. Albert hadn't felt it since Karen returned home, and his family began the process of healing. He had gotten bogged down along the way. Watching his siblings find answers highlighted the lack he had himself. Their willingness to forgive contrasted with his own unwillingness that had lain hidden for so long. It wasn't hiding anymore, and he needed to own up to it. Sooner than he wanted.

In helping these kids, the tide of despair had paused for Joe. Albert looked forward to waking up to a fresh perspective and finding that joy filling his own heart. There was a lot in front of him to get past this depression. He knew that medication, counseling, and focusing on God were all a part of the picture for his healing. He took the cup of cider Abigail held out to him.

She patted him on the arm. "You'll find your way. Don't fret."

"How..."

"You're pretty easy to read, kiddo." She returned to her preparations in the kitchen.

Two of the young girls followed her and he could hear Abigail begin the process of passing on to them something of what she held dear. She wasn't allowing the absence of her daughter to keep her locked in a world that didn't give. Looking back at the boys gathered around Joe, he thought of his own kids and excused himself to call his family.

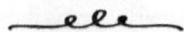

Albert pushed back from the table and patted his stomach. Once the kids had arrived, chaos had reigned for the rest of the day. Even through the meal, laughter and jesting were the rule. Albert watched, wishing this kind of familial interactions took prominence in his own home. He knew it was largely due to his own depression and inner turmoil that it didn't. But it would change. *Lord, change me. I want to hope again. To be filled with joy.*

"Let's show these kids to their lodging. Boys in the cabins. Girls will be in the house." Joe rose from his seat. "Who wants to go on a sleighride afterward?"

A chorus of voices cheered the idea with only two dissenters.

Joe eyed the girls, who sat on either side of Abigail.

"Can we just hang out with Mrs. Abigail?" The older of the two girls leaned against Abigail's shoulder.

Joe laughed. "I think my wife would like that. If you don't want to go on the sleighride, you can hang out in your cabin or here at the house. Just let us know where you'll be. If you're going on the sleighride, layer up, then meet us in the barn. Albert and I will get the team hitched to the sleigh."

The next morning, Albert sat on the edge of his bed well before the sun was up. He hadn't been able to sleep, thinking about his recent conversations with Joe. His heart ached for the old man. Joe had made mistakes, but Albert knew that no matter what had happened between the man and his kids, restoration lay at the door of the younger generation to make things right. Joe had done all he had in his power to do.

Resentment grew in his heart. Taking a deep breath, he swiped the air like one would swipe away a cobweb. As if he could make this all go away. *Right.* His agitation grew. All of this was because of his dad. Even as Joe talked, it sprang to life in Albert's heart. He had never forgiven the man who raised him. Despite all he had done to make things right. The next move was Albert's.

Swearing, he got up and stomped to the kitchenette in his cabin. He pulled out the bag of coffee grounds and started a pot. He had a while before he was expected at the house, and it didn't appear he would be able to sleep. *God help me. Yesterday I felt the first tugs of hope in a long time. And this morning, I feel like I'm back at square one. When will I stop flip flopping?* From what his counselor had said, what he was experiencing was normal with depression. But he didn't like it. *Lord, help me to forgive.*

CHAPTER THIRTY-FOUR

Elinor

At twelve o'clock, Elinor pulled to a stop in Dad's drive and parked behind James's car. Right on time. She stepped out into the crisp fall air and stuck her hands in her pockets. Haley got out from the passenger side while Charlie and Annie jumped out of the back seat. Pulling jackets snug around their bodies, they waited for the others to join them.

Karen, Alita, and Hope, along with Clarice and her grammie, pulled up next to them. Clarice flung open her car door and jumped out. She ran in circles around the cars, followed by Annie and Charlie. They stopped to give Elinor a hug, and then ran up the porch stairs and back down to her grammie as Haley helped her out of the car.

"This is going to be such a greaterful day."

Charlie and Annie took up a chant as they skipped around Clarice. "Greaterful, greaterful. What a greaterful day." The kids grabbed their bellies and laughed.

"Child, I don't know where you come up with your words." Grammie's face lit up.

"My teacher says I have a big imagination."

"She doesn't know the half of it." Grammie sighed.

"Can we go inside now?" Clarice twirled. "When will we see the horses? Can we go on a ride? Or will we pick out the tree today? Can we—"

"Slow down, girl." Elinor tousled Clarice's hair. "How about we go in and see how far along the food is? If we have time, we can give the horses a treat before we eat."

"Yay!" She ran past all the others, up the porch stairs, and pulled open the door. "We're here."

By the time the others made it up the stairs, Charles was at the door to welcome them. They piled into the house and began taking off jackets and gloves. A crash, followed by laughter, sounded from the kitchen.

"What is going on? Is there anything we can do to help?" Karen gave her dad a hug.

"Sounds like you might need some." Alita stuck her gloves in her pockets.

"Absolutely not. We have it all under control." Charles planted his hands on his hips.

"You sure about that?" Elinor chuckled.

Charles raised his eyebrows. "You doubt our abilities?"

"Yeah." The girls all laughed.

"I guess you'll have to judge for yourself. But for now, stay out of the kitchen and dining room."

Haley shook her head. "Pride goes before a fall."

Charles laughed. "Make yourselves comfortable. Go visit the horses—"

"Yay! Horses!" Clarice put her coat back on.

"—or go on a walk. We'll ring the dinner bell when it's ready."

Clarice tugged on Elinor's hand. "Let's go. Can we take carrots?"

"I'll grab the carrots." Karen started for the kitchen door.

"Nice try. I'll get them." Charles barred the way and stared down his daughter.

"What is so secretive?" She attempted to bypass him.

Charles wiggled his eyebrows. "All in due time."

"Fine. Anyone else want to come?" Karen pulled on her gloves.

"If you gals don't mind, I'm going to sit." Grammie made herself comfortable on the couch.

The rest of the girls pulled on coats and gloves and headed down to the stable. The kids raced to the stable, then clambered up the rungs of the corral. Leaning her tummy against the top rail, Clarice spread her arms wide and looked up at the sky. Annie and Charlie mimicked her antics.

Glancing over her shoulder at the troupe of ladies heading her way, Clarice waved everyone toward her. "Come on."

"Hold your horses, kiddo." Elinor laughed.

"Can I hold your horses, too?" Clarice laughed, held onto the top railing, and leaned back, looking at Elinor upside down.

Karen ran up, wrapped her arms around Clarice's waist, and swung her around.

"Whee." Clarice giggled. "More."

Karen set her down. "That's about all I have in me. Other than these." She pulled out the carrots and they headed into see the horses.

Elinor handed Clarice and Annie each a carrot as the dinner bell rang, and they fed the last two horses before heading to the door.

Clarice paused and gave the bay horse in the end stall a pat on his neck. "I'll be back later."

Racing each other, the kids reached the porch ahead of the grownups and hurried indoors. By the time the adults caught up, only Charles at the door and Grammie on the couch waited for them in the living room. Giggling and laughter seeped out from behind the door to the formal dining room.

"The kids get to see what's for lunch before we do?" Elinor stood there, fists on hips.

Charles shrugged.

"I smell a rat. What's going on?" Karen threw her coat onto the coach where the others' wrappings were piled.

Charles let out a belly laugh. "I guess I can't keep you in the dark forever. Come on." He led the way to the dining room and threw open the door.

"Surprise!" Joanna jumped out into full view and spread her arms wide. Blond hair flowed down to her shoulder blades in loose curls, and a floral skirt hung to her ankles.

Karen stared at her sister. "Joanna? How? I thought—"

"Just give me a hug." Joanna opened her arms.

Karen, Elinor, Haley, and Alita gathered around their sister for hugs. Someone cleared their throat and the ladies turned around.

"Hi." Alexis Petrakis, former chef at the bed and breakfast, stood to the side, hands in his pockets and wearing a sheepish grin. Mediterranean good looks still demanded to be noticed.

"What are you doing here?" Karen's eyes widened.

Joanna went over to stand beside him. "Everyone, I would like to introduce my husband to you."

"Say what? And you didn't invite us to the wedding?" Elinor crossed her arms.

Joanna held up her hand. "I'll tell you the whole story later. For now, I need to introduce you to another someone special." She glanced behind herself and waved someone forward. A young girl stepped into view and snuggled under Joanna's arm. "This is Alexis's daughter, Hannah."

Hannah hid against Joanna. A bit older than Albert's kids, she seemed to lack the confidence that Charlie and Annie had. Thick brown hair graced the top of her shoulders, and she kept her gaze down as though she were afraid.

"I think she's a bit overwhelmed with all the new people." Joanna stroked Hannah's hair.

Clarice came from behind and put her arm around the girl, who was a bit older than herself. "Don't worry. You'll get used to them. They're nice."

The girl nodded but didn't leave Joanna's side as Clarice went around the circle and told her who everyone was.

Elinor raised her eyebrows. "When do we get to hear the whole story?"

"Once we serve up the food." Charles pulled out his chair at the table. "You're going to love what Alexis whipped up."

"So...Alexis was your secret weapon for Thanksgiving dinner." Karen glanced over at her dad as she gave her sister's husband a hug.

"Gotta use what's available, and when I heard they were coming..."

"How long have you known?" Karen shook a finger toward her dad.

"I was sworn to secrecy." Charles grinned. "Now come on. Let's eat before the food gets cold."

The dining room filled with laughter as the family found their places around the table.

"I'm so glad you're back Miss...Mrs. Joanna." Clarice giggled, then peeked around Joanna at Alexis, sitting at the end of the table nearest the kitchen. "Are you really married? Where will you live now? Are going to stay? Can I come see you all the time now?"

"Clarice." Grammie patted her hand.

"Oops." Clarice covered her mouth. "Sorry. Grammie says I have to learn how to hold my tongue." She laughed. "That would just be gross. Who wants to hold their tongue?"

Joanna pulled her into a hug. "I'm so glad you're here. I've missed your chatter." Joanna tapped the end of Clarice's nose.

Clarice beamed at her friend and snuggled into the hug. "I've missed you."

Elinor helped Karen get Hope settled into her highchair, then went around the table and sat between her dad at the head of the table and James. She glanced at her husband. He and Barry talked across the table in animated tones about the upcoming football game later in the day. She appreciated James's distraction saving her from the tension living between them since their talk last Sunday. She still hadn't decided if she would participate with the CPC project Saturday. But today was about being thankful.

Charles clinked his glass with his fork and held out his hands. The family linked up around the table and bowed heads as Charles said grace.

"Dear Heavenly Father, Thank You for this day. To gather and remember all the blessings You have given us. Thank You for bringing Joanna and her new family back home." Charles paused, his voice full of emotion. "Be with Blake. Keep him safe from all harm. Let him know he is loved. Thank You for this food. In Jesus's name, amen."

"Amen. Dig in." Charlie's declaration broke the silence and a happy noise lifted around the table.

"Alexis, I think you're on." Charles turned over the lead to his new son-in-law.

Alexis scooted his chair back from the table. "I'll go grab the turkey, that's the last of it. Go ahead, start the line for the buffet, by the time you get to this end, I'll be carving up the bird."

"Joanna, I just have to ask, how much of this did you do?" Karen bumped Joanna with her elbow as they stood in the buffet line.

"That's a good question." Elinor leaned in to hear the answer.

Joanna laughed. "You think Alexis needed my help? He can cook circles around me."

The girls waited with raised eyebrows and crossed arms.

Joanna held up her hands. "Promise. I didn't help. Well, maybe open up a can or two."

They all laughed as they scoped out the food, filled their plates, and headed back to their seats.

Charles caught Barry's attention. "Didn't you visit Blake last week?"

Barry nodded. "He wasn't as belligerent as usual. Didn't talk much, though. Seemed to have something on his mind. He asked about you, Alita." Barry addressed Alita across from him.

"I'm hoping to head out there next week. Haven't been to the prison since I went with Elinor earlier in the fall. I hope he doesn't get mad."

"Want some company?" Elinor leaned forward so she could see Alita on the other side of James.

"That would be great. Aren't you getting ready for that retreat, though?"

From the corner of her eye, Elinor caught James watching her. "Let's talk about it more later. I'm sure we can figure something out."

James leaned over to her. "Does that mean you have time for the CPC after all?" He looked her straight in the eye, expecting a straightforward answer.

She had no answer that would satisfy him. "Let's talk about it later, please." Elinor hated the tension between them, but there was only one way to end it. A shudder ran up her back.

"You girls still in for shopping tomorrow? Joanna raised her voice above the chatter.

"Absolutely." The girls chorused their assent.

Karen leaned forward with her elbows on the table. "Let's have a girls' sleep over at my place tonight, so we can get out early."

Silence descended as the guys realized they were being called upon for kid duty. "What about the game?" Barry threw that thought out on the table and voices raised in cheerful complaint. After a few minutes of haggling, the men agreed to watch the kids together at Dad's as long as the older kids helped with Hope.

"Let's only go till noon." Karen added. "After that, pizza and Joanna's...excuse me... Mrs. Petrakis's story."

"It's a deal." Joanna clapped her hands. "Girl time. And then Saturday...Dad you still up to hauling us around in that old sled if we get that promised snowfall?"

"A sleighride?" Clarice jumped out of her chair and ran around the table. "None of my friends get to go on a sleighride. Wait till I get back to school and tell everyone."

Joanna caught her around the waist as Clarice tried to pass for a second round. "How else are we going to hunt for a Christmas tree for the bed and breakfast?"

Cheers busted out from all the kids. Charles clanked his fork on his glass again until everyone calmed down. "One last important detail. In order to give you ladies an opportunity to do your part in this great meal, you are all on dish duty. We'll be in the family room watching the game."

The men laughed as a collective groan went up from the women.

Karen raised her voice. "Typically, the women do both."

"Nice try, honey." Barry put his arm around his wife. "You ladies are leaving us with the kids tomorrow. I think you can handle dish duty today."

"Fine." Karen held up her hands in surrender. "But really, we do appreciate all of your hard work on the meal."

The other women joined her in their appreciation and the conversation picked back up as they chatted about plans for Christmas.

CHAPTER THIRTY-FIVE

Elinor

"Pizza's here." Joanna called out from the kitchen.

Elinor hurried to the kitchen to help bring in the food. Black Friday shopping had gone longer than planned. The lines had been maddening. Pizza would go a long way toward soothing their shopping monsters. And, of course, hearing Joanna and Alexis's story. Joanna had refused to share anything until tonight, no matter how hard they had plied her with questions while they stood in line this morning. Elinor laughed. The day had been a blast.

"What tickled your funny bone?" Joanna picked up the platter of vegies.

"Thinking about how much fun today was. Did they bring the right kind of pizza?"

"Yes, I ordered the right kind of pizza." Joanna patted the stack of boxes in her hand.

"I wasn't...."

"Chill." Joanna laughed. "Just teasing. They brought your favorite pizza. Can you grab the plates and napkins?"

"Got 'em." Elinor followed Joanna back to the library and set them on the corner table.

With everyone gathered around the food, Joanna offered a prayer of thanks before they loaded up their plates and spread out around the library.

Karen elbowed their older sister. "Spill the beans, Joanna. No more excuses."

Joanna laughed.

"And don't leave anything out." Haley crunched on a celery stick.

Joanna raised her eyebrows as she took a bite of pizza.

"Can't get out of it that easy." Elinor shook her finger at Joanna.

"Can't a girl eat?" Joanna mumbled around the food in her mouth.

"In between details." Alita added her own encouragement for Joanna to start talking.

"Fine." She set down her pizza and pulled her knees up to her chest. "You already know about the rehab and that I worked there for a bit after I completed the program."

The girls all nodded.

Joanna's eyes sparkled. "And I'm pretty sure you knew Alexis and I liked each other."

"On with it." Elinor moved her hand in a quasi-princess wave.

"What you didn't know...well, except for Karen...Alexis was married."

"What? How could he lead you on? Lead all of us on?" Alita shook her head as though vastly disappointed.

Joanna held up her hand to stop them. "He didn't mean to." She looked at her ring. "God directed him to help me. As a friend. Crazy, when you think about it. And it wasn't an issue until he began having feelings toward me and it became obvious to everyone but me that I was growing attached to him. All a part of God's plan to bring us together, I suppose. Anyway, Alexis came clean with me. That's what matters. He was honorable."

"I'm confused. What about his family?" Haley leaned forward.

"They were estranged. When his daughter was a baby, his wife took her and disappeared. They had been gone ten years by the time he came to the Applewood Hill. He hired an investigator to track them down. That was why Alexis left when he did, and I thought it was the last I would see of the one man who treated me like a lady. The one man who showed the love of God to me with no strings attached. He accepted me for who I was. I loved him and had to let him go. A new experience for me."

"The investigator found his family?" Alita got up and refilled her plate.

Joanna nodded then held up her hand. "I call a break in the story for sustenance." She picked up her slice of pizza.

"Good idea." Haley refilled her plate.

Everyone helped themselves to more pizza, then ate in silence until one by one, they got up and threw their plates away.

Haley sat next to Joanna on the floor. "You left off with the investigator finding his family. How did you and Alexis reconnect?"

Joanna reached over and took Karen's hand. "This last spring, Alexis contacted Karen to find out where I was, then he showed up at the rehab center with Hannah."

"What about his wife?" Elinor leaned back against the couch.

"Unfortunately, she was an addict, and even though she made a show of wanting to work through things when he caught up with them, in the end, she overdosed. After a couple of months of it being just the two of them, he and his daughter headed my way."

"Wow. And his daughter was good with that so soon after her mother died?" Alita got up and stretched. "I'm getting too old for the floor." She plopped down on the sofa.

Joanna took another bite of her pizza before continuing. "She wasn't much of a mother. I think Hannah was just glad to have someone to take care of her. She's blossomed with all the love. Besides, we didn't get married right away. She had time to warm up."

"I still don't understand how you ended up married." Karen stretched her legs out in front of herself.

"He and his daughter rented a cabin near the rehab. He volunteered his talents cooking at the center."

"I bet they loved that." Karen laughed.

"You better believe it. They've offered him a full-time position if he comes back."

"Think you will?" Elinor nudged Joanna with her toe.

"Still talking over our options."

Karen nodded. "Finish your story."

"His daughter went to a summer camp for the first time in her life. She loved it. Made real friends for the first time in her life, too. The three of us started hanging out with the idea that this was about getting married. We included Hannah in the process, because Alexis wanted to be sure she would mesh with us as a family and that we weren't jumping in without counting the cost. It only took a month to know." Joanna wiped a tear from the corner of her eye. "The day she called me Mom, we knew." She took a minute to collect her emotions. "But I had to finish out my commitment at the rehab center. After that, we didn't want to wait. Figured if we came home first, it would turn into a huge event. We wanted to go ahead and establish a home for Hannah. We got married two weeks ago. And here we are."

Elinor reflected on how much her sister had changed. How many mistakes she had made, and still someone loved her enough to spend the rest of his life with her.

If someone loved Joanna that much, wasn't it possible, James loved Elinor enough? Despite how he had reacted years ago as a young believer to his girlfriend's abortion? Hope bubbled to the surface of her heart. Maybe she could trust him with the whole story.

Taking a deep breath, peace settled into Elinor's heart. She would serve at the CPC tomorrow with her family. And then, once the retreat was over, she would tell him everything. Grabbing her phone, she sent James a quick text to let him know her decision about the CPC before she helped clean up the library.

CHAPTER THIRTY-SEVEN

Elinor

Charlie, Annie, and Clarice raced to the library and stared up at the tree reaching to the eight-foot ceiling with barely enough room for a star.

"Think this one will do, kids?" Elinor came in behind them.

"How are we going to reach the top?" Clarice stared at the tree with eyes wide in wonder.

Elinor laughed. "Grandpa Charles will have to use his ladder."

Clarice jumped up and down, clapping her hands. "Can we start? Can we? Please?"

"Slow down. Not everyone is done with lunch. Come on back into the dining room for dessert." Elinor stood by the door and waved them through.

"I'm going to beat you girls." Charlie sprinted toward the dining room.

"Hey, girls. Wait up a minute. Can you do me a favor?"

Both girls nodded.

"Hannah is very shy. Can you include her in stuff today? She's part of the family now."

"I like her. She's nice. Quiet, but nice." Annie looked at Clarice. "Let's see if she wants to help us with the ornaments later."

Clarice nodded, and the two girls took off for the dining room.

Elinor watched the girls hurry off. Yesterday, the CPC volunteer work had gone better than anticipated. The family had sorted through all the donations and made order out of the disorganization. She even agreed to be part of their family team to volunteer there once a month, easing a little of the tension between her and James. Perhaps they would get through all this kid stuff after all. Closing the door behind her, Elinor followed the kids.

"There's my girl."

Elinor startled when James spoke from behind her. She turned with one hand on her hip and raised an eyebrow. "What do you mean sneaking up on me?"

James pulled her into his arms. "Let me make it up to you." He leaned in and kissed her right cheek. "That is to make your heart beat erratically." He kissed her left cheek. "That is for leaving you unattended for the last..." He glanced at his watch. "...oh, the last five minutes."

Elinor giggled.

He kissed her forehead. "That is to thank you for coming to the CPC with us." He kissed the tip of her nose. "That is for being so incredibly wonderful."

Elinor locked eyes with his. This. This made her heart thrill. As he pulled her tighter and their lips met, she melted into his arms.

"Aunt Elinor...oops."

Elinor looked behind James at Annie. "Did you need something?"

Annie covered her mouth and stifled a laugh. "Karen wants to know if you want cheesecake or pie."

"Cheesecake."

Annie grinned and ran back to the dining room. James and Elinor looked at each other and laughed.

"Not exactly the dessert I was hoping for." James kissed her neck near her right ear.

A shiver trailed up Elinor's spine. "We'll just have to continue this later tonight." She grabbed her husband's hand and dragged him, groaning and complaining, down the hallway. Before entering the dining room, she turned and gave him a well-deserved kiss.

"Will that keep you till tonight?"

"Just barely." James followed Elinor to the dessert table.

"Cherry or peppermint?" Karen's server poised above the two choices of cheesecake.

"Peppermint. My favorite." Elinor took her plate and sat near Haley. "How's it going?"

"Good. The kids loved the sleighride yesterday. As a matter of fact, they're having a lot of fun this year."

"Without Albert?"

"It's so peaceful. I kind of feel guilty. Especially since it's Thanksgiving."

"Have you heard from him?"

Haley nodded. "We talked late on Thanksgiving. He sounds better. More at peace."

The two women ate in silence a few minutes before Haley set her fork down. "Do you think this has to do with your dad?"

Elinor shrugged. "Honestly, he never seemed bothered about how we were raised, but then again, he was always the strong one and the one who just did the right thing no matter what. Maybe he just didn't talk about it."

"What about you? How did you handle it? You seem to have it all together all the time."

"If only you knew." Elinor laughed.

"What was the hardest thing to deal with?"

"Kind of the elephant in the room, isn't it?"

Haley nodded.

"Well..."

"If you don't want to talk about it..."

"No, it's fine. I guess I never felt like I could be me. Never felt loved or accepted for who I was. I always had to be somebody else."

"Dad's actions certainly cast a wide net of consequences."

"That's what anger does." Elinor focused on her cheesecake, hoping this topic would end soon.

"How did you overcome that?"

Elinor shot Haley a sideways glance, wondering what was behind her question. "Still working on it."

"It's a journey. I hope you get it figured out." Haley placed a hand on Elinor's arm.

"Thanks. Me too."

Karen clapped and everyone quieted. "The kids are pulling at the reins to decorate the tree. How about we move dessert and coffee into the library?"

"Sounds good to me." Elinor got up from the table, leaving her cheesecake barely eaten.

Joanna and Alexis volunteered for clean up while the rest of the family trekked to the library to help with decorations. Grammie took a spot on the couch to watch while Elinor directed traffic. Her dad had already strung the lights on the tree early this morning before church. This afternoon, they would hang the garland and the ornaments, and place the star in its rightful place.

Alita helped Karen with the garland while Elinor opened the boxes full of ornaments. Thankfully, they were all nonbreakable. The kids could help with those as far up as they could reach. The rest would take an adult's arm. That left the star, which was traditionally Barry's job.

Elinor stood back and watched the magic happen. This year's Applewood Hill tree was destined for things other than a *Better Homes and Gardens* Award. Well worth it to see the kids enjoy it so much. Especially Clarice and Hannah.

"Mrs. Elinor, can I help hang the star?" Clarice danced from one foot to the other as if music pounded in her head.

"I think we better leave that to the tall people"

"I know how to climb a ladder."

"I'm sure you do. But this tree is very tall. Let's leave it to the grownups."

Clarice's face fell into a dejected expression as she turned back to the other kids. Within seconds, she was leading the joy parade again. Elinor wanted the same deep-down-inside, nothing-can-stop-it, joy. But her secret weighed on her like a bag of sand holding a bouquet of balloons secure when she remembered her promise to herself to tell James everything after the retreat.

"Hey, you cold?" James laid his arm across Elinor's shoulders.

She shook her head and leaned against his shoulder.

"I can go get one of your sweaters for you."

"I'm fine. Just stay here with me."

"As you wish." James hummed a portion of a vaguely familiar tune. "Haven't had a chance to tell you. I talked to the bank early last week."

Elinor glanced at him and raised her eyebrows.

"About getting a home loan."

Elinor's curiosity won over the annoyance she felt that he hadn't checked with her before talking to the bank. "And?"

"You remember that house we looked at?"

"Yes."

"We actually qualify for a loan for that house."

"Is that what you want?" Elinor was unsure how she felt about a house that big,

He shrugged. "It's nice. But we both have to like whatever we get."

"You're serious about this."

"I think it's time. Don't you?"

Elinor couldn't deny that she relished the idea of living in her own house. One she could decorate in her favorite colors. They could entertain. And it would provide them absolute privacy for a change. She grinned. "That was an amazing house. Is it still on the market?"

He nodded and offered a sheepish grin. "I called the agent, too."

"Mr. Sneaky." She punched him in the arm and laughed.

"Want to go see it again next week?"

"We have to get ready for the retreat, but I could arrange a couple hours off one afternoon."

"Perfect. I'll make an appointment with the realtor."

She gave him a quick peck on the cheek. "That's for thinking about us."

"What about this side?" He offered the other cheek.

"Getting cheeky, are you?" She laughed and kissed his cheek." That's for always knowing how to make me laugh."

He put his hand around her waist and pulled her close.

"Ewe." The collective exclamation of the kids stopped James' intended purpose.

"Can't wait to have our own house." Elinor whispered in his ear.

James nodded. "Your dad may not see us at the family gatherings for a while."

Elinor giggled and stepped out of his arms.

He held up his hands. "I'm being good."

Clarice laughed. "You're funny." She dangled an ornament from her finger. "Can you lift me up so I can put this high up on the tree?"

"Sure, kiddo." He glanced back at Elinor. "I can just see us decorating our own tree with our own kids someday."

She watched him lift Clarice up to hang the ornament, and warmth spread through her like when you step out into the heat of a summer day after being in the air-conditioning. Even though it hurt to dream for a child she would never carry, she could try for James.

Smiling, she handed Clarice another ornament. "I heard the plural in that."

"Caught me dreaming." James lifted Clarice again.

Charles walked up beside Elinor and whispered, "You'll make a great mother someday."

"Time will tell." Shrugging, she joined Grammie on the couch.

Grammie reached over and placed a hand over Elinor's. "God has good things for you, child."

Elinor shook her head slightly at the woman's kindness. *God, what good can come of what I've done?*

The woman reached up her hand and turned Elinor's face toward her. "No matter what you've done, God still loves you. And you have a family and husband who love you. Do you think they're going to stop for any reason?"

"How...?"

"Your longing to be completely loved. Your fear of losing. I saw it in my own mirror for years. There, there. I was trying to encourage you. Not make you cry." She dug in her purse and pulled out a small packet of tissues. "Here, sweetie."

Elinor tugged out a tissue and wiped the dampness from her face.

"I watch you with Clarice. You were born to be a mother."

"But I can't."

The woman nodded. "There are lots of ways to be a mother." Grammie patted Elinor's hand. "You just pray and wait on the Lord. He will guide your steps. Go where He says even if it doesn't make sense."

Elinor's heart softened. She knew the woman spoke truth.

She excused herself and headed to her apartment. She needed to make peace with her past, but it felt like trying to stop a speeding freight train. A knot formed in her stomach as she thought about the coming week. The retreat couldn't be over fast enough. She paused at the doorway. Maybe if she just told James now. She shook her head at the improbability of finding time anytime soon to talk about something so important. Best if she waited. *Lord, give me strength.*

CHAPTER
THIRTY-SEVEN

Elinor

E linor had enjoyed taking a break from her work at Applewood Hill over Thanksgiving weekend, but the retreat was approaching in three days and this place needed to be decked out in Christmas cheer.

"These go on either side of the registration desk." Elinor handed Joanna a wreath and picked up the other one before heading to the foyer.

She and Joanna had already put in several hours of work and still had three shelves full of decorations to go through and put up around the place. She had hoped to get out for a mini date with James to tour that house again, but it didn't look like a possibility today.

"Where did you find these? They're beautiful." Joanna held up a matching pair of turtledoves, each perched in the branches of a small tree bouquet.

"On one of my treasure hunts."

Joanna laughed. "Still frequent that one stop out near the state park?"

"Yep." Even though they hadn't always gotten along great over the years, on occasion Joanna would join her for a treasure hunt. That had been a favorite stop in those days. Once, they found an old wall hanging made from a toilet seat decorated with biker memorabilia. What some people thought worth making bemused her. For a practical joke, they brought it home and Blake had instantly claimed it as his own, hanging it out in his workshop garage.

"I wonder where that toilet seat ever went. Do you think Alita still has it?"

Joanna sputtered out a laugh. "She hated that thing."

"I still can't believe we bought it."

The girls broke out in laughter.

"I thought you two were working." Alexis and James joined them in the foyer.

"Looks like we're doing more work than you two." Elinor looked down on them from her stepladder.

"I don't know about this guy." Alexis jabbed James with his elbow. "But I've been cooking, and I came out to tell you that lunch is ready."

"And I've been pulling out all the boxes of decorations, if you didn't remember."

"Which I greatly appreciate." Elinor came down from the ladder.

James grabbed her around the waist and pulled her to him. "I guess you'll have to make it up to me."

"Sounds intriguing, but not till I get all this stuff put up." She stepped out of his embrace. "Alexis, I'm hungry. What's for lunch?"

"Grilled cheese and tomato soup."

"I thought Chef Alexis was on the job."

"Chef Hannah fixed lunch today. Wanted to impress Joanna, I think."

Joanna tucked her hand around Alexis's arm. "Well, let's leave this stuff here and go eat. Can't keep the chef waiting."

They trouped into the kitchen and took their dished-up food from the young chef.

"This looks amazing, honey." Joanna gave Hannah a hug.

"Try it." Hannah wrung her hands in front of her and looked up at Joanna with anxious eyes.

"Joanna set her plate and bowl down and took a bit of the soup. "Wow." Her eyes widened. "Elinor, James, try it." She turned back to Hannah. "What did you put in it? This isn't how I make tomato soup."

"You like it?"

"Absolutely." Joanna took a bite of the sandwich. "Yum. It's unique, too. What did you add?"

Hannah looked at her dad, who nodded. "It's a secret. I can't tell."

Joanna laughed. "I see your dad is teaching you well."

Hannah hunched her shoulders and grinned. She held her hand in front of her mouth and whispered to Joanna. "I'll tell you later when no one else is around." She glanced at Elinor and James. "You are my mom." Hannah looked down at the floor.

Joanna knelt in front of her and pulled her into a hug. "You bet I am. And I love hearing you call me Mom."

"You do?"

"I'm so happy that you want to."

Hannah wrapped her arms around Joanna. "Don't ever leave me."

"I'll never leave you or your dad. I love you both so much."

Alexis knelt and drew them both into his arms.

Elinor and James took their food and slipped into the breakroom to give them space but were soon joined by the new family. Hannah sat squished against Joanna, not saying a word while the adults talked and ate.

"Joanna, you still want to go see Blake?" First one to finish, Elinor pushed her dishes to the center of the table.

"Do you have time?"

Elinor nodded. "Once we get past this retreat. Want to go next Monday?

"Perfect."

Turning to the men, Elinor stepped back into the role of supervisor. "When we get done here, can you guys help with the garland on the stair railing?"

"We are at your service. What else?" James stacked his dishes.

"All we have after the garland is the rooms. I think Joanna and I can finish the rest."

"Just holler if you need any help." Alexis added his dishes James' stack.

"I can help, too." Hannah spoke up for the first time since they sat down.

"I think we can find something for you to do." Elinor gave the young girl a smile.

Hannah clapped her hands. "Yay."

Joanna pulled the young girl into a side hug. Jealousy poked up its head in Elinor's heart. The joy she witnessed between Joanna, Alexis, and Hannah stirred a desire in Elinor to have a family. She caught her bottom lip between her teeth smacked it down. She couldn't even begin to hope for a family until she told James everything. Would Remí reveal her secret to James?

"What's twirling in your mind?" James leaned her way till their arms touched.

Elinor looked across the table to find Joanna watching her with raised eyebrows. "Just making a mental list of what needs to get done yet. Back to work, everyone." After taking the dishes to the kitchen, she went to the storage room to check on how many boxes were left. Two boxes for each room. "James?" Elinor did an about face and collided with him. She placed a hand over her heart. "You startled me."

"What's going on?"

"I'm just zoned into getting this done."

James nodded. "What did you need?"

"Before you do the garland, can you take these boxes to the bedrooms. They're labeled where they go."

"As you wish." He leaned down and gave her kiss. "More later. I promise. I'll grab Alexis and get these moved for you. Anything else?"

"I need to talk to you tonight." The words were out before she could regret them. If she wanted to save her marriage, then she had to tell him before the retreat.

"What's up?"

Elinor glanced out the storage room door at the kitchen full of workers. She shrugged. "Just stuff. Will tonight work?"

James wrinkled his forehead but nodded. "Of course. After supper. But for now, I think I better get started on this honey-do list you gave me."

Starting in the honeymoon suite, Joanna, Hannah, and Elinor busied themselves pulling decorations out from the boxes that James and Alexis brought up.

Joanna held up a snow globe and turned to Elinor. "These new?"

"Found the entire Christmas collection at an estate sale. Couldn't pass it up."

Elinor had been elated when she came across them. That Saturday had been long with nothing to show for it. Then she saw the collection depicting various Norman Rockwell-like Christmas scenes. She bought then on the spot. Since it had been the end of the day and she wanted the entire collection, the family came down in price. Otherwise, Elinor wouldn't have been able to afford it with the budget she had.

"What did Karen think?"

"She hasn't seen them yet."

"Don't be surprised if she nabs some of these for her own collection."

Elinor laughed. "Maybe I better glue them down."

"Glue what...oh my goodness. They're beautiful." Karen walked around the room admiring the collection. She picked up a globe with a scene of a young couple ice skating on an outdoor rink in front of the Christmas tree at the Rockefeller Plaza in Manhattan. She gasped. "Can I have this one? Oh...I guess you should have glued them down."

Elinor laughed. "It's yours. I thought you might like that one. It even winds up and the skaters move around the ice."

Karen twisted the key. "It's Beginning to Look a Lot Like Christmas" filled the room.

"Didn't you and Barry have special memories there?" Joanna took a closer look at the tiny figures inside the glass.

Karen nodded. "Lots of memories in the city. Thanks." She hugged her new treasure to herself and started to leave. "Oh, I came up to see if Hannah would like to help me with Hope for a little bit."

"Can I, Mom? Can I?" Hannah jumped up and down.

"Go ahead. And have fun."

Hannah wrapped her arms around Joanna's waist in a quick hug then left with Karen.

"Motherhood looks good on you." Elinor closed an empty box.

"Never expected it. But it feels right. What about you? You're a natural with Clarice. You planning to have your own?"

Emotions caught in Elinor's throat. She turned away from Joanna to hide her inescapable response. "We haven't even been able to fully enjoy being newlyweds. Not with living where we work. Especially that first year in this suite."

"I hadn't thought about that."

"We're talking about buying a house."

"That would be great. And someday, you *will* make a great mom." Joanna gave Elinor a hug and grabbed the empty boxes to toss into the hallway. "That's it for this room. What's next?"

"I'm calling it Grandma's Christmas room."

"Can't wait to see why." Joanna followed Elinor to the next room down the hall and helped open boxes. She laughed when she spied the figurines depicting grandmas of all shapes and sizes in various stages of celebrating Christmas. "Perfect. These will look..."

"Knock, knock." Haley poked her head in the room. "Elinor, there's a Remí Bonnet at the front desk. Needs to talk to someone about the retreat. You'll love his accent."

Elinor tucked her head and turned away from her sisters. James must have gotten done with the garland or he would have been close enough to take care of it, but no way was she going to invite trouble by going down there to check. "Are you in the middle of cleaning? Do you have time to find James? I need to finish up this room."

"I can finish up in here if you need to take care of it."

"James has been taking care of the business side of the retreat. I would prefer letting him deal with it." Elinor wasn't sure that her nonchalance convinced Joanna, who watched her with narrowed eyes.

"No worries. I'll go find him." Haley's footsteps faded down the hallway.

Joanna stopped Elinor's hands from picking up another figurine. "What's going on?"

Walking over to the window, Elinor pulled the curtain open. Leaning against the sill, she stared out across the orchard. Trees, laced in white, held arms up to the sky, twisted in a dance of joy. She was tired of her secret. She longed to have that sister relationship she could trust to tell everything, but the words stuck deep inside her where they had stayed hidden for so long. "I can't talk about it. Not yet."

Joanna came up beside her. "I'm here if you change your mind."

Warmed from the inside, Elinor nodded. "Thank you." Maybe somewhere along the way, Joanna had grown into the big sister role at last. Leaning on Joanna's shoulder, Elinor allowed the tears to fall in the safe embrace of a sister's love.

CHAPTER THIRTY-EIGHT

Elinor

E linor pulled back the curtains to a beautiful, clear day instead of the hoped-for snow and ice storm that would have forced Remí's group to reschedule. What would that have accomplished? Nothing. After taking a last drink of her coffee, she set the mug in the sink and headed out into the bed and breakfast.

Apprehension leading her thoughts, she considered all the interruptions that meddled with her being able to talk to James once she decided to lay her secret out on the table. Monday, Remí and his wife stopped by and insisted on taking James out for dinner while they talked over final details. Asleep by the time James came to bed, another opportunity to talk disappeared.

Tuesday, two key staff members quit. She spent the morning calling staffing agencies and the afternoon interviewing. James helped Alexis in the kitchen, assuring all supplies were well stocked. By nightfall, too exhausted to talk, James asked if it could wait till morning.

Wednesday morning, they woke to the fire alarm blaring. A kitchen fire caused by the carelessness of one of the new staff members put everyone on alert. Fire trucks arrived, and chaos reigned until lunch. Elinor called in the family to help. Alita and Dad arrived within the hour to take the newly vacated spots. Hiring new staff would just have to wait.

By nightfall, the smell of smoke gone, all other preparations complete, the opportunity share her heart with James was lost. She only hoped the weekend passed without her secret coming out another way. *Lord, I need a lot of help. My plans just keep falling through.*

Elinor stopped by Karen's office in the kitchen and touched base with her about the schedule for the day. Next, she found Alexis stirring a concoction on the stove that released an aroma that most likely came from heaven. Alexis agreed to guest chef for the retreat, and Elinor looked forward to once again being treated to his specialty dishes. After reviewing the plans for the RJB group, Elinor took note of food items Alexis needed for a dish he planned to add to the menu. Haley could get those from the store.

Leaving the kitchen, she found Joanna, who agreed to oversee the housekeeping staff for the weekend and verified that everyone scheduled had shown up. A quick peek inside each room satisfied Elinor that the guests would indeed find that part of their stay satisfactory. Heading down the stairs, she heard voices in the foyer. Remí's deep, rich accent reached her ears above all the others. A cascade of memories poured over her. She hurried downstairs and slipped into the bathroom. Leaning against the wall, she squeezed her eyes shut and tried to will away the memories wreaking havoc on her life.

It had all started with her senior trip to Europe with a handful of high school seniors she didn't care to know. She had only wanted to get away from home. Shortly after they arrived in Paris, there was an opportunity to be extras in a movie being filmed in the city of love. Not wanting to be left out, she joined her classmates. Remí walking onto the set and the eyes of every woman there were glued on him. He, with time for only one. Her.

Turned out, his father was the producer. Remí carried clout. She and her classmates enjoyed playing actors and actresses with the benefits of his favor. Filming complete, he invited her to tour his home country of France with him. No one else. Just her. Seeing her way out of returning home sooner than she wanted, she ditched her classmates and went for the ride of her life.

Six months later, the glamour and parties over, his unsolicited favor slowed to a trickle. The solitary nights spent in secret rendezvous were done. Her pregnancy had been confirmed and so ended any chance of being the main thing in his life.

Placing a hand on her empty belly, she pushed herself away from the wall.

She couldn't afford to be near the man. Not if the mere sound of his voice stirred her like this. Keeping out of sight of anyone in the foyer, Elinor returned to the kitchen to locate James and Barry to help with the luggage.

"Elinor, could you take this to the young couple in the library? They're waiting to meet with Karen and Barry to discuss planning an upcoming event."

"Sure." Taking the tray loaded with tea and snacks that Alexis held out, Elinor headed toward the back hallway that led directly to the library. Distracted, she backed through the swinging door and came close to running into Remí and his wife. She almost lost her grip on the tray. She took a step back.

"Elinor." His eyes lit up when he saw her. Then an instant of what appeared to be sadness filled his eyes.

She nodded at Remí, barely glancing at his wife. "Excuse me, I need to deliver this tea."

She slipped past, delivered the tray to the library and hurried toward the kitchen, going through the foyer this time to avoid another awkward encounter.

As she passed the registration desk, Remí's familiar voice called to her from the door of the empty conference center. He, too, had circled around.

"We might as well get this over with. You can't avoid me the whole time we're here." Elinor shrugged at the registration clerk and walked past him into the main hall of the

conference center. Turning back to her left inside the room, she headed to a grouping of two chairs that sat at an angle not easily seen from the door. She took a seat shielded from view by a large plant; she motioned for Remí to sit opposite her.

The man sat with the grace of a someone trained to impress wherever he went. "I finally found you."

Willing herself not to fidget, she sat in silence as he observed her.

"Does your husband know about us?"

She glared at him. "Does your wife know about us?"

"Touché." He looked down and brushed off apparent dirt from his pants.

"What do you want, Remí?" The sound of his name coming out of her mouth reminded her of other times she had asked him what he wanted. Shame crept up her neck. She grabbed a strand of hair and twirled it around her finger. She tugged and the feelings mounting against her clouded. She couldn't let him see what he did to her.

"I want to know where our child is." The words came in almost a whisper, just like he made known his desires all those years ago.

Elinor never had been able to resist him. Today, she had to stand her ground. "I think your exact words to me were 'your child.' And you made it clear what you wanted."

"I was hoping..."

"What else did you think I would do?"

"I thought you might leave in order to keep it."

"Not an it." She looked away, then back to meet his eyes. "Then why didn't you just tell me to go?"

He leaned his head back against the wall. "I never should have listened to my father."

They sat in silence, watching each other like prey and predator.

"So that day I came back, and you were sick?"

"I wasn't feeling so well after I did what you wanted."

"I'm truly sorry." He reached over and touched her knee.

She leaned her knee away from his touch. "You think that makes it all better?"

"Of course not. What else do you want me to say? I am sorry." He leaned forward with his elbows on his knees. "If only I could just go back."

"The damage is done. Forever. Get it?"

His gaze dropped to the ground at his feet. "My wife tells me there is only one way to banish the demons inside me."

"Oh, she has a way of getting you off the hook of what you did, does she?"

"No. She doesn't know the why, just that I am tormented."

"Tormented?" Elinor's voice rose.

The look he gave her almost had Elinor believing. But he was good at that. "Then what?"

"A way to find forgiveness."

She huffed. "From me?"

He shook his head. "From God."

Elinor felt like a brick had just slammed into her. *Forgiveness? For driving her to an abortion? Let him off the hook?* She wanted to run far away from the man in front of her. Just like she had all those years ago. Maybe she should just disappear. James would be better off anyway.

She grew nauseous. She could never leave James. But would he leave her once he knew? The idea of continuing to keep this secret draped shame over her like a pall over a coffin. She stood. "Please, don't say anything." Then she hurried from the room. James stood just inside the doorway. He furrowed his brows and tilted his head.

She ran into the nearest bathroom, held her hair back and threw up into the toilet. *How much had James heard? Had he heard about the abortion?* After rinsing out her mouth and splashing water on her face, she slumped to the floor and wept.

She had managed to cover up her misery for so long with busyness and fashionable dress and the love of her life. But now the floodgates were open. Fresh tears fell as she sucked in sobs that fought to be unleashed.

CHAPTER THIRTY-NINE

Elinor

E linor sat stiffly in the pew. She had avoided Remí and his wife for the past two days. If James heard anything, he hadn't said a word, though their interactions were stilted, and she often caught him watching her with a look of confusion. She had waited too long. Now the shame hung like a veil between them. How could she tell this man she loved more than life itself the truth about her past? Afraid she was already losing him, she squeezed James's hand when he took hers in his. At least he still wanted to touch. Night times were bittersweet when he snuggled against her and she could pretend that everything was fine. A solitary tear fled the capture of her eyelids.

"You look tired." James leaned over and whispered in her ear.

She nodded and forced herself to offer a smile. "I'm looking forward to getting past the retreat." At least that was true.

He held onto her hand through the entire service. More tightly than usual, as though hanging onto something he thought he might lose otherwise. The pastor got up to preach and she zoned him out until she heard that word that had been nagging her spirit.

Forgiveness.

Lifting up her head, she focused on what he said.

"It's a choice. A day by day, won by the sweat of your brow, choice. The Spirit gives us the strength, but we have to accept His help. One day, you'll wake up and realize your heart has caught up to your choice. Until then, you have to choose to walk it out moment by moment. And we can't forgive others until we accept God's forgiveness. For those of you doubting His forgiveness, there is nothing so bad that God won't forgive. He doesn't stop loving us because we make mistakes."

The rest of his words were lost as she contemplated her own choices. *Lord, please forgive me. And if it's possible, help James to forgive me.*

The kitchen bustled more so than usual on a Sunday afternoon as the staff prepared the final lunch buffet for the RJB group. Elinor and James inspected prep work in the kitchen, then checked with Joanna concerning the wait staff. Lunch would be served on time. They took a moment to grab a plate of food and disappeared into Karen's office for a half-hour reprieve. Elinor savored the peace that momentarily settled between them.

No sooner had they reclined in their chairs than Remí poked his head into the office. He took in their meal in front of them.

"I apologize for interrupting, but could I talk to you a moment, James? I think we may have an issue with one of our menu items." Remí locked eyes with Elinor as James got up.

Elinor closed her eyes to break the hold he had on her. Glancing up, she caught James staring at her. She looked away and the men left. *I can't do this.* Her breathing hitched in her chest. She had nothing in her to pretend anymore. Even if the RJB Investments group was checking out before supper.

Leaving her plate of food on Karen's desk, she grabbed her jacket and hurried outside. On the porch, she wrapped her arms around her waist and leaned forward as her gut tightened in panic. Breathing slowly, she sat in a nearby chair until the pain decreased. She hadn't felt this much anxiety since she left Europe. She hurried across the pavement toward Karen's house, where she planned to hide out for as long as she could manage. She couldn't talk to James. Not yet.

"Elinor?"

She glanced behind her.

Bijou, Remí's wife, gave her a tentative wave. "Wait up. I want to talk."

Right. Elinor changed course and headed for the gazebo. At least they might have a semblance of privacy here for whatever insults or accusations the woman wanted to throw at her. Keeping her back turned, she waited.

"I'm guessing you don't want to talk, but..."

"You think?" She glanced over her shoulder then back into the shadowed spaces of the woods.

"It's obvious you have history with my husband."

Elinor laughed to herself. *Little does she know.*

"Shortly after Remí and I married, I found a note pushed to the back of one of his chests of drawers. It was from an Elinor apologizing for leaving. I confronted Remí and he said it was years ago. He tossed the note into the trash. I was convinced. Until he retrieved that note from the trash when he thought I wasn't looking. When I stopped by a couple weeks ago, I put the puzzle pieces together. Are you that Elinor?"

Elinor thought about the woman living with Remí all these years, knowing only whispers of something she had heard through a long-ago note. She relented her stance and nodded.

"Look, this is awkward for me, too. I'm sorry."

"For what? This is all on your husband."

"Causing you distress, for one. I'm just looking for answers to his torment."

Elinor was only too happy to help her understand the torment his actions had caused her. "He said I was...an inconvenience." The bitter laugh that came out of Elinor sounded far away and sad to her own ears. Laughter didn't belong in this conversation, but it came unbidden and somehow felt like the only authentic response. "He lied to me. I did what I did because I believed his promises. But when he came back after..." Elinor's voice fell to a whisper. "...I killed my baby..."

Silence engulfed the space between them.

"Go on." Bijou's voice—soft, hesitant—encouraged her to continue.

"I knew by the way he talked to me that he and I would never be together. I was just something on the side. I guess I was right."

"I understand how you feel."

"Do you, now?" Elinor raised her eyebrows.

"More than you know."

Elinor huffed.

"It was expected that we marry. But a year and a half after the ceremony, we found out we couldn't have kids. He said it didn't matter." Bijou leaned against the railing next to Elinor. "He changed then. Nothing dramatic, but he was easier to live with. When he was around."

"What happened?" Despite her determination to just listen, Elinor wanted to know.

"He started meeting with private detectives to look for you. He didn't know I knew. But between the note and whispered conversations I overheard, the growing distance between him and his father, I pieced it together. Then there were the trips without me. The dinners without me. The tables were turned, Elinor. Now you were the main thing."

"Not me. The child. That was all he wanted."

"Perhaps." Bijou waited. "What about your husband?"

"What about him?" Elinor crossed her arms.

"You haven't told him?"

"No." Elinor shook her head.

"Secrets only destroy a relationship."

"It had better stay a secret until I decide otherwise."

"Of course. I just...I don't know." Bijou placed a hand on Elinor's arm. "You have something good here with James. Don't do what I did. That's all."

The woman's touch felt like fire. Elinor dropped her arms. "He said you talk of forgiveness."

Bijou nodded. "It's how I've found peace in all of this."

"How do I forgive something like this? Forgive Remí? How do I forgive myself?"

"With God's help. One day at a time."

"God?"

Bijou shrugged. "I've had a lot of time to think, and I started going to church."

Confusion settled in Elinor's heart. She remembered what the pastor said about God's forgiveness, but did it apply to this? Her part and Remí's? How could it? Turning away from Bijou, she noticed James on the porch, watching them.

Tears clouded Elinor's vision as she fled toward the back entrance of Karen's house, only to find it locked. Leaning against the doorframe, she banged on the door. When no one came, she slid down to sit on the porch and pulled her knees up to her chest with her forehead resting on top. She stayed that way until someone knelt beside her. Elinor glanced up.

Joanna sat close beside her and wrapped her in a hug. "Remí?"

Elinor nodded and allowed her sister to pull her closer.

That was where Karen found them. "James sent me over to check on you. Let's get you inside, Elinor." After unlocking the door, she stood aside while Joanna helped their younger sister into the house.

CHAPTER FORTY

Elinor

E linor climbed into the car with Joanna, thankful her sister was driving. She didn't want to visit Blake, but this was the first chance Joanna had to see him since she got back from Colorado. Elinor wanted to support Joanna, like she had supported Elinor last night. Joanna and Karen had let Elinor cry until there was nothing left inside. Then they had listened.

The story tumbled out of her like a handful of dice. As evening approached, Karen called James and let him know Elinor was spending the night at her place and not to worry. It had been a relief to tell the truth to someone. And her sisters made her promise to follow through with telling James. But she was stuck somewhere between hope and fear.

"Are you feeling better this morning?" Joanna put her car in gear and headed out of the Applewood Hill parking lot.

Elinor shrugged. "Glad the retreat is over."

"Did you talk to James this morning?"

"No. He was busy with a client when I went to our apartment to change." While she had changed in the bedroom, she heard him enter their apartment, yet he didn't seek her out. As much as she didn't want to see him, his not seeking her out concerned her. Sniffling, she gazed out the window. *Have I destroyed his trust?*

"You promised to tell him."

Elinor wanted to tell Joanna to bug off, but she knew that without a bit of prodding, she would likely put this off too long. "Yeah. I will."

"Not going to be a best time."

Elinor nodded.

Joanna reached over and placed her hand on top of Elinor's. "Love you, sis. Don't sell James short. You guys will be fine."

"I hope so."

Checked into the prison by noon, Elinor and Joanna waited on a guard to bring in Blake.

"Are you nervous?" Elinor sat in the chair indicated by a guard and turned to Joanna.

"A little I guess." Joanna shrugged. "Not sure why. He was the one who instigated breaking our codependent sibling relationship. Just not sure if he's willing to try and have a healthy one."

"Wasn't Alita the one who pushed that? What does she think now?"

"We haven't talked much. Another conversation I need to have. A lot to apologize for there."

"Our family is a mess, isn't it?"

"What family isn't? At least Dad decided to change and has been praying for each of us since. We've come a long way since Karen came back to Westfall."

"True." Elinor reflected on the recent history of her family. Her mother, coming back home and forgiving her dad. Karen returning home, then forgiving Barry after he changed and followed her to the Midwest. Albert on his sabbatical seeking healing. And Joanna...if she could change, wasn't there hope for Elinor? A timid smile tugged at her heart. She hoped James's heart had enough room to allow her to grow.

Joanna elbowed Elinor out of her thoughts.

Blake walked through a door and sat in a chair on the other side of the glass that sat between them, and locked eyes with Joanna. He offered a lopsided grin and picked up the phone.

Elinor watched the exchange with interest. The last time she came, Blake had been so defensive with her. He seemed changed somehow.

Joanna picked up the phone on her side of the window. "Hey."

"I wasn't expecting to see you."

"Just got back from Colorado."

"You look good."

"Thanks." Joanna tapped her fingers on the counter.

"That a ring I see?" He leaned forward to look at her hand.

She held up her hand and wiggled her fingers.

"Who's the guy?"

"Remember the chef at the Applewood Hill?"

"Hmm. You happy?"

"I am."

"Good." Blake looked down at his hands. "I..." He started to scoot back his chair.

"Don't go. What were you going to say?" Joanna placed a hand on the glass.

He slumped in his chair. "I'm sorry."

"Me too."

Blake nodded.

"Let's be friends again?"

"I'd like that. But different this time."

"Agreed. So..."

Blake tilted his head. "What?"

"How are you?"

"You know. It's prison." He glanced at Elinor as though he had just realized she was there. He nodded then looked back at Joanna.

"Dad said you're meeting with the chaplain?"

"He cornered me."

"And?"

Blake's laugh was harsh. "What? You think meeting with someone who has never spent the night inside a prison much less been convicted of a crime like mine would have anything to say that I would listen to? Preacher Man is much more believable than the likes of him."

"Preacher Man?" Elinor joined the conversation.

"One of the inmates. He earned his nickname preaching forgiveness and being kind to your enemies. The thing is, that's the way he lives." He chuckled. "He can get away with it, considering how big he is."

"And?" Joanna leaned forward.

Blake shrugged. "Not much to tell. So, what else is going on with you?"

Elinor relaxed in her chair as Joanna filled Blake in on how she ended up married and with a daughter. Blake engaged without that edge of anger ever present with him. He seemed genuinely interested. Elinor wondered if the change would last. She hoped. Alita would be glad to hear. Lost in her thoughts, she was surprised when the guard told Blake his time was up.

"Already?" Blake looked over his shoulder.

"Don't give me any trouble." The guard crossed his arms. "Two minutes."

Leaning closer to the glass, Blake looked at both his sisters. "Tell Alita I love her." He pushed his chair back. "See ya." He got up and exited through the door on his side of the glass.

Joanna linked arms with Elinor on the way to the car. "He's doing better than I expected."

"Better than the last time I was here. Hope it's real."

"Me too. Hey, do you mind if we stop by and see Clarice and Grammie once we get back to Kansas City?"

Elinor glanced at her watch and shrugged. "Fine by me. Can we stop at a flea market on the way?"

"Road trip time." Joanna unlocked the car doors. "First stop, ice cream."

"Absolutely." Elinor climbed into the car. A fleeting thought drifted through her head about talking to James. A shiver crawled up her spine. She knew the time had come to talk to him about her past. How could they move on otherwise? *God, give me courage to tell him the truth.* Elinor shook off any more thoughts about her marriage. For now, she needed a break.

Two scoops of ice cream and three flea markets later, the girls and a trunkload of treasures stopped in front of Clarice and Grammie's house.

"Can you believe how much they expected to get for that vase at the last flea market?" Elinor got out of the car.

"One-hundred-year-old crystal. Right." Joanna laughed. "They didn't know they were up against the guru of flea markets." Joanna pointed at her sister.

"Why thank you." Elinor slipped her hand through Joanna's arm as they headed up the sidewalk.

She looked up and down the block. Streetlamps blinked as they turned on, lighting up the otherwise darkening street. The neighborhood boasted well-built smaller homes. Most of the residents were older. Still, they took care of their property, often hanging onto homes that had been in their families for years. But things were changing. Landlords were buying up houses and renting them out to those who didn't care as much. At least Grammie's block was in good shape, still holding its value for now.

"The house looks dark. Think they're out?"

"Doubt it. Probably just in the family room in back."

Before they reached the top step, the porch light came on and the door flung open. Clarice raced out and wrapped her arms around Joanna. "You came."

"What's up, girl? Why are you crying?"

"Grammie won't wake up. But I prayed that you would come, and you did."

"Where is she?" Joanna grabbed Clarice's hand and hurried into the house.

"Back in the family room in her big chair."

Elinor followed and watched as Joanna checked the old woman's pulse and breathing. "She's breathing. Grammie, can you hear me? Elinor, call 9-1-1. Clarice, go pack a bag with what you need, then after we get your grammie to the hospital, you're coming with me."

Clarice nodded and ran off upstairs.

Within minutes, the sirens wailed down the street. Clarice clambered downstairs and ran to check on Grammie. "Please be okay, Grammie. Please." Clarice kissed her grandmother's cheek.

Holding tight to Joanna's hand, she moved to the side as the paramedics came into the house and began checking Grammie over. A police officer confirmed that Joanna and Elinor would care for Clarice, and then he headed out after the paramedics as they loaded up the older woman. Joanna and Elinor checked that everything was turned off and locked up, then followed the ambulance to the hospital.

Joanna handed her car keys to Elinor and climbed into the back seat next to Clarice. Sobs grabbed at Elinor's heart. She watched Joanna through the rearview as she comforted the young child. She wondered if Joanna and Alexis would take Clarice in even with Hannah with them. Probably. Seemed like that was who Joanna was these days.

Not long after getting to the hospital, Alexis and Hannah joined them in the almost empty emergency waiting room.

Hannah sat next to Clarice and put her arm around her. "You can sleep with me in my room at Grandpa Charles' house."

"Really?" Clarice hiccuped.

Hannah nodded. "Really."

"Thank you." Clarice leaned against Hannah and rested.

Alexis, Joanna, and Elinor invited the girls to join them, and they prayed. Then the girls found something to watch on the television while the adults chatted.

"Grammie seemed overly tired at Thanksgiving. I should have paid it more mind." Joanna wrapped her hands around her husband's.

"Don't beat yourself up, sweetheart."

"You're right. I'm just glad we decided to stop by tonight."

"Joanna Hannigan?" A nurse stood nearby, waiting for someone to answer.

"That's me."

"She's stable now. But we need to check her into the hospital for observation."

"Can I see Grammie?" Clarice jumped up from her chair and ran over to stand in front of the nurse.

"You must be her granddaughter."

Clarice bobbed her head up and down. "Can we take her home now?"

"Not yet, but your grammie wants to see you. You need to keep it calm for her. Can you do that? She told us how energetic you are." The nurse grinned.

"I'll do my best." She stood tall and straight and acted like she pulled a zipper across her mouth.

The nurse laughed. "Your best will do. Joanna, can you come with her? The doctor will meet you in the room and fill you in on her condition. Her grandmother signed the paperwork so you can hear from the doctor yourself."

Joanna and Clarice followed the nurse down the hallway and disappeared through a set of doors.

Elinor watched Alexis and his daughter poring through a magazine together. They were a perfect fit with Joanna. Elinor was happy for them, though a bit of envy for something just as beautiful as what they had reared up inside her.

She glanced at the time on her phone. It looked like tonight wouldn't be the night to talk to James. Again. A mixture of relief and regret rose like bile in her throat. *God, help me make a way to talk to James tomorrow. Please help me. Help my marriage.*

CHAPTER
FORTY-ONE

Albert

Albert turned on his blinker, checked traffic, then turned left onto the highway. He glanced in the rearview mirror to make sure the boxes of food donations he and Joe had picked up for the local shelter weren't tumbling around in the bed of the truck.

Settling into the drive, his mind wandered to the kids who had come to stay at the ranch while their bus was repaired. The weekend after Thanksgiving had been busy taking the kids on hikes, sleighrides, and horseback rides. Albert enjoyed the change of pace. Even though he had been one of the adults in charge, it felt more like vacation than work.

Smiling, he remembered the evenings around the fire. Somehow, he found his way to leading devotionals every night. The kids seemed to eat it up. Three of the boys cornered him during free time, and they ended up in deep discussion about temptations they were facing at home, at school, and in front of their computer screens. That was what he loved. True ministry, not another program.

He tapped his thumb on the steering wheel and glanced over at Joe. Head leaning back against the headrest and hat pulled down over his eyes, he rested.

Glancing in the side mirror, Albert switched lanes and passed a semitruck as his mind meandered back to processing the weekend. Programs made him tired. It didn't matter if there were enough people to serve, the church seemed bound and determined to have programs. Would that culture ever change? He shook his head. One thing this weekend showed him, he could do what he loved, what God made him to do, without being a pastor behind a pulpit.

"We there yet?" Joe stirred on the seat beside Albert.

"You sound like those kids this weekend."

"Ha. Those kids have nothing on me."

"True. You're grumpier."

"Watch it, young man."

The two laughed as Albert backed into the space next to the shelter's back door stairs. After climbing out of the pickup, he came around and opened the tailgate. They had driven to the other side of Alamosa this morning to pick up a load of food donations for the shelter. While they were loading, Joe got a bit winded. He insisted all he needed was a decent breakfast, since they'd taken off without one of Abigail's morning feasts. They stopped at a diner, and it appeared Joe was right, as his energy increased after food and copious amounts of coffee. Joe had been slowing down since Albert had arrived at the ranch, but Joe resisted his wife's insistence that he go to the doctors.

"I'm fine." He had practically yelled at her before he stomped off. What could they do, but pray?

"Hey, Joe. Feeling any better?"

"Fit as you, young man."

Albert grabbed a box form the back of the truck. He hoped the older man was right.

One of the men from the ministry propped the door open and came down to help them unload. "Thanks for picking these up for us. We would have been short staffed if one of us had gone." He lifted a box from the bed of the truck. "Speaking of which...do you have time to come in and help serve lunch?"

Albert glanced at Joe, then nodded. "Sure. Too bad Abigail isn't with us. She enjoys talking to the ladies." After hefting a box up, he followed the man up the stairs into the facility.

The three of them unloaded the vehicle in short order, then both Joe and Albert donned the aprons handed to them and reported to the dining hall. Joe was assigned to dish up food and Albert to clean tables.

The door opened and within minutes, the line outside moved into the warmth of the building. The solitude of the street became community as volunteers connected with men and women living on the street. Smiles replaced downcast looks and the occasional belly laugh infected the atmosphere with joy.

Meeting the homeless in their moment of need, Albert found joy in ministering to them. A hug, pat on the back, or a prayer. It didn't take much to lift their spirits.

Toward the end of the scheduled serve time, an old man and woman walked in together. But not together. They kept about two feet between them, but it was like an invisible rope wouldn't let them get away from each other.

Albert watched for a while then went over to one of the regular volunteers. "Looks like they have a story."

The woman nodded. "It's sad. Wouldn't know it, but they've been married for over fifty years."

"Wow." Albert stuffed his hands in his pockets. "But?"

"Hard to miss, isn't it? We don't know all the details, but a while back, they lost everything."

"Lots of people survive that. How did they end up at such odds with each other?" Albert stepped aside as one of the volunteers came through with a tub of dirty dishes.

"From the conversations I've had with them, I think the problem is unforgiveness. But here's the twist. They each blame themselves, not the other person. But think the other blames them. And they won't believe it when we try and set the record straight. Shame oozes out of them. They need to talk to each other instead of stumbling around in the dark together. After a while, we stopped trying to convince them. We just love on them."

Albert nodded. "Why do you think they stay together?"

"After fifty years?" She shrugged. "Probably still love each other underneath it all. Besides, all they have is each other." Leaving Albert to his own conclusion, she grabbed a rag and started wiping down tables.

Albert grabbed a cup of coffee and sat down across from the couple, where they sat with two seats between them. They stared at him. He stared back. What made them willing to live like this instead of getting back on their feet? He smiled at them. They glared back.

"Name's Albert." He held out his hand.

They ignored his offer of a handshake and kept eating.

Lord, what can I say that hasn't been said? What do they need to hear?

Albert drank the last of his coffee, then got up and filled two cups and set them in front of the couple. What better way than to get straight to it? He lifted a silent prayer before he spoke. "Do you guys want to keep living like this?"

The woman paused with food lifted halfway to her mouth. A tear ran down her cheek, then her fork clattered to her tray, and she looked down at her lap. She shook her head. The man glanced at his wife, then shook his head. The woman sniffled.

Albert reached out and touched each of them on the arm. He looked at the man and pointed to the chair next to his wife. The man closed his eyes for a moment then nodded. Scooting over his tray, he moved to the seat next to his wife. She sucked in a breath, then rested her face in her hands as tears fell in earnest. The man reached awkwardly and patted her on the shoulder.

Her shoulders shook.

Albert wondered what had been buried so deep for so long that would keep people in chains like this. He met the man's gaze. "You ever been a church-going man?"

He nodded.

"I think you know what to do."

He nodded again.

"I'll be over there if you need anything." Albert indicated a table close to the coffee then got up to leave them alone.

The staff manager watched him from behind the counter. He nodded and pointed up. Albert nodded back, then found a place to sit. Joe joined him and they prayed as mercy took over at the table where shame had held two people hostage for far too long.

Thank You, Lord, for breaking through to them. Thank You for bringing me to this moment at this place. Albert glanced at Joe. *Can You break through in this family? Bring Joe and Abigail's kids home?* He gave thanks to God in his heart that he had been a small part in bringing God's grace to this place.

That night, Albert struggled to fall sleep as he contemplated his future. He knew it was nearing the time to go. There was peace in his heart, and most days, joy too. Somewhere along the way, forgiveness took prominence over the resentment and anger about the past. He needed to embrace whatever his future looked like. Working with the kids and having a part in the restoration of a relationship got him to thinking about seeking out something other than pastoring. But what? All he knew was that his life needed to change. Thoughts of returning to his family filled his heart as he finally drifted off to sleep.

Pounding on the door jerked him awake. He sat up on the edge of his bed and pulled on his jeans. The urgency of the knock...he grabbed his shirt and hurried to the door. Joe had told him to sleep in this morning, take a break from the early morning routine. What was wrong? He flung open the door to find Abigail standing there with her housecoat hanging out from underneath her down coat. Winter boots unlaced on her feet. Tears streamed down her face.

"It's Joe. I called 9-1-1, but...I don't know...they're telling me what I should do, but I...I...need help." Sobs broke from her lips. "What if...?"

Leaving the door standing open, Albert grabbed his jacket and phone and stuck his feet in his boots. "What happened?"

"I don't know. When I came down this morning, he was in his big chair in the living room, I thought waiting for breakfast. But then...I can't wake him, Albert. I'm afraid."

Albert placed his hand briefly on the older woman's shoulder. "Pray." Then he took her phone and bolted for the big house. "This is a friend. I'm headed to Joe now. What should I do?"

"Check to see if he is breathing and if he has a pulse. You may need to start CPR. Just keep me on the phone and tell me what is happening. I can let the paramedics know."

"Will do." They needed a phone in the cabin. It would have saved precious minutes. He slammed open the door and rushed into the living room. He knelt beside the chair. *Lord, let this man live. He has done so much to help so many.* "Joe? Can you hear me?"

No response. Albert checked Joe's pulse. Still strong. James relayed this to the 9-1-1 operator.

"Stay with him. Keep checking his pulse and breathing. If anything changes, let me know. I'll stay on the line with you till the paramedics arrive. They should be there in twenty minutes."

Abigail rushed through the door and slammed out the cold air. "I'm going to get dressed so I'm ready to go. Then what should I do?"

"Just come talk to him. He needs to hear your voice." Albert prayed as he waited.

Abigail returned within fifteen minutes and sat next to her husband. "When will they get here? This is taking too long."

Albert checked with the operator.

"They should be here any time now."

"I'll go watch for them." Leaving Abigail on her knees, pleading to God for her husband, he went to the door. "They're pulling in."

"Thank God." Abigail got up off the floor to make room for the paramedics.

The house became a beehive of activity as the paramedics checked Joe over. Within half an hour, they had stabilized him, loaded him in the ambulance and headed to the hospital in Alamosa.

Albert turned off all the lights and locked up with the keys Abigail had handed him, then they followed the ambulance to the hospital. Joe had to be all right. Praying he didn't get stopped, he pushed the pedal down and sped up.

Once they arrived, they checked in with emergency personnel, who instructed them to wait until someone came out to let them know how Joe was.

"What will I do without him, Albert?"

He put his arm around her shoulders and pulled her into a hug. "Don't go there. Let's pray." Heads touching, he led her in prayer for the health of the man she loved. He prayed that somehow their kids would find their way home and that restoration of relationships would be full and complete.

Within an hour, the doctor informed them Joe was stable, but they wanted to check him in for observation and to and run tests the next day. Abigail and Albert were allowed to go to Joe's room. Throughout the day, Albert stayed nearby, taking care of whatever Abigail needed. His heart ached at the thought of her having no one. *God, where are her kids?*

"Albert?" Abigail patted his arm.

He jerked awake and sat up straight. "Sorry. I shouldn't have fallen asleep."

"And why not? It's been a long day, young man." She smiled at him with peace flowing out of her.

"Did you hear anything?"

She shook her head. "But as I sat here and prayed, I remembered something about one of the paramedics. He looked familiar. Reminded me of the man who helped us out after our boys left all those years ago. Mike. You remember me telling you about him?"

He nodded, not fully following what she said. But then he recalled the picture and how much the man reminded him of Gabe. He sat up straight. There was a woman and two men paramedics who piled into the house to take care of Joe. Closing his eyes, he dredged up an image of them huddled over Joe. One of the men had turned and asked him a question. That wasn't Gabe. The other one never turned, and he wore a cap. Wait. The same type of cap that Gabe had left behind.

"Can you go find out if that was him? He used to tell us how much he liked to help save people, so it would fit. But not sure why he wouldn't have said something to me...maybe it was just too hectic."

"Probably."

"Well, go on. And bring me back a donut, please." She turned back to one of her friends who had stopped by to visit.

Albert stood and stretched. Where would he go to find out about a paramedic? He walked out to the information desk and chatted with the receptionist about it. She directed him to the appropriate person to get information from. He picked up a donut from the cafeteria and delivered it to Abigail before heading to that department. But first, he wanted to follow a hunch.

At his car, he dug around in the trunk until he found Gabe's hat he'd left behind. The Regional Medical Center. *What do you know?* Slamming the lid shut, he went back into the hospital and found the emergency department.

No man by the name of Mike or Gabe worked there. And no one by another name fit the description.

A paramedic standing nearby raised his eyebrows at his questions. "Your friend must have a guardian angel."

Shaking his head, Albert walked away. God did send angels to minister to His children. And if anyone needed ministering to, it was Joe and Abigail. Deciding to accept the fact that God had been at work, Albert hummed a worship song on the way back to Joe's room. If God was at work, perhaps it was time for Joe's kids to come home. He smiled at the thought of that reunion. *God, is there something*

You want me to do to facilitate that happening before I go back to my family?

When Albert arrived back at the hospital, he told Abigail what the paramedic said.

She laughed. "I always knew we had a guardian angel."

Nothing took her joy the rest of the day. Even when the doctors came in to talk to them.

"The tests indicate a mild stroke or TIA. We're going to run another test to confirm and then we'll talk again and decide what to do. For now, focus on rest." The doctor patted Joe's knee.

After the doctor left, Joe turned to Abigail and held her hand. "Go home and get a good night's sleep."

"I can't leave you."

"You mean you won't. I will be fine. Not planning any long trips. Besides..." He turned to Albert. "...how long does it take you to get to the hospital in that fancy vehicle of yours?"

Albert laughed. "Fifteen minutes, tops."

"See? Albert will make sure you get here if I wake up and decide I need you in the middle of the night."

Abigail looked from one man to the other like a chastised young girl. "Fine. But I don't like it." She kissed Joe on the cheek, picked up her things, and walked to the door. "Are you coming, Albert?"

Joe laughed. "I married me a spitfire, didn't I?"

Albert waved as he followed Abigail into the hallway.

CHAPTER FORTY-TWO

Elinor

C larice and Hannah, each dragging Joanna by one hand, burst into the formal dining room at the Applewood Hill, where most of the Hannigan clan was gathered for a midweek breakfast together.

"We get to go see Grammie today." Clarice clapped her hands as they stopped in front of Elinor. "Do you want to come with us?" She looked at Karen. "You, too."

Karen laughed. "We could meet up with Haley and Alita afterward."

"Already called them. They'll meet us at Bobby's Plate for lunch." Joanna pulled Hannah into a side hug.

"Yay!" Clarice and Hannah danced around the room.

"What about us guys?" Alexis came in behind Joanna and wrapped his arms around her waist.

"There's a game on." Charles added his two bits.

"Sounds like that's settled." Elinor stood and gathered plates.

"What if I object? I mean, I hardly see my wife anymore." James walked in as plans were being bantered about and stopped next to Elinor.

Longing for a sign that all was well, she glanced at her husband. The muscle in his jaw twitched despite his smile. Like it did when he was upset. She hated this. They hadn't had two minutes to talk since the retreat, what with everything that had happened with Clarice's grammie. A part of her felt relieved and yet she knew nothing would heal without facing the truth. *I should get this over with.*

"I can stay if you want."

"You would do that?" James turned her direction.

"Of course." Elinor tried to smile encouragingly.

He met her gaze for a moment then closed his eyes. Although voices buzzed around her, the room seemed wrapped in silence as she waited for his response.

He kissed her cheek and whispered in her ear. "We can talk when you get back tonight." Then he turned and smiled at the others. "I know better than to get in the way." He gathered up plates and headed toward the kitchen. "Have fun."

After a morning of Christmas shopping and visiting Grammie, who was doing much better, the girl crew stopped at Bobby's Plate, one of Westfall's well-kept secrets known for the best homestyle food in town. Joanna perused the menu a bit, then called Alita to see what was holding her up.

After a quick exchange, Joanna stuck her phone back in her pocket. "She can't make it. Something work related. Who's ready to order?"

"We need more time." Hannah spoke up and Clarice nodded.

Looking over the girls' shoulders, Joanna pointed out her favorites on the menu.

"Yuck." They spoke together and giggled.

Joanna laughed. "You guys are like two peas in a pod.

"Say what?" Clarice amped up the attitude.

"You know, just alike." Elinor piped in.

"We are not just alike. She has yellow hair and I have dark hair. She is in fifth grade and I am in fourth grade. Where do you get off saying we're just alike?" Clarice rolled her eyes.

Hannah gasped and looked around at the grownups.

"You like the same food." Joanna pointed out.

Clarice narrowed her eyes. "Well, I guess."

"You both like to sing and dance."

Hannah bobbed her head up and down and turned to Clarice. "I can't wait to see your Christmas pageant. I've never been in a pageant. I bet it will be fun. Can we go early to get a good place to sit, Mom?"

Joanna laughed. "And you both like to talk."

Clarice tilted her head, put one finger on the corner of her mouth and looked up at the ceiling. Then she giggled and hugged Hannah. "I think she's right."

Hannah returned the hug and giggled along with her new friend.

"What should we order?" Clarice pointed to the picture of a pile of fries with gravy on them. "This?"

Hannah nodded, although she didn't look to sure.

"Trust me girl, you'll like these." Clarice bent her head close to Hannah and they proceeded to talk about something like it was top secret.

Elinor looked at Joanna over their heads and mouthed "Adorable."

Joanna nodded. "Right?"

The waitress stopped by the table with water and took their orders, then headed back to the kitchen.

"Can we go to Grandpa Charles' tomorrow?" Clarice looked up at Joanna with her hands held together like she was praying.

"Please?" Hannah joined her in pose.

"How can I resist this?" Joanna looked around at the other ladies.

"Can you take us to the treehouse, too?" Hannah glanced over at Clarice.

Clarice nodded. "You're doing good, girl."

Elinor squelched a laugh. Joanna wasn't able to squelch hers. Soon, they were all laughing. Clarice and Hannah looked around the table and joined in too. Several of the other patrons gave them odd glances, but no one seemed to mind.

Darkness crept up on them as Joanna and Elinor pulled into the drive of the Applewood Hill. They had all decided to go to a movie before ending their time together back here at the bed and breakfast. *Wonder* had been well worth their time. Haley and Karen had already made it back. Elinor checked her phone. Plenty of time to have that talk with James. *I will do this.* Peace settled on her. Tonight was the night. Finally.

Joanna glanced in the rearview mirror at the two girls leaning against each other, eyes drooping. "Girls. Who wants dessert?"

Their eyes opened in a flash. "We do." They climbed out of the car and then raced to the house.

Elinor looked at Joanna and raised her eyebrows, then took off at a sprint.

Joanna almost caught up with her before they reached the porch. "No fair. You had a head start."

Elinor shrugged and headed inside. "Where is everyone?"

With Joanna on her heels, they followed the murmuring sounds of voices and found the family in the library. The kids were gathered in one corner, playing quietly. James watched over their shoulders. The other adults were scattered around. Sitting on a love seat, Dad wept quietly. Karen sat next to Barry, shaking her head, face masked in disbelief. Elinor's eyes landed on Alita, curled in a ball on the couch, Haley next to her.

"What is going on?" Joanna walked over toward Alexis next to the window.

James joined Elinor where she stood in the doorway. "There's been news about your brother."

"Albert?"

He shook his head. "Blake."

"What happened?" Elinor turned at the sound of Joanna crying out. Alexis held her in his arms.

"There was a fight in the prison. Blake was killed."

"No." She shook her head. "We were just there. He was fine."

"It happened this morning. We don't know the details yet." He pulled Elinor into his arms.

Her mind resisted the idea that her oldest brother was gone. They were never close, never truly knew each other, but as their dad led the way to healing in their family, she held out hope that one day she would at least have a peaceful relationship with him. And where did this leave the hopes her family held out for his turning to God. *Haven't You been listening to our prayers God?*

Melting into the embrace of her husband, she clung to him for comfort, hoping that once details came out, they would understand why this happened.

CHAPTER FORTY-THREE

Albert

A t first light this morning, Abigail found Albert in the barn. "Are you ready to go, young man? I've been gone from the hospital long enough."

Albert looked over the top of the stall. "Just need to finish this stall. You already have breakfast?"

"I can eat at the cafeteria."

"I'm still going to be a few minutes, go ahead and grab something. Doesn't have to be fancy."

"You won't be long, though, will you?"

He shook his head.

"Good. I'll be ready to go when you're done." She paused at the door to the barn and turned around. "Thank you, Albert. For being here and taking care of me and...everything."

"You're welcome."

She nodded and left for the house.

An hour later, Abigail was back beside her husband, content to tell the nurses how to do their job. Albert excused himself to head back and take care of the daily chores around their place.

As he drove back to the ranch, Albert allowed his mind to wander. Abigail had been satisfied that there was no Mike paramedic, convinced God was at work for them and had sent their guardian angel to protect Joe. Albert had a suspicion God was up to more than either Joe or Abigail had an idea about. Along with the chores he needed to do, he planned to do a bit of snooping. He didn't think they would mind, if things worked out the way he suspected. And he didn't want to mention anything to get their hopes up before he was sure.

At the ranch, he felt compelled to look around before chores, starting with the lineup of framed photos and albums Abigail had all over the family room. It didn't take long to find the picture of Mike. Looking closely, Albert decided Mike and Gabe could have been related. He decided to accept the unexplainable. Moving on, he found the most recent family album. There weren't many pictures in it, but one was telling. There, front and center, was there daughter, Jennifer. *Just as I thought.*

Running down to his cabin, he dug around in his duffle bag for the business card he had picked before he left the Hole. He prayed as he dialed.

Jennifer picked up after three rings. "Hole in the Wall Diner. What can we serve up for you today?"

"Hey Jennifer, it's me, Albert. Your long-lost cook."

"Please tell me you're coming back."

"Afraid not."

"Bummer. We closed down last week when the guy who took over for you left. Don't know what it's going to take to get someone here to stay. Sorry. You probably called about something besides hearing my troubles. What's up?"

Albert lifted a quick prayer, then jumped right in. "Forgive me if I'm speaking out of turn, but is your maiden name Miller?"

Albert waited past the pause on the other side of the line.

"Yes."

"Long story, but I ended up working at your parents' ranch." He persisted when silence met his statement. "Your dad is sick." A gasp came through the line. "He's stable, but I think...well, I think it's time all you kids came home."

Jennifer spoke through sobs. "You don't know what it was like. Growing up there."

"I think I do. More than you know. From what your mom and dad shared...he reminds me of my dad. But Joe has changed."

"Right. Do you believe a man like that can change?"

He had been holding on to the same doubt. But in that moment, he realized it wasn't about trusting the man. It was about trusting God. And as confidently as he could tell Jennifer that Joe had changed, he could equally believe the same about his dad. Swallowing past the emotions caught in his throat, he gave the only answer he could.

"Yes. Absolutely."

"I don't know."

"Call your brothers and at least talk about it? Talk to your husband?"

"I'll call you later and let you know. I can reach you at this number?"

"I'll have my phone with me." Albert stuck his phone in his jacket pocket and headed out to take care of his chores.

***

Albert watched Abigail and Joe play a game of cards. Their laughter buoyed his spirits. It had been six hours since he talked to Jennifer, and still, he hadn't heard back. Had he made a mistake calling her?

Glancing at his watch, he got up from his chair. "I'm going down to the cafeteria. Want anything?"

"A hamburger, fries, and milkshake."

Abigail play-slapped her husband's arm. "You know you can't have that. Doctor's orders."

"A man can wish, can't he?"

"How about I see what kind of deli sandwich they have? Nothing fried." Albert leaned against the doorframe.

"Fine. You two are conspiring against me."

"Who's the spitfire now?" Abigail swatted at her husband's shoulder, then looked at Albert. "Get me the same, please."

Albert meandered down the hallway, checking his phone for messages as he got onto the elevator. He stuck his phone in his pocket. On the ground floor, the door to the elevator opened and Albert came face to face with Jennifer and her husband waiting to get on. Albert grinned as he stepped off the elevator and shook their hands. He motioned for them to follow him to a group of chairs, and they all sat down.

"Glad you guys decided to come. Didn't expect you so soon."

She nodded. "Bill said since the diner was closed anyway, we might as well come now. Only took us an hour to get on the road once we decided. How is he?"

"The doc says he should make a full recovery."

"Mom?"

"She's tired but hanging in there. They're going to be glad to see you. Are your brothers coming?"

"Tomorrow. But I couldn't wait. I had to get here as fast as I could, or I was afraid I wouldn't come at all." She twisted the Kleenex she held in her hands. "Thank you. For being here for them. For calling me. I needed a kick in the pants."

"We all do from time to time." He nodded toward the elevator. "Want me to come with you?"

She shook her head. "I think I need to do this on my own."

"I understand. I came down to get food. I'll take my time before I come back up."

She stood and gave him a quick hug. "I feel like you're family now. See you in a bit. Say a prayer for us while you're eating."

"Absolutely."

Albert watched them get on the elevator before he got his food, then chose a table near a window. Before he ate, he said a prayer for the family who were reuniting after all these years. Knowing that Joe and Abigail were being looked after, Albert unwrapped his sub sandwich and enjoyed a leisurely lunch. Fresh snow drifted down, big fat snowflakes hitting the window and melting as they slid to the bottom of the framed view. He would miss this part of the country. And the people. But as much as Joe and Abigail felt like family, they weren't his. He longed for the embrace of his own.

Someday, he would bring his family here for a vacation. Joy ignited his heart as he thought about it. For the first time in a long while, he looked forward to spending time with his family. Fully present for whatever the future held. Taking a sip of his soda, he tapped the weather icon on his phone. Scrolling through the forecast, he realized there was a deadline on this trip. A front was forecast for next week. He wanted to get ahead of that. He figured maybe two more days before he headed back.

He checked his watch. It had been forty-five minutes since Jennifer and her husband had gone up to Joe's room. He tossed his trash in the can, then went back through the line and got Joe and Abigail's food. His phone rang while he waited on the elevator. Haley's name showed up on the screen as the elevator door slid open. He stuck the phone back in his pocket, planning to call back when he could focus. Before he reached the door to Joe's room, his phone rang again. It was Dad this time. He let it go to voicemail and stepped into the room. Jennifer sat on the edge of the bed holding Joe's hand. Abigail stood next to her, arm draped over her shoulder, tissues in hand.

Joe waved him over. "I understand we have you to thank for this?" He pointed at their daughter and her husband. Tears rimmed his eyes.

Albert shrugged. "Once I put two and two together, I didn't think there was anything else I could do but call them."

Joe reached for Albert's hand and squeezed.

Abigail walked around the bed and gave Albert a hug. "How can we ever thank you?"

"I'm just thankful I came this way and that I stopped at that diner and met your kids. It seems that God had a plan all along."

"He always does." Abigail returned to her spot next to Jennifer and gave her daughter a

hug. "Did she tell you the boys are coming tomorrow?"

"I'm looking forward to meeting them." Albert's phone rang again, and he glanced at the screen. Elinor. *Why is everyone calling me? Are the kids okay?* "Excuse me." He walked to the other side of the room and swiped the answer button. "What's up?"

"Finally."

"What's up? Are my kids—"

"It's not your kids. It's Blake."

"What happened?" Albert glanced at Joe and Abigail who watched him with concern.

"There was a fight at the prison and...Blake was killed."

"What?" Confusion coursed through Albert's body.

"That's all we know right now. Can you head home? We need the family together."

"Yeah. Of course. Tell Haley I'll call her later tonight." Albert disconnected the call and looked up at his friend in the hospital bed. "My brother, the one in prison, was killed in a fight."

"Time for you to head home, son." Joe pointed a finger at Albert.

He nodded. "What about the stock?"

Joe's son, Bill, stood up. "Show me what to do. I can handle that part."

Jennifer joined her husband. "My brothers will be here tomorrow. They'll help, too."

Abigail came over and put an arm around Albert's waist. "But you have to promise us something."

"Anything for you." Albert put his arm around Abigail's shoulders.

"Bring your family and stay awhile. You know you always have a cabin waiting for you."

Albert gave her a hug. "I'll plan on it." Hoping to get on the road before first light in the morning, he said his last goodbyes and headed out with Bill to the ranch.

CHAPTER FORTY-FOUR

Albert

Albert pulled up to the church as the sun dipped below the horizon. He checked his watch. Blake's memorial was supposed to start in an hour. Not enough time to go to the house first. He texted Haley to let her know he was here.

He got out of the car and walked around the parking lot to stretch his legs. The drive had been long from Colorado, with him stopping only for fill-ups and short rest stops. He was glad to be home. Just wished it weren't filled with grief.

Gravel crunched as Albert's dad pulled into the parking lot. Waving, he got out of his car. Albert nodded.

Charles walked toward his son. "How was your retreat?"

"Good. Very good."

"Glad to hear." Charles stuffed his hands in his pockets and nodded toward the church. "Never expected this."

"Yeah." Albert leaned against his dad's pickup. "Ever find out what happened?"

"They're still investigating. It was hard enough seeing him go to prison. Now..." He looked toward the sunset. "How do we do this?" He removed his hat, ran a hand through his hair, and plopped the hat back on. "I know what to say at a memorial when the life has been well lived, but not for this." He shrugged.

"Talk about your heart for Blake. How much you loved him. The changes you made to reach his heart. People need to hear about that kind of grace."

As he spoke, Albert felt a spark of joy ignite in his heart. His dad had done that for all his kids. For him. He let out a pent-up breath. "Dad?"

Charles looked Albert in the eye.

"It means a lot. What you've done to bring our family together and to see healing occur in each of our lives. The effort you've made to make amends. And I need to tell you that I forgive you."

Charles pulled his son into a hug. "Thank you, son."

Albert stepped back from his dad's embrace. "And for what it's worth, I believe, given time, Blake would have, too."

Charles looked toward the sky and silence enveloped them for a moment. "I would like to believe that, too. But it's hard after everything I put him through." He brought his gaze back to Albert's.

"Then hope. Perhaps in his last moments, he did."

Charles nodded. "I'll try." He glanced over his shoulder at the sound of cars pulling into the parking lot. "I'm going on in. Collect myself a bit."

"See you inside."

"Daddy." A duet of voices called from across the parking lot.

Albert grinned and walked toward his family. Annie ran toward him and jumped up in his arms, wrapping her arms around his neck. Charlie slammed into him with a hug around his waist. How could they show him such love after the way he had treated them?

"I have missed you guys so much." He kissed Annie on the cheek and set her down, tussled Charlie's hair, then walked over to Haley and pulled her into his arms. "And you, my lady..." He bent his head and kissed his wife like he hadn't in who knew how long. Like thirsty ground drenched in rain, his soul swelled with satisfaction. He was home.

"Ew." Charlie and Annie giggled.

Albert kissed their mother again.

"Albert." Haley whispered in his ear. "Maybe we should save this for later?"

He glanced over her shoulder and saw church members looking their way. "I guess we are drawing attention."

Her face turned red, and he laughed.

"It's good to hear that laugh. So good." She wrapped her arms around him and leaned against his chest.

"It feels good to laugh." He motioned for the kids to come close and pulled them into a family hug. "I'm sorry for the past...too long. Will you forgive me?" The hug tightened around him in response. The days ahead promised to be good. He released his family. "I guess we better go in. Huh?"

Albert held on to Haley's and Charlie's hands. Annie grabbed her mother's hand and they walked into the building as a family. In the foyer, a table had been set up with pictures of Blake. A larger one of him in uniform stood in the right back corner. Framed family photos on easels sat across the back. A photo album lay open in the middle. Albert flipped through the pages, remembering the good times jumbled in with a hurtful past. If not for the grace of God, where would they be now? Blinking back the tears, Albert followed his family into the sanctuary and found seats next to Alita, at the front behind others in the family.

Karen got up from where she sat with Barry on one side, Elinor and James on the other, and gave Albert a hug. "Glad you made it back."

"It was time."

"I still can't believe it. Elinor and Joanna saw Blake on Monday. We got the news on Tuesday."

"Dad said they're still investigating what happened."

"We thought about delaying the memorial till we knew more, but they said it could be a while. We thought it better to go ahead."

"Makes sense. There's Joanna and Alexis. I want to say hello before we start." He made his way to where Joanna and her new family sat.

Joanna's eyes lit up when she saw him, and she met him halfway. "You made it."

He drew her into a hug. "As did you."

She stepped back and nodded. "I did at that." She tilted her head toward her family and grinned. "My bright spot in all this."

He gave them a nod. "I'll meet your family later." He gave her another hug before they each returned to their seats. The past few years had certainly brought along a lot of changes to his family. Good ones he never expected. Forgiveness and healing permeating their family now instead of pain and regret. If only Blake had reached that place. Albert bowed his head and fought back the tears of regret that attempted to swallow him. Regardless of what Blake chose, Albert knew what his choice was. Hope, healing, and joy.

He lifted his head and listened as a longtime friend of his dad and pastor of a church in Kansas City spoke to the audience.

A quick look around told Albert that his family had a lot of support. Most of these were from his church. They knew his family's story, and despite their feelings toward Blake, chose to be here for them. Albert fought back the emotions fighting for control inside of him. How had he ever slipped into the place of despair he'd found himself in lately? He thought of Joe and Abigail and smiled at the reminder of God's grace, then turned his full attention to the memorial service.

The congregation sang two songs after a word of encouragement and hope from the interim pastor, then time was given over to the family to share. Alita shared a favorite memory of Blake and her hopes that while in prison, he had changed. She thanked everyone for coming, then his dad approached the podium, pausing before he spoke.

"I'm not sure what to say. I'm so sorry. I love Blake." Tears fell unhindered down his face. "I love him so much." Shoulders hunched, he wept.

Karen got up from her pew and went to him. Joanna followed close behind. They put their arms around the man who raised them with such turmoil. Elinor, Albert, and Alita got out of their seats and joined Karen and Joanna encircling their father, now forgiven.

The service gave over to the family's grief as the pastor offered a prayer. He invited the guests to the fellowship hall, where the family would join them for visitation. Silence descended on the family as the auditorium emptied and the sound of sorrow echoed around them.

"Remember when Blake brought home his first motorcycle?" Karen broke the silence.

One by one, snickers dared to stand in solidarity with her audacity to bring such a memory up at this time.

"As I remember, it never made it out of the garage." Joanna laughed.

Charles' laugh rose above the rest. "I remember how he used to pester all you kids."

Elinor huffed. "Wasn't so funny at the time."

Looking at Elinor, Joanna stepped back, breaking the tight circle around Charles. "I remember once he told you if you ran around the house five times, there would be two cows following you. You were off like the flash."

"Yep." Albert laughed. "You wanted me to run, too."

"I can't believe I was so gullible." Elinor shook her head.

After the laughter settled, quiet returned. Albert looked around at each of his siblings. "This is good. I like remembering that there were good times."

The others nodded in agreement.

"I guess we better go meet with the guests." Karen picked up her purse.

As they walked toward the back of the auditorium, a woman walked through the door and stopped. Her hair hung in long braids to the middle of her back. Her dark skin appeared light against the black of her clothes. In her hands, she held a small box. "Are you Blake's family?"

Karen nodded. "Did you come for the memorial?"

"Yes. No. I mean, I came here to see the family. I assume that's you?" She looked at those gathered around her.

Karen nodded. "And you are...?" Karen stepped closer to the woman.

"Melody. I need to give you something." She gave the box she held to Karen. "From my husband."

"Who is your husband?" Albert moved between the women. He wondered if this was payback for something Blake perpetuated.

"Steve. But they call him Preacher Man in prison." Melody smiled.

"Blake mentioned a preacher man when we were there earlier this week." Joanna tapped her fingernails against the pew.

"That would be my husband."

"Barry met a man named Steve when he was in jail in New York City. Gave him a Bible."

"That would be my husband." Melody grinned. "He's a believer because while he was in jail in New York City, someone he referred to as preacher man gave him a Bible. Steve was mighty pleased when fellow inmates landed that title on him." Melody's pride in her husband came through her voice. "He passed that Bible on to another inmate."

"Barry."

Melody nodded. "Steve and Blake figured out the connection 'cause Blake had the very Bible Steve gave to Barry."

"Barry said that if it weren't for that Bible, he might not ever have changed."

Elinor joined the huddle around Karen, now opening the box to reveal a small Bible.

Karen flipped the Bible open to the front. "This is the one." She flipped through the pages marked up with underlining and notes. "I don't understand."

"They didn't call my man Preacher to make fun of him. Everyone respected him because he lived what he talked. He and Blake have been studying the Bible together for a while."

"That's hard to believe." Joanna clamped a hand over her mouth and mumbled an apology.

Melody laughed. "Oh, girl, the truth sets people free even if they're in prison. Sometimes especially then, 'cause they can't run away from it so easy."

"You guys coming?" Barry walked in on the group, chatting and motioned for them to come.

"Barry, this is Melody, Steve's wife. The man who gave you that Bible when you were in jail." Karen stood up, clutching the Bible to her chest.

Barry looked at Melody, then back at Karen, who nodded, then he walked over and enveloped Melody in a hug. "I owe so much to your husband. Where is he now?"

"In the same prison Blake was in." She grinned when he looked at her with eyes wide open in apparent disbelief.

"No way."

Melody nodded and relayed what she had already told the rest of the family.

"So..."

"The night before the fight, Blake told Steve that he was ready to let God be in control of things."

Charles whooped. "Thank You, Jesus."

"And my husband wanted to be sure that you knew Blake died defending someone else."

"He had it in him." Charles nodded. "It just got lost."

"Thank you for bringing this to us." Karen handed the Bible to Alita. "You should have this."

Alita nodded and took the Bible before they all exited and went to greet the others who had come to comfort them in their grief, though joy now filled their hearts.

CHAPTER FORTY-FIVE

Elinor

Elinor watched James move through the kitchen, distracted. He barely saw her, much less talked to her. Although he supported her the last week, finding out about Blake and then his memorial service, for the most part, he had remained distant since the RJB Investments retreat. Polite, kind even, but not present with her. Today was more than simple distance. Did he somehow find out what she needed to tell him herself? She shuddered at the thought.

She touched James's arm as he passed her. "Can you grab the pan of potatoes and take them out to the dining room?"

"In a minute." He walked away from her touch and went to the storage room.

His sharp tone bit into Elinor's heart. Tears stung her eyes. Looking down, she busied herself with the task in front of her. Joanna reached across the counter and placed her hand on top of Elinor's. She glanced up and shrugged.

"Praying for you," Joanna mouthed underneath the radar of anyone's hearing.

Elinor returned to cutting up the vegies in front of her. The kitchen phone rang, and she went to pick it up, but James came out of the storage room and answered it. His expression grew stormy as he talked. Concerned there might be a problem with the upcoming week, she waited till James hung up.

"Something wrong?"

Looking at her, he narrowed his eyes. "It was Remí. Did you want to talk to him?"

The sharpness of his tone drove her a step back, hand at her throat. "What? How could I know that it was Remí? And why would I want to talk to him?"

He looked up at the ceiling then back at his wife. A struggle played out across his features and Elinor was uncertain what might win.

She put a hand on his arm. "I thought maybe there was a problem with one of our guests this week."

"Remí wants to come by before he returns to France. He's interested in his company using our conference facilities again in the future."

"I'm glad there wasn't a problem." She turned to gain as much distance as possible from this conversation that felt on the verge of exploding.

"I didn't say there wasn't a problem."

Elinor's emotions felt whiplashed. "Is it something I need to take care of?"

"You tell me."

"How should I know?" She glanced over her shoulder at the door to the dining room where her family gathered. "Can we talk about this later?"

"Sure. What's another delay?" James stalked to the stove and pulled out the chaffing pan of potatoes and headed into the dining room.

Elinor slumped against the wall. This was so unlike the James she had married. She wanted to pretend it would all go away without her doing anything, but it was time to act. She made a commitment to herself, her sisters, and to God to tell James everything. Tonight. *If*

I have to hogtie him and kidnap him. I will. Everything else would wait. *Help me. Please. I don't want to lose my husband.*

By the time Elinor joined the family in the dining room, the meal was underway; only a few still needed to fill their plate at the buffet. James watched her from where he sat between her dad and Albert. She offered a small smile. He looked down at his plate and resumed eating.

All her life, she only showed the better parts of herself, always protecting who she was inside. Until she shared with her sisters, she hadn't told her secret to anyone. And tonight, she planned to tell James. How would he respond? Would he turn his back on her like he had his long-ago girlfriend who had an abortion? She picked up her plate and mindlessly filled it with food, then found a seat next to Karen and tried to make sense of the conversation around her.

"...he told me he was being tried back in the Midwest, but I never even thought Steve might be around here." Barry scooted his plate toward the center of the table. "Nothing surprises God."

"What do you mean?" James looked across the table at Barry.

"He prepared the way for Blake to hear the truth. To find peace. All the way back in New York, he was thinking of Blake. Steve, the Bible, Blake in the same prison halfway across the country? God doesn't waste any difficulty in our life if we give it to Him."

"Hmm." James stabbed a bite of chicken and dragged it around in the sauce. "Some things seem too hard to give to Him."

Elinor kept her gaze aimed at the plate. Was he talking about them? She waited to see how the others might answer his sentiment.

"If Karen hadn't given our difficulties over to God, she never would have given me a chance to change. She never would have forgiven me. I hate to imagine where I might be now."

Hope stirred in Elinor. Would James give her a chance? She dared a glance his way. He stared at her with a look she had never seen before. There was an edge to his expression that hinted at anger. Tears stung the edge of her eyes, and she glanced down.

"Giving things over to God is so worth it." Karen squeezed Elinor's hand underneath the table.

Lord, open James's heart to forgive me.

"I know we're not a drinking family, but I want to offer a water toast." Everyone around the table laughed at Albert's announcement. "Thank you, Dad, for all you've done to bring healing to this family."

A chorus of "thank you" filled the room. Charles sat tall, visibly emotional as a stray tear or two made an appearance. He nodded and pointed heavenward.

"It's all God." Setting his glass down after taking a drink, he turned to Alita sitting on his left. "How are you doing?"

She looked at each member of the family. "I spent last night looking through Blake's Bible, all the notes he made. He was serious about changing. I am so thankful for Steve. I am so thankful."

Everyone nodded in agreement and sat in silence for a moment until the crashing of a plate broke the interlude.

"I sorry." Hope stood next to the buffet, the plate of cookies broken and scattered at her feet. Tears trickled from her eyes.

Karen began gathering the large chunks of broken plate and cookies lying on the floor and Barry scooped up their daughter in his arms and wiped her tears. "Accidents happen. Let's find you another sweet."

"Otay Dadda."

The two of them headed toward the kitchen. James got up from the table and followed. Elinor watched them go, hoping James was in pursuit of a bit of wisdom.

"Albert, what's up with you, man? Too much going on last night to fill us in on your trip." Alexis leaned back in his chair and Hannah climbed into his lap.

Albert pushed back from the table and picked up his coffee mug. "For the first time in my life, I had plenty of time for thinking and resting. It was wonderful." He took a drink of his coffee and set the mug on the table. "I realized that over the years I've been so busy taking care of everyone else that I never took care of my own relationship with God. I preached forgiveness to everyone else, but somewhere along the way, I failed to forgive. I didn't realize the bitterness that was stewing in my heart. And that led to the depression. Until I got away from all the distractions of taking care of everyone else, I was too busy to hear God." He nodded at Charles. "Forgiveness is the biggest victory during my retreat. That paved the way for everything else."

"Daddy said we get to go back to Colorado for a vacation." Annie wrapped her arms around Albert's neck.

"And stay at the ranch in a cabin and take care of the horses and go on hikes." Charlie pumped a fist in the air.

Albert laughed and tussled his son's hair. "Absolutely."

"And I got the love of my life back." Haley gave Albert a kiss on the cheek.

"Are you going back to your pastor job?" Joanna got up from her chair and went to the dessert table.

"We're still talking about it. The board wants a decision in January." He kissed the top of his wife's head. "We'll let you know once we decide something. I do need your prayers, though."

"What's up son?"

"It takes work to overcome depression. I hope and pray I can get off meds in the future.

But regardless, there will be counseling in addition and retraining my thinking. So, prayers are appreciated."

"Absolutely, man." Alexis put a hand on his shoulder. "You can count on us."

Everyone around the table nodded.

Elinor watched the exchange amongst her family. Even two years ago, you couldn't have convinced her they would be sitting around the family table sharing like this. She longed for the ease of openness they all seemed to now have. *Lord, help me.* A quiet peace settled in her heart as she pushed back from the table. No more delays.

James wasn't in the kitchen. She peeked out on the patio. Not there. Maybe he was in their apartment. Heading down the hall, she heard voices coming from the library. She paused. Barry was talking. Now James. She stopped at the sound of her husband's voice rising.

"I don't know if I can."

"Maybe you misunderstood what they were talking about."

Silence. Elinor drew her lower lip between her teeth, not daring to move. Finally, her husband responded.

"I don't think so. I heard them talking about their child."

Elinor gasped. He heard that part of her conversation with Remí? She stepped backward. Blake's death had drawn James back to her briefly, but now he seemed more distant than ever. She turned and fled to their apartment. She needed to get her emotions in check before she shared her side of the story.

She ran through the living room of her apartment to the bedroom and closed the door behind her. Falling to her knees, she cried out to God. *Lord, give me courage to say what needs to be said to the man I love. I've hurt him badly. God, forgive me. I'm so tired of carrying all this. I'm tired of hiding and pretending.* She collapsed on her bed and allowed the tears to come.

CHAPTER FORTY-SIX

Albert

"Got the carrot?" Albert held out his gloved hand.

Annie slapped a carrot in his hand and giggled.

He stood directly in front of the snowman, examining the lopsided head. Where to put it? He stuck the fat end of the carrot into what appeared to be the middle of the ball of snow. Charlie let out a belly laugh. Annie giggled.

"Turn and smile for the camera." Haley directed from behind them.

Albert looked at his kids. "On three, turn and make your silliest face."

The kids nodded in agreement.

"One, two, three."

They turned and instead of a camera pointed their way, snowballs flew at them. One hit Albert square on the forehead.

"I'm going to get your mother." Albert chased Haley around the yard till he tackled her, and they fell to the ground laughing. The kids ran over and scooped snow on top of him.

"Hey, no fair. Three against one?" He struggled to his feet and bent over with his hands resting on his knees. He laughed until it turned into a belly laugh he couldn't stop. Sitting down in the snow, he rested his arms on his knees. "Anyone game for hot chocolate?"

"And s'mores?" Annie and Charlie pleaded together with hands clasped under their chins.

"Absolutely."

"Race you to the house." Haley scrambled to her feet, grabbed Albert's hand, and held him back when the kids took off. "Let's enjoy the walk."

"Sounds good to me." He tucked her hand under his arm and began the stroll back to the house. "Now that we have a minute to ourselves..."

"Finally." Haley laughed a gentle windchime-worthy laugh.

"Have I told you lately how much I enjoy your laugh?"

She shook her head.

He leaned over and kissed the top of her head. "I want more days like this."

"That would be nice. What are you thinking?"

"Other than a Colorado vacation? I don't want to be a pastor."

"Are you sure?"

"It's not like I would stop pastoring. It's what I do. I help people. But I'm ready to do it out from behind a pulpit."

Haley looked out across the countryside.

Albert turned Haley toward him. "What's going on?"

She shrugged. "It's a relief. I don't want to go back to the way things were and I guess I was a bit concerned that if you went back to pastoring, the same issues would be at your heels again."

"Is there something else?"

"What's it going to look like? I mean we've made it these past few months because the board kept paying your salary during the sabbatical, but we have to earn a living."

"We're going to be fine." He pulled her into his arms and rested his chin on the top of her head. "What do you think about apples?"

"What?" She pulled back to look at him.

"Dad's orchard manager left last year, and he's been doing the work since then. But he's ready to turn it all over. Not just managing it. He wants to deed it to us."

Haley's eyes opened wide. "Wow."

Albert laughed. "Exactly."

"Do you want to do that?"

"I think so. But I want to talk to Dad about it more and I want you to be sure, too, before we decide."

She tucked her hand into the bend of his elbow as they resumed walking. "I don't have to think too hard. I'm so thankful to have you back and I don't want that to change. If running an orchard will accomplish that, I'm all for it."

"Let's keep it under our hats for now."

"That's a good—"

Snowballs splatted against their coats. Laughter rang out from behind the bushes as another round of ammunition was launched their direction. Albert and Haley ducked. Springing into action, they ran for cover and went to work making snowballs.

"You don't know what you just got yourself into." Albert called across the open space.

Laughter answered their challenge along with another volley of snowballs.

"I think they have help." Haley laughed as she chucked another snowball toward their opponents.

"I need a distraction. I'm going in." He scooped up an armload of snowballs.

Haley nodded and ran out into the open, taunting the kids. An adult head popped up over the top of the hedge. James. Now this was new. Staunch British properness put in its place. Haley laughed and ducked behind her cover and waited, tossing the occasional snowball. Within a few tosses, Albert confirmed his success.

"Ahh..." was followed by the crunching of snow as James fled from cover with hands waving in the air. "I surrender."

"That was fun, Uncle James. Let's get hot chocolate." They each grabbed one of his hands and began dragging him toward the house.

"Hold up, there. I came over to talk to your dad."

Charlie and Annie hung their heads.

"How about I stick around after that?"

"Yay!" The kids grabbed Haley's hands and ran for the house. "We'll get it ready. S'mores, too."

Albert watched his family run for the house. "What's up?" He glanced toward James.

"It's Elinor."

"Let's walk." Albert led the way around the back of the house toward the path he had cleared for Haley to walk on her trail. "Tell me what's going on."

"I don't know. Barry said I needed to get more facts, but Elinor isn't talking."

"I'm lost."

"Remember the retreat we had? I overheard Elinor talking to the guy who owns the company. It sounded like they knew each other. Extremely well."

"How well?"

"He asked her about their child."

"Oh. That's got to raise a few questions. For the record, I have no clue what that's about. Have you talked to her?"

James shuffled his boots in the snow, kicking up small piles. "I haven't had time. Between the retreat, then Blake..."

"You can't let things get in the way of talking to her."

"The other day, the guy called to set up an appointment to discuss future use of the bed and breakfast. The way she reacted..." He rubbed his eyes. "I did ask her about it, but she just put me off. Then later, I found her in the apartment crying. I've never seen her cry like that. I can't help but think she was crying over that man."

"These are all assumptions. You need to talk to her. And listen. Really listen."

"I know you're right. It's hard...I love her so much."

Albert placed a hand on James's shoulder. "She deserves to be heard."

James nodded. "I'll talk to her. There's a full house the rest of this week at the bed and breakfast. There won't be the space or time for an uninterrupted talk. After the guests are all checked out, I'll do it."

"I'm going to hold you to it."

"Thanks. I need it." James made a U-turn on the path. "Better get back for treats before

the kids come hunting for us."

CHAPTER
FORTY-SEVEN

Elinor

E linor kicked off her shoes as soon as she walked into her apartment. She needed to stop wearing heels when the days were as long as today. She hadn't stopped since breakfast. This past week was a bear, too. Full house all through the week as well as a conference on Saturday. It was busier than the RJB retreat.

James had remained tense the entire time. She attempted to create time for them to talk. For her to confess what happened all those years ago. But they were constantly interrupted. They only spoke when they needed to exchange information about the guests. At night, he came to bed after her and left before she woke.

She walked to the window to look out at the moonlit snow. The weatherman promised it would be white from now through Christmas. Perfect for a couple in love to curl up in front of the fireplace together and hide from the world. *God, help us make the time. He can't go on believing the worst.*

A muffled thump came from the bedroom. "James?" Elinor headed toward their room. She opened the door and her eyes fell on her photo album opened on the bed. She dropped her hand from the doorknob. James stood with his back to her, looking out the window. She crossed to the bed and glanced down at the open page. Her and Remí touring France. At the vineyards, at his place. It was obvious they were together. And then the one she had a stranger take before she told Remí about the baby, her hand lay protectively over her stomach. Tears stung the back of her eyelids. *Oh, God, don't let me be too late.*

She joined him at the window and touched his arm. "James?"

He shrugged off her touch and walked away, not looking at her.

"Can we talk?" She took a step to follow him.

He paused at the door. "Why? You've been happy keeping your secret for this long. Aren't you afraid I'll ruin your little tryst?"

She stepped back as though he had slapped her. "What are you talking about?"

He pointed at the photo album. "You can't deny the evidence."

Her emotions reeled under his angry scrutiny. "That wasn't—"

"Wasn't what? I watched how he looked at you. I felt your response when he was nearby. You avoided him at all cost. And why? Unless you had something to hide."

"But..."

He shook his head. "How can I trust anything you would say right now?"

Her breathing quickened. She caught a strand of her hair and tugged. "Please...I love you."

"Feels like just words coming from your lips."

Elinor recoiled. She had never seen him get this angry before. Was she on a short list for him to shake off like so much dust on his coattails? He'd shared his past and expected her to move past it. Where was that same grace for her? "It was a long time ago."

He held her gaze. "Was it? I heard you and Remí talk." He turned away.

She sucked in a breath. "Did you hear everything?"

"I heard enough."

"Evidently not."

He turned back to glare at her. "What about his child? You told me you can't have children and yet you did."

She hung her head. *It's too late.* He would hate her for ending the life of her child.

"That's what I thought. Another lie." He walked out into their living room.

"But—"

"I don't know if I can do this anymore." He stopped at their front door.

"Please don't leave like this."

He glanced over his shoulder with a look she couldn't fathom and then he was gone.

She wanted to chase after him, but fear held her back from revealing her heart. There was a part of her that believed that under the right circumstances—if he saw her for who she was—he would leave in a heartbeat. But he was leaving already. *I have to stop him. Lord, help me.*

Barefoot, she ran after him, heedless of the glances of strangers, employees, and family. The screen door banged against the porch wall as she ran outside. Her eyes met James's gaze and held as he backed out of his parking space. And then he looked away as he sped down the drive, his tires spitting gravel behind him.

"James...don't leave." Numb, she sank down on the steps and wrapped her arms around herself. She thought she had been devastated when Remí left all those years ago, but that was nothing compared to what she felt now. *God, what am I going to do?*

"Elinor?" Alexis came up behind her. "Did something happen? Do you want me to call your sisters?"

She shook her head. "I'll be fine." Ducking her head, she hurried back to their apartment. *What if James doesn't come back?* She sank onto the carpet and leaned against the front of the couch. Tears ran unchecked. Curling herself into a ball, she slid to the floor and allowed all the pent-up sorrow to weep out of her. Years of regret and shame bombarded her. The double life growing up, the affair with

Remí, the abortion, the secret she'd kept hidden from everyone all these years. For the first time in her life, she knew what it meant to be loved, and her secret was going to ruin it all.

As the sobs eased, sleep pulled her into its warm embrace until the dreams taunted her with images of a child - a younger version of Remí - running through a vineyard. She called to him as he ran away from her. As she chased him, the vineyard faded and instead of pursuing a child, she was searching for James. Each time she drew near, he faded. Her breathing raced as she fought the panic. Reaching out for him, her hand closed around empty air. She had to find him to tell him the truth. She turned as someone called her name. Who was looking for her? Remí stepped out from behind a tree. She gasped and fell back against a tree, long hair tangling in its branches. She couldn't get free.

"Help me." She struggled against the branches that refused to let go.

"Elinor."

"James? You came back?" She peered into the shadows but saw only the dim shape of someone just out of reach.

"Elinor. It's me, Joanna."

Shaking her head against the invading reality, Elinor opened her eyes. Darkness stretched across the floor, a near full moon the only light. She struggled to remember why she was on the floor with her sister beside her. She sat up and looked around the room. "Where's James? I need to find him before he leaves."

Joanna sat next to her. "I heard you cry out from in the hallway. "Want to talk?"

"I ruined it. I threw it all away."

"You told James?"

Elinor shook her head. "I waited too long. He found out on his own. Not the whole story.

Just enough..." Sobs broke out of her soul, and she leaned against Joanna. "I messed up. Bad. I should have told him sooner. Life just kept interrupting."

"That man loves you like crazy. He'll be back."

"If only that were true." Elinor shrugged.

"Oh, Elinor. It is. He's a good man."

"He doesn't trust me or anything I tell him. He said so."

"Hmm. Give it time. He'll come around."

"I hope you're right. James deserves to hear the whole story."

"Trust God with this. He's all about healing hearts and relationships."

Elinor leaned against her sister and closed her eyes. "Do you have to go?"

"I can stay a while."

"Thanks."

"You got it. Let me just text Alexis so he doesn't worry, then I'll make tea."

CHAPTER FORTY-EIGHT

Elinor

James never came home last night. Joanna stayed till dawn. A pot of tea, a long sister conversation about messing up, starting over, and the grace of God, along with a viewing of *The Princess Bride* built a will in Elinor to get James to sit down and listen to the whole story. But in the silence of the apartment after Joanna left, Elinor grew restless. She needed to get this over with soon, but how could she make sure that James would listen?

Pacing the floor, she considered her options. "Drats. I can't wrap my mind around what I should do." A drive usually helped her clear her head. A glance outside the window confirmed the weatherman was accurate—plenty of snow, but the fall was slow and gentle, the snowplows likely able to keep up. Shouldn't be any problem to go on a drive in the country with her snow tires. The snow created a more peaceful atmosphere, anyway.

She dressed warmly in layers with long johns and wool socks underneath to keep her warm. She would call their apartment phone from the car and leave a message, letting James know she would be back and that she wanted to talk. Hopefully by then, he would be willing to listen. On impulse, she grabbed an overnight bag and stuffed it with a change of clothes, toiletries, a book, and her journal. In this weather, you never knew. She might have to stop somewhere for the night.

On the way out to her car, she stopped by the kitchen. Thankful to find it empty of family members, she filled up a travel mug with hot chocolate, sneaked an egg sandwich ready for the guest breakfast buffet, and headed outside. After putting her things in the car, she started the engine and grabbed the snow brush to clear the window. By the time she finished her task, the car was blowing mildly warm air out of the vents. *Good enough.* After climbing in, she stuck in a Piano Guys CD and pulled out for her head-clearing drive in the snow-covered countryside. Peace filled her heart as she wound her way along the roads. Today, with God as her help, all would be told.

Elinor decided to head back home after about an hour of mindless driving. She glanced at the gas level, she pulled into a Pay and Pump gas station to top off the tank first. Hopping out, she looked at the sign directly above the digital screen. Pay inside? She groaned and headed in.

A young man with a cap pulled down over his ears sat at the register. He looked up in surprise. "Didn't expect anyone out in this weather."

"It's not that bad. You just need to be careful."

"I take it you haven't been listening to the weather reports?" The young man turned and pointed a remote toward the TV hanging in the corner.

The image of a weatherman and a map filled the screen. "Time to hunker down, folks. These roads are going to be piled high in no time. This storm has a history of a large dump. Don't go far from home and be sure you have emergency supplies in your car in case you get stuck."

A sinking feeling overtook Elinor as she realized she'd never left that message for James. He would worry. She pulled out her phone, then paused as she realized that hope had tiptoed into her heart and a song of joy had begun its serenade. As sure as she was that James would worry, she was sure that he still loved her and that he would come around and listen. *Thank You, Lord*. She smiled as she tapped the icon for her husband. There was a future for them. Skip the apartment phone. She wanted to hear his voice.

"Ma'am?"

She held up her hand, indicating he should wait.

"Our wireless is out."

The sinking feeling returned in full force as she looked at the young man. "Do you have a landline?"

He pointed to a phone on the wall. She picked up the receiver. No dial tone. She set the receiver in the cradle. What was she going to do? She never should have taken off in the snow without telling someone. "Is there a nearby hotel?"

He shook his head.

She walked to the door and looked out. Already, the snow had grown more intense. There was no way she could make it home now. A blast of cold air ushered someone else into the building.

"Son, you ready to head home?"

Elinor turned and met the woman's gaze. She had the kindest eyes she could ever remember seeing.

"Lord, have mercy. What are you doing out here in this weather? Never mind. Ain't nowhere else to go. You're coming home with us. Now don't you worry none, we're not weird or anything. God loving folk. You can ask our occasional pastor. Nothing personal, just distance and this place." A wave of her hand indicated the convenience store. "Our home is small, but warm and full of good food and company. Nothing else for…"

"Mom…" The young man spoke in a whine.

"Oh, son. Never mind my chatter. Haven't you learned yet, there's nothing you can do about it at this stage." Her laughter invited Elinor to enjoy the moment. "We live just out back. You can pull your car to the side of the building then walk on over." She pointed out the door to a house situated at the end of the parking lot. "What you think? Do you dare brave staying with strangers? By the way, name is Nancy. Son here is John." He gave a quick nod as she rattled on. "What's yours?"

"Elinor. And yes, I would like to take you up on your offer." Staying in the car was not an option. *Lord, keep me safe.*

"Good." The woman's eyes twinkled. "Lock up, son. We're having company."

He gave his mom a mock salute, but his warmth and love toward her was obvious as he walked around the counter and locked the front door, turning the sign to "closed."

Elinor followed Nancy to the side door, then hurried through the blowing snow to her car and pulled it to the side of the building. Fortunately, on the side away from the drifts. She grabbed her overnight bag from the back seat and joined her hostess in their trudge across the parking lot.

The wind caught the door and slammed it against the side of the house as they attempted to go inside. Blowing snow followed them into the warmth of the house and quickly melted on the floor around them. Elinor kicked off her boots and hung her coat next to Nancy's, then followed her into a smallish family room with a roaring fireplace throwing off the chill that followed them from the outdoors.

"Have a seat. I'll get coffee to warm you up. It doesn't take long to get chilled to the bone with that wind."

Elinor sat down and pulled out her phone. No bars. "Nancy, do you have a landline in the house?"

She shook her head as she sat a mug of coffee on the side table next to Elinor. "It's been out since morning. The wind always knocks it out. Need to get ahold of someone?"

Elinor nodded. "My husband. I think I'll try and leave a message with roaming on. Maybe it will get through."

"You go ahead. I'll dish up the soup. Sound good?"

Elinor nodded and clicked on the icon for James. "James, I hope this gets through. I'm safe. I stopped at a Pay and Pump gas station on route 9 a bit west of 159. It's about an hour from home. A kind woman took me in when it became apparent that I couldn't make it home. Don't worry. I'll call as soon as there's a connection." She added the woman's phone number to the message then left her phone on in case service was restored and set it on the side table.

Nancy handed Elinor a mug of soup. "What were you doing out on a day like this all by yourself?"

"Long story."

Nancy pointed out the window. "Looks like we've got a while."

"Just a misunderstanding."

"Had plenty of those while my husband was still around."

"Mom, I'm back." The door slammed shut as Nancy's son entered the house. "When's supper?"

"That boy is always hungry." She chuckled. "Food is in the crockpot, son. Help yourself."

"Thanks. Then I'll be headed out to my studio. Unless you need something?" He poked his head around the corner.

"We'll be fine, John. Thanks for asking." Nancy faced Elinor. "He's a good son. So thoughtful. Studying art. Has his own studio over the garage. I was surprised he made it home for Christmas. I think he has a girlfriend, just hasn't got up the nerve to tell me."

"Are you talking about me, Mom?"

Nancy laughed. "Smart as a whip too. Nothing for you to worry about, son." She settled into her chair with a deep sigh. "This is nice. The company of another female and plenty of time to chat."

CHAPTER FORTY-NINE

Albert

Albert pulled around back of the bed and breakfast around midmorning and climbed out of his car. The snow was getting heavier, and the forecast predicted a heavy dump before the day was done. Where would Elinor go in this weather?

James had shown up at his place last night and, uncharacteristic for James, he had rehearsed his entire fight with Elinor. Then, he went through the list of all the reasons he was right. All the reasons Elinor didn't deserve another chance. Albert listened, and it soon turned into all the reasons James loved Elinor. He knew Albert had been right and he had messed up by making assumptions and accusations and needed to make it right. Albert hadn't said a word. He wondered at the mysteries of how God worked. But now there was a mystery they needed to solve. *Lord, help us find Elinor. Keep her safe in this weather.*

James had stayed at Albert's last night to cool off and make sure he approached Elinor with the right attitude, and was looking forward to that talk this morning. But when he got home around breakfast time and found her absent, he called Albert.

"Any word yet?" Albert waved at James coming down the steps.

He shook his head. "No message and I can't get through to her phone. I'm about to go crazy. The weather is getting worse by the minute. What if her car broke down? What if...what if I don't get the chance to make it right?" I have no idea where she is, and she thinks I'm done with her." He shivered and crossed his arms. "How could I be so careless with my words?"

"Don't go there." Albert placed a hand on his shoulder. "Listen, I have an idea. Charlie's idea actually. Do you both have a Find My Friend app on your phone? Don't know if it will work in this weather, but it's worth a try. And have you called the state troopers yet?"

"I think Elinor did download something like that. Would you mind calling the troopers while I check on the app?"

"Sure. Let's head inside." Albert trudged up the steps with James close behind, then they went to the library where Albert notified the troopers.

James located his Find My Friend app and a few minutes later, a location popped up on his screen. "Found her. Looks like she's almost an hour away."

"Might want to wait this storm out."

"I have no idea if she is safe. She could be stuck in a ditch. I have to go to her."

"I understand." Albert stood. "You go get layered up and grab whatever else you might need if you get stuck or find her and you're both stuck. I'll pack food for you and update the authorities. And let the family know to pray."

Elinor woke when cold air chilled her arms, and the front door slammed shut. Wrapping the blanket tighter around her, she began to doze off again until a familiar voice whispered her name. Her eyes flew open, and she looked into the eyes of her love. "James. I knew you would come. Did you get my message?"

He squatted next to the couch. "Once I was outside the convenience store."

"Then how...?"

Remember that Find My Friend app you downloaded on our phones?"

She nodded.

"And I think there were quite a few people praying."

She widened her eyes. "My family."

"And Nancy." He nodded his head toward the woman standing in the doorway. "Thank you, Nancy. God led me to the right place."

"He surely did, child. Now young man, why don't you warm yourself up by the fire while I go prepare your room. I think you two need to talk." She glanced out the window. "And it looks like you're stuck here."

Elinor laughed at the woman's directness, relieved not to be hiding behind a shield of lies any longer. She looked back at James to find him watching her intently.

He leaned down for a kiss. "I've missed you." He kissed her again then sat back on his heels. "The last few weeks have been agony for me. I'm so sorry." He bowed his head until his forehead touched hers.

Elinor stroked his face. "I have a story to tell you." She sat up and patted the couch beside her.

"And I'm ready to listen." He sat and put his arm around her shoulders.

"I've been afraid for a long time. Afraid of being pushed out of people's lives. Afraid of not being wanted because I wasn't good enough. I suppose a lot of that was because of my dad. I ended up living a double life. Plain Jane, obedient Jane at home while the stylish, edgy version showed up for school. And for my senior trip to Europe. I felt like I was finally free."

"That's where you met Remí?"

Elinor nodded. "I threw all caution to the wind when he invited me to tour France with him. I left the tour group and called Dad.

Left a message on his phone that I was staying overseas for a while."
Memories flooded back and emotions knotted in her throat.

James rubbed her shoulder. "I'm not leaving."

She nodded. "It was wild. You saw the pictures. He took me to
all the famous places. At first it was platonic. But when he started
taking me to see those places that weren't on every tourist map, more
personal places, he moved it to a...more intimate level. As starved
for love as I was, I went along with it. I allowed myself to believe
everything he said. All the forever stuff."

"Enough to make a young girl see stars?"

She nodded. "I don't know if I can..."

"I love you no matter what and I'm not going anywhere. But you
need to tell the whole story. And I need to hear it. We have to base
the rest of our life on truth." He stroked her cheek and wiped away
her tears with his thumb. "I'm not letting go." He held her gaze until
she relaxed.

She couldn't believe he still loved and wanted her. Her instincts
yelled at her to run, but hope won out. "I got pregnant. I thought
he would be happy, but it was just the opposite. He yelled at me.
Accused me of trying to trap him. Told me if I would...get rid of
it..." She lowered her head into the cradle of her hands. "How could
I...Oh, God, forgive me...I had an abortion."

"Sweet Elinor."

Wrapping her arms around herself, she rocked back and forth as
the full force of what she had done slammed into her heart and an
ache swelled within her to hold her child she'd so easily sacrificed on
the altar of wanting to be loved.

A harsh laugh escaped her throat between the sobs. "How could
I have believed his lies?" Leaning into the crook of her husband's
shoulder, she let out the grief that had built up for over two decades.
James held her close and whispered soft reassurances of his love.

Distraught over the choice she had made, the weeping came in
waves until, fully exhausted, she drifted to sleep in her husband's
arms. When she woke up, she was lying on a bed and the shadows of

a stormy midday surrounded her. James's breath warmed the back of her neck. A glance at the nearby clock told her she had been asleep for two hours. She shifted on the bed.

"Love you." James's soft whisper warmed her heart.

"Me, you." She turned onto her other side to face the man she loved.

He kissed her gently. "I'm so sorry."

"For what?"

"I didn't give you the same chance you gave me to move on from my past. I'm a different man than I was when I chose to walk away from my girlfriend rather than forgive."

Tears ran down her cheeks.

He wiped her tears with his thumbs. "You've got a lot of grieving to do, and I'll be right beside you."

She sucked her lower lip between her teeth.

"What is it?" He tucked her hair behind her ear.

"Do you think God will forgive me?"

"Oh, sweetheart." He drew her into his arms. "Of course."

"Are you sure?"

He pulled away and looked her in the eye. "Do you believe I still love you?"

She nodded.

"Is God's love less than mine?"

She shook her head, and a tiny smile escaped her lips.

"Then He must love you, because I know I do." James smiled. "Would He refuse to forgive one of His children He loved who asked for forgiveness?"

Her smile grew as joy whispered her name. She shook her head.

"We're walking this together."

"I don't know why you love me so much..."

He turned over on his back and held up a finger. "First, you are an amazing woman. You are kind and generous. You're funny. You complement me perfectly." With each new reason, he held up another finger. "You laugh at my British humor. Very important, you know."

Elinor giggled.

"You love God. You are gentle. You are...you." He looked her in the eye. "Besides all that, you cook well, you're smart, you're gorgeous...shall I go on?"

Elinor beamed.

He wiggled his eyebrows. "But you got me."

"That I do." She circled her arms around him and relaxed into his embrace that she had avoided far too much the last few weeks. "I've missed this spot."

"Me too. Do we have to leave?"

"Not till the storm clears."

"That will have to do." He brought his lips to hers as they melted into each other's love for the rest of the afternoon.

CHAPTER FIFTY

Elinor

Charles prayed over their Christmas brunch feast, then raised his head and looked at the family gathered around the table. Elinor nestled next to James. Once the snowstorm had abated and they returned to the Applewood Hill, she and James enjoyed the reconnection fostered by their time stuck at Nancy's during the storm. In her good-natured motherly way, Nancy provided hot meals, words of wisdom, and plenty of space. Claimed she needed to rest. *Ha.* Elinor was on to her. John, Nancy's son, had trekked over to a friend's house not too far away and didn't return while they were there. Those two days were God sent and healing to her heart, not to mention her marriage. She and James came to some important decisions. Plans she wholeheartedly agreed with. A plan for a great future.

The clamor for food was in full swing. Egg casserole, bacon, fresh squeezed orange juice, and cinnamon rolls. Elinor looked around the table at each of her siblings and wished Blake were there but was thankful Alita had joined them and still considered them her family.

Joyful banter rounded the table. Last night, Clarice's Christmas pageant at the Huddle had been a perfect beginning to their celebration. Even though Blake was gone, they were assured of his choosing to follow God. They would see him again. She hummed to herself in anticipation.

"What are you humming about?" James leaned over and whispered in her ear.

"I want to tell everyone what we've decided to do."

"Which part?" He wiggled his eyebrows and grinned.

"All of it." Elinor placed a hand on his arm. "Can we?"

"How can I resist you?" He gave her a quick kiss on the cheek. "Now?"

"Why not?" She clapped her hands silently and smiled at the love of her life. She still couldn't wrap her mind around how much he loved her and how good God had been to them both throughout this journey.

James clanked his knife against the side of his glass. The family looked his way and quieted their conversations. "We have something to share with the family and thought this was as good a time as any."

"Thought you two might have something to share." Karen grinned across the table at her sister.

Elinor glanced at James with raised eyebrow.

"Go ahead. You're bursting at the seams." He chuckled.

"We're going to build a house."

"Congratulations!" Charles clamped a hand on James's shoulder.

"Don't worry, Karen, we're still going to work at the Applewood Hill. We just need our own space. And more of it."

"You're pregnant?" Karen grinned at her from across the table.

Elinor shook her head. "We've decided to adopt."

"That's wonderful." Karen placed a hand at her throat.

"I didn't even know you were thinking about it. Was it that presentation at church?" Charles picked up his mug of coffee.

Elinor sucked in a breath and blinked back tears. This would be harder than she anticipated.

Joanna placed an arm around her sister and gave her a gentle squeeze. "You don't have to say anything if you're not ready."

James took her hand in his. "I'm right here." He looked at the others. "Maybe the kids shouldn't be in here for this."

"I'm on it." Barry took Hope out of her highchair and set her on the floor, free to roam, then waved Annie and Charlie over. "Could you all take your cousin into the other room awhile and let her play?"

"Yay" Annie and Charlie yelled in unison. They scooted off their chairs to catch up with Hope. Hannah followed close behind.

Elinor gripped Albert's hand as the family looked her way. She cleared her throat. "During my senior trip to Europe, I met a man. Thought I was in love. That was why I didn't come home as planned." She glanced at her father and met his gaze of unrestrained love. "I got pregnant, but he didn't want the baby. He suggested I..." She shook her head against the memories assaulting her anew. She wiped the tears streaming down her face. "...I got an abortion. There were complications...and...I can't have kids." Her shoulders shook as she allowed family to see her grief. She leaned into James and held on to the fact that he still loved her, no matter what her family thought.

Chairs pushed back from the table and her family gathered around her. Prayers lifted for her comfort, healing, and looking forward. Love filtered into her heart and filled the longing she always carried to belong. Hope turned back the edges of sorrow, and joy peeked out. She smiled through tears when her family returned to their seats, waiting for her to share more.

"We're planning a remembrance ceremony for my baby in the spring. I would like it if you all can come."

Heads nodded all around the table and words of affirmation encouraged her plans.

Joanna cleared her throat in the silence that followed Elinor's words. "I have a feeling most of us will be making changes next year. Why don't we all share what's in our plans?" Joanna looked at Elinor.

"Absolutely." Elinor smiled and leaned forward to look past Joanna and her family at her sister-in-law. "Alita, what will you do now?"

Alita set her utensils down. "You all have been amazing. Taking me in and treating me like I belonged. But...with Blake gone now...I'm thinking about moving out to be near my boys in Wyoming. We had a good visit when I went out earlier in the year and our relationship is starting to heal, so it won't be right away, but I'm hopeful." She closed her eyes and nodded. "I want to be around my boys and my grandbabies."

"We'll miss you, but that sounds like the place you need to be." Joanna offered Alita a smile.

"Thanks. It'll be hard to leave, but you're right."

Karen pointed a fork at Albert. "What about you, brother dear?"

"Well..." Albert looked at Haley. "I'm not going back to pastoring."

An immediate bombardment of questions bounced back and forth across the table.

Albert held up his hand as if in surrender. "I give up. I'll tell you. No more torture. Please, stop. Really, I'll tell."

Laughter filled the dining room and all eyes landed on Albert.

"Now, where was I? Hmm...let's see...what was I talking about...maybe..."

A balled-up napkin bonked him in the forehead. "Enough already." Karen laughed as Albert took on a wounded expression.

"You assaulted me."

"Albert." The family spoke as one and glared at him before breaking down laughing.

"In addition to our vacation in Colorado, we're going to...oh, wait, I almost forgot. Something I need to do before I tell you the rest of our plans." He walked over to the buffet and retrieved a gift box out of the cupboards underneath, then returned to the table and handed it to Haley.

"What's this? I thought we were opening gifts in the other room."

"Open it and you'll find out."

Using her fingernails, she cut the tape and took the lid off. She stared at its contents. She pulled out stacks of family pictures. "Where did you get these?"

"I had a lot of help from the family. I asked them to make copies of any pictures they had of our family over the years." Albert looked down at the ground.

Haley got up from the chair and threw her arms around Albert. "Thank you for the pictures."

"I'm truly sorry for being so careless."

Haley silenced him with a kiss. "It's all forgiven. I'm just glad you came back whole."

Smiling, Albert pulled her to his side and looked around the table. As for the future, we're going to run Dad's orchard."

"You mean your orchard." Charles looked around the table. "I'm deeding the orchard and the manager's house to Albert. It's time I turned it over to someone younger."

"What are you going to do, Dad?" Karen reached for another cinnamon roll.

"Travel. I'm thinking I might visit South Dakota."

Karen raised an eyebrow. "Isn't that where..."

"...Helen is. Yes."

"Oh, this is getting good. Do tell." Barry elbowed his father-in-law.

"I've kept in touch with her."

"And..." Barry leaned closer.

"She's a good woman." He looked around the table. "It's been over three years since your mother passed. Can I have your blessing to pursue Helen? I mean, I don't know where it will lead, but it would be nice to spend the rest of my life with someone by my side."

"Of course, Dad." Karen reached across Barry and placed a hand on her dad's arm. The rest of the family added their assent.

"Good. Now, I believe it's Joanna and Alexis's turn to share what's happening." He balled up a napkin and lobbed it at the couple.

Joanna ducked and laughed when it hit Alexis in the face. "You probably have already guessed. Given Grammie's condition, we're going to adopt Clarice."

"Is Grammie coming over with Clarice later today?" Elinor dodged another napkin lobbed her way.

"Clarice is bent on it. Wants to show off the tree to Grammie."

"What's next for you guys, besides growing your family?" Karen poured more coffee in her mug.

"We're not sure how it's all going to look, but we plan on running a ranch for disadvantaged kids. Dad is turning over the stables to us. He also gave us land to build a home on. We'll live with Dad until it gets done."

"That's great." Elinor gave her sister a hug.

"Alexis, does that mean I can persuade you to come back and cook at the Applewood Hill?" Karen pleaded with her eyes.

"We'll talk."

"Good enough." Karen smiled at her favorite chef.

A balled-up napkin sailed across the table and landed in Karen's coffee.

"Oops. Where did that come from?" Albert looked all around the room.

Karen balled up another napkin and threw it at Albert. They busted out laughing.

"Anything new with you guys?" Albert tossed the napkin at Barry.

"I'm thinking about going back to school. Debating about what to study."

"And we're pregnant." Karen interjected with a smile.

"Woohoo." Joanna high-fived her sister. "It's about time you guys had another one. When are you due?"

"Early summer."

Joanna groaned. "Let's put in an order for no tornadoes."

"I'll just make sure you stick close to me come May." Karen reached across the table and placed a hand on top of Joanna's.

"Have you chosen a name yet? Or is it too early? Do you even know if your baby is a boy or girl?" Elinor pushed her plate away from the edge of the table.

Karen laughed. "We started talking about it as soon as we found out."

"Are you telling?"

Karen looked at Barry then back at the family. "I think you all know why we chose Hope's name." She reached for Barry's hand. "We went through this major upheaval in our marriage and yet God brought us back together. He gave us hope, not just for me and him, but for the whole family. And now look at us." She looked at her dad. "Thank you. For not giving up. For pressing us to work through things. For loving us. Five years ago, who would have thought we would be sitting around a Christmas brunch enjoying each other's company? Even laughing together. Anyway, last week we had an ultrasound and found out we have another girl on the way. We finally had a chance to talk last night and stayed up late debating names. We wanted one that fit what God is doing in our family."

"And..." Elinor laughed.

"We chose Joy."

Understanding reflected from each set of eyes as they looked between themselves. God had indeed done a deep work in their family.

"Mom, Dad...is it time for presents yet?" Charlie stood in the arched doorway leading into the living room, holding Hope. Annie and Hannah stood next to them.

Laughter erupted in the room as adults and children headed for the library to open gifts. Karen linked arms with Joanna on one side and Elinor on the other. "This is good. The laughter. I can feel the hope."

Joanna nodded. "And I don't feel broken anymore. Peace covers our past."

Elinor laughed. "And He's giving us a future filled with joy."

"That's what happens when we allow God to rewrite the story." Albert came up behind his sisters and gave each a kiss on the cheek. "And I never want to go back to the way it was."

Thank you

We hope you enjoyed reading Where Healing Starts by Angela D. Meyer. If you did, please consider leaving a short review on Amazon, Goodreads, or BookBub. Positive reviews and word-of-mouth recommendations honor an author and help other readers to find quality Christian fiction to read.

Thank you so much!

If you'd like to receive information about The Mosaic Collection's new releases and writing news, please subscribe to *Grace and Glory*, Mosaic's monthly newsletter.

About Author

ABOUT ANGELA D. MEYER

 Angela D. Meyer writes fiction that showcases God's ability to redeem and restore the brokenness in our lives. Now that her two children are grown, she spends her life writing instead of homeschooling, stays active at church, and is plotting what to do with the rest of her life. She enjoys sunrises and sunsets, hanging out with friends, a good laugh, and reading. Someday, she would love to vacation by the ocean.

Learn more about Angela's books on her **website** Sign up for her **newsletter** to be among the first to hear about her new book releases.

Also By

OTHER TITLES BY ANGELA D. MEYER
From The Mosaic Collection:

The Jukebox Café (short story in Hope is Born: A Mosaic Christmas
Anthology)
This Side of Yesterday
Jillian's Refuge (short story in Song of Grace: Stories to Amaze the
Soul)
Returning to Christmas (short story in A Star Will Rise: A Mosaic
Christmas Anthology ll)
Reinventing Josie (short story in All Things New: Stories to Refresh
the Soul)
Reclaiming Tomorrow (Short story in Whisper of Peace: A Mosaic
Christmas Anthology IV)
Where Hope Starts, Applewood Hill Book 1
Where Healing Starts, Applewood Hill Book 2

Acknowledgments

Almost thirteen years ago I penned the first words to the Applewood Hill series. Nine years ago, the first book in the series was published for the first time. Three years ago, the rights reverted to me for the first two books in the series. And now, Where Joy Starts, book three in the series comes to you for the first time for your reading enjoyment.

From the first book to this final one in the series, I've had a lot of help.

To God, thank you for opening a door when I least expected it and most needed it, giving me a nudge to pursue my dream. To my first publisher, thank you for believing in and publishing my story. And thank you to my writing sisters in the Mosaic Collection for all your support since I joined Mosaic three years ago! I love being a part of our group.

To my family, thank you for supporting me on this journey.

And to my editor, Lesley Ann McDaniel, for making my book shine.

COMING SOON
FROM THE MOSAIC
COLLECTION

For as long as she can remember, Rose Galway has been a captive, controlled by one man or another. To her, though, God is the one holding the keys, refusing to set her free despite the desperate pleas she has sent heavenward. Detective Laken Jones has known hardship too, including the daily trauma of racism. Still, nothing he has gone through compares to what Rose has endured. He wants nothing more than for her to experience hope and healing and maybe even happiness in her life. But first he has to find her. Laken is willing to risk everything to set Rose free. And to help her find her way to God. Even if that means letting go of her—and the future he envisions for the two of them—forever. (TW: human trafficking, some violence)

"Are you hungry?" Melissa turned back to the stove and cut off the pilot.

"Starving!" Loyal said as she reached over and grabbed a slice of bacon from the plate.

The room grew silent. Loyal leaned up against the refrigerator looking at Melissa.

"Thank you." Loyal said.

Melissa looked up at Loyal with a confused looked.

"For taking care of me... thank you."

Melissa smiled. "I know if it was me drunk and funky you would have done the same thing."

"I guess you don't know me that well because I ain't cleaning up vomit." Loyal said, laughing.

Melissa laughed because she knew her friend was right. She would have probably just sprayed her with the water hose.

"What made you be so friendly with drinking anyway?" Melissa asked.

"Girl, shit has been crazy lately." Loyal sighed. "I don't even know where to start."

Melissa handed Loyal a plate of scrambled cheese eggs, grits, bacon and toast. "Well we've got time." Melissa said grabbing her plate and walking out of the kitchen.

Loyal followed her to the living room. They both sat and ate breakfast as Loyal filled her in as much as possible. She told her about Iras' mother showing up, all the way down to Iras accusing her of having an affair with Kino.

• • •

"I know I should have been there for you, and I'm sorry." Melissa said after hearing everything she was going through. "I just needed to—"

"Needed to what?" Loyal asked. The tone of her voice changed when she remembered that Melissa abandoned her. "You just disappeared without even an explanation."

A single tear feel down Melissa's cheek.

"Melissa what's wrong?" Loyal asked.

Melissa didn't answer. She put her head down as the tears begin to flow.

Loyal was seeing another side of her friend.

"That Monica lady you spoke of…"

"Yea, what about her?"

"I never told you how I got my scars, have I?"

"Come to think of it, no." Loyal said. "You never did, and I never asked. I figured if you wanted me to know you would tell me. But what does that have to do with Monica?"

"I was only six-years-old. I didn't mean for it to happen…."

Summer 1987

"Monica, wake up! Monica! I'm hungry!" Melissa yelled trying to get her big sister's attention.

Monica rolled over in her bed ignoring her little sister's request.

"Monica, Please?" She continued.

Monica reached for her watch on the night stand. "Ugh…Seven a.m." Monica said after seeing she had only been sleep for two hours after coming in from a night on the town with Angel. "Where's Aunt Laura? Tell her to make you some food." Monica pulled the covers over her head.

"She left." Melissa said.

Monica sat up in the bed. Melissa was standing on the side of her bed wearing an oversized tee shirt and two ponytails in her hair. She looked at her little sister and smiled. She was the only real family she had left. Melissa was the product of her father's second marriage.

Her father was killed by Melissa's mother shortly after she was born. They were taken in by a foster parent who told them to refer to her as Aunt Laura. As far as Melissa was concerned, Laura was her real aunt. Melissa was too young to understand what happen to her parents, but Monica knew better. She remembered everything from the late night arguments, to the parade of women her dad kept. As a husband, he was everything she didn't want in a man. Monica knew that when she got older she would demand the respect from her husband. But as a father, Monica adored him. He gave her any and everything she wanted. He always made her feel safe and no matter how many women he had in his life, Monica always came first. In fact, her father always told her never to let any man walk over her.

Monica loved her father; she just wished Melissa had a chance to get to know him like she did. Melissa had most of her dad's features. She even picked up his grey eye color.

"Mel, how about you watch my TV for an hour, and then we can go out to eat at a restaurant."

Melissa's eyes lit up with joy. She loved spending time with her big sister because she knew a new toy was always in the plan.

"Okay!" Melissa said as she climbed into bed with her sister.

Monica turned on the TV to Fat Albert and went back to sleep.

Three hours passed and Monica was still sleeping. Melissa didn't want to keep bothering her sister, but her stomach kept growling. Melissa looked at her sister sleeping so peacefully. She got up from to bed and went down stairs to the kitchen to get a bowl of cereal. Melissa opened up the refrigerator to retrieve the milk, but there was none. There was hardly ever any food in the house. She was really hungry and felt her stomach began to sink. She opened the egg carton, grabbed to eggs and then closed the refrigerator door. She had never cooked on the stove, but was preparing to mimic what she seen her aunt and sister do. She got a pan from the cabinet under the sink and placed it on top of the stove. Melissa could barely see over the stove; she decided to push up a chair to stand on. Reaching down, Melissa turned the knob on the stove to turn on the fire…

Monica woke up in her bed and looked around the room. She knew Melissa was there watching television before she went back to sleep. Monica climbed out of her bed and headed towards the bathroom. When she stepped into the hall way, it was as smokier than a crack house. Monica could barely see the stairs. She called for her baby sister several times and panicked when she didn't get a response. Rushing down the steps, Monica called for her again.

"Melissa!" She choked on all the smoke that filled the living room. "Mel! Mel, baby, where are you?" Monica tried to catch her breath but there was hardly any clean air to breathe. She saw the flames coming from the kitchen and screamed.

"No, no. Melissa!" Monica felt her body go numb and she fell to the floor.

"Melissa!" Monica started to feel dizzy and the room started to spin. She heard a loud boom at the door followed by a voice.

"Is anybody in here?" A man yelled.

Monica was too weak to answer. *God please don't let him leave me in this burning house.*

"Hello?" The man yelled, again. He spotted Monica lying on the living room floor when he entered the house. He picked her up and carried her outside.

"I found one." He yelled, running out of the house.

Outside looked like a scene from a movie. A neighbor noticed the smoke coming from the back of the house and managed to call the fire department. It was a fire fighter who rescued Monica. He put her on the stretcher the paramedics had waiting at the bottom of the steps. Monica felt a cool breeze hitting her face. She began to breathe and cough, realizing that she had not found her baby sister.

Monica used all of her strength to tell the paramedics that her little sister was still in the house. By the time she managed to get the words out, another fire fighter was walking out with another body cradled in his arms. The fire fighter put the body on another ambulance.

"This one still has a pulse." He shouted.

They closed the back of both ambulances and headed for the hospital.

Loyal's jaw dropped. The news of Monica being Melissa's big sister took the cake.

"When I saw her in the boutique that day, I froze. I wasn't sure if my mind was playing tricks on me. I haven't seen my sister since the accident."

"Melissa, I am so sorry. Here I am being pissed off at you for not being here for me, and I'm the one who wasn't being a good friend. There should be nothing we don't know about each other at this point."

"When I was put into the group home, I told myself that the past was going to be just that. I became a new person, and seeing Monica took me back to that vulnerable place. She was all I had and she just left me. My aunt Laura would always say she had better things to do like getting high. When I was old enough, I went looking for Monica. I searched for her all over the city and finally found her. She was living with some dope dealer, burned out. She was so high off that shit, Monica didn't even recognize me. I wanted to help her but when the guy came in and saw me there, he got mad and beat her right in front of me." Melissa's tears turned into water works.

"I watched him beat on my sister like she was a punching bag. I wanted to kill him. I picked up a brick that was on the floor next to the bed and hit him in the head from behind. When he was out cold, I tried to get Monica out of there but she turned on me. She started yelling at me and hitting me for knocking him out. And when I saw her crawl over to his body to hold him, my heart shattered. I ran out of there so fast and never looked back since."

"So, that means you are Ras' aunt?" Loyal couldn't bring herself to words.

"I guess so."

"Wow!" Loyal sat back. God had a way of pulling them altogether anyway. Loyal felt like a fool after finding out about Melissa's past. She knew she had to let Iras know about his precious Monica. She didn't want to take another chance of him not knowing it all.

****

As the afternoon began to reach its peak, the ride home from Atlantic City seemed to get longer. There was a lot of police action on the Ben Franklin Bridge. Two lanes were blocked off, which only left one lane open for traffic. As Angel and Pablo drove past the cops, Angel noticed the yellow tape around the wooded area.

"They must have found a body or something." Angel said looking on at the scene.

"Mostly likely they did." Pablo said, agreeing with her. They finally got passed the traffic and headed into downtown Philly.

"I need to make a stop." Pablo said pulling up to an apartment building in the Chinatown section of downtown.

Angel nodded her head and leaned her seat back. Pablo's quick stops always took about twenty minutes, so Angel got comfortable.

Pablo got out of the car and disappeared into the building. She turned on the radio. Kanye West was just going off right before C-Dub, the radio host came on.

"You're tuned in with C Dub on Hot 98 for the mid-day old school jams. Before we get back to the music, this just came in: a young woman was found dead on the Ben Franklin Bridge. Police say she was found by two teenage boys while they were hiking. They are not releasing her name at this time, but are asking anyone who knows about this to contact the New Jersey police department."

Damn, we just rode passed there! Angel thought. She sat up in her seat and turned the radio down when she saw Pablo storming back to the car. From the looks of it, something was wrong.

"Take my car," he said. "I'm going to be here for a while."

"Are you sure? What happened in there?" Angel asked.

"Don't worry about it. I'm handling it. I'll be home later." Pablo said before going back into the building.

Angel climbed into the driver seat and started the engine. "What the hell could have happened?" She left the parking lot and did just what Pablo said.

When she got to the house, she turned off the car and grabbed her pocketbook from the back seat. She wanted to make sure Pablo was ok so she pulled out her cell phone. She looked at a black screen.

"Damn," she mumbled, completely forgetting that she turned her phone off last night. Pressing the side button, Angel powered on her cell and a voicemail symbol instantly popped up. Angel called her voicemail and turned on the speaker phone.

"You have one new voicemail message. New message: "....that's how it started out Kino but I swear I would never do anything to hurt you. I love you!" Meeka said.

"You're lying, bitch!" *Smack!* "If I wouldn't have gon' to see Smoke, your ass would still be plotting. Is that what you call love?" Kino asked.

"I was going to tell you, I swear." Meeka pleaded. "I just didn't know how. I fell in love with you and my heart wouldn't let me do it. I knew you wouldn't believe me."

The phone went silent. Angel looked at the screen and saw the on-call button lit so she knew it was still recording.

"No, no, no! Kino, don't do this!" Meeka cried.

"You want to know what happen right." Kino started. "First, we cut every inch of his body with a razor blade. Then we took turns hitting him like a piñata with a chain."

"Oh god, Trey! Not mi primo!" Meeka cried. She didn't know what hurt more; the fact that she knew Trey suffered, or the reality of her being a trader. She fell in love with the man who caused her family much pain.

"And finally, when we got tired of his ass, my boy Iras put one right in the middle of his eyes. And now, you can send him my regards!"

Pop! Pop! Pop!

Angel sat in the car in stunned. Her ears had to be deceiving her. She just heard Meeka's murder. She ended the call and dialed Meeka's number back hoping that she would answer.

Kino looked at the ringing phone on the pool table. It was the first time it rang since he took it out of Meeka's dead hands. Iras sat quietly on the pool table as well. Even though they had an awkward night, Kino had to confide in his boy about what went down with Meeka. Tension was still in the air from Iras' blow-up the night before, but Kino had no one else to call. They both sat in the warehouse staring at the phone as it rung.

"I snapped Ras! That bitch played me all along." Kino said trying to convince his self that what he did was right.

"Okay. But your sloppy shit is what's going to get you caught up." Iras snapped back. The room got silent again just as another call came through.

"The same number keeps popping up; it's got to be them Death Trap mutha' fuckas'. They got to know something's up." Kino said.

"Why did you keep her phone anyway?" Iras asked.

"Her phone fell out her hand when I popped her. It was on, like she was calling somebody. I picked it up and listened to see if I heard anybody. It was nothing but dead silence. I was about to leave it but my prints were already on it. I don't need anything tying me to that shit."

"But you popped her out in the open? That was smart." Iras said, sarcastically.

"There wasn't anybody around!"

"And what about Smoke? What if he talks?"

"That mutha fucka ain't saying shit!"

Iras shook his head. "So now you trust other niggas with your life?"

"Would it be better I trust the nigga who thinks I'm fucking his bitch?"

"Admitting your guilt?" Iras asked.

"Ras, you know there ain't shit going on between me and Loyal. What would make you think some shit like that?" Kino snapped. "We've been boys since the womb. You're buggin' if you think I'm that nigga."

"I'm buggin?" Iras huffed. "You're rocking bitches to sleep in the open and I'm buggin?"

"Fuck that shit, Ras! What's done is done. We need to clean this shit up. I'm just going to hit up ya pops." Kino said pulling out his cell.

"No!" Iras stopped him. "My pops don't need to know shit, we can handle this. Besides, I promised him I would stay far from this shit."

"What the hell are we going to do?" Kino asked.

"Call Buttah… tell him to come to the warehouse. He'll know what to do." Iras said before disappearing up the stairway.

CHAPTER EIGHTEEN

"Everything is cool on our end." Eric said. "Wait. Run that by me again. Yeah. No problem. I'll get to the bottom of it." He said before ending the call.

One thing he didn't like was a bad business deal, especially when it's on his end. Pablo assuring him that Buttah never made the drop didn't sit too well with him. Eric picked up his office phone and dialed Buttah's number. He got up from his desk and walked over to his office window overlooking downtown Philadelphia.

"Come to the office. Yes, now." Eric hung up the phone and walked back to his desk. He pressed the intercom button on the phone.

"Yes, Mr. Taylor?" A lady said over the speaker.

"Cancel my meetings today, Shelly. And you can take the rest of the day as well."

"Yes, sir. Can I get you anything?"

"No, that's ok. See you tomorrow."

Eric poured himself a glass of cognac and sat down at his desk waiting for Buttah to walk through the door. He sat his glass on the desk next to a picture of him and Iras. Picking up the photo, Eric stared at it remembering the day it was taken. Iras had just turned eighteen and they were celebrating his acceptance into Hampton University on a full scholarship.

Eric loved his son and wanted nothing but the best for him. The day Iras chose not to go away to college was the day his life did a one-eighty. Eric knew exactly what Iras got down with, even though Iras tried to keep it secret. Eric wasn't stupid. He knew he had to let his son make his own mistakes. It'd been a couple of days since he last spoken to his son. He picked up the phone and dialed Iras' number.

"Yo, Ras. It's me, just checking on you. Hit me back when you get this." Eric hung the phone up. He immediately assumed he was with Monica and that added fuel to the fire that was already brewing inside of him.

****

"Fuck!" Iras said, pounding his fist on the pool table. "I knew this nigga wouldn't keep his mouth shut. Buttah told my pops!"

"How do you know that?"

"I ain't talk to him in a couple of days, why is hitting my jack now?"

Kino looked over at his boy. Something wasn't right with him. He hasn't been himself for weeks now. His paranoia level was through the roof. Iras was always fearless, shoot first and ask questions later. Even down to the incident at the party; how he blew up thinking he was having an affair with Loyal.

"You told Buttah you didn't want Eric to find out." Kino started. "So why would you think he would tell him, he didn't even get here yet to find out the whole story."

"Buttah's loyalty is to my pops, not me. He doesn't keep anything from him." Iras explained.

"That's you're godfather, his loyalty holds fast to the Taylor family." Kino said. "This ain't you, man. What the hell is going on with you?"

"Ain't shit going on with me. When the grass is low, the snakes will show. And it looks like everybody around me is trying to be the King Cobra." Iras said walking towards Kino.

Kino didn't budge when Iras came into his personal space. The tension was thick. Kino's emotions were already on edge after what he just went through with Meeka, and this was the first time the thought of him rocking his best friend to sleep came to mind. He had the feeling Iras was playing a completely different ball game. One thing he did know was if it came down to it, it wasn't going to be him lying there lifeless. The sound of footsteps coming downstairs broke their attention.

"Whatever it is, it ain't worth it." Buttah said, feeling the animosity as he entered the room. He walked over and leaned up against the pool table.

"Now tell me what's going on, and make it quick because I have to meet up with E." He said lighting a cigarette.

"King cobra!" Iras said to Kino before heading up the stairs.

"Young Blood?" Buttah called Iras.

Iras ignored him and left out of the warehouse. Buttah looked back at Kino with confuse eyes.

"Don't ask." Kino shook his head. "I got bigger shit to worry about."

Kino began to fill Buttah in on the whole fiasco that went down; from Meeka, to Iras.

****

Loyal pulled up to the condo. It was the first time she been there since the night of the party. She walked in on Monica doing aerobics in the living room.

"Whoa! You scared me." Monica said out of breath. She picked up the remote and turned the television off. "You should have knocked. I wasn't expecting anyone." Monica said, wiping the sweat off her forehead with the towel.

"Why would I knock? I live here."

"You do?" Monica responded walking passed Loyal and into the kitchen.

"Where's Ras?" Loyal asked ignoring her smart comment.

"Emanuel is out at the moment. Is there something I can do for you?"

"No at all." Loyal said. She headed towards the bedroom.

"Oh umm, I have my dress lying on the bed. Try not to touch it, will you? From the looks of it, I can tell you don't handle things well."

It took everything in Loyal not to put Monica in her place. She didn't want to say anything that would upset Iras even more. Loyal went into her room and shut the door.

****

Meeka's death was the top story on the news. Angel turned off the television after coming to the conclusion that it was Meeka's body that was found. She tried to pull herself together long enough to call Pablo and inform him of his daughter, but for some reason she didn't have the heart to. She felt responsible for letting her get in that deep with Kino.

What hurt her even more was the thought of Pablo blaming her as well. She was in love. The feeling she had for Pablo ran deeper than the ocean. He was a good man at heart, and she would do anything for him. Things were about to get deep, and fast. Not only was she out to avenge Trey's death, now Pablo's daughter. Someone was going to feel her pain one way or another.

****

"Wait here, I'll be right back." Buttah told Kino. Buttah got out of the car and headed into the high rise building where Eric's real estate office was located. Buttah walked into Eric's office and the sound of Tupac's, Me and My girlfriend, was sounding from the speakers. Eric turned the volume down low enough for Buttah to hear him.

"Since when do we not keep our end of a deal?" Eric asked, making direct eye contact with Buttah.

"What's that supposed to mean?" Buttah asked, knowing exactly what Eric was referring to.

"Did you make the drop?"

"The drop was made that night, E."

"Pablo is saying otherwise."

"See, I knew it was something about that mutha fucka!" Buttah said as he started to pace the room. "So now we got a problem?"

"No. I'll handle it."

"Give me the word, E. And I'll handle him." Buttah said nodding his head.

"I said I will handle it. I'll hit you up later." Eric said sipping his drinking.

Buttah turned to leave out. Once he was in the clear, he pull out his cell.

"Fuck!" He whispered after getting Trina's voicemail. Buttah got back into the car and pulled off.

Kino noticed the nervous look on his face but decided not to butt into his business.

"Young blood, I got something I need to handle right now. I'll swing back pass to get you later on to fix your little problem."

"Alright, cool." Kino said.

Buttah let Kino out at one of the trap houses he operated.

"Hold things down over here until I get back." Buttah said before pulling off.

He had to find Trina and that money quick. Not telling Eric that Trina stole the money and disappeared would make him look weak. Trina never pulled a stunt like this.

"I can't believe I trusted that bitch!" Buttah yelled out, punching the steering wheel. Murder was his one mission.

"The best thing for her is to stay under the rock where she is hiding because when I find her, I'm going to make sure she never steals from me again."

****

Loyal woke up from the sound of laughter coming from the living room. That nap felt so good. She climbed out of the bed when she heard Iras' voice.

"This nigga funny as shit." Iras said, laughing. He and Monica were watching the Kings of Comedy. Loyal's presence caused them to break their focus from the movie.

"I forgot you were in there." Monica said acting surprised.

Loyal didn't respond to her. "Can we talk?" Loyal asked looking at Iras.

He was avoiding her eye contact.

"Iras, are you hungry? I can make you something to eat before I leave." Monica said getting up and heading to the kitchen.

"I'm still stuffed from lunch. That steak was on point." Iras said getting up and walking over to Monica. "Just call me when you get home."

"You don't have to worry, I'm grown. I can handle myself." Monica kissed her son on his cheek.

Loyal couldn't stand the way Monica was all over her own son. *She acts like that's her man or something.*

Iras walked Monica out to her car and waited until she pulled off. Loyal was sitting on the sectional when he returned.

"Funny seeing you here." He said as he shut the door behind him.

"I didn't come here to argue, Ras."

"Why are you here? I didn't see or hear from you in over a week, and now you come back and expect things to be cool?"

"I needed to clear my head. That bull shit you pulled wasn't called for. You know there is nothing going on between me and Kino. He's you're best friend."

"That's what made it so easy. I trusted him around you."

"Ras, just stop!" Loyal snapped back. "I get it. You're pissed. But this isn't about me or Kino. Be a man and tell me what's really going on with you, because whatever it is, I'm not going to stand here and reap the consequences."

"Maybe we need to chill for a while. Shit's been crazy lately and—"

"Chill? Chill! You know, ever since Monica came into your life, you act like nothing else matters. Like she got you all wrapped up on her finger."

"Keep my mom out of this. You don't even know her."

"No, you don't know her!" Loyal wanted to tell Iras what Melissa told her, but she paused when she saw the tears building up in his eyes. "I know you're hurt, but taking it out on everybody is not the answer." Loyal said, changing the tone. "Whatever it is, we can work through this." Loyal grabbed his hand. "You should know by now, that I'm not going anywhere. You can't push me away that easily."

Iras felt stupid for his actions. Loyal had his back from the start and deep down he knew she was a rider for her man. He pulled her in close to him and kissed her on the forehead. Loyal was relieved, and now was undecided if she wanted to open another wound. She decided to let it go, and he will find out about Monica when the time was right.

CHAPTER NINETEEN

Eric walked into his house and threw his keys on the mail table. He had been at his office most of the night making arrangements to fix Buttah's fuck up. He knew from the time Buttah walked into the office something was up. Eric can read people like a book. Buttah's nervousness sent off vibes that alerted him. He didn't know what happen, but he knew Buttah was up to something. Eric was able to wire the money to an account for Pablo to access it. He wasn't going to tell Buttah. He wanted to see how far he was going to keep this charade going.

He walked passed the living room not bothering to turn on the lights. A piece of mail he was reading held his attention. He didn't even notice Monica sitting in a recliner in his living. Eric walked upstairs to his master bedroom. He doubled back when he noticed a light on in another room. Eric instantly felt an eerie vibe and pulled out his 9mm hand gun. He crept to the lit room and cocked his gun back. If someone was in there, they definitely weren't getting out, alive anyway.

Eric kicked open the door and went in with his gun blazing. He quickly scanned the room only to find there was no one there. Lowering his gun, Eric sighed. "I need a vacation."

Things have been different since he found out that Monica was back. His own son was acting different. Eric turned the light off and shut to door as he left out the room.

Ding dong!

Eric looked at his watch. It was almost 2am and he wasn't expecting company. He went down stairs and could see the flashing red and blue lights through the window on the door. He placed his gun on the mail table before opening it.

"Can I help you officer?"

"Sorry to bother you so late, but you might want to check your car." The police officer said pointing back to Eric's Benz parked in the driveway. "I made that mistake before and killed my battery. Worst feeling is when you're in a rush to leave and your car won't start." He said referring to the lights still on inside Eric's car.

"Thanks a lot officer." Eric said as he stepped out of his house.

"That's a mighty fine vehicle you got there." The officer said, admiring the car as they walked up on it. "What year is it?"

"2010." Eric said, not knowing why he was outside at 2 am with a cop discussing the basics of his car. Eric opened the car door and climbed in to turn off the light. He hit the lock button before closing the door. "Thanks again, officer. I'm about to take it down. I had a pretty long day."

"You have a good night, now." The officer said as he watched Eric walk back into the house.

Briefly, he stared at the house before heading back to his car. As he got closer, he heard the dispatch calling his unit.

"Unit 514, over." He answered.

"514, what's your 20?"

The officer didn't want to give up his location. He was in a neighborhood where he had no business being, waiting for Monica to come out of the house.

"Chief Dilucci?"

"I stopped to get a bite to eat at the 7-11, over." Joe said.

Pop! Pop! Pop!

Joe dropped to the ground after hearing the sound of a gun going off. He pulled out his gun and ran to Eric's front door. He kicked in the door and found Monica standing over Eric's bleeding body.

"Baby, what the hell are you doing?"

Monica didn't respond. The look in her eyes was a look Joe had never seen before. Monica stepped over Eric's dead body and squatted down so that her face was almost touching his.

"We could've been a happy family." Monica whispered, sarcastically, before spitting in his face. She stood up and looked over at Joe. "Aww, baby. You look like you saw a ghost."

"What… why did you kill him?" Joe said in a panic. "You were supposed to just find the money and get out. How am I going to explain this?"

"You won't!"

Pop! Pop!

Joe's body dropped to the floor when Monica sent two bullets to his head. Monica dropped the gun beside Eric's body and left the house. She removed the white leather gloves she wore and put them in her pocket. After one last glance, she headed out the door and to her car parked two blocks away.

As she walked passed the police car, she heard the dispatch put a search out for Joe. She reached her car and pulled off going to the only place where she knew she would be safe.

****

"Ras! Wake up. Someone's at the door!" Loyal rasped as she shook Iras put of his sleep. She was abruptly awakened from hers when she heard the loud banging.

Iras jumped up when he realized the time of morning it was. He reached over, opened the draw on the nightstand, and grabbed his protection. He walked to the door and looked out the peephole.

Monica stood on the other side waiting, anxiously. The second Iras opened the door, Monica pushed passed him and began pacing the living room floor.

"It's gone! It's all gone!" She cried.

Iras shut the door, making sure to secure it. "What's gone? What happened?"

"Everything. My apartment, my clothes, my money! He took everything and trashed the place."

"Wait, slow down," Iras said. He grabbed her to stop her from pacing. "Who took everything?"

"Nathan, my landlord that's a want-to-be pimp. I told him I would have the rent next week." Monica sold the story as if it really happened.

Iras pulled his mother into his arms. "You can stay here tonight. I will handle everything in the morning."

Monica buried her face in Iras' chest. She closed her eyes and saw Eric's face flash in her head. *He is my son!* She thought.

"You can sleep here on the couch. Try to get some rest." Iras told her before heading back to his bedroom.

"Who was at the door?" Loyal asked when he returned to the room.

"Monica."

"Your mother?" Loyal said sitting up in the bed.

"Yes, my mother."

"What is she doing here this time of the night?"

"Something happened to her apartment. Look, I'll explain in the morning, but she's going to sleep here tonight." Iras turned off the lamp before laying down in the bed.

"Ras, I need to tell you something." Loyal said.

"Can it wait until the morning, I'm tired?"

"It's about Monica."

Iras turned over and looked a Loyal. "What about her?"

Loyal wanted to tell Iras everything she knew about Monica; about the drugs, and about Melissa. She didn't want to keep it a secret any longer but when she looked into his eyes, she could see that now wasn't the time. When it came to Monica, Iras didn't see any wrong. Loyal didn't want to make it seem as though she wasn't giving Monica a chance.

"I-I think we should just let her stay with us. The guest room hasn't been used in a while." Loyal said. *What the hell am I doing?* She immediately thought.

Iras leaned up and kissed her. "I love you."

"Love you too, Ras." Loyal laid down in the bed and cuddle him from behind. *This better be worth it!*

****

Buttah had been up all night, driving. He was determined to find Trina. He checked just about every hotel in Philadelphia. Each minute that passed, he grew angrier. He was going to enjoy ending her life.

"This bitch thinks it's that sweet. Like she can just rob me and get away with it!" Buttah said, playing the entire situation over and over in his head. It was almost 4 a.m. when he pulled up to a 24 hour dinner on South Street. He went in and sat at the last booth in the back.

"Good morning," the waitress said as she placed a napkin, silverware and a menu on the table in front of him. "Can I start you off with a beverage?"

"Just a coffee, please."

"Alright, take a look at the menu, and I'll be right back with your coffee." The waitress walked away.

Buttah couldn't help but noticed how plumped her ass was. For a white girl, she was caked up. Buttah pulled out his cell and called Eric.

"Yo E, it's me. Look, I wasn't one hunnit' with you earlier today. Some shit went down with Trina and the drop money. I'll explain later, but right now just know that I'm going to fix it. Hit me back when you get this message."

Buttah closed the cell phone. He felt a little more at ease now that he got that off his chest. He knew Eric wasn't going to be pleased when he heard the message, but it was something he had to do. The feeling of him betraying his best friend was worst then losing the money. The waitress came back with the coffee.

"Ready to order?" She asked, pulling out a pencil and a notepad.

Buttah opened up the menu and scanned over it. "I'll have two scrambled eggs, turkey bacon and toast."

"Alright, it will be out shortly." The waitress took the menu and disappeared into the kitchen.

Buttah took a sip of his coffee and nearly spilled it when he noticed a beautiful woman walk into the diner. She sported a blue three piece suite and glasses. Her hair was tied back into a bun. She looked as if she worked in an office setting. Buttah watched as she walked to a booth where another person wearing a black hoodie sat. He couldn't tell if the other person was a man or a woman. He assumed it was a woman by the small body frame. They sat with their back toward him and had their hood pulled up. Buttah knew it was not the time to meet new people, but she was something he couldn't pass up. When the opportunity presented itself, he had every intention of making a new companion.

****

"What the hell took you so long? I've been waiting here for almost an hour." Trina said. She told her best friend and partner in crime, Keilani, about hitting the jackpot. It was there biggest payout yet.

"Damn girl, relax. You look more nervous than a baby daddy on trial for child support." Keilani said, flopping into the booth. "Why did you want to meet here?"

"This is the only place I knew Buttah wouldn't be. Right now he's probably in and out of all the hotels looking for me. Did you get the tickets?"

"First class to Atlanta. We're out in 4 hours." Keilani said pulling out two plane tickets.

"I will feel so much better when we are on the plane." Trina said as she sipped her drink.

"Well, I'll tell you one thing; it's about time you cashed out. Another month and I was damn near bout to just come in there blasting." Keilani said, jokingly.

Trina smiled. They have been best friends for as long as she could remember. Trina was also the god mother of Keilani's six-year-old son, Akahi. Keilani was like a sister to Trina. They started blind-robbing men when Keilani was diagnosed with breast cancer. Keilani went through so much treatment that she was tired, literally. She made the decision to fight her diagnosis on her own. She asked Trina to get this money with her so that one day when her body couldn't fight it anymore, Trina would have what she needed to take care of Akahi.

"On some real shit T, I'm ready to live. No more 'getting it'. We got enough for me, you and Akahi to live comfortably."

"I feel you." Trina nodded. "Besides, something about this one just doesn't feel right. This nigga Buttah is too connected. Let's just get Akahi and be out. We can start new life when we get to the A," Trina said pointing two fingers down forming the letter. "I need to use the little girl's room, get the check so when I come back we can roll."

Keilani nodded her head.

Trina put her glasses on and slid out of the booth.

Buttah noticed the girl's company walking away. He got up and took the only chance he had while she was alone.

"Excuse me." He said, standing in front of her booth.

Keilani looked up and instantly knew who he was. She looked over at the duffel bag Trina left sitting on the chair, then back up at him.

"I can't help but notice how beautiful you are. I apologize if I'm offending you, but your husband must be a very lucky man."

Keilani just smiled. She reached behind her back discreetly putting her hand on her berretta tucked in her pants. Her heart was beating out of her chest.

If only he knew his money was a foot away from him, she thought. "Thank you for the compliment. And yes, my husband is a very lucky man." Keilani said, hoping he would go away.

"Okay, but if you ever need an ear to vent to when he's not appreciating what he has, here's my card." Buttah slid his business card in front of her.

Keilani picked the card up and slid it into her pocket. She got up from the booth and reached over for the duffel bag.

"Allow me." Buttah said reaching for the bag.

Keilani felt as if the air supply was gone when Buttah picked up the duffel. He handed her the bag, and she put it on her shoulder. The jingling bells hanging on the door caught their focus when someone rushed out.

"Your friend seems to be in a rush." Buttah said after seeing the hooded person she was sitting with storm out of the diner.

"Yeah, we've got somewhere to be. It was nice to meet you Buttah." Keilani said as she turned to walk away.

Buttah watched her as she left out. He smiled at the front row view he had of her backside. Slowly, his smile faded when he realized she called him Buttah.

"I never told that bitch my name." He uttered. Buttah pulled out his semi-automatic and ran out the diner. He looked up the street and saw a car speeding off. He hopped into his car and followed behind them.

"That was too close!" Trina exhaled as she took off her hood and glasses.

"Out of all the food spots in Philly, you had to pick the one he was going to be at." Keilani said.

Trina shook her head. "Just my luck, right?"

"It's a good thing that nigga don't know who I am. I thought I was going to have lay his ass down right there." Keilani said as she came to a stop at a red light.

"Let's just pick up my godson so we can get out of here. Next time we might not be so lucky."

Pop! Pop! Pop! Pop! Pop!

Buttah let off a whole clip when he pulled up alongside their car at the light and saw Trina. He got out the car and open Keilani's door. Keilani's body fell out and onto the street.

"Lani!" Trina screamed. Her eyes popped and her body trembled in shock.

Buttah reached in the car and grabbed the duffel bag from Trina's lap. He put his gun to Trina's forehead and pulled the trigger.

Trina jumped when she heard the gun click.

"God must be on your side today, but I will see you again." Buttah said after realizing he was out of bullets. He hit her across the face with the butt of his gun, got back in his car and pulled off.

Trina's mouth was bloody. She climbed over the seat and got out of the car to check on her best friend.

"Lani! Lani, baby wake up!" Trina rolled Keilani's body onto her back. Her eyes were still opened. Blood already began to form a pool in the street around her. Trina pulled her body into her arms and cradled her. She sat in the street rocking her best friend's body as if she were a newborn baby.

"You can't leave. I need you. Akahi needs you," Trina cried.

Sirens began to fill the air. Trina reached into Keilani's pocket and pulled out the plane tickets. She didn't want to leave her there, but she couldn't be there when the police showed up. She kissed Keilani on the cheek and closed her eyes lids so that she could rest peacefully.

Trina ran back towards the diner and got into the rental car. She was going to get Akahi and get out of Philadelphia.

****

Buttah sped over to Eric's house. His adrenalin was pumped throughout his body. There was no doubt what he was going to do to teach Trina a lesson for robbing him, but first he wanted to return the money to Eric. Buttah arrived at Eric's house and saw cop cars and yellow tape everywhere. He slowed down to get a look at the scene. The front door was wide open and police officers filled the house. He couldn't tell by looking if Eric was okay or not, but the scene said it all. There was a murder, Buttah just hopped that Eric was the one putting in the work.

Buttah parked his car around the corner. He grabbed his cell and called Iras. It was almost 6:30 am but he didn't care.

"Buttah, the fucking cops are here telling me my dad is dead! What the fuck is going on?" Iras said soon as he answered Buttah's call.

That news hit him like a tidal wave, "I don't know, Ras."

"Don't bullshit me, Buttah! They want me to come identify a body that might be my father. What the fuck is going on?"

"I don't know. I wasn't with him. I just rode passed his crib just now and it looks like a fucking murder scene. Listen, I'm on my way there." Buttah said before hanging up the phone.

He punched his steering wheel letting out his frustration. A crazy night was turning into a crazier morning. Buttah was going to get to the bottom of it. The one person who he could think of that may have wanted Eric dead was Pablo. Money will put a price on anybody. If Pablo was after them, Buttah knew he might be next; but he planned to pay Pablo a visit first.

CHAPTER TWENTY

"….Yea, though I walk through the valley of the shadow of death, I will fear no evil: For thou art with me; Thy rod and thy staff, they comfort me..." The preacher's voice faded out of Pablo's ears as he watched his only daughter being lowered into the ground. Family and friends threw white roses on top of the cherry wood casket. Pablo got up from his seat and walk off. Seeing his only baby girl laid to rest was ripping him apart. Angel and two of his workers quickly followed behind him. They all piled into the stretch Cadillac awaiting near the grave site. One of Pablo's men signalled the driver to pull off after everyone was in.

Pablo was silent. He stared out the window as they passed through the grave yard gates. His worst fear had become his reality. Tango and George also rode quietly, waiting for their boss to speak. Tango was Pablo's head Honcho. Anything Pablo needed done, Tango made sure it was done. No request was too much. Tango had been with Pablo since their days in Miami. He was first hired as a body guard for Pablo's mother. In Miami, Pablo was a wanted man. He took over the drug scene when he came from Puerto Rico. Attempts were made to end Pablo's life, but none were successful. One night when Pablo stopped by his mother's home the door was ripped off the hinges. He went in and saw the place trashed. Furniture was flipped over, paintings that once graced the walls were thrown to the floor, and glass tables were shattered. Luckily, his mother was on a cruise at the time, but the thoughts he had of what could have happen to her if she had been home made him uneasy. That's when he realized that he was on another level. His family had become targets to get to him. That's what made him hire Tango. When Pablo's mother passed away, he kept Tango around. Tango's loyalty was solid.

George on the other hand was fairly new. He was bought on the scene about a year ago. He was Pablo's brother-in-law. He was married to Pablo's youngest sister, Maria. He was from the Mid-West. Pablo saw a business opportunity and jumped on it. George was connected. With him, he could expand his empire.

"Every witness, news reporter and anyone else that may know of my daughter's death— I want to speak with them." Pablo said, breaking the silence. His eyes never left the window. "Somebody knows something. Whoever is connected, they're dead."

Tango nodded his head to the orders. Philadelphia's murder count was about rise, and all at the hands of Pablo. Angel's heart began to beat, rapidly. Her palms were sweaty, and her air supply suddenly seemed to shorten. She knew Pablo wouldn't take it too well if he knew she was the one who came up with the plot that eventually got Meeka killed. She wasn't sure if Pablo's love for her would be enough to save her life. The way he spoke in the car confirmed that no one was safe. He was willing to put it all on the line to find his daughter's killer and anyone involved.

How can I tell him it was Kino without giving me up? She thought.

The driver pulled up to a gas station near the church where the service was held.

"I got you, boss!" Tango said before he and George got out the car. Pablo didn't respond. The driver pulled off once again. Pablo looked over at Angel who was consumed in her own thoughts. He pulled her closer to him and place a sweet gentle kiss on her forehead.

"You are the only person who I feel like I can trust right now." He said. "I often wonder if I wasn't paying Tango and George, would they still be around. If I'm buying their loyalty. But you, I know for sure you're here for the right reasons. From here on out, you don't have to worry about anything. You belong to me. Anything you want, just say the word."

Angel's eyes began to fill with tears. Knowing that she had something to do with Meeka's death was killing her. She loved Pablo. Her love for him grew deeper each day. He was the man she had always dreamed of being with. When she looked up at Pablo, his face was full of fresh tears. It was the first time she'd seen him cry.

"I'm always going to be here for you, too. I love you, Pablo." Angel said before laying her head on his shoulder.

I've got to fix this! She thought. *I have to finish what Meeka started…*

****

Iras and Loyal sat at the table with the director of King's Funeral home. Planning Eric's home going service had taken a toll on the both of them. Iras had beaten himself up ever since he heard the news of his father's death. All he could think about was the argument they had about his mother.

"So the total cost will be $15,159." The director stated.

Loyal looked over at Iras waiting for him to respond.

"Well, we've got to send him off right now, don't we?" Monica said walking over from them sofa. She stood behind Iras and massaged his shoulders. "His father meant so much to him."

Oh please, give me a break! Loyal thought, rolling her eyes.

"We, at King's Funeral home, cater to our customer's needs. Losing a loved one is hard, but we promise to make the home going service one you can be proud of." The director assured.

"Well, it's settled then." Monica said. "Sweetheart, I need to take a nap, do you mind if I rest in your room? The mattress in the guestroom is so hard on my back."

"My place is your place," Iras said.

Monica kissed her on the cheek before heading back to the bedroom.

"Thank you again for all your help," Iras told the director as they both stood from their seats. Iras walked him to the door.

"If you have any other questions, feel free to give me a call."

Iras nodded, "Will do."

They shook hands one last time before the director headed out.

"Ras, you know I don't like anyone else lying in my bed." Loyal said once the director was gone. She didn't want to cause a scene in front of their guest.

"Now is not the time, Loyal."

"When is it ever a good time? Every time I mention something about Monica, you brush it off. I feel like a stranger in my own home."

"She's my mother, Loyal. Damn, is it that hard for you to like her?"

"I never said I didn't like her."

"You don't have to say it." Iras said as he walked passed her. He collected the funeral papers from the table. "You don't think I notice the looks you give her whenever she's around. Or the instant attitude you get when she comments on anything."

"Your mother is the one who has a problem with me!" Loyal stormed over to him.

"You don't even know her!"

"And how well do you know her, Ras?"

Iras didn't answer. He exhaled deeply trying not to flip out on her. "Loyal, I've made the mistake of pushing one parent out my life and now he's dead—gone. I am not going to do the same with her because you two are having a menstrual dispute."

"I'm not asking you to fall back from your mother. I'm asking you *not* to fall back from *me*. I hate competing for your attention, but Monica makes it hard not to." Loyal's emotions were starting to surface. She never wanted to admit it, but she was a little jealous of Monica. In Iras' eyes, Monica was perfect. There was a time when he felt that way about her. She felt him slowly slipping away, but didn't have the answer as to why.

"When I get back, all three of us are going to get to the bottom of this. We're going to talk and work it out." Iras said.

"Where are you going?"

"I've got to meet up with Buttah. But I will be back in a few hours. I promise we are going to get through this." Iras picked up his keys from the coffee table and left the condo.

Monica stood by the bedroom door listening to every word Loyal and Iras said. The smile on her face confirmed her satisfaction. "Time to turn up the heat on Ms. Loyal!" Monica said as she took a seat on the bed. She reached into her pocket and pulled out a little clear bag that contained a white powered substance. She opened the bag and emptied it on the back of her hand. Lifting her hand up to her nose, Monica used her free hand to pinch one of her nostrils. She inhaled the drug in one deep snort. She held her head back allowing the drug to run its course. It was the third time she had gotten high since she murdered Eric. Her nerves were driving her crazy, and all of the voices in her head was paranoid. The only time she could remember feeling relaxed was when she invited the white candy into her body. Monica rolled her head slowly in a circular motion as a warm numbness travel throughout her limbs. A tingling sensation sparked between her legs instantly making her moist. Monica laid back on her son's bed. The room felt as if it too had mellowed out. To her eyes, a warm tint covered the room as if the sun was setting over the horizons. Her ears heard the calming tunes of Bob Marley's, *No Woman No Cry*. The smell of freshly squeezed pineapple juice bombarded her nostrils. She loved the ride she boarded. It was a feeling she was all too familiar with.

Monica closed her eyes. Slowly, she unbuttoned the dark denim jeans she had on and slid them down just enough to expose her throbbing kitty cat. She slipped two fingers between her pussy lips and teased her pulsating pearl. Her cool fingers against the warmness was the perfect combination…

Maybe he's right, Loyal thought. *I mean, it was her past and people can change.* Loyal walked to the bedroom taking the initiative to make amends with Monica. All she wanted was for her relationship to get back to the way it was before Monica came into the picture. Loyal knocked on the door and waited for a response.

The music in Monica's head blasted so loudly, she didn't even hear the knocking. She was too occupied with bringing herself to a climax of ecstasy. Her breath sped up slightly as she grinded her hips against her fingers. She slipped her free hand under the light green V-neck and massaged her hardened nipple.

Loyal knocked on the door again and after not getting a response she opened it. Stunned with shock, she halted in her footsteps.

Monica looked up at Loyal. She didn't even flinch when she saw her watching. A sinister grin spread across her face as an explosion erupted between her legs.

Loyal noticed a few pack of cocaine on the floor by Monica's foot. "What the fuck are you doing?"

Monica leisurely stood up and fixed her clothing. She grabbed the drugs that had fallen out of her pocket and stuffed them back in. "What do you want little girl? And didn't your mother teach you how to knock before you enter a room."

Loyal couldn't believe what she just witnessed. *People change, my ass! This bitch in my house with that bullshit!* She was livid. There was nothing Monica could do or say to make her forget what she walked in on.

"Monica, I've been very patient with you. I've tried to make you feel comfortable in our home, but there are somethings I will not tolerate."

"Oh, so now you want to get a backbone?"

"We have to be able to get along for—"

"Cut the bullshit," Monica interrupted. "Let's not pretend we're friends. Iras ain't nowhere around. Be real with yourself for once." Monica said walking passed her and into the living room.

"You want me to be real? The only reason I tolerate your ass is because of Iras." Loyal said following behind her. "The disrespect stops now!"

"Oh please, bitch. You don't have enough credentials to demand respect from me. You try and play a big girl's game, you gon' end up getting your feelings hurt." Monica said lighting a cigarette.

Loyal walked over to Monica and snatched the cigarette out her mouth. "Well in this game, I make the rules! There is only room for one woman in his life, and I've already claimed that spot. So back the fuck off!" Loyal said, snapping the cigarette in half. She grabbed her purse and car keys then headed to the door. "Oh and you've got a little something right there." Loyal said pointing to the coke residue her nose, and slamming the door behind her.

"Game on, bitch!" Monica hissed, staring at the front door. Loyal was becoming a problem, one that Monica needed to get rid of and fast.

CHAPTER TWENTY-ONE

Angel sat outside of Eric's funeral in her brand new cherry red Buick Enclave. She watched as people piled into the church to say their goodbyes. She didn't know Eric too well, but she wanted to support Pablo in paying his respects. Angel waited in the car because she didn't want to view another dead body. Meeka's funeral was just three days ago, and she wasn't ready for another sad atmosphere.

A white SUV pulled up in front of the church. Angel recognized Buttah when she saw him climbing out of the front seat of the truck. She remembered back to the day she met him at the restaurant with Pablo. The look on his face reminded Angel of the look Pablo had at Meeka's funeral. She could tell murder was on his mind, and anyone who stepped in the way was going to get rocked.

Angel noticed another guy getting out of the back seat. He was the splitting image of Eric. *He must be Eric's son.* Angel thought. The guy turned and offered his hand to a woman getting out to the car. He placed his arm around her and headed into the church.

Angel's heart skipped a beat when she spotted Kino getting out after the girl. She watched Meeka's killer as he went inside the church. She had no idea he was connected to Eric. Affiliated or not, she knew what she had to do to make it right. The rain began to hit Angel's windshield. Death was hovered over the city, and it was far from over. Angel was preparing to bring hell to earth.

Monica greeted the guest as they entered the church. She saw people who she hadn't seen in years; some who she enjoyed seeing and others who she purposely kicked off her radar. The stares she got from some of the woman reminded her of the time when she and Eric was together. Every girl in the neighborhood wanted to be the lady on his arm. Monica strutted passed the crowd and took a seat on the front row next to her son and Buttah.

Buttah looked over at Monica. *I still can't believe she had the nerve to come back!* He thought. Buttah has seen Monica at her lowest point. He thought she would be dead before the day she would give up drugs. His thoughts were interrupted when he spotted Pablo walking up the aisle to view Eric's body. He instantly reached for his hip where his gun sat in its hoister.

Monica noticed Buttah's gesture and looked down at Buttah's hand. She quickly grabbed his arm before he got all the way up from the seat. She pulled him back down and shook her head. She didn't know what was going on but she had every intention to find out once the funeral was over. Whatever it was, it wasn't worth making a scene at Eric's funeral.

Pablo looked over at Buttah and gave him a nod before taking a seat in the back. Little did Buttah know; Pablo was there out of respect. He respected Eric for keeping his word and not backing out of a deal, even after there was a mix up with the money. That was a piece of information Eric held back from Buttah.

Kino looked down at his buzzing cell phone. It was the third time in the past half hour a private number popped up on his screen. He got up from the seat and headed outside to answer his phone. Normally, he didn't fuck around with private numbers, but he was curious as to who was blowing his phone up. As soon as Kino walked out the church and flipped open his phone, it stopped ringing. Kino became suspicious. He developed paranoia ever since he found out that everything Smoke told him was true. Meeka was blood of the *Death Trap Mafia*, and their head honcho, Mr. Gomez, was no joke. Even though not too many people knew what he looked like, his name rung bells. Kino knew it was a matter of time before they find out who murdered their princess. He beat himself up at how sloppy he handled the situation. He let his emotions stand in the way of his thinking. He needed to clear his head and most of all he needed his piece. He didn't want to bring it to the funeral, but with the way things were going he felt stupid for not having it. The church wasn't too far from where his car was parked. He decided to walk back to get it.

If they did catch me out here now I guess it's just my time.

Angel watched as Kino left the church. Her plan worked perfectly. She kept calling him from a blocked number in hopes that he would step out to take the call. She pulled out the .45 caliber that Pablo had given her for protection. She wanted to end his life the moment he stepped out of the church, but Kino deserved a long, slow, painful death for what he did to Meeka.

Starting the engine, Angel slowly followed behind him, staying far enough behind not to be spotted. The rain poured harder, and Kino ran into a nearby bodega. Angel pulled the car over when she saw him go into the store.

"It's coming down out there, huh?" The old Latino said. He pulled a paper towel from behind the counter and handed it to Kino gesturing for him to wipe his face.

"Thanks a lot." Kino said, taking the paper towel. *I am really bugging!* He thought.

"What brings you out in this type of weather?" The Latino asked.

"I was at a funeral."

"Well, that's no Bueno. No wonder the sky opened up so much." The man shook his head.

The hard rain only lasted a minute or two; as if it were just passing through.

"Well, I better get back to the service. Thanks again for the paper towel." Kino said when he saw the rain starting to let up. The man nodded as Kino walked out of the store.

Bitch never ran in my blood, and I don't expect it to start now. Kino decided to head back to the funeral. *If it's my time to go, then it is what it is.*

Angel watched Kino ad he walked right by her heading in the direction he'd came from. Her trigger finger twitched as she gripped her gun tighter. Just as she was ready to let out the entire clip, a pregnant woman came running out of the store.

"Excuse me! Did I hear you say you were at a funeral?"

Kino turned around. "Yes…"

"You wouldn't be talking about Mr. Eric's funeral, would you?"

"You knew him?"

"He saved my life!" The woman said. She started walking with Kino.

"How did he become your lifesaver?" Kino asked.

"He used to be my landlord. Well, me and my ex-boyfriend. I was in a very abuse relationship. Mr. Eric happened to be in the apartment complex at the time me and my ex got into a heated argument." The lady continued. "To make a long story short, he gave me a place to stay— rent free, so that I could get away from him. If it wasn't for Mr. E, my unborn child and I would be dead right now. When I heard he passed away, I was heartbroken. I walked passed the church wanting to pay my respect, but I wasn't sure if they would let me in."

Kino knew Iras' dad was a good dude. So good, you almost forgot he had his hands in so much negativity.

This bitch is in the way! Angel thought. As much as she wanted Kino dead, she wasn't about kill an innocent woman, pregnant at that. "Fuck!" She spat in frustration. Angel drove around the block and back to the church. The lady walked with Kino the whole way there.

"I'll see you again, mutha fucka." Angel said, putting her gun away just as she saw Pablo coming out of the church.

"Ok, we can go now." He said as he climbed into her car. Angel didn't want to let Kino go that easily. She knew he might be hard to find if she let him out of her sight. She saw him and the pregnant woman walk into the church.

"Baby, I have to use the ladies room. Do you think they will mind if I go in?" She asked Pablo.

"No, it should be fine. I'll wait here for you. I need to make a call."

"Ok, I'll be right back." Angel headed up the church steps and through the tinted glass doors. The pew was packed. Eric knew a lot of people. She saw the pregnant woman standing at the front, viewing Eric's body. Angel scanned the room for Kino, but he was nowhere to be found.

"I'm going to get some air. I can't take this anymore." Buttah said as he got up and stormed out. He was so upset he didn't even notice Angel standing by the entrance. Monica got up and followed behind him making sure he was okay.

Angel's eyes widen in shock. It was as if she was looking into the past when she laid eyes on the one person she'd thought she would never see again.

"Monica?" Angel said in a faint whisper. Rapidly, she blinked her lids making sure she wasn't hallucinating. Nope! It was her best friend, and her features grew clearer as Monica moved closer.

"Monica!" Angel called out.

Monica was stunned. She gasped as tears built up in her eyes when she saw Angel standing there. The two women swallowed each other in their arms.

Angel couldn't hold back any emotion as she held tightly to Monica. "What happened to you? You just stopped coming to see me. I thought you were dead." Angel cried out.

The commotion they made caused people to turn their heads and focus on them.

"Excuse me, ladies. Out of respect for the family, do you mind stepping out the door to continue your conversation?" One of the ushers from the funeral home asked.

Before Monica could respond, police officers stormed into church. A white woman wearing a long black trench coat and a man walked up to the front to where Iras was sitting.

"Emanuel Taylor, you are under arrest for the Murder of Eric Taylor and Officer Joe DiLucci." The detective said. He pulled Iras to his feet. Two other cops came behind him and cuffed his hands behind his back.

"What?" Loyal shouted, standing to her feet.

"I didn't kill my pops! Get your hands off me." Iras said, trying to yank away from the cops. They slammed Iras down to the ground. "Come on man, I didn't do shit! Ahh!" Iras yelled from the pain of the cop's knee pressing down on his back.

They lifted Iras back to his feet and read him his rights. The guest watched as the police escorted Iras out of the church.

Loyal grabbed her clutch and quickly followed behind him. Monica stood there like a deer in headlights when she saw her son being put into the back of the police car.

"I need to get to the police station! My son didn't kill anybody!" Monica said. "He's a good man!" The usher consoled Monica as she burst into tears.

Loyal rolled her eyes at the acting Monica was giving. The last thing she needed right now was more drama from Monica's ass. Loyal called Kino's phone as she walked to the truck they came in. Kino didn't answer. Buttah got in the truck with Loyal and the driver pulled off following behind the police car.

"Why would they think he killed his father?" Loyal broke down. At that point everything she was going through had let itself out. So much bullshit was already in play and now Iras was being arrested for murder.

Kino wanted to answer Loyal's call. He was coming out the restroom when he saw the cops coming into the church. He instantly assumed that they were looking for him, so he made his way to a back door and slid out. He had to get out of Philly for a while until things cooled down.

CHAPTER TWENTY-TWO

Trina almost missed her exit trying to read directions she had written down. She had only been in Atlanta a little over a week and was not at all familiar with the city. After dropping Akahi off at the daycare center, she was meeting up with Corey. Corey was a guy she dated a while back before she got into the robbing game. Even though she was thirteen years younger than him, she knew Corey was different. He too moved to Atlanta from Philadelphia when he was accepted to Clark Atlanta University, and got a degree in business.

Trina thought off him on the plane ride and looked him up when she was settled into the hotel. Surprisingly, he wasn't that hard to find. He taught a course at the university three days a week. He was the one who recommended the day care for Akahi.

Trina took the exit and pulled over to the side of the road. She looked around for a sign to help her go in the right direction, but she was in fact lost.

"Ugh!" She moaned and balled up the paper. She pulled out her cell phone and dialed a number. "Hello, Corey? When I get off at exit seven do I make a left or right? Uh-huh. Okay. And you're right there? Great, I should be there in a few minutes, then."

Trina hung up her phone and followed the directions Corey gave her. No doubt, Corey was waiting for her at the small shopping strip he guided her to. Leaning up against his car, he smiled as he watched her parked the car and walked over to him.

"Hey you!" Corey said.

"Hey!" Trina responded, hugging him.

"You making out okay?"

"Hell no, this city is too damn big."

Corey laughed. "It's not so bad once you get used to it."

"Yea, I guess." She said, putting her hands on her hips. "But I am hungry. What's good out here to eat?"

"Hop in. I know a breakfast spot not too far from here." Corey opened the door for Trina to get in. She admired that about him. For as long as she known him, he was always a gentleman. He would probably stay far away from her if he knew the kind of shit she was into now days.

They pulled up to *Mama Joe's Flapjack House*.

"If this isn't country, I don't know what is!" Trina said referring to farm right next to the restaurant.

"They make the best food in town." Corey said laughing. They walked into the restaurant and the smell of pork filled the air. They took a seat at the first booth by the door.

"So how long do you plan on staying here?" He asked.

Trina shrugged. "Not sure yet. This trip was kind of sudden. It was Keilani's idea to move to Atlanta and it doesn't feel right without her."

"Where is she? I haven't seen her in years."

"She's dead…"

The waitress came over to the table and placed two menus in front of them. "What can I get y'all?" The girl said with a heavy southern accent. She looked about nineteen-years-old. She had apple red hair and two gold teeth in the front of her mouth. She was pretty, but would probably be a knockout with a makeover.

"Are the pancakes any good here?" Trina asked the waitress.

"Pancakes? You're not from around here I see." The waitress said, laughing.

"It's their specialty. The best in the US." Corey said.

"You will love them, trust me. What kind of meat do you want with them? We have pork and turkey bacon, and pork and beef sausage. We also have fried catfish."

"I will have the turkey bacon, please."

"And I'll have the same…" Corey added.

The waitress took the menus and went to put in their orders.

"Sorry to hear about Keilani." Corey said. "How did she pass?"

"In my arms." Trina put her head down as she remembered that very day. It was all still new to her and even though she hadn't seen Corey in years, she didn't mind being so open with him. Corey grabbed her hand. Trina looked up at him and saw the concerned look on his face.

"Tell me what happened." He said to her, rubbing the back of her hand.

"You probably would hate me after I tell you this."

"Try me." He rested back in the booth.

Trina hesitated.

"You didn't kill her, did you?" Corey asked.

"No! Hell no. She was my sister!"

"Well then what happened?"

Trina took a deep breath. She was about to tell Corey the truth; the whole truth.

*****

"I haven't worked out in years," Monica complained.

"Don't worry, you'll be cool." Angel said laughing at her friend as she struggled trying to keep up with the treadmill. It was the first time they really had a chance to hang out. It had been over twenty years and both of them had much to share. Angel finally told her about Mac and being in prison.

"Angel, you could have come to me. We could have dealt with Mac together." Monica said after hearing about Angel's abuse from her father.

"Then both of us would have been in jail. Trust me; you don't want anything to do with that place." Angel assured.

Monica got off the treadmill trying to catch her breath. "Well believe me, the road my life took me down wasn't a walk in the park either." Monica never went into detail about her drug problem.

"So where is Mr. Pablo now? I would love to meet the man that tamed your tiger!" Monica joked.

"He's handling business in Miami. He hasn't been the same since his daughter passed." Angel said turning off her treadmill.

"It's sad isn't it? People are dropping like flies," Monica said, wiping the sweat from her forehead. Monica's comment gave Angel the shivers.

If it wasn't for me, she'd still be alive. Angel thought. Even though Angel and Monica were close, she kept it to herself about how Meeka died. She didn't want to chance nothing getting back to Pablo. Monica was her girl, but she didn't know if she was the same girl who she rolled with back in the day.

"Well, that's why he has you. Just make sure you are there for him. Death is hard enough. Lord knows Emmanuel didn't take his father's death to well."

Angel nodded her head thinking about how she really betrayed the one man she'd ever loved.

"I need to hit the sauna after this," Monica said. "Do they have one here?"

"Yup, and it's a great way to end a workout." Angel replied.

The two of them went into the locker room and took off their sweaty gym clothes. Angel tried not to stare when she noticed how skinny Monica was. She couldn't really tell when she was fully clothed, but naked, Monica was a pencil.

Monica saw Angel staring at her through the mirror and quickly wrapped a towel around her body.

"Um, the sauna is this way…" Angel said, trying to ignore the awkward moment.

"I'll meet you in there; I just need to use the bathroom." Monica said.

"Okay."

When Angel was out of sight, Monica pulled a small bag of cocaine out of her locker. She got down on her knees and poured it in a line on the bench. In one breath, she inhaled the entire line. She sat on the floor taking in the impact the drug delivered.

Years of rehab down the drain.

Mind your business; you want it just as bad as I do. You need this, you will die without it.

"No, No, No, No, Noooo!" Monica yelled. She couldn't control the voices in her head as easily as she used to. She was hearing them more and more since she murdered Eric. She grabbed her hair and fell back on the floor. She looked up at the ceiling and saw Eric's body hanging from the light. Blood dripped down to the floor and she tried her best to dodge it. The more she tried to dodge it, the harder it became. Blood started to cover her feet. She removed her towel and tried to scrub is off, but it wasn't working.

"Ahhhhh!" Monica curled her naked body in a corner.

Angel came back in the locker room to see what was taking Monica so long. She saw her friend having a nervous breakdown on the floor.

"Monica, what's wrong?" Angel sat on the bench and grabbed her.

"Get your hands off of me!" She yelled.

Angel had no idea what was going on. People started piling into the locker room trying to find out what the commotion was.

Angel saw the small bag on the floor beside Monica. She quickly grabbed it before anyone else had a chance to notice. At that point, Angel knew Monica was on drugs. She knew it had to be a reason why she was so skinny. She was always thick and healthy.

"Should I call an ambulance?" One of the workers asked.

"No, she'll be fine. And what the fuck is everybody staring at?" Angel snapped. "This ain't no fucking theater."

Angel's attitude cleared the room. She grabbed Monica by her shoulders and shook her.
"Monica! Monica!"

Monica looked up and saw Angel standing there. She looked down at her feet and the blood was gone. Her hallucination seemed so real.

"Come on," Angel lifted her to her feet. "I'm taking you home."

CHAPTER TWENTY-THREE

"What the fuck is taking so long?" Iras snapped at his lawyer, Malcolm Goldstein. "It's going on almost two weeks now."

"This case is not as simple as you think. They have a witness who identified you at your father's house the day he was murdered."

"I told you, I stopped there earlier that day but he wasn't home."

"Why didn't you tell the police that from the start?" Malcolm asked.

"Whose side are you on?" Iras asked sitting up in his chair.

"All I'm saying is if there is something you need to tell me, I'm all ears. Your hearing is in a couple of days, and I would rather not have any more surprises."

"And all I'm saying is that you work for me. My peoples are paying good money to fatten your pockets. I didn't kill my father so get me the fuck out of here. It shouldn't take this god damn long for a bail hearing."

"Do you know you your father is? My guess is they are trying to make an example."

"Well then, shut it down. Or I'll have to get a lawyer who can." Iras said before getting up and walking towards the guard. The guard opened the door to escort him back to his holding cell.

"Goldstein. When you talk to Loyal, tell her I said thank you and we gon' make it!" Iras said before leaving out the room. He knew Loyal was going through it. But he knew he could count on her to make sure she held him down while he was down. She hired Goldstein and made sure the bills were paid. No matter how many times he fucked up, she was still there. She showed him time and time again that she is wife material and when it all blows over, he was going to make sure it was permanent.

****

"Look, Auntie Trina!" Akahi said looking out the window in excitement. "The world is so tiny from up here."

"That's because we are flying with the birds." Trina responded.

"I want to learn how to fly, that way I can visit mommy whenever I want to, right auntie Trina?"

"Kahi, where mommy is, we can't go yet."

"You said she is with God right?" Akahi asked.

"That's right…"

"Well mommy said I was her angel, and angels can visit god."

Trina smiled at her god son. She wished it was as easy as a child made it seem. The facial expression Akahi made reminded her so much of Keilani. He had one dimple on his left cheek just like his mother. Akahi turned and continued looking out of the window. Trina looked over at a sleeping Corey. She was glad that he decided to come to Philadelphia with her to visit Keilani's grave site. The sudden turbulence woke him up and he caught her looking at him.

"You're admiring my good looks?" Corey asked.

"Nope, I was just looking to see if that drool was going to make it to your shirt." Trina said, jokingly.

The two shared a laugh as he nudged her arm. Corey was eye candy. He resembled the rapper T.I. Corey always had a girl chasing after him, but never wanted a hood girl until he met Trina. From the moment he laid eyes on her he wanted her. Trina didn't know this, but Corey was still madly in love with her. He promised himself now that she was back in his life; he would never let her go again.

The plane ride was only a few hours. They arrived in Philadelphia a little after 5 p.m. They checked into a hotel ten minutes away from the airport. Trina didn't feel safe being back in the city. She wanted to hurry up and visit Keilani's grave so she could leave before Buttah found her. Corey had another engagement on his agenda. He planned on paying Buttah a visit from the moment Trina spoke of him. Trina didn't know, but Corey and Buttah had history. Corey was in the business of sticking people up, and tried his luck with Eric and

Buttah. His attempt to murder both Buttah and Eric years back when they were coming out of a movie theater didn't go the way he had planned.

To Trina, Corey wasn't known to be a killer, and he didn't want her to think of him any other way then what she knows of him now. He was going to make sure Buttah was not one of her ninety-nine problems.

****

"Yes, I understand. Thank you, Mr. Goldstein." Loyal said before hanging up the house phone. Iras' hearing was coming up and she wanted to make sure everything was okay. She laid her head on the table.

"What did he say?" Monica asked.

Loyal was startled. She didn't know Monica was standing behind her that whole time.

"Who?" Loyal responded.

"Wasn't that Emanuel's lawyer?" Monica asked, walking over to the table. "What did he say?"

"He was just reminding me about the hearing date." Loyal said. *Like I'm really going to tell you.*

"Well, let me know if anything changes. You and I both know that you are far from capable of handling things." Monica said, walking over to the couch.

"I've been handling things just fine before you got here, so I am very capable of doing so!" Loyal said.

Ding Dong!

That's what you think. Monica thought as she opened the door. "Hey! Come on in!" Monica greeted Angel.

Angel gave her a hug and walked into the condo. "You have beautiful place! How long have you been here?" Angel said, admiring the layout of the living room.

"Girl, this is my son's place. I'm staying with him for a while."

"Your son has good taste…"

"Unfortunately, not in women." Monica said, sarcastically.

Loyal grabbed her keys off the table and walked over to Angel. "Hi, I'm Loyal, the bad taste!" Loyal said looking at Monica.

Angel felt the tension in the room and tried to lighten to mood. "Ms. Loyal, I'm Angel. Nice to meet you."

Loyal nodded her head and opened the door. "I'm going to meet with Buttah, if Iras' lawyer calls back, tell him to call Buttah's cell because I can't find mines."

Angel's eyes shot over at Loyal when she said the name Iras. She instantly thought of the voicemail message she heard and Kino's voice saying: *my boy Iras put one right in the middle of his eyes!*

"Who is Iras?" Angel asked Monica when Loyal left out.

"Oh, that's Emanuel's middle name. Everybody calls him that." She replied.

You have got to be fucking kidding me! Angel thought. First, she finds out that Meeka's killer is connected to Pablo's business partner, and now the person she promised Teresa she would find is the son of her best friend. Things couldn't get any more complicated. She didn't know Iras, but just to know he is Monica's son was enough.

"Angel!" Monica said, breaking her thought. "Are you okay? You don't look too well."

"Umm, yea- yes. I'm good. Can I use your bathroom?"

"Yea. It's to the back on the left."

Angel walked to the bathroom and shut the door. *Monica's son!* She thought. *Meeka's dead! I dint know Trey but I gave Teresa my word.* The decision of remaining loyal to Teresa or Monica was becoming an even bigger issue. Monica was her right hand back in the day, but for the past couple of years Teresa has filled that position. If it wasn't for Teresa, she would have never met Pablo. *Iras already made his bed. I awe Pablo. Meeka is dead because of me.* She thought, trying to convince herself that the decision she was about to make was the right one.

Angel flushed the toilet and ran the water to give the illusion of using the restroom. She looked at herself in the mirror. "It's settled; Good night Iras!"

CHAPTER TWENTY-FOUR

Buttah pulled up to his house looking for a parking space. He couldn't pull in to his garage because a big red security system company truck blocked it. He found a spot on the next block down and parked. As he walked back to his house, he spotted a guy wearing the security company's uniform talking to his neighbor.

"Since when has it been ok to block people's property?" Buttah yelled over to the security guy. The guy put one finger in the air gesturing that he will move it in a minute.

Buttah shook his head and went into the house. The moment he shut the door, Loyal pulled up to his block. The security guy was getting into his truck and moved it up. Loyal didn't see Buttah's car in the driveway so she pulled to check if he had gotten home yet.

Buttah answered the door on the first ring. "I didn't think you were home. Where is your car?" She asked, giving him a hug.

"That damn truck was blocking my driveway; I had to park down the street."

"You're getting a new system?"

"Shit, with all that's going on I need to get some type of surveillance…" Buttah paused.

"What's wrong?" Loyal asked seeing the look on Buttah's face.

Talking about surveillance made Buttah remember Eric's system. Buttah was the only one who knew about it. Eric didn't want anyone to know his house was being videotaped.

How the hell could I forget about that? He thought. "I need to make a quick run, I'll be back." Buttah ran out the door and to his car. Just his luck, when the truck moved from in front of his house, it doubled parked on the next street and blocked his car in. Luckily, for him the guy was still in the truck. Buttah got in his car and beeped the horn. The truck moved back to let him out of the parking spot.

Twenty minutes later, Buttah arrived at Eric's house. It looked as if he still lived there. It was the first time he'd been there since the night of Eric's death. He knew he only had a short period of time before the Feds find out about Eric's secret surveillance system. Eric kept his cameras running twenty four-seven. Buttah stepped over pieces of glass and traces of stained blood on the floor. He went upstairs to Eric's office, turned on the computer, and logged in to the surveillance system. Buttah was the only person besides Eric who knew the access passwords. He searched the date of the incident and the screen displayed the six rooms Eric had cameras.

Buttah saw Eric talking on the phone in one on the small windows on the screen. *Damn E!* Buttah thought. His vision blurred from the tears building in his eyes. He promised Eric's older brother Isaiah that he would always look after him. Even though they were grown, he still felt obligated to do so. Now that Eric was gone, he felt like he let Isaiah down. Buttah continued to watch the screen. Eric left the house, and for a while there was no action. He fast forwarded the video to see if the murder was caught on tape. He played it when he saw someone wearing a sweat suit with the hood pulled up and dark glasses come through the front door. The person went upstairs in the guestroom, searching through closets, lifting mattresses, and empting drawers. The room was a mess. They moved to the next room, which was Eric's bedroom. They did the same damage as they had done in pervious room. *What the hell is he looking for?* Buttah thought. He tried to make out who it was. The person went into the last room and paused when they opened the door. They turned on the light and slowly walked in the room. A mural painted on the wall held the person's attention. It was a painting of Eric and Iras as a child. That was Iras' old room and even as a teenager, Iras kept the mural. The room was set up as if he still lived there. Surprisingly, the intruder didn't trash the room. Instead, the person ran out of the room and slammed the door shut behind them. Buttah watched as they ran down the steps and pulled off the hood.

"A bitch?" Buttah said after seeing the hair when the hood came off. She pulled out a cell phone and began pacing the floor. Buttah paused the video and zoomed in. He nearly fell out the chair when he recognized Monica on the tape.

"What the hell is she doing here?" Buttah said as he resumed the video.

Monica toured the rest of the house, looking in the refrigerator and taking a sip of milk straight from the carton. She went into the garage and got into Eric's 1985 Caprice Classic. She popped open the trunk and looked through it. Finally, retired to the living room and laid down on the sofa. After fifteen minutes of her not moving, Buttah assumed that she had fallen asleep. He fast forwarded to when she began moving. Almost nine hours had passed in the video. Monica got up and looked out of the window. Buttah could tell that it was dark outside because the night vision icon was on the screen.

"Why didn't she mention she was there anyway?" he said to himself. They were all questioned by the authorities and Monica never bought it up.

Shortly after, Eric walked in the house and picked up his mail. Buttah watched as he walked right passed Monica in the shadows of the living room.

Eric went up the steps pulling out his gun along the way. The suspense was as if Buttah was watching a horror movie. He couldn't hear anything because it was just video surveillance. Eric walked into the Iras' old room. Buttah got nervous after realizing he was about to watch his best friend's execution. Eric left room and went down stairs to the front door. Intensely, Buttah stared at the screen waiting for what he knew what was about to happen. Eric left out the house with a cop. Monica picked up Eric's gun that he sat on the table before going outside.

"No! Please don't tell me...." Buttah uttered. His breathing increased, and butterflies swarmed his stomach when Monica pointed the gun at the door. When Eric came back into the house, without hesitation, he lunged at her. Before he could make a connection, Monica shot him.

Buttah stopped the video and got up from the desk in a panic. "Monica killed him?" He asked himself, trying to wrap his head around the idea. He turned off the computer and headed straight for Iras' lawyer's office.

"First things first: clear my god son's name." He pulled out his phone as he sped downtown.

"Hey Loyal, you're not going to believe this shit. Monica killed Eric. I saw the surveillance video. Meet me down at the lawyer's office. I will be there in twenty minutes." Buttah closed the phone hoping that she would get the message soon.

Corey dipped in and out of the lanes trying to keep up with Buttah. The security company truck wasn't fast at all, but he wheeled it like a professional race car driver. His plans where intervened when he saw a woman go into Buttah's house after he had waited around almost all day to spot Buttah. He even went door-to-door pretending to sell alarm systems until finally Buttah had come home. When that plan was ruined, he decided to follow him and wait for his shot.

Corey pulled over a block away from where Buttah stopped. He saw Buttah run out the car and into a tall building. Corey got out the truck and walked to Buttah's car. He pulled on the door handle and just as he expected it was unlocked. Buttah seemed to be in such a rush, he didn't secure his car. Corey shook his head at how easy it was to catch niggas slipping. He climbed into the back seat and waited for Buttah to return.

Ding! The elevator door opened up, letting Buttah off at the sixteenth floor. Buttah ran to the office and barged threw the doors.

"Can I help you, sir?" The receptionist asked noticing the urgent look on Buttah's face.

"I need to speak with Mr. Goldstein."

"I'm sorry, but he is already gone. He will be in court the rest of the day." She said.

Fuck! He thought. "I need you to call him."

"Sir, he's in court and I'm sure he will not answer. I can leave him a message. What is this pertaining to?"

"Tell him I got information on the Taylor case. Important information. I need him to call me the moment he steps out of court." Buttah left out the office before giving the receptionist his name. He got back into his car and took a deep breath. He put his head back on the headrest and closed his eyes. He thought about his best friend and how his son's mother had a nerve to end his life. He automatically got the urge to repay the gesture to Monica, but to kill her would only complicate things even more. *I'll let that bitch just rot in jail.* He put the key into the ignition and started the car.

Pop!

Buttah's body slumped over the steering wheel. Without saying a word, Corey sent a hallow strait to the back of Buttah's head. He got out the car and walked back to the alarm truck as if nothing had happened.

CHAPTER TWENTY-FIVE

Two days later…

"You still haven't found your phone?" Melissa asked Loyal as she combed her hair in the mirror.

"Nope. I called Sprint and they are sending me a new one, though." Loyal said. "But to be honest, I really don't want to talk to anyone right now. Shit has been crazy. Your sister has been working my last nerve."

"She is not my sister. Just because she is blood doesn't make her my sister. *You're* my sister!" Melissa confirmed. "You didn't tell Iras did you?"

Loyal shook her head no. "Your secret is safe with me."

"Besides, you've got too much to worry about now. Don't be stressing over my family tree. Wouldn't want my niece or nephew getting sick now do we?" Melissa said touching Loyal's stomach.

Loyal was shocked. She hadn't told anyone she was pregnant yet.

"What? You don't think I notice when my best friend gains weight, and eats everything in sight. And let's not forget the mood swings. You just haven't been yourself lately." Melissa said as she tied her hair into bun. "Does Iras know?"

"No, I was waiting for the right time to tell him, and then all this happened."

"How far along are you?"

"About two months, I think." Loyal said. "I haven't been to the doctor's yet. After the third test came out positive, I pretty much had my answer."

"I'm going to be an auntie!" Melissa said with a big smile.

"Well, technically you already are." Loyal said jokingly referring to Iras.

Melissa smiled and shook her head. "I love you girl!"

"Love you to, Liss!" Loyal said. "Well, I better get going. Got a big day tomorrow, are you coming to the hearing?"

"I can't make any promises, but I will try. If Monica is going to be there, I don't think that is a good place for a family reunion."

"You're right. I'll call you later." Loyal left out and went home. The only thing on her mind was sleep. She wanted to be refreshed and alert as possible at Iras' hearing.

****

Beep. Beep. Beep. Beep.

The sound of the hospital machine was all that made a noise. Kino sat and watched Buttah as he laid in the hospital bed in a coma. He came back to Philly when a nurse recognized Buttah and called him. She used to work at the strip club as the barmaid. She and Kino hooked up a few time but it didn't turn out to be anything serious. She told Kino that Buttah had been shot in the head. Kino knew it had to be the DT mafia. Too many people around him were dropping. His partner in crime was behind bars, so this was one war Kino planned to fight alone. He wasn't sure if Loyal knew about Buttah, but she hadn't answered any of his calls. He was going to check on her to make sure she was okay when he left the hospital.

"Well, looks like you're awake now." A nurse said as she entered the room. She looked at Kino and rubbed his shoulders. "How are you feeling, honey?"

"I'll feel a lot better when he wakes up." Kino admitted, looking over at Buttah.

"He's pretty lucky, you know? You would think a close range shot like that would have done more damage." The nurse walked over to the window and closed the curtains.

Kino looked over to the nurse who was writing something in her chart. "Is he going to be ok?"

The nurse closed the chart and sat it on the table. She walked over to where Kino was sitting so she didn't have to speak so loudly. "Your father is going to be fine. The surgeon was able to remove the bullet without any permanent damage." Kino told the hospital that Buttah was his dad.

"Will he remember anything?" Kino asked.

"It's hard to tell at this point. Let's just hope for the best." She replied.

Kino stood up from the chair. "I'm going to come back in the morning. Please call me if anything changes, or if he wakes up."

"No problem." The nurse smiled.

Kino left the hospital. He opened his cell and called Loyal once more. Her voicemail came right on. *Damn!* He couldn't help but to think the worst. Hopping into his car, Kino headed straight to Loyal's house

****

Loyal tossed and turned in her bed. Even though she was tired, she was having trouble falling asleep. And it didn't help that it was only going on 8 p.m. She got out of her bed and went into the kitchen, walking passed Monica who was sitting in the living room on the sofa.

Loyal poured a glass of water. She grabbed her stomach when she had the urge to throw up. She bent over the sink and ran the hot water as she bought up everything she'd eaten.

Monica walked into to kitchen and leaned against the counter. "Is it Kino's?"

"Excuse me?" Loyal said with a confused look.

"The baby. Is it Kino's?" Monica repeated.

"I've had enough! After tomorrow's hearing you need to find another place to stay. You're not welcomed in my house anymore!"

Monica watched as Loyal walked into the living room grabbing the cordless phone. She went back into the bedroom and shut the door. Loyal dialed Melissa's number and got no answer. She was two seconds away from beating Monica's ass, and she needed some fresh air. Loyal called her own cell phone hoping that she would hear it ring. Her voicemail came right on, and Loyal realized she hasn't checked her messages since she lost her phone few days ago. She pressed the pound key and it played the first message. It was Iras' lawyer telling her to return his call. She deleted the message and went to the next one. It was from Buttah.

"Hey Loyal, you're not going to believe this shit. Monica killed Eric. I saw the surveillance video. Meet me down at the lawyer's office. I will be there in twenty minutes.

Loyal dropped the phone after hearing Buttah's message. The room began to spin and her heart beat sped up. She couldn't believe what she just heard. She picked up the phone and called Buttah. The last time she spoke with him was a few days ago when he rushed out of his house.

When she didn't get an answer, she put on her sneakers. She needed to know if what Buttah was saying true and he was the only one who could answer that. She opened her bedroom door.

Boom!

Monica hit Loyal over the head with a cast iron frying pan. Loyal was out cold. She heard the message Buttah left when she was ease dropping from the kitchen phone.

"I told you not to get in my way!" Monica said kicking Loyal in the face. Blood poured from Loyal's nose and mouth. Monica tied Loyal's hands behind her back and put a pillow case over her head. She dragged Loyal's body to Loyal's car and lifted her into the trunk. She got in the driver's seat and pulled off.

Just as she turned the corner, Kino pulled up to the condo. He left his car running as he hopped out and ran up to the front door. Kino banged on the door but got no answer. He started getting nervous, not sure if Loyal was ok or not. He went to the only person who he could go to. With no one around to give him any real updates, he went to pay Smoke a visit. If anyone knew something, it was him.

When Kino got to Smoke's club, he saw three men walking out and getting into a white car. He wasn't sure who it was so he waited until they were gone before getting out of his own car. He ran into Smoke's club and was surprised there weren't any guards at the door. He hurried back to Smoke's office and opened the door.

"Oh shit!" Kino jumped back when he saw Smoke and all of his men stretched out on the floor. There was blood everywhere. Kino backed up and ran out. He knew it was a matter of time before they would find him. *These DT niggas won't stop*! "Think Kino, think! Where could Loyal be?" Kino rapidly snapped his fingers. "Melissa!"

****

"I put that work in!" George said lighting a cigarette. Smoke and his boys didn't know what hit them.

Tango got word from one of Smoke's men that he knew who killed Meeka. Pablo, George and Tango paid Smoke a visit. No matter what was put on the table, Smoke didn't give up Kino. Smoke had a silent respect for Kino, and his ego didn't make it any better. Smoke wasn't one who did well with taking orders.

Pablo knew it was a matter of time him and Smoke had it out, anyway. Smoke used to work with Pablo but they agreed to stay clear from each other when it didn't work out. That agreement was breached when Meeka came into play. Pablo thought about Angel. He didn't want her around when he turned the city red so he lied and told her he was going away for business. She didn't know that he was still in the city. Once he was done, he planned on moving them to Paris and give her the   life   she   deserved.

CHAPTER TWENTY-SIX

"Ugh," Loyal moaned.

"Well it's about time you woke you. I was beginning to think I killed you." Monica said laughing.

Loyal tried to adjust her eyes to the dark room. She could barely see through her swollen eyelids. Loyal tried to moved, but couldn't. Monica bonded her wrist and ankles to the chair she sat her in, and the duct tape on her mouth prevented her from saying anything.

"You're not so tough now, huh bitch?"

"Umm!" Loyal moaned from the blow Monica gave to her head. Tears started to flow down Loyal's face. All she could think about was never seeing Iras again and having his baby. She knew Monica was eventually going to take her life. She remembered the message she heard from Buttah before Monica knocked her out. Monica turned on the light. The room was filthy. Graffiti writing covered the walls and a dirty mattress laid on the floor. The only window in the room was boarded up. The syringes and crack pipes littering the floor let Loyal know that she was in a crack house.

Loyal heard movement behind her and turned to see what it was. A black-haired man sat in the corner of the room, getting his fix. She looked back at Monica who was shoving something up her own nose.

"I have to go to my son's hearing. You be good while I'm gone, okay?" Monica said grabbing Loyal's cheeks.

Loyal hated her with a passion. She watched Monica as she left out of the room. Loyal cried harder the second Monica left. She didn't want to give her the satisfaction of seeing her breakdown.

God, please get me out of this! Loyal thought. She was about to miss Iras' hearing. She started rocking in the chair trying to free up her hands. There was no use. Monica tied her wrist so tightly that her hands were going numb from the lack of blood circulating in them. She had no idea how she was going to get out of this, but she knew if she didn't do something fast she would die.

****

Kino woke up in his car outside of the hospital. He had been searching for Melissa almost the entire night. He knew where she lived at one point of time but he never been to her new house. After no luck, he went back to the hospital and pulled into the parking lot. He didn't want to take any chances falling asleep in the hospital just in case someone found him in there. DT mafia was connected, and he didn't want to risk going up to see Buttah one last time. He wanted to find Loyal before he got out of town for good. He remembered the message Loyal left for him a week ago. She told him the date and time of Iras' hearing, and that day was today. He started his car and headed to the city hall building where the hearing was being held.

****

Iras walked out with the bailiff wearing an orange jumpsuit. The bailiff escorted him to the table where Mr. Goldstein was sitting. Iras turned around looking for his support. The only person he saw in the first row was Monica. Loyal and Kino was nowhere in the room. Iras was hurt. The people he thought would sit by his side was nowhere to be found at the time when he needed them the most.

"All rise!"

Everyone in the court room stood as the judge entered the room and took a seat.

"The people VS Emanuel Taylor." The bailiff announced.

"How do you plead?" The judge asked.

"Not guilty, your honor!" Iras answered. The judge wrote something down.

"Bail set at fifty thousand dollars. The trail will begin in one month from today." The judge said without even looking up.

Iras looked back at Monica. She nodded her head with approval. The bailiff escorted Iras back through the door they had come from.

Mr. Goldstein walked over to Monica.

"So now what?" Monica asked.

"If you can post bail today, he will be out as soon as tomorrow." Goldstein said.

"Done!" Monica was prepared to do just that. She left out the court room and got on the elevator.

Kino walked into the front of the building and stopped at the receptionist desk. "I'm here for the Taylor hearing." He said to the man.

"Take the elevator up to the sixth floor and make a right. Courtroom J."

Kino hurried over to the elevator and pressed the button.

Ding!

The elevator door opened up and Monica stepped out. "Kino!" She said when she saw him waiting there. "Where were you? The hearing is over."

"I tried to make it here as fast as I could. What happened?"

"The judge made is bail for fifty Gs'. I need to find a bondsman to get my baby out of that place!"

"No, I know where we can get the money. Ras keeps his stash in his crib." Kino said. "I'll meet you there."

"I need to check on something first. Take the key and do what you got to do. I will be there shortly." Monica said handing him the key to Iras' condo.

"Monica, have you seen Loyal?" Kino asked as they walked out of city hall.

Monica pretended she didn't hear his question. Kino noticed her slight tension when he asked about Loyal.

"Monica." He called.

"Yea?"

"Do you know where Loyal is?"

"Last time I spoke to her she was going to stay with a friend for a few days. I thought she would be here but I didn't see her up there. But I will meet you at the condo soon, okay." Monica said as she walked away from Kino.

Something didn't feel right. Red flags went up in Kino's head when he saw Monica get into the driver's seat of Loyal's car and pulled out a phone.

Kino walked toward his car and spotted a woman leaning against it. He stopped in his tracks not knowing who the woman was. He reached behind his back attempting to grab his gun, but remembered he left it in the car to get pass the metal detectors. Kino kept his eyes on the woman. She turned her face towards his direction. Relieved, he let out a deep breath when he saw that it was Melissa. She spotted him and wave for him to come over.

"I've been looking for you? What are you doing out here?" Kino asked when he approached her.

"I was coming to support Ras. But wasn't sure which building he was in. I saw your car and fingered I'd wait for you. Is Loyal down here?" Melissa asked.

Truth was she spotted Monica coming out of the building and turned before she recognized her.

"I was going to ask you if you've seen her." Kino said opening the car door. "Get in."

Melissa hopped into the passenger seat.

"Something doesn't feel right." Kino said.

"What's wrong?" Melissa asked.

"I just ran into Ras' mom and asked her if she's seen Loyal. She said something about her going to stay with a friend, but then I see her getting into Loyal's car." He looked back to see if Monica had pulled out of the parking space yet. She was just pulling off and rode passed them.

"Take this ride with me." He said as he pulled off and followed Monica.

CHAPTER TWENTY-SEVEN

Loyal heard footsteps coming up the stairs. Her heart began to beat, uncontrollably. She didn't know what Monica was going to do to her.

"Did you miss me?" Monica said as she entered the room. "I got some good news. Iras will be out tomorrow. Aww, but you won't get to see him now, will you?"

Monica walked over to Loyal and sat on her lap. "That's okay, soon he'll forget about you anyway!" She whispered into Loyal's ear. "Can I tell you a secret? I killed Eric, and….I'm going to kill you too." Monica said, smiling. "What's that? I can't understand you." Monica said trying to make out Loyal's mumbling. She snatched off the duct tape that cover Loyal's mouth. As soon as the tape was off, Loyal threw up all over Monica.

Monica jumped up and punched Loyal so hard that the chair tilted over. She bent down close to Loyal and lifted her shirt, exposing her bare chest.

"Hey! Hey!" Monica yelled, trying to wake up the man in the corner. He lifted his head and squint his eyes.

"You like this?" Monica asked, fondling with Loyal's nipples.

The man slowly got up and stumbled over to Loyal.

"No!" Loyal cried. "Somebody help me!"

"Enjoy!" Monica said before heading down the steps.

Kino and Melissa watched as Monica came out the house and got back into Loyal's car.

"I'm going to check the place out." Kino said when Monica was out of sight.

"What is there to check out? It's a crack house for God's sake!" Melissa said.

"Just stay here. I'll be right back." Kino reached over and pulled out two hand guns from under his seat. "You ever use a gun?"

Melissa started getting nervous. "No, Kino what's going on?"

Look, just take this. If something don't feel right to you, use this and get the fuck from out of here!" Kino didn't want any surprise visits from Meeka's family while he was out in the open. He went into the house with his gun ready to pop anybody that stood in his way. He looked around the first level of the house. The smell of garbage and urine made him gag. He was all too familiar with that stench; after all, he ran one of Buttah's houses. He heard noise coming from the upstairs and slowly walked up.

Monica circled the blocked and came back to the crack house. She forgot she told Angel to meet her there. She needed someone to watch the house and Angel was the only one she could trust. She turned off the ignition and waited for Angel to arrive.

"Shit!" Melissa said when she saw Monica come park. "What the hell is she doing back so fast?" Melissa had no way of letting Kino know that Monica was back.

Pop! Pop! Pop!

When Melissa heard the gun shots, she saw Monica get out the car and run in the house.

Kino stood over the man's dead body. He walked in on the guy ramming his hand into Loyal's vagina. Kino bent down to help Loyal. She was relieved to see him. She thought she was going to die in that room.

"Get me out of here!" Loyal cried.

"I will! You're safe now!" Kino assured her.

Pop! Pop!

Kino's body fell on top of Loyal. She looked up and saw Monica standing there with a smoking gun pointed at her. "Maybe I should just kill you now! You are becoming a pain in my ass!"

Monica walked over to Kino and picked up his gun. She stepped her foot on the bullet holes in Kino's back.

"Ahh!!" Kino screamed from the pain. "Monica, what the fuck— why are you doing this?"

"You should have minded your damn business, Kino. Now I'm going to have to send your ass to hell too." She pointed one gun at Kino's head and the other at Loyal.

Pop! Pop! Pop! Pop!

Monica dropped to her knees when the bullets entered her body. She laid there in a pool of her own blood. Melissa dropped the gun and fell to the floor. Her legs instantly went numb after shooting her sister. She crawled over to Monica's body and lifted her into her arms. Monica and Melissa made eye contact for the first time in over twenty years. Monica's eyes opened wide when she looked into Melissa's face. Neither of the women could manage to say a word. Monica's body began to shake. She managed to raise her hand a placed it on Melissa's cheek, touching her faint burn scars from the fire. Monica let out a slight smile and managed to mouth the words 'I love you' before her eyes rolled to the back of her head. Melissa laid Monica's body down and kissed her forehead. She never stopped loving her sister; her love for Loyal was just a little bit stronger. She knew she made the right choice.

CHAPTER TWENTY-EIGHT

Seven Months Later

Loyal pulled up to her new home. Things were coming along well after Loyal and Iras' recent move to Atlanta. Monica had managed to turn their perfect world upside down, so this move was something they both needed. Loyal sat in her car and rubbed her growing belly. She and Iras had come a long way, and now they were preparing for their baby girl to arrive. She was finally in a happy place, mentally and emotionally.

Loyal got out of her car and walked up to the door. There was a card taped to the screen with her name on it. She pulled it down and opened the door to enter her home. She sat her purse and keys on the table next to the door and opened the card. It read *SURPRISE!*

"Now what could he be up to this time?" Loyal said as she put the card in her purse. Ever since they got engaged, Iras expressed his love for her a different way every day. He told her he never wanted her to forget, or feel unappreciated.

Loyal walked into the family room expecting to see her fiancé or gift waiting for her. But there was nothing.

"Baby?" She yelled out. She headed up the staircase looking for Iras. "Babe, where are you?"

Loyal heard the water running in the bathroom as she walked passed. Iras' cell phone rang from their bedroom. She went in their room to retrieve it. She looked at the caller ID and it read Kino.

"Hello?"

"Hey, baby girl. How you doing?" Kino asked already knowing who she was.

"I'm good! Your boy is in the shower."

"Oh alright, tell him to get with me when he's finished."

"I will." Loyal responded.

"How's lil' mama doing?" Kino asked referring to her unborn child.

"Lil' mama is good, it's big mama who's in pain." Loyal said, jokingly.

"But it'll all be worth it."

"Oh no doubt, god daddy!"

"That has a nice ring to it." Kino said, smiling.

"Let me go, but tell Ras I'm on the first flight out there in the A.M."

"Ok, see you then!" Loyal said before hanging up the phone. Loyal walked back out to the hall way.

"Ras, I'm home!" She yelled. *He probably can't even hear me under that water.* She thought. She walked to the bathroom and opened the door. Her heart skipped a beat when she saw Iras' dead body slumped over the tub.

Her body went completely numb.

"Ahhhhh! No! Baby!" She cried as she rushed to him. Her hands trembled as she rolled him over on to her lap. "Baby!" Loyal cried out. She suddenly had trouble breathing. "HELP ME!" She screamed, but there was no one else in the house. She looked up and noticed the words "Surprise Bitch" written on the wall with his blood. Those words pierced her heart like a knife.

"God, what did I do to deserve this?" She cradled Iras' body and rocked him like a baby. At the same time, she felt her baby girl kicking inside of her......

EPILOGUE

June 9, 2010
Dear diary,

Why? Why is this happening to me? It wasn't supposed to be like this. We were supposed to live a long life together, have children and build our home. My baby is gone! I'm going to say my last goodbyes, and if that bitch even show her face at this funeral, I will personally send her to meet her maker!

Loyal closed the diary without reading the rest of the passage. It was the first time she'd opened it since the death of her fiancé, Iras. *This year went by so fast.* Loyal thought to herself as she looked over the obituary of the only true love she had ever known. Emanuel Iras Taylor. April 27th, 1987 to June 3rd, 2010. Stuffing the obituary back into her diary, Loyal could feel the familiar burn of tears pricking the back of her eyes. She hated the reminder of the dark place her mind was in that day, but it was the truth. She was ready and willing to kill for hers.

Loyal placed the diary back into the lock box she stored in her master bedroom's walk- in closet, in a safe disguised as a stack of shoe box. After sealing it shut, she took a few steps to the opposite side and began searching through racks of clothing. With a host of choices and designer labels, Loyal's closet could've easily been mistaken for a high-end fashion boutique.

"Where is it?" She uttered, separating each hanging garment to get a better look. Today, she'd plan to visit Iras' grave site, and wanted to wear his favorite blouse of hers. Even though he was no longer here in the flesh, Loyal still dressed to impress only him.

"Here it is." She snatch the cream, laced, crop top from the hanger, and held it up in front of her to view. For such a simple piece of fabric, Iras loved the top on her. He'd stare at her, and observe the way the soft material clung to her body, hanging just above her navel. Loyal never really understood why he loved it so much, but it was one extra thing she did to make him smile. Iras was her baby. He was the definition of true, unconditional love.

After picking out her attire, she placed it on the king-sized bed and went to check on her little one sleeping in the next room. She had given her nanny, Thelma, the day off. Loyal didn't want any company on this day. This was something she felt she needed to do alone. Standing at the cheery wood crib, she peered over her daughter, Nijah. At only eight-months-old, Nijah had already began taking the features of her father. Loyal wanted nothing more than to have her family complete. She vowed to always keep Iras' memory alive so that her daughter would know the kind of man he was.

"Thank you, Iras." Loyal said to herself as she looked down at her peaceful sleeping beauty. At that moment, a smile brushed crossed Nijah's face, and Loyal could feel the presence of her deceased love.

"I love you too, Baby!" Tears filled her eye sockets, fogging her vision. After placing a kiss on Nijah's forehead, Loyal headed to the bathroom to shower.

Forty minutes later, both she and Baby Nijah were ready for their trip. It was a first time visit for the both of them. Loyal grabbed the Louis Vuitton baby bag and doubled checked to make sure her black and chrome berretta was still in the secret compartment she had specially made in the lining. Iras taught her well. The life he lived forced her to be prepared for anything and everything. Loyal was his rider, to say the least. Loyal lifted Nijah into her arms and headed down the black wood staircase. The same stairs she vividly remembered him making love to her their first night there. Even after finding Iras dead in their bathroom, moving from their Atlanta home was out of the question. Their last memories were spent within the walls, and that alone was priceless to her.

Loyal walked through the spacious kitchen and through to the two car garage where she kept her black 2011 Acura MDX, with the deep tinted windows and black leather interior. She strapped Nijah into the car seat and then got in the driver's seat. Reaching above her head, Loyal she set the house alarm from the sensor clipped to the sun visor.

"You ready, ma?" She asked her daughter, looking at her through the rearview. Nijah laughed; one of the most pure things Loyal had ever heard. The joy her heart felt anytime Nijah cooed, reminded her how precious life is.

"I will always protect you, baby girl." Loyal said as she slipped the key into the ignition. "Believe that!"

She turned the key.

BOOM!

Monica sat outside in her all white Aston Martin watching the flames consume the house. She anticipated a bigger blast from the one that presented itself. She pulled out her cell phone and hit the send button. The phone rang twice before she heard the silence.

"It's done…done…done…."

Loyal sat up in her bed breathing heavily. She immediately touched her stomach reassuring herself that baby Nijah was safe. She looked over at Iras sleeping peacefully on the other side of the bed. Loyal reached over and turned on the lamp that sat on the nightstand. Iras woke up from her movement.

"What's wrong?" He asked, adjusting his eyes to the light.

"I need water." She said slowing down her breathing.

"Another bad dream?" He asked as he sat up in the bed. Loyal nodded her head. Her body was warm and she had already broken out into a sweat. Iras rubbed her back trying to comfort her. Her nightmares were frequent ever since they found out that Monica wasn't dead. Her dreams felt so real that she would sometimes wake up crying.

"I'll get you some water." Iras said.

"No, I can get. I got to pee anyway." Loyal said as she got up out the bed. She walked into the bathroom and cut on the light. She stood at the sink and looked at herself in the mirror. Her skin was flushed.

A trip to the spa is definitely in tomorrow's agenda! She thought. "Get yourself together, girl!" She said to herself. Loyal turned on the water and bent over to rinse her face. The cool water felt refreshing. She stood back up and was greeted by another reflection through the mirror. The woman scared the shit out her, literally. She looked down and saw that her water had broken. Before Loyal could do anything, two bullets were released into the back of her head from the pistol with a silencer attached.

Angel stood there staring at Loyal's dead body with the smoking gun still pointed at her. She kneeled down and placed Trey's picture on top of her, and made her way out of the house. She couldn't bring herself to murder her best friend's son; but to even the score she took the love of his life. Her mind wasn't yet clear, but a huge weight was lifted now that she avenged Trey's death.

"I'm on my way Pablo, headed to the airport now." She said into the cell once she got into her car. Even though she still kept the secret about Meeka's death, in her mind, killing Loyal made things right and it was the start to her healing.

I truly hope you have enjoyed my novel. Thank you for the support and love! ~Tammy Capri